HERE'S WHAT READERS ARE TELLING US ABOUT THE FIRST BUG MAN NOVEL!

■

"I read this book on vacation this past weekend, and once I began, I couldn't put it down. The writing is clever, intelligent, humorous, and suspenseful. The words are so visual that the whole time I was reading, I was picturing the book as I would a movie. I'm already looking forward to the next Bug Man mystery." —MD

"I've read every Grisham novel and loved them all; however, not since *The Firm* have I enjoyed a book this much." —LA

"I loved Nick Polchak! He is quirky and fascinating. The humor is great and the story had a ton of fun twists and surprises." —DG

"Being a big fan of the TV show *CSI*, I looked forward to the release of this novel. But it blew my expectations away! If Bug Man is any indication of the types of novels Howard Publishing will publish, this new series will be a fantastic hit!" —SH

"I can honestly say that I was held by every page. The characters were so unique and believable. I learned a great deal about insects in a very pleasurable format." —LD

"I could hardly put it down—when I get one this good it always makes me mad at myself because I finish it too fast and it is over." —WH

"How wonderful to discover a hero who hasn't stepped out of the pages of *GQ*. His human frailties and quirky personality give hope to mere mortal men! My hat is off to Tim Downs. A masterful job!" —RF

"I loved the Bug Man. What ht character—well done." —DC

CHOP SHOP

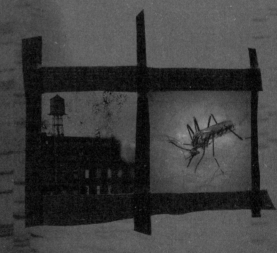

A BUG MAN NOVEL | 2

HOWARD
Fiction

TIM DOWNS

CHOP SHOP © 2004 by Tim Downs

All rights reserved. Printed in the United States of America

Published by Howard Publishing Co., Inc.
3117 North 7th Street, West Monroe, LA 71291-2227
www.howardpublishing.com

In association with the literary agency of Alive Communications, Inc.
7680 Goddard Street, Suite 200, Colorado Springs, CO 80920

04 05 06 07 08 09 10 11 12 13   10 9 8 7 6 5 4 3 2 1

Cover design by David Carlson Design
Interior design by Gabe Cardinale
Edited by Ed Stackler

ISBN: 1-58229-401-1

For my father-in-law Bill Burns,
my research assistant in Pittsburgh and Tarentum,
who once climbed across a burning bony pile
and lived to tell the tale.
Thanks, Dad.

And for Joy—always for Joy.

ACKNOWLEDGMENTS

I would like to thank the following individuals for their assistance in my research for this book: Joe Dominick, chief deputy coroner at the Allegheny County Coroner's Office; Dr. Shaun Ladham, forensic pathologist at the Allegheny County Coroner's Office; Pat Kornick at the Center for Organ Recovery and Education in Pittsburgh; Jane Corrado and Burt Mattice of Carolina Donor Services; Teresa Derfus of the Marshfield Clinic, Personalized Medicine Research Project; Tim Altares of the Bureau of Abandoned Mine Reclamation, Pennsylvania Department of Environmental Protection; Chuck Farneth, former tugboat captain on the Three Rivers; Bert Dodson Jr. of Dodson Exterminators; Christian Heinrich of Cary Emergency Medical Services; Cheryl Sims of Wake Surgical Center; Sam Thomsen of North Coast Idea Company for his help on computer surveillance; Bob Crutchfield for his knowledge of surgical centers and equipment outsourcing; Ralph

ACKNOWLEDGMENTS

O'Donnell of Shred-It in Raleigh; and all the others who took the time to respond to my e-mails, letters, and calls.

Thank you to Dr. Neal Haskell for his continued generosity and forbearance in helping me with the technical details of the amazing science of forensic entomology.

And thanks to all the others who helped make the publication of this novel possible: my literary agent, Lee Hough of Alive Communications; story editor Ed Stackler for his critical insights; and the staff of Howard Publishing for their kindness, friendship, and hard work.

University of Pittsburgh Medical Center, 1973

The young man set his glasses down beside the sink, then bent down and cupped handfuls of cold water against his face. He fumbled for a strip of coarse, brown paper towel, straightened, and studied himself in the mirror. *You can do this*, he said to himself. *There's a first time for everybody. Come on, Julian, you did a PhD in bioethics at twenty-five. You can do this.*

"Good morning!" he said aloud. "I'm Dr. Julian Zohar."

Too eager. For crying out loud, their daughter died thirty minutes ago! He replaced his glasses and turned back to the mirror.

"I am Dr. Julian Zohar," he said solemnly. "First of all, let me say how sorry I am . . . how very sorry I am . . . how *terribly* sorry I am to hear about little Angela"—he picked up a file folder, flipped it open, and ran his finger down the page— "little *Angelita*." *Nice work, Julian. At least get the kid's name right.*

He took a deep breath, composed himself, and began again.

"I am an organ procurement coordinator for the Center for Organ Procurement and Education." *Man, what a mouthful.* He flipped open the file folder and scanned it again:

Father: Tejano Juarez, age 31, landscape maintenance.

Mother: Belicia Juarez, age 26, domestic services.

"I'm Dr. Julian Zohar," he mumbled, "and you two are probably a couple of wetbacks who barely finished the sixth grade before you squeezed under a fence somewhere in west Texas. Organ procurement coordinator. Organ pro-cure-ment. *Comprende* 'procurement'? Sure you do."

He tossed the folder beside the sink and began to pace back and forth in the rest room, gesturing in the air as he spoke.

"Well, hello there! I'm Julian Zohar. I was just passing by, and—what's that? Your four-year-old daughter drowned this morning in a drainage ditch? Say, that is a bit of bad news. But speaking of people who don't need their vital organs anymore—can I have hers? Oh no, not all of them, just her kidneys. *Riñones,* I think you call them. I can? Well, that's very big of you! Now, if you'll just scratch your names here on this multipage release form, I'll be on my way. And so sorry about Angie, or Amy, or whatever her name was."

He stood silently in the center of the rest room for a moment, then turned back to the sink. He opened the spigot, plunged both hands under the stream, and watched the water run off. Minutes went by.

Finally, he looked up at his image once again, slowly leaned forward, and pointed at his own face.

"I am Dr. Julian Zohar," he said deliberately. "I learned less than an hour ago about the tragic loss of your daughter. I cannot tell you how sorry I am. I have no way to comprehend your feelings of loss and grief. But I came here today to tell you that your daughter's death does not have to be in vain. Even now, even in death, she has the ability to save another little girl's life. Just a few miles away from here, over at Children's Hospital of

Pittsburgh, there is a little girl dying of end-stage renal disease. Your daughter is the right size, the right blood type, and they are reasonably histocompatible. I am asking you to release your daughter's kidneys for transplant. Without them, that other little girl will die—and you have the power to prevent it. One little girl died this morning. Please don't let there be two."

Just then the rest-room door swung open with a pneumatic sigh. In stepped the figure of a priest.

"Please forgive the intrusion," he said. "I'm looking for Julian Zohar."

"You've found him."

"I'm Father Anduhar," he said, extending his hand. "I received a call this morning about the Juarez family—about their loss."

"I didn't call you," Julian said.

"The family services coordinator called. I understand that you're preparing to approach the family about organ donation. In such cases, it's often helpful if a member of the clergy is there to assist."

"No thanks." Julian stepped past the priest and pressed the hand blower with the butt of his palm.

"May I ask why not?" the priest said above the low roar.

"Sorry," Julian said, rubbing his hands smoothly one over the other.

The priest waited patiently for the roar to subside. "Why not?" he asked again.

Julian turned to him. "I'm about to ask a mother and father to allow a surgeon to cut out their daughter's kidneys. Their daughter is dead. They *know* that, but they don't *feel* it yet. Clinically speaking, there's a very fine line between life and death; emotionally, there's no line at all. The last thing I want is a priest talking to them about 'the resurrection of the body unto life everlasting.'"

The priest shook his head. "You misunderstand. The Catholic church wholeheartedly endorses organ donation—"

"It's not what you endorse; it's what you *represent*," Julian said. "You tell the family, 'Angelita lives on! She can hear you, she can see you. Talk to her, pray for her.' *I* tell the family, 'Angelita is *dead*. She cannot hear, she cannot feel—so give me her kidneys. Let someone use them who *is* alive.' You encourage people to dwell on the dead; I want them to think about the living. No thank you."

The priest shook his head. "If you fail to care for the dead, you fail to care for the living."

Julian stepped toward the door. "You go ahead and sprinkle your water and wave your incense. Say your prayers for the dead—me, I work with the living."

The priest stared after him in astonishment. "Remarkable. You have no faith at all, do you?"

Julian turned back again. "Let me tell you what I have faith in," he said. "One year ago, a Swiss biochemist named Jean Borel discovered an amazing immunosuppressant called cyclosporine. It's made from a common soil fungus. Up until now transplants have been hit or miss, but when cyclosporine hits the market, it's going to revolutionize transplant technology. No more massive tissue rejection, no more 20 percent survival rates. Can you imagine? People living ten, twenty, thirty years longer; people surviving cancers and overcoming genetic defects; people extending the duration and quality of their lives because they can get *parts*. And not just kidneys and the occasional liver; I'm talking about intestines, lungs—even hearts. *Hearts*!

"And when all this happens, Father whatever-your-name-is, you know what the greatest barrier to transplantation will be? People like you: people who encourage others to focus on the past instead of the future. Because even with all that wonderful technology, people will still have to be *willing* to give up their organs—and that has to change."

"What do you mean?"

"Not all cultures are as individualistic as we are in the West. Here, we assume that each individual should possess sovereign rights over his own body—even after death. In more communal cultures—more *enlightened* cultures, in my view—they believe that the community should assume the rights to your body at the moment of death, and the community should then be free to use your body for the greater good."

"That's frightening."

"You think so? What frightens me is the idea that the dead should have power over the living. That's your world, not mine. I want to make people understand that it's not just a privilege to donate an organ, it's an obligation."

"You're going to tell this family that they're *obligated* to surrender their daughter's kidneys?"

"I'm going to tell them whatever it takes," Julian said.

"That is immoral and unethical."

Julian smiled. "I have a PhD in bioethics," he said. "You want to talk ethics? What's the greater good here: that a family should be permitted, through ignorance or selfishness or superstition, to allow perfectly good organs to perish, or that those organs should be used to save another human being's life? What do you think, Father? Should one little girl die today or two?"

The priest said nothing. Julian turned and pulled open the door.

"I think you are a very great fool," said the priest.

"I am the future. You are the past. Now if you'll excuse me, I have a life to save."

■

Julian peered through the waiting-room window at the grieving Juarez family. There were six of them huddled loosely around an orange vinyl sofa in a tableau vivant; Julian studied the setting the way a painter would analyze the composition of a painting.

Seated in the center was a gray-haired woman; she held her head in her hands and bobbed back and forth, wiping at the corners of her eyes with the tips of her fingers.

Grandmother. The beloved matriarch. The tent peg of the family, the one with the strongest sense of loyalty and tradition. She can turn the whole family if she wants to.

A younger woman sat stroking the old woman's back, reaching across to pat the face of a crying sibling, stopping only to cover her own face and let out a shuddering sob.

Mother. The backbone of the family, the one who holds everyone else together. No matter what she feels, she'll do what she thinks is best for the rest of them. She's the lever, the one who can move them all.

Three children orbited the grieving women like little satellites. The oldest, a girl, stood weeping beside her mother. Her younger brother cried more gently, grieving more over his mother's pain than over a death he could not yet comprehend. On the floor, an even younger boy sat blissfully flipping through the pages of an activity book.

Daughter. The only one of the three who's really a player. She's the catalyst; she holds the family's heart. If she trusts me, the rest will follow. I can reach them all through the daughter.

To the left, standing at a distance and facing away from the rest of the family, stood a small, sinewy man with a copper face and a tangled mustache. He was dressed in work clothes: sagging denims that hung down over mottled gray boots, and a faded gray T-shirt with a gaping collar. He stood with his hands jammed deep in his pockets, pacing back and forth in quick steps like a stallion that wants to bolt but has nowhere to run. His eyes alternated between confusion, grief, and rage—but rage was winning out.

Father. The alpha male. He has all the anger; he's the wild bull. I can ride him, or he can trample me. He has the ego; he's the one to stroke.

Julian took a deep breath, tucked the file folder under his arm, and rapped on the glass.

"Good morning," he said as evenly as possible, "I'm Dr. Zohar."

The father stopped and looked at him, his eyes brightening.

"There is news?" he said excitedly. "Something has changed?"

Suddenly the entire tableau broke apart before Julian's eyes. The mother sprang to her feet and rushed toward him, grasping Julian's forearm with both hands. The children swept in behind her like flotsam in the wake of a boat. The father charged forward and then halted, staring in wide-eyed anticipation.

And then, worst of all, Julian saw the grandmother struggle painfully to her feet and shuffle forward. He had made the old woman rise—and for nothing.

A terrible moment of silence followed.

"No—there's no change. Angelita is still . . . I mean, I'm not that kind of doctor."

Julian felt the mother squeeze his arm again, and then release. He saw three pairs of youthful eyes turn to her for explanation. He watched the older woman's shoulders round and her body sag as though she might drop right where she stood. Worst of all, he saw the rage returning to the father's eyes. Julian bit his lip. By raising their hopes, even for an instant, he had caused them to look backward. Now his job would be twice as hard.

"Then what do you want?" the father growled. "Leave us!"

"I just stopped by . . . to see if . . . if there's anything I can do," Julian stumbled.

"What can you do? You can bring my little Angelita back to life. Can you do this? No? But you are not that kind of doctor."

The women had returned to the sofa now, weeping freshly and glancing resentfully back at Julian.

"I came to tell you that your daughter's death does not have to be in vain."

The father turned to his wife and shrugged. "*¿Qué quiere decir?* 'In vain.'"

"Inútil," she translated. "'Useless.'"

The father whipped around in a fury. "Angelita's death was not *useless*. What do you want from us? Is this how you help?"

"No. I'm sorry. Please—let me explain." He stepped to the sofa, smiled, and rested his hand on the little girl's head. She ducked away and leaned against her mother.

"There is another little girl. She is very sick. She is in a hospital right now, not far from here. Angelita can help her."

"Angelita can help no one. Angelita is dead."

"She can still help. A *part* of her can help."

The mother squinted at Julian in confusion—until a look of horrified recognition began to spread across her face like gangrene.

Julian saw it. Seconds were critical now; he plunged ahead.

"We want your permission to remove your daughter's kidneys. The doctors want to transplant them—*place* them—into the little girl who is sick. This can save her life."

The father turned again to his wife and mother. There was a flurry of Spanish between them: *"Angelita . . . los doctores . . . sus riñones . . . trasplante."*

The old woman groaned.

The father stumbled back as though he had been punched in the gut.

"Is this why Angelita is dead?" he said. "Did the doctors even try to save her?"

"Mr. Juarez, of course they did. The doctors here did everything in their power to—"

The father charged forward, jerked the file folder from under Julian's arm, and handed it back to him. "The girl in the hospital," he said. "What color is she?"

"Mr. Juarez, it makes absolutely no difference—"

"What color is she?"

Julian fumbled open the folder and ran a finger down the first page, focusing on nothing at all. He knew the answer before he opened the folder.

8

"The little girl . . . this particular little girl . . . seems to be of Caucasian descent."

"Anglo!" the father spluttered. "Angelita is dead so an Anglo can live!"

"Mr. Juarez, this has nothing to do with race—nothing whatsoever." Julian listened to the sound of his own words. The harder he protested, the more hollow the words seemed to sound.

"Mr. Juarez, listen to me. Angelita is dead. She feels nothing."

"*I* feel! *I* feel!"

"You have the power to save a little girl's life."

"And you! You had the power to save *my* little girl's life!"

"Mr. Juarez, try to think of the other girl's family."

The father stared at Julian in amazement. "My Angelita is dead less than one hour. You come to me and say, 'Please! Give me her *riñones*! We will cut her open! And then you ask me to think of *another* little girl? Get out! Get out of here!"

Julian turned silently to the door and stepped out. As it closed behind him, he looked one last time at the family of Angelita Juarez, a little girl whose perfect little kidneys, through a series of chemical changes, would soon be reduced to two lumps of decomposing waste.

Waste.

Angelita was dead—and so was the little girl across town.

North Carolina State University, May 2003

Nick Polchak stood with his nose less than twelve inches from the blackboard, his right hand waving a stick of chalk like a conductor's baton. From time to time he stopped abruptly, and the chalk would tap out a hypnotic staccato; then he would suddenly arch away from the blackboard, study his most recent series of scratchings, make a few quick edits with his left hand, and begin again. He spoke directly to the blackboard, as though students might somehow be trapped behind it. In fact, they were behind him, fighting off heat-induced slumber and cursing the fate that had forced them to take General Entomology during a summer session while more fortunate classmates were right now stretching out on the sands at Myrtle Beach.

"While all bugs are insects, not all insects are bugs," Nick confided to the blackboard. "True bugs belong to the suborder Heteroptera; these include lace bugs, squash bugs, chinch bugs, red bugs, water bugs. The tips of their wings are membranous, but only the tips—insects with entirely membranous wings belong to the suborder Homoptera, which includes cicadas, treehoppers, aphids, and lantern flies. Both orders, of course, are characterized by sucking mouthparts—"

"Dr. Polchak," a weary voice interrupted, "will this be on the final?"

The chalk stopped tapping. Nick turned slowly and looked over the class as if he were shocked to discover someone sitting behind him.

"Who said that?"

The soft shuffling of papers and shifting of bodies abruptly stopped; all eyes turned to the blackboard. Nick Polchak was a legend among students at NC State. He was a professor who had been censured by his own department so many times that he had achieved an almost mythical status. Nick was a forensic entomologist in a department of horticulturalists and livestock specialists, a man whose private research on human decomposition had spawned a dozen campus legends about missing undergraduates and shallow graves deep in the Carolina woods. But the best-known thing about Nick Polchak, the thing that every student knew about, was his eyes. Nick wore the largest, thickest glasses anyone had ever seen, and they made his chestnut eyes appear enormous. But it was more than size—it was the way the eyes moved. They floated and darted like synchronized hummingbirds; they scanned and penetrated like orbiting probes; they disappeared completely when Nick closed his eyes, then suddenly reappeared twice as imposing as they were just a moment ago.

Nick's entomology courses were among the most popular on campus. Everyone wanted a chance to look at him—but no one wanted Nick to look back; those eyes were just too much to bear. Whenever Nick turned from the blackboard—an event that was mercifully rare—every head was bowed and every pen was busy. Everyone knew that Nick Polchak loved insects more than anything in the world. He was the Bug

Man—and someone just asked the Bug Man if bugs would be on the final exam.

A young man in the second row, squeezing himself down into the recesses of his writing desk, looked up to see twin moons rise in the sky above him.

"It seems a bit *premature*," Nick said, "to be asking in the first week of a course whether 'this will be on the final.' It shows tremendous . . . *foresight*."

Nick blinked, and the brown moons vanished—then they flashed open again, even larger than before.

"What you're really asking me is whether *this*"—he gestured to the blackboard—"is worth *knowing*." Nick cocked his head to one side and studied the young man's face as though he were searching for those sucking mouthparts. "Insects comprise the largest class in the animal world," he said. "Ninety-five percent of all animal species are insects. There are about a million known species; there may be *thirty* million more waiting to be discovered. They are distributed from the polar regions to the rain forests, from snowfields in the Himalayas to abandoned mines a mile underground. They flourish in the hottest deserts, on the surface of the ocean, in thermal springs—even in pools of petroleum. The smallest insect is less than a hundredth of an inch long; there is a kind of tarantula that weighs a quarter of a pound and measures eleven inches toe to toe. It has fangs an inch long. It eats *birds*. Is any of this worth knowing?

"Did you know that ants and termites alone make up 20 percent of the entire animal biomass of our planet? Did you know that one out of every four animals on earth is a beetle? Your little town of Raleigh has a population of what—a quarter of a million? There may be two million insects in a single acre of land. Insects eat more plants than all the other creatures on earth. Without insects, we would be living in an ecological nightmare—mountains of rotting organic matter everywhere. Without insects, half the other animal species on earth would probably perish—yours included. My species rules this world; you are a member of an annoying minority group. When you ask me if this is worth knowing, you're asking me if life *itself* is worth knowing."

Nick studied the young man's face. Like all undergraduates, he knew how to look suitably repentant; it was one of their most basic survival skills. This one looked like a cocker spaniel that got caught peeing on the rug. He was sorry—so *very* sorry—that even phys ed majors like him had a three-hour science requirement.

Nick let out a sigh. "Let me bring it down to your level," he said. "The kissing bugs of Central and South America can consume twelve times their body weight in blood. That's the equivalent of a Sigma Chi drinking two hundred gallons of beer at one party."

The entire class let out a cheer.

Nick turned back to the blackboard. "I should never have turned around," he said. But before he could return to his private lecture, another student, sensing the opportunity, spoke up.

"Dr. Polchak, what are your office hours? I can never find you."

"My office is here in Gardner Hall, room 323. Knock on my door; if I answer, those are my office hours. If you really need to whine about something, talk to me after class."

"But I can never *catch* you after class. Am I supposed to talk to your back while you're running down the hall toward your lab?"

Nick nodded. "That works for me. Now can we get back to this? I've got a lot of material to cover. And *yes*," he said with a nod in the direction of the cocker spaniel, "this *will* be on the final. The only thing I will not require you people to remember is *useless* knowledge—and in case you're wondering, there is no such thing as useless knowledge."

But as the classroom quieted once again, an unusual sound drifted forward from the back of the room. Heads began to slowly turn—Nick's last of all. There, spread-eagled atop a cool, black laboratory island, was a student fast asleep. He lay on his back, mouth open, with a little pool of spittle beside his face.

A piece of chalk snapped in two.

"Did I ever tell you," Nick said slowly, "about a case I had several years ago? It was in Colorado, in an area near a meat-processing plant. The men who worked there carried an unusual type of knife, something like a boning knife, and they were very adept with it."

As he spoke, Nick started back through the classroom toward the sleeping student.

"They found one of their employees in the bottom of a nearby ravine with his gut sliced open. The body had been there for several days. After seventy-two hours, forensic entomology is the most reliable way to determine postmortem interval, so the local medical examiner asked me to come in before they moved the body."

As Nick passed each row of students, he gestured for them to follow.

"I could see the body from the top of the ravine, lying in an opening between some small trees. It looked as if they had painted a chalk line around the body, like they do to mark the placement when a body is finally removed—only the body was still there. When I got closer, I realized what it was. The long gut wound had allowed a massive maggot infestation in the abdomen, and the maggots had completed their third instar—they had eaten all they could hold, and they were leaving the body, looking for a safe place to pupate. There were so many maggots exiting all at once that they formed a white outline, slowly moving outward toward the trees."

Nick was standing over the lab table now with the rest of the class gathered silently around. He spoke quietly, glaring down at the oblivious student. Nick opened a drawer and removed a scalpel and a pair of forceps. With the forceps he gently lifted the boy's shirt near each button, and with a quick flip of the scalpel sent each button tapping across the table. Now he used the forceps to peel back the shirt, leaving the bare chest and abdomen exposed. The student brushed an imaginary fly from his nose, licked his lips, and let out a long, moaning snore.

"I examined the abdomen. The wound stretched from the breastbone to the groin—just the kind of incision a man would make who's used to gutting Herefords. The maggot mass was enormous, the largest I've ever seen. I wanted to measure the temperature at the core of the mass. I slid in a probe—it was almost 120 degrees at the center! But maggots can't regulate their own body temperature, and that's about the point where thermal death occurs, so the maggots were circulating away from the core as fast as they could. The cooler ones were wriggling their way toward the center while the overheated ones were struggling to get out, venting their excess heat on the surface like tiny radiators. It was amazing! The entire mass looked like a pot of boiling ziti.

"Then all of a sudden, I felt something land in my hair. I brushed it off without thinking about it—then it happened again. Then something hit my arm . . . then my back. Finally, something landed on my neck, wriggled for a minute, and rolled down my back. I looked up . . ."

Nick stood beside the boy's head, leaning ever closer as he spoke. He held the gleaming scalpel directly in front of his face, and the volume of his voice began to slowly rise.

"When maggots flee a body, they instinctively look for a drier place to pupate. To a maggot, *dry* means *high*, so they climb anything they can find: a rock, a bush—even a tree. Thousands of maggots had inched their way up the surrounding trees, crawled out to the tips of the lowest branches, and now they were dropping off. It was raining maggots, and they were landing on my neck and rolling down my back. And there's only ONE thing in the WORLD that I HATE more than MAGGOTS DOWN MY BACK . . ."

15

The boy's eyes popped open. Two great brown meteors crashed down on him, mere inches from impact, led by the flash of surgical steel.

Nick spoke in a low, rumbling tone: "DON'T-*EVER*-FALL-ASLEEP-IN-MY-CLASS."

With a quick flip of his hand Nick placed the cold, blunt butt of the scalpel on the boy's breastbone and drew it firmly down the center of his abdomen. The boy shrieked, clutched at his chest with both hands, and rolled off onto the floor. Nick looked up at the rest of the stunned students.

"Now then. Does anyone *else* have a question?"

■

Dr. Noah Ellison, chairman of the NC State Department of Entomology, tapped his spoon against the side of his coffee cup; the various members of the faculty committee took their seats and shuffled into silence.

"We have a number of items on our agenda this evening," Dr. Ellison began. A man directly across the table raised his hand slightly and, without waiting for recognition, plunged ahead.

"Perhaps I might suggest an appropriate starting point," he said with a dripping Southern lilt in his voice. "Let's see now. We could begin with research reports from our various agricultural extension stations. Then again, we might consider the budget allocations for new equipment in the graduate laboratories. Now, what was that other item? It escapes my mind just now—oh yes, now I recall." He shot a glance toward the end of the table, where Nick Polchak sat slumped in his chair with a copy of the *Journal of Medical Entomology* open on his chest. "We could discuss Dr. Polchak's decision to dissect a student in his class this morning. Yes, let's begin with that."

Nick closed his journal. "I didn't actually dissect him," he said, "though the idea does open up some interesting research possibilities. Some of these undergraduates, I'm sure no one would miss."

"Why, Dr. Polchak," the man replied, "rumor has it that you have an entire woodland forest filled with decomposing undergraduate students. Whatever would you do with another?"

The man glaring at Nick was Dr. Sherman Pettigrew, tenured professor of Applied Insect Ecology and Pest Control. Dr. Pettigrew had several years of seniority on Nick, and he had strongly opposed the decision to hire Nick in the first place—but his "foresight went unheeded," as he liked to put it, and now he took every available opportunity to remind Nick that he was not, and never would be, welcome. He despised Nick's arrogant iconoclasm; he was horrified by the very idea of *forensic* entomology; and most of all—though he would never admit it—he resented Nick's popularity with students.

For Nick's part, Sherman Pettigrew represented everything he hated about academia, traditional entomology, and the South. Sherman Pettigrew was a large man, in his midfifties, but with the face of a child: round, soft, and still bulging in places that should have long ago turned to muscle and sinew. It gave his face a look that Nick found hard to take seriously, even in an argument. He had the old Southern habit of always wearing white: white shirts, extra starch, with the cuffs buttoned tightly about his wrists; white cuffed pants with knife-edge pleats; white socks; white shoes—that's what irritated Nick the most—and an ever-present white linen handkerchief for mopping beads of sweat from his pudgy forehead. His choice of apparel did his physique no favors, and only added to his babylike appearance. "Light colors make a room look bigger," Nick once said to him. "Don't they have decorators in the South?" Nick had an entire collection of nicknames for Dr. Pettigrew—the Great White, the Bulgy Bear—but since their very first faculty meeting together, Nick had addressed him as "Sherm"—not Sherman, not Pettigrew, and never, ever *Dr.* Pettigrew.

"Perhaps you find this amusing," Dr. Pettigrew replied. "I, for one, fail to see the humor in it. Even as we speak, there is an aggrieved family meeting with the university's counsel, deciding whether or not to take legal recourse—legal recourse as in *lawsuit*, Dr. Polchak. While your colleagues are submitting papers to academic journals, you may find yourself submitting to a deposition."

"I read *your* last paper," Nick said. "'*The European Corn Borer: Larval Parasitism in Selected North Carolina Hosts.*' What a snoozer."

"Dr. Ellison, I really must protest—"

The aged chairman of the entomology department knew that it was time for a judicious intervention, but he hated to interrupt. For Dr. Ellison, the ongoing verbal volley between Dr. Polchak and Dr. Pettigrew was the highlight of these endless committee meetings, and he resented the role he was forced to play as peacekeeper and hand-slapper.

"Nicholas, Dr. Pettigrew does have a point. We really cannot make a habit of attacking our students with surgical instruments."

"He fell asleep in my class," Nick said sullenly.

"Perhaps there is a reason for that," Dr. Pettigrew offered.

Nick glared at him. "I'm sure the European Corn Borer has them bouncing off the walls in your classroom, Sherm."

"Gentlemen," Dr. Ellison said. "I think we're all in agreement that Dr. Polchak's disciplinary action this morning, while memorable, was a tad . . . *extreme*. We are now in the position of having to decide what to do about it."

"There is only one thing to do about it," Dr. Pettigrew said. "I move for the immediate dismissal of Dr. Polchak."

A groan arose from the entire faculty committee.

"A failed coup attempt." Nick whistled. "How embarrassing."

"That also is a tad extreme." Dr. Ellison frowned at Dr. Pettigrew. "However, some form of punitive action is necessary.

I'm sure you understand, Nicholas, that to avoid legal action, the university must be able to demonstrate that you have been chastised in some appropriate way."

"You could make me take one of Sherm's classes," Nick suggested.

"Nicholas, you're not helping."

Suddenly, Nick took on a look of deep remorse. "There's only one alternative," he said. "Official censure. I'll have to give up my classes for the summer and go away somewhere."

"This is patently unfair," Dr. Pettigrew interrupted. "Everyone here knows that Dr. Polchak hates teaching. And every time he is 'officially censured,' he goes off to do whatever he pleases while the rest of us are forced to assume his class load."

"What else can we do, Sherm?" Nick said solemnly. "After this kind of tragedy, can we all just go back to business as usual? What would it communicate to the grieving family if today I vivisect little Bobby, and tomorrow I'm back teaching as usual? No, something must be done. I say we send me away. I say we apologize to the boy's family. And I say we send him to Sherm's class and let him sleep as much as he wants to."

Dr. Ellison wanted to smile, but his role required him to maintain a sober countenance. "I think there is something to what Dr. Polchak has suggested," he said. "Very well, Nicholas, you will once again be officially censured by this department and by the university proper—"

"*That* hurts," Nick moaned.

"And you will forfeit your summer classes—*and* all remuneration associated with them."

Nick winced. That did hurt.

"And if I may make one more suggestion," Dr. Pettigrew smiled. "It seems to me that Dr. Polchak could put some of this free time to good use—perhaps in some constructive activity that will help him to reconsider his errant ways."

"Such as?"

"We all know the priority our department places on community service activities—especially our K–12 educational seminars. So far, Dr. Polchak has avoided them like the proverbial plague. There's almost a month before the public schools dismiss; perhaps his involvement in this area would have a redeeming effect—a *calming* effect on him."

Under the table, Nick rolled his journal into a tight scroll and squeezed. Dr. Pettigrew smiled, taking special delight in this particular torture.

Dr. Ellison turned to Nick. "Nicholas?"

"Agreed," Nick said through clenched teeth.

With the issue settled, the committee adjourned briefly for refreshments. As Nick passed Dr. Ellison, he bent over and whispered in the old man's ear.

"So I have to go away," he said. "Does anybody care *where* I go away?"

CHAPTER
2

Pittsburgh, Pennsylvania, May 2003

Riley McKay's heels clicked and echoed down the hollow corridor of Fairview Elementary School. The shoes hurt. She curled her toes and wriggled her feet from side to side in a vain attempt to stretch out the unbroken leather. She longed for the comfortable Nikes she wore at the Allegheny County Coroner's Office each day, but there were strict rules about the appearance of pathologists participating in community educational programs. It was Health Day for the second-graders at Fairview Elementary School, and in the opinion of her supervisor, such an auspicious occasion was no time to be a slouch.

The blue glow from the windows at the far end of the corridor created a tunnel-of-light effect. It reminded Riley of the hallway that led to the autopsy room back at the coroner's office: worn linoleum endlessly buffed to a dull shine; cinder-block walls layered with so many years of thick, glossy paint that the texture of each block had almost disappeared; and heavy oak doorposts and lintels that bore the scars of hundreds of daily collisions. The walls were dotted with odd-sized bits of paper too—but at Fairview Elementary the papers were chalk and crayon drawings, not headshots of trauma victims and reminders from the histology lab.

Riley shook her head. She expected her pathology fellowship program to include some extracurricular duties—evening hours, extra weekend rotations, additional paperwork, and administrative chores—that just came with the territory. But why ask an MD with five years of pathology residency to conduct a seminar that any of the deputy coroners could do? Why ask her to—

Just then a classroom door burst open, and a young boy ran directly into her, straddling her with his arms like a blind man walking into a pole. He instinctively wrapped his arms around her waist, then recovered and looked up at her sheepishly. Riley looked down into his beautiful eyes and brushed the sandy hair back from his face.

"I got to go to the bathroom," he said.

Riley smiled. "When you got to go, you got to go."

He grinned back. Riley hoped for one more hug before he left, but he slid past her and raced off down the hall.

"Where's room 121?" she called after him.

"Next one down!" he shouted back. "Ms. Weleski!"

Riley rapped on the thick glass panel embedded with a crosshatch of black safety wire. A pleasant-looking woman sprung up from a seat in the back of the room and pushed open the door.

"Ms. Weleski? I'm Dr. Riley McKay from the Allegheny County Coroner's Office. You asked for someone to speak about our 'Cribs for Kids' program?"

"Yes! Yes!" She took Riley by the arm and pulled her inside, effervescing with an enthusiasm perfected by twenty years of daily exposure to seven-year-olds. "Thank you ever so much for coming! But I'm afraid we're running a bit behind. Our first pre-senter showed up a bit late," she said with a roll of her eyes. "He's just getting under way now."

"No problem. I can wait," Riley said with a smile and a wink. She wedged herself into a chrome-and-plastic desk beside the teacher, squeezed off her shoes, and reached down to massage her aching arches.

"My name is Nick Polchak," said a voice from the front of the classroom. "I am a forensic entomologist. Can anybody tell me what that means?"

Silence.

"OK," Nick said, "how about just the entomologist part? Does anybody know what an entomologist does? I'll give you a hint: it comes from the Greek word *entomos*, meaning 'one whose body is cut into segments . . .'"

Still nothing.

Riley looked up to see a tall man with angular limbs and large hands. His appearance was casual, as if he had just stopped off on the way to a Pirates game. To Riley it looked as if he dressed quickly, and once dressed forgot what he had put on. *No one's setting a dress code for him,* she thought. He wore a faded plaid oxford, sleeves rolled up to the elbows, over a gray Penn State T-shirt. His shorts were weathered and worn, the ragged edge more the result of wear than style. Everything about him seemed to say, "It's not about how I look; it's about what I do." Riley smiled in agreement.

Then she noticed his eyes.

Nick Polchak wore the thickest eyeglasses Riley had ever seen. Behind them his brown eyes floated like two buckeyes, flashing off and then on again as if they might be communicating some mysterious code.

"Dr. Polchak," Ms. Weleski said in a pleasantly pleading tone. "Perhaps you could make it more—" She held both hands palm-down and made a patting gesture in the air. Nick looked at her blankly, then slowly turned back to the class.

23

"When you finish with a soda can, what do you do with it?"

"You throw it away," came a voice from the second row.

"Wrong," Nick said. "That's what your parents did with it. What do *you* do with a soda can when you finish with it?"

"You recycle it," said another voice.

"Why do you do that? Why do you recycle it?"

"So you don't waste stuff." The pace was quickening now.

"Exactly. Now—who can tell me what happens to you when you die?"

There was a long pause here. The class was suspicious, wondering if the man with the buckeyes might be trying to trick them.

"They . . . bury you," one brave soul ventured. "Or they burn you up. That's what they did with my grandpa."

"Ah!" Nick held up one long index finger. "But what if they can't *find* you?"

"Why can't they find you?"

"What if you're in the woods, and no one knows you're there, and you have a heart attack? Or what if someone shoots you four times, dumps your body in a drainage ditch, and covers it with debris? I had a case exactly like that, where—"

Ms. Weleski made a sharp coughing sound in the back of the room.

"Or what if you're in the woods, and no one knows you're there, and you have a heart attack?" Nick said again. "What happens to your body then?"

No one had the slightest idea.

"Then you're *recycled*," Nick said triumphantly, "because nature doesn't like to waste stuff either. And what do you suppose recycles you?" Nick swept the classroom with his huge brown eyes.

"Insects do," he said. "They *eat* you."

There was an audible gasp from the classroom, most notably from the corner where Ms. Weleski sat. It was all Riley could do to keep from laughing out loud.

Suddenly Nick clapped his hands together and the entire class jumped in unison. "Let's do a little demonstration. I need somebody to be a dead guy." He turned to a small, doe-eyed boy in the front row. "How about you?"

"Don't want to be a dead guy," he grumbled.

"Not a real dead guy—just pretend. Come on up here and lie down on the teacher's desk."

Ms. Weleski tried to quickly stand, but the little desk rose up with her like a hoop skirt. "Dr. Polchak," she protested, "please be careful . . . I don't think it's a good idea if you—" But by now the boy was sprawled out across the desk, staring mournfully at the ceiling above.

"OK, we got a dead guy," Nick said. "Now, how did he die? Anybody?"

"He got his head chopped off," one little girl offered cheerfully.

The little boy propped himself up on one elbow. "Do I look like I got my head chopped off?" Nick put one hand on his head and pushed him back down.

"OK, he got his head chopped off," Nick said. "Now, as soon as he hit the ground, certain kinds of flies began to—"

"What happened to his head?" said a voice in the front row.

"Forget the head. A raccoon carried it away."

"Raccoons eat heads?" someone whispered.

"Yes—and hands and feet too—but that's another story. Now, certain kinds of flies will land on the body, and what do you think they do?"

"They eat you?"

"No. They lay eggs on you so their *babies* can eat you."

Riley had to cover her face with both hands. She let one long snort escape, which she did her best to disguise as astonishment.

Nick picked up an eraser and held it over the boy. "Here comes the momma fly. She smells blood, she lands, she lays her eggs—thousands of them, and they look just like that cheese they sprinkle on your food at Olive Garden."

The boy on the desk lifted his head. "I like Olive Garden."

Nick pushed him back down. "You have no head, remember? Now, when each of the eggs hatches, it becomes a maggot. And each maggot has two little hooks on one end, like this." Nick held up two curled fingers like quotation marks. "They try to eat you, but you're too darn tough—so they puke out this digestive fluid, and it dissolves the tissue that's in front of them."

Ms. Weleski was free of her desk now. "Thank you, Dr. Polchak! Thank you, thank you for coming to see us today—"

"And then the maggots begin to scrape, and scrape, and—"

"Class, can we all say a nice thank-you to Dr. Polchak for visiting our health fair today?"

Nick blinked at her. "But I haven't explained the life cycle of the maggot yet, and how we use it to determine postmortem interval."

"Thank you, Dr. Polchak! Thank you!" Ms. Weleski led the stunned class in a chorus of appreciation, while at the same time beckoning Nick cheerfully toward the door.

"OK." Nick shrugged. He turned to the class one last time. "Don't forget, when it's time to go to graduate school, remember NC State. Go Wolfpack."

Riley watched as the door closed behind Nick, and Ms. Weleski momentarily braced herself against it as if to prevent a forced reentry. She turned to Riley with a look of utter despair. "Dr. McKay," she said, "what is *your* topic?"

A tiny voice inside of Riley longed to say, "The Autopsy: A Guided Tour." But her kinder self got the best of her, as it always seemed to do with Riley, and she simply said, "Cribs for Kids, Ms. Weleski. How your second-graders can help contribute cribs to underprivileged families with infants."

Ms. Weleski heaved an audible sigh and stepped away from the door, but Riley stared at the door a moment longer.

He's the one, she said to herself.

CHAPTER
3

Tarentum, Pennsylvania, June 2003

Riley knocked on the front door of the tiny brick-and-siding split-level, then turned and stood with her back to the door. Before her, row after row of gray shingled rooftops descended away from her, down toward the mountainous coal pile and the railroad tracks that snaked along the Allegheny River.

There was no answer. She followed the sidewalk around the left side of the house and there, tucked back among the sycamores along the steep hillside, she saw a lovely old greenhouse that must have been constructed decades ago. The frame was made of flaking iron once painted a pale shade of green. The panels looked to be the original glass, spotted and speckled and smoky around the edges, as though only the centers were ever wiped clean. Down the center of the ridge line ran a pair of hinged panels that could be opened or closed to control the temperature inside. Riley thought it looked very much like the town that contained it: once a thing of beauty, now just a skeleton, a monument to better days and more bountiful times.

In the midmorning sun, the glare from the glass was blinding. Riley lowered her sunglasses, ducked her head, and stepped inside. Even with the ridge vent wide open, the heat was sweltering and the humidity even worse. Standing in the center of the greenhouse, oblivious to her presence and to the tropical climate around him, was the man with the enormous glasses. Beside him stood a man of similar age and of Indian descent, who mopped constantly at his dripping brow.

"This is oppressive. Worse than *Kolkata* in May," the man complained. "Nick, why don't you open a window?"

"There are no windows," Nick said.

"This is a *house* of windows. Do they have no hinges in Tarentum?"

In the doorway, Riley reached out and rapped against the glass wall. "Dr. Polchak? I'm Dr. Riley McKay. I'm a pathology fellow at the Allegheny County Coroner's Office. May I come in?"

"You are in," Nick said. "Dr. Riley McKay, meet Dr. Sanjay Patil: molecular biologist, Pitt Panther, and part-time whiner." Nick turned back to his overheated companion and handed him a plastic container. "Tuesday," he said. "No later."

"Impossible," Sanjay replied. "You have given me half a dozen specimens, and you want an RFLP on each of them by Tuesday? I tell you it is not possible."

"Let's ask her," Nick said, nodding toward Riley. "When you order a DNA typing at the coroner's office, how long does it take to get lab results?"

"Two weeks," Riley said. "And that's only if you flirt with them."

Nick looked at Sanjay. "Do you want me to flirt with you?"

Sanjay placed the container in a black specimen case, exactly like the one Riley held at her side, and headed for the door. "It was a pleasure," he nodded to Riley as he passed. "See what you can do for him; it is truly a job for a pathologist."

Nick turned to Riley. "Thanks a lot, Dr. McKay. Sanjay used to do the impossible for me all the time because he didn't know any better; now you've told him it's impossible. What am I supposed to do now?"

"I guess you'll just have to start being reasonable," she said.

Nick cocked his head and looked at her. When he did, Riley saw his eyes begin to dart and roll—like the BBs in a little puzzle, she thought, only infinitely larger. The soft brown orbs first traced the contour of her body, then slowly scanned her vertically from head to foot, halting momentarily at special points of interest. Suddenly they slashed back and forth across her, as if making a series of surgical incisions; then the eyes made a sequence of slow, sweeping motions over her, wiping up after the procedure, coming to rest at last on her face.

Riley exhaled sharply, unaware that she had been holding her breath. No one had ever looked at her—no one had ever looked *through* her like that before. It was like having a CAT scan. No—it was like having an autopsy. He was taking her apart and reassembling her with his eyes. She felt that somehow Nick Polchak knew her now, knew her inside-out, and she had some catching up to do.

"You look . . . familiar," Nick said.

"I should. I was in Ms. Weleski's class the other day at Fairview Elementary School."

Nick let out a groan.

"I thought it went very well," Riley assured him. "Especially the part about the little hooks on the maggots that scrape and scrape."

"What was *your* topic? What's the coroner's office handing out these days?"

"'Cribs for Kids.'"

"See, that's not fair," Nick said. "You probably use PowerPoint, don't you? With slides of pathetic little toddlers sleeping on tile floors. Let's see what you can do with a maggot infestation."

Riley smiled. "You know, I had a little trouble finding this place."

"What, you mean Tarentum? Second star to the right and straight on 'til morning."

"It's a little . . . tucked way."

"'Tucked away' as in 'buried.' Dead things deserve to be buried, Dr. McKay. Tarentum is almost a ghost town—but you should have seen it seventy-five years ago, before the steel mills and glass factories began to close down."

"Riley."

"Excuse me?"

"You're a doctor, I'm a doctor. We cancel each other out. Let's make it Riley and Nick, OK?"

Nick nodded. "I assume you didn't come all the way from Pittsburgh just to critique my classroom presentation. What have you got for me?"

"Red off that table and I'll show you." She stepped forward and lifted the black valise.

"Wait a minute," Nick said. He carefully moved a glass terrarium containing a single black spider, rearing up on its hind legs like a lion.

"What's that?"

"An *Atrax robustus*—a Funnel Web Spider. It's one of the two deadliest spiders on earth. It's killed thirteen people in Australia, one in less than two hours."

She stared at him, blinking.

He shrugged. "I just thought you might not want to knock it over."

"Good idea. Thanks." Riley looked the table over a little more carefully this time, then set down the valise and began to remove a series of containers: the smaller ones were made of glass, the larger ones plastic; some had screw-on lids, and others had snap-on tops with holes punched in the center. Nick picked up each one and examined it carefully. In the bottom of each glass vial was a pile of paste-white larvae of different sizes and shapes. He carefully pried back the lid from one plastic container and peered inside. In the bottom was a layer of brown-and-white vermiculite; on top of it rested a piece of aluminum foil folded up on the sides and crimped at the top like a little lunch sack. Nick didn't have to open it; inside would be a small square of damp paper towel, a palm-sized slab of beef liver, and a handful of maggots eagerly scraping and scraping . . .

"This is very good," he said. "Who did the collecting?"

"I did."

"No kidding? Hats off to your fellowship program. You wouldn't believe some of the garbage I get from coroners and crime-scene investigators: unlabeled specimens, leaking jars, containers full of dead larvae because they had no air holes, completely desiccated specimens . . . and then they say, "Analyze this for us!"

Nick held one small glass vial up to the light. In the bottom of the ethanol lay a half-dozen plump, white maggots. A neat, handwritten label encompassed the vial, and a second label stuck out of the fluid inside.

"You even double-labeled." Nick smiled. "Smart girl."

"And I wrote the labels in pencil so the ethanol doesn't eradicate the ink."

"Well, thank you for coming all this way to show me your Diptera collection," Nick said, handing the vial back to her. "Is there anything else?"

"Yes." Riley smiled. "Analyze this for us!"

Nick smiled back. "For us? Or for you?"

The smile disappeared from Riley's face.

"The Allegheny County Coroner's Office is a big operation," Nick said. "Forensic entomology isn't new to your people. Who's your regular bug man? Who do you use?"

Riley set the vial down with the rest of the containers. "Sometimes Neal Haskell out of central Indiana. Sometimes Steve Bullington from Penn State."

"I know them both," Nick nodded. "Good men. So tell me,

Dr. Riley, why does a pathology fellow go outside of regular channels to request an entomological evaluation? And why does she drive twenty miles all the way from downtown Pittsburgh just to deliver the specimens herself? Don't they have UPS at your office?"

Riley said nothing.

"And why do I bet that you'll be paying me by personal check, and not by a bank draft from Allegheny County?"

"Those are good questions," Riley said. "Do you need answers before you'll do my evaluation?"

Nick paused. "Not as long as you have two pieces of identification with your check. So what are you looking for—a postmortem interval?"

"I'm looking for . . . anomalies."

"Anomalies—as in, 'something out of the ordinary.' I assume you collected these from a dead person? *Something* was out of the ordinary."

"I want to know everything an entomological evaluation can tell me. Time of death, place of death, manner of death."

"All of which can ordinarily be determined by the coroner's office."

"Ordinarily."

Nick studied her intently. "I have so many questions," he said.

"So do I. Will you help me?"

"Three hundred and fifty dollars," Nick said. "I'll need a week. Maybe two."

"That long?"

"I'm just being *reasonable*. It's the new me."

"Can't your assistant help out?"

"You mean Sanjay? He can't make larvae grow any faster. Besides, Sanjay is not my assistant. We went to grad school together at Penn State. Now he's a research biologist at Pitt. He's helping me with a little research project: We're doing DNA fingerprints on flies of forensic significance. In their larval form, most flies are impossible to tell apart. The DNA sequences will let us distinguish different species even in their earliest stages of development. Cutting-edge stuff."

Just then there was a sound from the doorway. Riley turned to see the figure of a short, stout woman in a screaming floral dress, beaming from ear to ear. She was—*loud*, that's the only word Riley could think of. Her lipstick was too red, her pearls were too large, and her hair was too high—but she had an altogether warm and inviting manner. The woman cleared her throat a second time.

"Nicky, aren't you going to . . ." She gestured to Riley.

Nick said nothing.

"Nicky! Who is this lovely woman? Tell your mother."

"Mama, I'd like you to meet Dr. Riley McKay. Dr. McKay, the flashing siren standing in the doorway is Mrs. Camilla Polchak, ruler of all Poland—or at least all the Polish people living in Tarentum and Natrona Heights."

"*Mama?*" Riley whispered to Nick.

"Four hundred dollars," Nick whispered back. "Keep it up."

"A *doctor*," Mrs. Polchak beamed. "And not just one doctor, two doctors, in fact! Just look at the both of you!"

"Mama," Nick said. "Why don't you just throw rice on us and get it over with? We'll try to produce a grandchild by Christmas."

"What are you talking about, grandchild? Did I say grandchild? I just like to have a pretty face to look at sometimes, not just those two big portholes of yours." She dismissed Nick with a wave of her hand and took Riley by the arm. "Such a pretty face," she said. "And what do I have to look at around here? Bugs. Flies and spiders and things I don't want to tell you."

"Mama . . ."

"Nicky is blind," she said, ignoring him. "The glasses—did you notice? A small thing. But let me tell you, under those glasses is a very handsome man. You stay for tea."

"What? Oh. I would love to, Mrs. Polchak, but I have a very busy day."

33

"Always a busy day," Mrs. Polchak scolded. "Too busy, maybe. Too busy to have a cup of tea with a lonely old woman?"

Nick rolled his eyes. "You should go into real estate, Mama. You could make a fortune."

Mrs. Polchak glared at him. "Why should I work? I have a rich doctor for a son! But no, you have to be a doctor for dead people—a doctor who makes no money. I ask you, what kind of person wants to be a doctor for dead people?"

"Ask her," Nick said. "I'm a bug man myself."

Mrs. Polchak looked at Riley in silence.

"I'm a forensic pathologist," Riley explained. "Just a fellow, actually."

Mrs. Polchak did a double take. "No man worth a *zloty* would call you a 'fellow.' Nicky, I ask you—is this a fellow?"

Nick looked her up and down. "Looks like a fellow to me."

"*This* is why I have no grandchild," Mrs. Polchak said. She turned and headed back across the yard toward the house.

Riley looked at Nick. "You live with your mother?"

"I'm just visiting," Nick replied. "Honest. I have my own car and everything."

"We'll have tea another time," Mrs. Polchak called back from the house.

"Another time, Mrs. Polchak. Thank you."

"Promise me. Promise me another time."

"I promise," Riley said, smiling at Nick. "I have so many questions."

Cruz Santangelo crawled on his belly across the damp limestone surface. He reached forward with both arms and then pulled, pushing forward at the same time with his toes, propelling himself slowly forward like a swimmer. A hundred and fifty feet above him, rainwater trickled down through cracks and fissures, leeching carbonic acid from the soil, dissolving layers of calcium from the limestone, leaving behind foot-high fissures and cracks that run three miles long and four hundred feet deep through the Pennsylvania hills.

Santangelo watched the green reflective strips on the soles of three other cavers ahead of him. Suddenly the light on his helmet blinked off; he raised his head slightly and tapped his helmet against the rock only inches above. The light flashed on again, and the long shadows reappeared on the rolling ceiling and floor that undulated together like two stone blankets.

"What's the problem back there?" one of the forward cavers called back, his voice thin and strained.

"No problem," Santangelo said quietly.

"Well, keep that thing on! We're in a hurry here—you know the weather forecast!"

Santangelo shook his head. They should be back with the women in the Tour Cave, standing erect on the nice wooden boardwalk, oohing and aahing over theatrically lit stalactites and flowstone and soda-straws. They had no business tackling a virgin crawlway; they had no business caving with *him*. But he had been forced to suffer their presence all day long, a safety requirement of the Laurel Cavern authorities: *caving in groups only*.

One of the men wore nothing but a simple pair of blue jeans and a thin flannel shirt. Another actually wore shorts—*shorts!* The fool had no idea that despite the summer temperatures above, fifty feet below ground the cave would stay an even fifty-two degrees year-round. Less than fifteen minutes after their original descent the man had begun to grumble about the penetrating cold and dampness, and he had been whining and complaining ever since.

All three men wore ordinary tennis shoes—not a decent pair of climbing soles among them—and none of them thought to bring a watch. Santangelo never did; but then, he was a veteran caver, and he knew how to compensate for the time-distorting effects of utter darkness—that is, except when he was distracted by the constant chatter of three anxious neophytes. Now none of them knew how much time had elapsed, and they were hurrying back toward the cave entrance just as fast as the unyielding stone would allow.

"Can you believe this?" one of the men laughed nervously. "We sure know how to spend a Saturday!"

"I tell you one thing, you're buying tonight!" said the man to his right.

"You're on!" his friend shot back.

"You guys can do what you want," the third man shivered. "I just want to get *warm*. I swear, I'm numb from the waist down!"

Their voices crackled like electrical wires; they spoke with ever-increasing energy and volume. They were venting fear, Santangelo knew, bouncing their voices off the stone the way bats do. But the stone gave nothing in return, and the absolute stillness—the absence of even the tiniest echo—was shredding the nerves of all three of them. Santangelo despised them; their incessant blabbering violated the perfect blackness like arrogant tourists shouting across the aisles of a great cathedral. *They're whistling past the graveyard,* he thought, *and if you're not at home in a graveyard you have no business being down here.*

"Quiet," Santangelo whispered.

"What? Who said that?"

"I did. Listen."

From the darkness beyond the narrow cone of their lights came a soft, shuffling sound. It was a kissing sound, a rubbery sound, like the sound of wet soles on a hardwood floor. It grew no louder, but it came steadily closer.

"Hey!" One man arched up suddenly, forgetting his narrow confinement; there was the dull crack of plastic on stone, and his light disappeared. "Something ran across my hand!"

"What was it?"

"I see it! There's another one!"

Santangelo tipped his headlight down at the limestone floor. A small, greenish gray form wriggled past his left hand. He watched it pass; it had four fingers on each foreleg, each ending in a tiny suction cup. Its body was slender and tapered, and mucous-covered skin stretched smoothly over the head where eyes would ordinarily be.

"Lizards!" one of the men shouted. "There must be a hundred of 'em!"

"They're cave salamanders," Santangelo said quietly. He reached forward with both arms, compressing his shoulders as tightly as possible, and began to roll onto his left side; his shoulders wedged between the ceiling and floor. He closed his eyes and exhaled slowly, relaxing, elongating his body. He felt his right deltoid scrape past the coarse stone ceiling, and he rolled over onto his back.

"They're everywhere! Where are they coming from?"

"Rocks. Cracks. They don't like to be seen." Santangelo slowly rotated his helmet from side to side, studying the rippling ceiling. Ten feet to his left the stone rose abruptly and then descended again, forming a sort of bubble six inches higher than the ceiling directly in front of his face. He began to work his body toward it.

"Why are they running toward us?" a panicky voice shouted back.

Centered under the bubble now, Santangelo pulled both heels under him, wedging his knees tightly between the ceiling and floor—then he reached up and switched off his lamp. "They're not running toward you," he said. "They're running away."

An instant later the wall of water hit them. The water itself reached them almost before the sound, and the flood caught the three men before their minds even had time to comprehend the nature of their impending deaths. Santangelo heard a half-scream, a muffled shout, and then the cavern was silent again.

The water hit Santangelo's helmet hard and cold. His knees scraped across the stone ceiling, but the force only wedged his legs tighter, and his position held. He arched his back and let the force of the water lift him up toward the bubble. He lay perfectly still, the water caressing his back in pulsing gushes, his arms waving at his sides like drifting seaweed.

He felt his right arm brush against denim, and then a series of kicks and jabs from a pair of flailing legs; seconds later they passed. He saw quick beams of light sweep across the ceiling like searchlights, and then disappear into the darkness. Suddenly he felt the full weight of a body jam against his back, forcing him even tighter up into the air pocket above. The body was rigid and desperate—kicking, groping, clawing—and then just as suddenly the current pushed the body off to the left and away. But as it washed past, one frantic hand caught his left forearm and held on, clutching at the last remnant of life in the subterranean graveyard. The hand jerked hard twice, and Santangelo imagined a voice saying, "Can't you help? Are you just going to let us all die?"

He felt the grip slowly release, and then all was still and quiet again.

He pursed his lips and breathed slowly into the air pocket, in through his nose and out through his mouth. He floated in the dark water, feeling gusts of current and bits of debris wash over his back, grateful that the blackness had at last swept through the cathedral and washed its sacred floors clean.

It was more than an hour before the water subsided, draining silently away into even deeper and darker recesses of the earth. Santangelo lay motionless, slowing his pulse and controlling his breathing just as he had done a thousand times on the firing range, waiting for the telltale pause between heartbeats before squeezing off a round at a silhouette of a man's head three hundred yards away. When the receding waters at last lowered him gently back to the stone floor, he switched on his light and swept the crawlspace from side to side. It was completely empty. He rolled onto his stomach and began to work his way back toward the cave entrance.

■

An hour later, Cruz Santangelo stood by the cavern opening, unzipping his sodden coveralls and peeling them down to his waist. He removed the ascenders from his nylon line and dropped them into a duffel bag. He took out a towel and began to blot at his wrinkled skin. He looked into the sky; to the south, lumbering gray thunderheads rolled off toward the West Virginia border.

Behind him, a mud-splattered SUV crunched to a stop. Windows rolled down, and three anxious faces peered out.

"We're looking for three men," the women said. "Have you seen them? Can you help us?"

"We went down together," Santangelo shrugged. "Last I saw them, they were headed the opposite direction."

The car slowly rolled away.

There was a beeping sound from the duffel bag. He pulled out his pager and checked his text messages. The single memo read: ZOHAR: MANDATORY: THURSDAY 2300: FOX CHAPEL YACHT CLUB.

CHAPTER
5

Dr. Jack Kaplan sat slumped behind the wheel of his Porsche 911 Turbo, drumming his thumbs on the steering wheel in time to the thundering pulses of two fifteen-inch subwoofers. Half a block ahead he watched two squad cars, lights flashing, a thin band of yellow tape fluttering in the breeze between them. One officer restrained a weeping mother and daughter; another knelt beside a reclining body, while a third reached through the window of his black-and-white cruiser.

It was almost 2:00 a.m.; Kaplan's shift at the UPMC Trauma Center had ended at midnight, and adrenaline still coursed through his veins like jet fuel. He had spent the last two hours slowly cruising the city, listening to his police scanner, hoping for some medical emergency that might keep him from having to return home to yet another sleepless night.

He looked impatiently at the two officers; they seemed to take forever. "C'mon, boys," Kaplan grumbled. "It's the Golden Hour."

At last, he heard his police scanner crackle.

"*Scene secured. Med One can approach.*"

A block and a half ahead, a pair of headlights blinked on, and an orange and white EMS rig began to roll slowly toward the scene. Kaplan revved his own engine, shoved the stick into gear, and pulled away from the curb. His silver Porsche and the cube-shaped EMS truck arrived simultaneously.

A paramedic and two EMTs scurried over the rig, gathering equipment from a series of side compartments: a bright orange backboard with nylon restraining belts, a torpedo-like oxygen tank, a trauma kit, a Kevlar med bag, and Advanced Life Support equipment.

Kaplan approached the scene at a jog, neatly scissors-kicking the yellow barrier tape, holding his credentials in front of him like a shield.

"Dr. Jack Kaplan," he said to the kneeling officer. "I'm a trauma surgeon at UPMC Presbyterian. What have you got?"

The officer reached up, steadied the credentials, then nodded to Jack. "Male, Caucasian, twenty-eight," he began. "He's a local resident—"

"I don't need his life story," Kaplan said. "I want to know why he's lying here in a pool of blood."

"Multiple stab wounds to the chest."

"Pulse?" Jack opened his medical bag and began to pull on a pair of greenish blue latex gloves.

"Yes—at least, I think so."

"You *think* so. That's kind of important."

Kaplan ripped open the shirt. He wiped a sterile pad once across the bloody chest and watched; three small scarlet fountains reemerged through horizontal slits just below the rib cage.

"The attacker was a big man," Kaplan said. "See the angle of the wounds? That's a thrusting stroke. If he came at him overhead, the ribs would have stopped at least one of them."

The EMS team approached now; the officer rose and stepped back away from the body.

42

"Do you mind?" the paramedic said to Kaplan. "We got a job to do here."

"Your job is to assist *me*—I'm signing off on this one."

"And just who exactly are—"

"Ask him." Kaplan nodded to the officer. "We're old pals. Now, backboard this guy, block him, whatever you've got to do to get him on the truck—but get a cuff on him and get me a pulse *fast*."

The EMS crew went to work. Within a minute the body was restrained, lifted to a stretcher, and headed for the truck.

"We've got an erratic pulse," the paramedic said, "and his BP is dropping off the charts."

"Keep the straps clear of the chest area," Kaplan said. "On the truck I want you to tube him, and I want two IV lines. You've got ALS equipment? Good—get a heart monitor on him right away."

The stretcher rolled in head-forward and locked into place. The paramedic turned for the driver's door—Kaplan stopped him.

"Uh-uh. You're in the back with me."

"Wait a minute, this is *my* rig—"

"And you've got the most medical training. You're in the back." He turned to the two EMTs. "Who's the third man here?" he said. They glanced at one another, and the man on the left sheepishly raised his hand. "You're out," Kaplan said. "You bring my car—I'm not leaving it in this dump. The keys are in it. Touch the radio and I'll remove your spleen—scratch it and I'll use a chain saw." Kaplan turned to the remaining EMT. "You do know how to drive?" The man nodded. "Then do it. UPMC Presbyterian," he called back to the officer. "Let the family know."

"Hold it," the paramedic broke in. "Presby is ten minutes farther away."

"Keep talking and it'll be fifteen minutes. Get in the truck."

The doors closed solidly like the doors of a meat locker; bright overhead lights flickered on, and the siren started its keening wail. The truck rolled slowly forward and then rapidly accelerated. The paramedic slid down the long vinyl bench on the right, connecting and adjusting the heart monitor; it was on less than five seconds before emitting a high, even tone.

"Cardiac arrest!" the paramedic shouted. "I'm going to defib!"

"No you're not," Kaplan said. "Not with a penetrating injury. Betadine the chest area—all of it, from the clavicle down."

"Why? What are you going to do?"

"A thoracotomy."

"A what?"

"I need you to switch places with me—now!"

The paramedic worked his way around the head of the stretcher. "What's a thoracotomy?"

"I'm going to make an incision right here," he said, drawing a line with his finger between two ribs. "I'm going to spread the ribs, open the pericardium, and repair any damage to the heart and coronary vessels. I'm going to clamp off the descending aorta to redirect blood flow to the lungs and brain, and then I'm going to reach in and massage the heart by hand until we get to UPMC."

The paramedic swallowed hard. "Have you done this before?"

"Nope. Always wanted to try it, though."

"Dr. Kaplan, we're not set up for that kind of surgery—our job is to stabilize and transport. We've got no instruments—one little tracheotomy scalpel, that's all, and maybe a forceps."

"Get them out. I need your trauma shears, too, and anything we can use for suction. I've got most of what I need with me—for the rest, we'll improvise."

"Will this work?"

"The survival rate is somewhere between 0 and 4 percent."

"Dr. Kaplan, we're *two minutes* from Allegheny General."

"I need more than two minutes. Don't you guys have a radio? Hey, driver! Give me something to work by back here."

"Allegheny General is set up for this kind of thing. Please—don't do this."

Kaplan said nothing. He placed the gleaming point of the scalpel near the sternum in the fifth intercostal space and drew it firmly down.

"You're killing him," the paramedic said.

"He's dead now," Kaplan shrugged.

Eight minutes later the twin doors of UPMC Presbyterian Trauma Center burst open, and the stretcher raced in. The paramedic was at the head, pushing and guiding, while an EMT hurried along at his side, steadying the IV bag and line. On the opposite side, Jack Kaplan walked quickly and evenly, with both hands extending into a gaping scarlet hole.

A tall, thin woman in a white lab coat swept in behind them. "Jack, don't you ever go home? Isn't a twelve-hour shift long enough for you?"

"I was gone for two hours," he said. "I got bored."

"What did you *do*?" she said, staring into the wound.

"A resuscitative thoracotomy."

"In the back of an ambulance? What were you thinking?"

Three more ER staff came alongside now, and the paramedic and EMT passed off the stretcher like a baton in a relay race.

"He's got multiple stab wounds to the chest," Kaplan announced to the group. "He was in arrhythmia at the scene and went into cardiac arrest in the ambulance. I opened him up and checked for cardiac wounds—the vessels were all intact, but I sutured one atrial laceration. I displaced the heart and searched for posterior wounds—there were none. And I've been massaging this thing for ten minutes now, and my hands are cramping— somebody want to take over for me here?"

Kaplan stepped away as the stretcher disappeared into the OR. He stepped to a waste receptacle and began to strip off his dripping gloves.

"Hey, Rosa," he called to a passing nurse. "You're looking good tonight. When are you going driving with me?"

"When I feel like putting a gun to my head," the nurse said without turning.

He was at the sink, scrubbing, when the paramedic and both EMTs approached.

"I just want to say one thing," the paramedic growled. "You didn't have to do that. You can explain it away to the family, maybe even to your doctor friends, but *you* know and *I* know. We were two minutes away from a fully equipped ER. You did it the hard way, and you did it just for the doing." The paramedic shook his head in disgust. "Don't ever ride on my rig again."

Kaplan looked at him without expression, then turned to the EMT at his side. "How did it drive?"

The EMT dropped the keys on the floor. All three men turned and left.

Kaplan stepped into the waiting area. In the center of the room, two women stood embracing and weeping. The older woman was fiftyish, heavy and thick-limbed, her eyes bloated and red. Kaplan's eyes moved quickly to the daughter, who looked twenty, maybe twenty-five, with the face and body her mother might have had a very long time ago. Both women looked up as he entered.

"I'm Dr. Kaplan," he said solemnly. "I was the surgeon in charge tonight. I took responsibility for your—" *Husband? Brother? Jack never even got a name. No matter.*

"It's lucky I happened along when I did. I just want you to know, I did everything I could, and he's in the best of hands now."

At this, both women began to weep openly. The mother turned to Kaplan with a look of infinite gratitude, her arms outstretched. Kaplan brushed past her and took the younger woman in his arms, comforting her as best he could.

There was a beeping sound at his belt. He glanced down at the luminous green LCD. It read, ZOHAR: MANDATORY: THURSDAY 2300: FOX CHAPEL YACHT CLUB.

The Allegheny River cuts a three-hundred-mile channel from New York state across western Pennsylvania to the city of Pittsburgh. The Allegheny's riverbed is solid rock, smoothed by some ancient glacier, and the water that flows across its siltless bottom is a clear greenish blue. To the south, the Monongahela River wallows its way toward Pittsburgh through a hundred and twenty-five miles of mud and clay, pumping its red brown water through the old Steel Valley that once belched out so much smoke and soot that the streetlights had to be turned on at noon. Both rivers were once choked with debris and industrial effluent; now both are clean again, lined with marinas and private quays dotted with weekend pleasure boats. The two rivers join to form the mighty Ohio at a place simply known as the Point, at the tip of downtown Pittsburgh.

Nick Polchak stood with his toes overhanging the concrete ledge, staring into the churning waters. To his right the water flowed clear green; to his left, muddy brown; straight ahead, the two colors swirled together in a watery palette and disappeared into the distance. The Point is one of the most dangerous places to swim in all of Pittsburgh; the two rivers collide like angry storm fronts to spawn tornadolike undercurrents—but the Point is also the most tempting place to swim in all of Pittsburgh, and each year a handful of the brave and the foolish surrender to temptation at the cost of their lives.

"Thinking of jumping in?" a voice said behind him.

"Every time I come here," Nick replied.

Riley McKay's hair was straight and whitish blond, cut off above the shoulders and pulled back from her face with a thin, tortoiseshell band. Nick cocked his head and took her measure, comparing this new image with the one burned into his memory just a week and a half ago. Her cheekbones were high and her skin was fair—the Scots blood in her, Nick thought. Her shoulders were broad, well-boned, and her lean arms hung down from them like stockings from a coat hanger. Her fingertips broke just below midthigh, a bit longer than usual; her hands were long and slender, and her fingernails were cut to the quick like a concert pianist—no, like a forensic pathologist.

She wore a straight, knee-length skirt with a back vent. Nick looked at her legs; they were tight and sinewy. When she shifted her weight from side to side, he could see the cut between the gastrocnemius and the soleus. Her ankles were slightly thicker than normal—a little swollen, Nick thought—and on her feet she wore a pair of bright white Nike cross-trainers. Her hair, her dress, even her simple jewelry—everything about her was less a matter of style than expedience. Riley McKay was a woman with somewhere to go and something to do.

Nick's eyes returned to her face. A spray of freckles lay across the bridge of her nose, the product of countless unguarded hours in the sun, and her eyes—Nick stopped abruptly. Her eyes were two distinctly different colors: one brown and one green.

"Like them?" Riley smiled. "My dad used to call me Three Rivers." She leaned forward and peered at Nick's enormous glasses. "What did your dad call you?"

"Blind," Nick said.

"Oh. Sorry."

Nick shrugged and handed her a manila envelope. Riley turned and stepped to the edge of the great round basin that occupies the center of the triangular Point. She raised one hand in the air, testing for overspray from the fountain, then sat down. Nick took a seat beside her.

She opened the envelope and removed the brief report. The title read, "Forensic Entomology Investigation: Report of Diagnostic Laboratory Examination." Underneath, the traditional demographic information—name, sex, age, case number—was all left blank. Under "Requesting Agency," Nick had written, "Personal Request."

She flipped through the few sheets of paper. "You can sit here and watch me read this," she said, "or you can tell me what it says. Do you have a postmortem interval for me?"

"No."

"Did you find any indicators regarding the cause of death?"

"No."

Riley looked at him. "Dr. Polchak, is this a social call?"

"I can't give you a reliable PMI until I rear the last of the blowflies to maturity. That could take another two weeks. As to cause of death, you've given me very little to work with. I can do a toxicology screening—but then again, so can you. You're from the coroner's office, aren't you?"

"Then why did you call me?"

"As I recall, you said you were looking for *anomalies*. I could have waited another two weeks to give you my final report, but I thought you might want to hear what I've found so far. After all, a woman who goes outside of regular channels might also be a woman in a hurry."

"You found something?"

"Yes. But if you'd rather wait for the final report . . ."

Riley waited, but Nick said nothing more.

She frowned. "Did anyone ever tell you you can be really annoying?"

Nick nodded. "Dad called me that too. I was just wondering: Why didn't we meet at your office today? It's just five blocks away, right up Fourth Street there. You've got reserved parking; you've got air conditioning. It's so hot in Pittsburgh this time of year, don't you think? Why meet outside? Why in such a public place? Why sit here by a fountain, where it's so hard to hear?"

"You have a lot of questions," Riley said.

"So do you—*time* of death, *place* of death, *cause* of death. Hey, I've got an idea: I'll answer one of your questions, and you answer one of mine."

"I'm paying you to answer my question," Riley glared.

"You're right, that's hardly fair. I know—how about a discount? I tell you what, I'll knock my fee down to *two* hundred dollars. That's got to help—how much does a pathology fellow make? And after all, this is a *personal* expense—"

"*One* question," Riley said. "But you answer mine first—and it better be a two-hundred-dollar answer."

Nick smiled. "You told me that the man's body was discovered in Butler County—that's a good twenty-five miles from metropolitan Pittsburgh."

"That's right."

"He didn't die there."

Riley's eyes widened.

"Is that worth two hundred dollars?"

"That depends," she said. "Keep going."

"The maggots you collected represent four different species of blowfly. You were lucky. All four can be distinguished in their larval form—I didn't have to wait for them to mature. The first was *Phaenicia coeruleiviridis*—a green bottle fly. It's a common carrion fly, one of the first to arrive after death. The second species was *Phormia regina*, the black blowfly. They usually arrive twelve to twenty-four hours after death. Both species are very common, very predictable, exactly what you'd expect to find in a rural setting."

"And the other two?"

"*Phaenicia sericata* is another type of green bottle fly. It's sort of the city cousin of *Phaenicia coeruleiviridis*. It's not unusual to find a few in a rural setting—maybe 5 percent of the specimens—but *sericata* made up half of the maggots you collected. You're sure you took a representative sampling of all the maggots that were present? You didn't give preference to any particular size or shape?"

"I was careful to include the largest specimens," Riley said, "but I also included a sampling of everything I saw, all sizes and shapes. That's the way they taught us."

Nick nodded. "The clincher was *Calliphora vicina*, the blue bottle fly. Blue bottles like shady places and urban habitats. Find a body in a basement, and you'll find blue bottles. The funny thing is, they make up 10 percent of your specimens. The presence of *sericata* in such high numbers might have been a fluke— I doubt it, but it's at least possible—but when you add the presence of blue bottles, there's no other explanation. Your boy spent some time in the city—some time *after* death. What was the cause of death listed on the autopsy report?"

"Is that your one question?" Riley asked.

"C'mon, that's hardly worth two hundred bucks. It's just a simple question."

"AMI—acute myocardial infarction," Riley said. "He was only thirty-five."

"Statistically unusual, but not unheard of," Nick said. "Here's the real problem: either the victim perished in an urban area and was later moved to the country, or he died in the country and was transported to the city and back again."

"Why would anyone do that?"

"Beats me." Nick shrugged. "That's the sort of thing the coroner's office investigates, isn't it? One thing is for sure:

someone else was involved in the circumstances surrounding this man's death, and that seriously calls into question the diagnosis of 'death by natural causes.' I'd take another look at that AMI if I were you."

Riley said nothing. The wind shifted slightly, and mist from the fountain drifted down on them like a descending cloud.

"And now for my question," Nick said brightly. "The category is 'Nagging Suspicions' for two hundred dollars, and the question is: Why don't you trust your supervising pathologist?"

Riley turned. "I never said I didn't trust—"

"You're a pathology *fellow*," he said. "That makes you low man on the totem pole at the Allegheny County Coroner's Office. These questions you're asking, they're very good questions—the kind of questions you should be asking the pathologist in charge of your fellowship program. But for some reason, you don't *want* to ask your senior pathologist. You don't want him to know you're asking these questions at all, do you? So you collect your own evidence—entomological evidence, the kind no one will miss. Very shrewd, Dr. McKay. Then you find your very own bug man, and you offer to pay him out of your own pocket. It looks to me like you want answers, but for some reason you can't find them in your own office. For two hundred dollars, my question is: Why not?"

Riley paused.

"Look," Nick said. "You went outside of normal channels to get an expert opinion. OK, here I am. I'm an outsider. I don't know anyone at the coroner's office, they don't know me, and I report only to you. If you can't talk to me, who else can you talk to?"

Riley looked at Nick's eyes, as if hoping to take some reading on the soul behind those enormous lenses.

"It started about three months ago," she began. "I was barely into my fellowship program. A man passed away at Allegheny General, a head trauma victim. When the call came in, the pathologist on rotation was my supervisor, Dr. Nathan

Lassiter. He ordered an autopsy. That was strange enough, since it was a physician-attended death. But then he denied me access to the autopsy—he gave me some nonsense about its utter simplicity having 'no instructive value.' He practically shut the door in my face."

"Is this your first experience with arrogant authority figures?" Nick said. "Welcome to my world."

"The thing is, the victim was carrying a valid organ donor card, and a request was made for his kidneys while he was still at Allegheny General—but Lassiter refused to release the organs for transplant. That happens from time to time: a pathologist can refuse to release organs for transplant when she thinks removal of the organ could destroy forensic evidence. But denying a *kidney* over a *head trauma*?"

"And when you asked him about it, he said . . ."

"That I was still in my residency, that I had a lot to learn. That some of these judgments require years of experience, et cetera, et cetera. It was all bluster and bravado. So I went over his head; I appealed to the coroner himself."

"I'll bet that went over big."

"My supervisor threw a fit. He started throwing around terms like *lack of respect, professional courtesy,* and *a track record of incontestable judgment*—that was my favorite. What was the coroner supposed to do, side with a wet-behind-the-ears resident over one of his senior pathologists? He backed his homeboy, of course, and I had to eat crow. It's been a steady diet ever since."

"There are other means of appeal," Nick said.

"Question the *coroner's* judgment?" Riley groaned. "Now there's a career move for you. Look, Nick, the Allegheny County Coroner's Office is one of the top five in the nation. Two of our senior pathologists are former fellows themselves, and—"

"And when you finish your fellowship, you're hoping to land a job there. I don't blame you. It would be nice, you being from Pittsburgh and all."

"How did you know—"

"You said, 'Red off that table,' remember? That's Pittsburgh talking."

"Dr. Lassiter has shut me out of a couple of autopsies," Riley said, "and he keeps pushing me out of the office, sending me out on errands or to do those community educational programs."

"You'll learn to love those," Nick said. "I know I did."

"It was a mistake to go over Lassiter's head. At least, I *think* it was a mistake. When he didn't back down at all—not even an inch—that's when it hit me that either he's hiding something, or he's just a sexist, egotistical, scum-sucking pig."

"Which is a very real option," Nick said. "Trust me, I know that species."

"I don't know what it is, but there's just something about him . . ."

"He smells funny."

"What?"

"Do you know how blowflies are attracted to a body? The decomposing tissues emit a kind of chemical indicator—no one knows exactly what it is. The blowflies lay eggs, the eggs become larvae, the larvae pupate and produce a new generation of flies. But the next generation will not be attracted to the same body. Do you know why? Because the tissues have been breaking down and drying out, and now they're emitting a different indicator. Blowflies find bodies because of the smell—something only they can detect—and it only lasts for a short time."

"You're saying that I should act quickly? Or that I remind you of a blowfly?"

"I'm saying that smells are reliable indicators of decay. And yes, Dr. McKay, you do remind me of a blowfly; after all, aren't you both forensic investigators in your own way? If Dr. Lassiter smells funny to you, I'd go with your instincts—the rest of the animal world does."

Nick watched Riley slide the report back into the manila

envelope, then stare off toward the confluence of the two rivers. He looked into her eyes, one green and one brown, and he wondered what sort of turbulence lay behind them.

"I have another question," Nick said.

"The deal was for *one*."

"I'm willing to pay for it. The category is 'Hidden Motives' for a hundred dollars. The question is: Why does this bother you so much? What's in it for you? What do you care if an arrogant pathologist makes a bad call?"

Riley paused for a long time. "I'm not ready to answer that question," she said at last. "I don't know you that well."

"That's a fair answer," Nick said, "but hardly worth a hundred bucks. How about one more try? My final category is 'Occupational Hazards' for a hundred, and the question is: How far are you willing to go with this?"

"I don't know," Riley said. "I guess it depends on what I find."

"Then you plan to go on looking?"

"Would you?"

"I once dissected an undergraduate student just to get out of teaching," Nick said. "I'm not the best person to ask about boundaries."

"I'm not very good at knowing when to quit either," Riley said. "But what am I supposed to do next? So I've got an *anomaly*. Am I supposed to run back to the coroner's office and start blowing the whistle again? That would finish me."

"I agree, timing is very important for you. The next time you blow that whistle, you better have something substantial to show for it. You better have *proof*."

"That's the problem," Riley said. "Proof is the product of evidence, and Lassiter controls all the evidence. When he locks me out of an autopsy, all I can do is read the report when he's finished—and the report says whatever he wants it to."

"You could urge the next of kin to request a second autopsy. They can do that, can't they?"

"Yes—but what do I say when they ask me *why*? Who pays

for it? And worst of all, what if it turns up nothing? Then word would get back to the coroner's office for sure."

"At least you have a couple of things going for you."

"Like what?"

"Like the fact that Dr. Lassiter is your supervisor, so you have ongoing access to him. Like the fact that you're part of a fellowship program, so you're expected to ask questions around the office—you're not nosy, you're a *resident*. You have knowledge of this anomaly—knowledge that Dr. Lassiter doesn't know you have. And doesn't Lassiter work a scheduled rotation? Then you'll know when he's up for an autopsy, and you can poke around and see what you can find."

"See what I can *find*. Nick, I have a medical degree, and I've done a five-year residency in pathology. I'm an experienced pathologist, but I still know next to nothing about forensics. I'm not exactly sure *how* to 'poke around.'"

"Whereas I am experienced in forensics," Nick said, "but I know far less about pathology. Maybe it would help if we formed a partnership: I'll do the forensics, you provide the pathology. Together, we'd make one mean forensic pathologist."

"Thanks," Riley said, "but to be honest, I can't afford to pay for your ongoing services. This is a personal expense, remember?"

"My prices are very reasonable. Didn't I just give you a 100 percent discount on my first bill?"

Riley looked at him. "You don't know me, Nick. I could be a crackpot for all you know. This whole thing could be just my imagination."

"The blue bottle flies weren't your imagination."

"Why would you want to do this? Why would you want to help me?"

"Because you remind me of me: you're smart, you're good-looking, and you're broke."

"I'm serious."

"OK," Nick said with a sigh. "If you must know, it's my

mother. She's been after me to join the Sons of Poland. She keeps trying to feed me pierogies—I hate pierogies. I'll pay *you* if it gets me out of the house."

"Nick. *Why?*"

Nick returned her gaze at last. "Bottom line?" he said.

"Bottom line."

He shrugged. "I like the way you smell."

CHAPTER 7

He pulled out of the driveway at exactly seven o'clock, the same time he did every Thursday night, after the same old argument with Melissa over his one night out with the guys. It's not like he did this every night—didn't he skip a poker night just a couple of months ago? Didn't he take the boys to a Penguins game?

So Melissa's got the kids all day. So what? What was *he* doing at PPG all day? And besides, a man needs to stretch his legs once in a while. Once a *week*, for crying out loud! Melissa's got her girlfriends; she's off to Starbucks at the drop of a hat—is one night a week too much to ask? Once a week is a bargain. For once a week, she oughta be *grateful*. He straightened a little and took a firmer grip on the steering wheel.

He took a left on Franklin, then a right on Kittanning, just as he did every Thursday night. He passed the same endless parade of indistinguishable row houses, all lined up like books on a shelf, each with its own overcrowded porch, overhanging roof, and tiny rectangle of neatly trimmed ryegrass.

Two blocks down, the neat little houses gave way to a different kind of neighborhood. Porch roofs began to dip and sag, long streaks of gray peeked out through peeling flecks of paint, and the occasional gutter drooped to the ground like a dying limb. After another two blocks the houses crumbled away entirely, leaving nothing behind but a graveyard of pawn shops, convenience stores, and razor-wired storage yards. In the stark mercury vapor lights, the early evening shadows cut like straight razors, and everything that wasn't black glowed the same electric blue.

He unconsciously leaned his elbow on the door lock, just as he did in this exact location every Thursday night.

At the end of Kittanning he would turn left again, away from the porn shops and the boarded-up churches, and into a better neighborhood. But at the end of Kittanning he did something he had never done before—he came to a stop. The left lane was blocked off by a flashing orange barricade, and a white-and-black detour sign pointed him in the opposite direction.

He slammed his hand against the steering wheel. What's wrong with those idiots at PennDOT? Why would anyone bother to repair a road in this shell hole? The whole place should be condemned; the whole neighborhood should be scraped level and buried in some landfill. He was the only car on the road—he was *always* the only car on the road. Do they think one lousy car merits road work? Go figure—your tax dollars at work.

He looked to the right. Just a block or two, then he'd take a left on the best-lit street he could find; two more quick lefts and he'd be back on track again. He shrugged and turned the wheel slowly to the right.

Two blocks down, a second detour sign beckoned him to the left. He turned up a narrow, lifeless, two-lane road walled in by empty back porches and buckling garage doors. In the dusk ahead, his headlights discovered a cherry red BMW, barely off the road, that leapt out from the shadows like blood on a newspaper. The trunk was open, and the car sagged limply to the left.

Beside the left rear quarter panel, holding a tire jack, stood a beautiful young woman with long, auburn hair. Her V-neck blouse was pristine white. As his car approached, she swept back her hair with the back of her hand, locked on to his eyes, and mouthed the words, "Help me—PLEASE."

He felt a rush of excitement. He pulled his car over just ahead of hers and looked quickly around the area the way a man does when he comes across a twenty-dollar bill on the sidewalk. He got out of the car, tucked his shirt front in tight, and approached.

"Need some help?"

"I feel like such a *girl*," she said. "I should know how to change this thing myself, but—it's so sweet of you to stop." She stood with one leg just in front of the other, like the women in the catalogs always do. She wore black stiletto heels, and her skirt was tight around her knees. He tried to imagine her squatting down to wrestle off a set of stubborn lug nuts. He smiled.

"You picked a heckuva place to get a flat tire."

"Didn't I, though?"

"Look," he said, considering their surroundings for the first time, "maybe I should drive you to the nearest Tire and Auto. They can help you out."

She turned up her lower lip. "It's just that I'm running so late," she said, holding the jack away from her like a dripping umbrella. "I was hoping you'd be one of those big, strong types—you know, the kind who has a whole garage full of tools back home. I guess that was kind of stupid of me."

He hitched up his pants. "Let me take a look at it," he said, taking the jack from her. He squatted down and began to pry off the hubcap with a rusted squawk.

"Is your spare in good shape?"

"I really don't know. I guess I should check that from time to time."

He glanced up at her. "Doesn't your boyfriend help you with these things?"

She winked. "Maybe that's what I really need—a spare boyfriend."

He started to say, "Are you from around here?" But then he looked at her again: smiling down on him like his very own moon, leaning back against the driver's door in that long S-curve. Whoever she was, whatever she was, she was not from around here.

He felt electrified. He felt feverish. His head was covered in a cold sweat, and he could almost feel his own pulse. She was so close to him, so completely present, that his senses allowed room for nothing else: not the tug of the shirt that clung to his back, not the grainy grit of the grease on his fingertips, not the weight of the tire in his hands—not even the sound of quiet footsteps that approached him from out of the shadows.

He glanced up at her again. He saw the smile disappear from her face, and he saw her cover her eyes with her left hand.

He felt himself slump forward against the tire, and then he felt nothing at all.

CHAPTER 8

"Good morning, Dr. McKay."

Nathan Lassiter was dressed in sea green scrubs, ready for the morning's round of autopsies. The Allegheny County Coroner's Office averages two or three autopsies every day of the calendar year. With luck they would finish by lunchtime, leaving the afternoon to review histology slides and begin the autopsy reports. Riley glanced at her watch: it was almost nine-thirty. She had already been there for an hour, reviewing the day's cases and arranging assignments with the autopsy techs and assistants. By now she was used to Lassiter's utter disregard for schedule—*her* schedule—but it still never ceased to irritate her.

"Good morning, Dr. Lassiter. I was looking over the chart—I've had a little time to kill. We've got three today: One is a drowning victim, a little four-year-old girl from Penn Hills. That's a sad one."

"I hate floaters," Lassiter said. "I'll leave that one to you. What else have we got?"

Riley looked up at him. Lassiter was fifteen years her senior. The hair coloring he used was two shades over the top, a kind of glaring chestnut brown that contrasted badly with his colorless face. The skin along his jawline was beginning to sag and pouch, and faint brown liver spots already dotted his temples. He dressed the way middle-aged men do when they lose touch with the times—when they lose touch with *women*. "We've also got a peri-operative death from Allegheny General," she said, "plus a homicide—gunshot to the back of the head. I assume we'll do the homicide first."

"*I'll* do the homicide first," he said. "You're heading over to the University of Pittsburgh Medical School."

"What? Why?"

"You're giving a lecture there today on the proper way to fill out a death certificate."

Riley tossed her clipboard onto the counter. "You've got to be kidding."

"Not at all. There's not a single class in all of medical school that teaches doctors how to fill out a death certificate. You wouldn't believe some of the garbage we get here: nonmedical terminology, indistinguishable causes of death—it's a serious problem."

"Dr. Lassiter, surely one of the deputy coroners could—"

"Not a chance," Lassiter said. "I've done the lecture; so have all the other pathologists. Why should you get special treatment?"

"This is bogus," Riley said. "My fellowship program requires participation in two hundred and fifty autopsies."

"Your fellowship program requires participation in *all* the activities of the coroner's office: crime scene investigation, toxicology, ballistics, *everything*—including community and educational activities."

"Come on, Dr. Lassiter. I did a hundred autopsies on natural deaths during my residency. Today we've got a homicide. Isn't that what I'm here to learn about?"

"You're here to learn about lots of things."

"Look, I've done *five years* of postgraduate training in both anatomical and clinical pathology, and I did a subspecialty in renal pathology—yet you keep sending me out on errands a schoolgirl could do. Why is that?"

"Because around here you *are* a schoolgirl—unless you want to take your five years of training and get yourself a nice job in a hospital lab somewhere. You're a pathologist, Dr. McKay, but you're not a *forensic* pathologist—not until you finish this fellowship program and take your boards."

"Then *let* me finish it! Let me stay here and do autopsies— that's what this fellowship program ought to be—"

"Don't tell me how to run your program!" Lassiter barked. "You think that med school lectures and community seminars are somehow beneath you—well they're *not*, Ms. McKay, and as long as I'm your program supervisor, you'll do anything and everything I assign you to do. Is that clear? Maybe in the process you'll learn that there's more to being a forensic pathologist than just performing autopsies. Maybe you'll learn a little *humility*."

Riley bit her lip hard. To have to stand there and listen to this man preach on the need for *humility*. It took all of her resolve to say nothing in reply. Lassiter was, after all, a senior pathologist and a member of the coroner's office staff. She knew that if she ever hoped to work there she had to hold her tongue—but not her imagination. In her mind's eye, she imagined Lassiter lying on his back on the cold, stainless steel autopsy table. She saw herself make the classic Y-shaped incision, from both collarbones to the sternum and then straight down the abdomen.

"I think we both have our assignments this morning," Lassiter said. "The sooner you leave to do yours, the sooner I can get started on mine—unless you have any *more* objections?"

Now Riley made the circular incision around his skull,

applied the bone saw, removed the skull cap, and found . . . nothing at all.

"Then get moving," Lassiter said. "The day isn't getting any younger."

Riley ran her tongue across her lower lip and tasted blood.

She wheeled around and charged down the hallway and up the stairs, ignoring a morning greeting from the chief deputy coroner. She headed for her tiny second-floor office, intending to stop just long enough to drop her lab coat and grab her purse—but on the way she passed the open doorway of Lassiter's office.

She looked back at the stairway. In a few minutes the autopsy would begin, and then Lassiter would be occupied for at least two hours—three or four if there were abnormalities. She glanced across the hall at the cubicles that filled the center office. She saw the tops of heads just visible above the fabric-covered panels. No one looked up; no one met her eyes; no one was watching.

She stepped back into Lassiter's office and quietly shut the door behind her.

She turned and rested against the door, surveying the office. Her anger had somehow left her, replaced by a strange sense of exhilaration. She felt lightheaded, almost giddy, the way she felt as a teenager playing a midnight game of Capture the Flag—but this was no game. She had acted impulsively; she had acted out of anger; she had entered Lassiter's private office without even knowing what she was looking for. *You'd better figure it out fast,* she said to herself. Her exhilaration was quickly giving way to gnawing fear.

And then she remembered—*autopsy dictations.*

During every autopsy, the senior pathologist wore a headset microphone and kept a running verbal commentary on a voice-activated digital recorder. These were his notes, the observations and details he would use to refresh his memory as he composed the final autopsy report. The recording sounded nothing like an organized presentation; it was always broken, choppy, filled with the pathologist's off-the-cuff remarks and unconscious reactions. Riley had heard comments made about a victim's attractiveness, or ethnicity, or even about his obvious guilt or innocence—comments that would never appear in written form. In the course of a two-hour autopsy, who knows what Lassiter might have said? His dictations might reveal evidence that never made it to his final reports.

Riley stepped around the desk and sat down at Lassiter's computer. She knew that the digital recordings were downloaded onto the pathologist's computer, where the session could be audibly reviewed or the file could be e-mailed to an outside vendor for transcription. On the monitor, a screen saver of a cherry red Dodge Viper was displayed. Riley jiggled the mouse and the image instantly vanished, replaced by the Windows Desktop. She quickly hunted through the dozens of icons, searching for the medical dictation program.

And then she heard the doorknob turn.

A pure panic-reflex caused her to jump to her feet just before the door opened wide. Nathan Lassiter stood looking at her without expression.

"Can I help you?"

Riley's brain flooded with adrenaline, and a thousand lame excuses and ridiculous explanations competed for her approval. But none of them was adequate—none was even close—and Riley stood there looking guilty and ashamed, like a little girl caught with a quarter pressed tightly in her hand and her mama's purse at her feet.

From the corner of her eye Riley saw the computer monitor, and she almost audibly gasped. The screen saver was gone; the Windows Desktop was still in view.

Lassiter charged forward. Riley quickly stepped out to block him from circling the desk.

"I came in to . . . leave you a note," she stumbled.

"You couldn't leave it with my secretary?" He moved forward again. Riley stepped as far forward as she could and still keep the screen in her peripheral vision.

"It was . . . personal in nature," she said.

Lassiter softened a bit. "Oh?"

"It was . . . an apology." She stood uncomfortably close to him now, but it was the only way to keep him from the computer screen.

"Well, here I am. Let's hear it."

Riley winced. "I just wanted to say . . . I'm sorry."

"Sorry for what?"

"For . . . for my attitude." Riley felt her stomach turn. She felt as though she were vomiting up each detestable word. "You're my supervisor, and I was . . . disrespectful." She eyed the monitor; how long does it take for a screen saver to reappear? Thirty seconds? A minute? She didn't know how much more of this sniveling she could endure. She was sure of one thing: Lassiter could listen to it all day.

"Well, I appreciate that," he said beneficently. "It takes a little perspective to see these things clearly, and I suppose that comes from experience." He reached out and placed one hand on her shoulder. It had all the warmth of a cadaver. From the corner of her eye, Riley saw a flicker of light and a change in hue from Windows blue to cherry red. She felt an overwhelming rush of relief, but she had no idea how to break off this touching encounter.

"OK," she said abruptly. "Gotta go." She stepped under his arm and headed directly for the door, exiting without looking back. She stopped briefly at her office, hung up her lab coat, and collected her purse. Then she hurried out of the building, looking for a suitable place to scream.

CHAPTER 9

T here was a steady, insistent rapping on the metal fire door that opened onto the parking lot at the Allegheny County Coroner's Office. Riley hurried to the corner of the autopsy room and pushed it open. There stood an expressionless Nick Polchak, a canvas backpack slung over one shoulder.

"Nick, what took you so long? I called you thirty minutes ago!"

"I live thirty minutes away," Nick said.

"You said you were going to be 'on call.'"

"You mean just sitting around day after day, waiting for you to call? And they say men are demanding."

She grabbed him by the arm and pulled him inside.

"Where is everybody?" Nick said. "The place is dead—no pun intended."

"It was a quiet night—there were no calls coming in—so I gave them some money and sent them all out for pizza and beer."

"You seem to personally fund a lot of interesting ventures. Remind me to tell you about a certain grant proposal."

"Nick, they left twenty minutes ago. They could be back any moment now."

"Then we'd better get busy. What have you got?"

"We had a body come in this morning. It was a gunshot wound to the rear of the head. He was apparently changing his tire, and they found him slumped over against his car—he picked a bad place to get a flat. Nothing was taken from the victim or his car; it looks like a drive-by shooting, possibly gang related."

"And the autopsy? I assume it was Lassiter's rotation."

She nodded. "I offered to assist, as always—this time he sent me to Pitt to teach medical students how to hold a pen. I reviewed the police report just before I called you. Estimated time of death was yesterday, around dusk. They talked to the victim's wife—he left home at exactly seven p.m. He was due at a poker game by seven thirty, but he never showed up. Lassiter did the autopsy late this morning."

"And?"

"The procedure is to issue a death certificate immediately after the autopsy, but all it indicates is the primary cause of death. The details of Lassiter's autopsy report won't come out for a week or two—but I talked to one of his autopsy techs. He said the cause of death was a single bullet through the occipital bone. There was an entry wound, but no exit—it was a small-caliber weapon. The size and shape of the wound suggest a short-to-intermediate firing distance, and it was straight-on—just what you'd expect from a drive-by."

"Nothing out of the ordinary?"

"Nothing the tech could see—nothing he was *allowed* to see. The only way we'll know for sure is to check for ourselves—that is, if you're still willing to help."

"What can I do?"

"I need a second pair of eyes. We can't reopen the body—we can't even use the autopsy room. We can't send any tissue samples to the histology lab, and we can't draw any fluids for

TIM DOWNS

a toxicology screen. All we can do is work from the outside. I can check for contusions, abrasions, additional wounds of any kind—I need you to look for evidence of insect activity. I'm looking for anything, Nick—anything that doesn't look consistent with a drive-by shooting. But whatever we do, we've got to do it *fast*."

The cooler door opened with a soft click, and a wall of icy air greeted them. The cooler was a single large room, long and deep, with a series of utility shelves and wire-rimmed, circular fans lining the far end. The walls looked like panels of Reynolds Wrap imprinted with poultry wire, a dull silver gray, and three stark incandescent bulbs dotted the midline of the ceiling. Packed in the center of the room were a half-dozen aging gurneys with white Formica tops and large, narrow wheels. Each one supported a human cadaver, sealed in a glossy blue body bag with a long black zipper directly down the center.

Riley pulled the door shut behind them and wheeled a single gurney into a small, open area.

"We have to do our looking in here," Riley said. "Sorry it's a bit chilly."

"My mom has no air conditioning," Nick said. "This is heaven." He pulled the zipper all the way to the feet and began to tuck the vinyl back away from the torso.

Riley started with the soles of the feet and worked her way up, searching for any telltale mark or scratch that might reveal a struggle, an antemortem wound, or a posthumous relocation of the body. Nick began at the opposite end, checking the eyes, ears, and nasal passages for infestation. He pried open the lower jaw and peered into the mouth with a penlight.

"This is interesting," Nick said.

"What?"

"There are eggs in the back of the mouth; blowflies go for the natural orifices first, and they often oviposit well back in the passageway. You said the time of death was after seven o'clock, around dusk? Blowflies usually knock off after dark, when the temperatures begin to fall. That would put the time of death as close to seven as possible. Looks like these ladies just got in under the wire."

"Hurry, Nick," Riley said. "We can debrief later."

Riley worked her way up toward the neck and cranial area, while Nick headed for the lower orifices; they stumbled into one another at the center of the body. When they bumped against the gurney, a tiny, paste-white object dropped into the crease at the bottom of the body bag.

"Now that *is* interesting," Nick said, smoothing the crease and lifting the edge of the body bag closer to his face.

"Do you need a magnifier?"

Nick tapped his glasses. "Got one—it's one of the perks." Under the powerful lenses, a single, barely moving larva came into focus.

"It's a first-instar maggot," he said, "the earliest stage of larval development. There are two possibilities: Either the temperatures remained warm enough last night to allow a blowfly egg to hatch, or it's a sarcophagid—a flesh fly. Blowflies lay eggs; flesh flies give live birth. They sort of squirt the maggots out, sometimes without even landing on the body. The big question for us is: where did it come from?"

"You already found eggs in the oral cavity."

"Yes—*deep* in the oral cavity. Flesh-eating flies are attracted to openings in the body—usually the natural orifices first, because that's where the gases are released that are the by-product of decomposition. But there are no orifices in the middle of the body, and yet we seem to have dislodged this little guy from somewhere."

Nick stooped down and grasped the thorax with both hands, hooking his thumbs under the lower back, rolling the body slightly onto its left side. On the back, just below the rib cage, was a long, curving wound that was roughly sutured shut. In the center of the wound, wedged tightly between the lips of flesh, were two more tiny maggots.

"Bingo," Nick said.

Just then they heard the click of the cooler door. Nick released the body, which settled thickly onto its back again. Riley lunged for the zipper, tugging it shut. She gave the gurney a shove with her hip, sending it rolling into the others. The cooler door began to swing open.

Nick turned to Riley, took her roughly in his arms, and kissed her.

Riley was so astonished that for the first instant she stood with her eyes bulging, her arms thrust down and back like a gymnast finishing a dismount, as rigid as one of the cadavers around her. Then, just as suddenly, she realized what was taking place and understood her part in it. She swung her left arm up around Nick's neck, closed her eyes, and kissed him back hard.

She heard a kind of snort from the doorway behind her, and then a giggling sound from out in the hall. "Sorry," a voice said. "Bad timing."

She turned to face them. Two deputy coroners and the dispatcher stood in the doorway holding a white cardboard box.

"We brought you back some pizza," one of them said. "Guess we should have brought extra." There was a smothered laugh and a trading of elbows.

"You two better take it easy," said another. "We can't have the stiffs thawing out in here."

Riley's face felt flushed and hot—something she hadn't experienced in a long, long time. She felt like a schoolgirl who had been caught behind the lockers with her boyfriend. She despised their adolescent snickering, and even more her temporary loss of hard-earned status—but there was nothing to do now but play her part out to the end.

"We'll be through here in a minute," she said.

"Doesn't look like it to me," someone whispered.

"Do you mind? Close the door on your way out."

The door closed firmly, abruptly cutting off the sound of rising laughter.

Riley glanced at Nick, peeled off her glove, and wiped her index finger across her lips.

"Well," Nick said. "I'd say this was very productive time."

■

Riley stepped through her apartment door, pausing to wrestle her keys from the deadbolt. Nick stepped into the doorway behind her and stopped, his eyes taking in the room in broad strokes.

"Nice place," he said. "It's a little Spartan."

"That's because I don't live with my mother."

"Ouch."

As Nick stepped into the room, he shoved his hands deep into his pockets, like a little boy cautioned not to break anything. He stood in the center of the room, turning and looking.

"You almost lost me on the way over here," he said. "You drive pretty fast. Why doesn't that surprise me?"

"I couldn't lose sight of *you*," Riley said. "There was a big blue cloud of smoke behind you. What in the world are you driving?"

"A car," he said.

"What *kind* of car?"

Nick frowned. "I really don't know."

Riley flopped onto the sofa and folded her legs underneath her. She straightened stiffly and grimaced, massaging her lower back with her thumbs.

"Back trouble?" Nick said, taking a seat across from her.

"Too many hours on my feet," she said. "What about that dorsal wound? I barely got a look at it."

"Very strange. You said Lassiter listed a gunshot wound as the primary cause of death. On the autopsy tape, there was no mention of any other major wounds?"

"None at all."

"Would a pathologist neglect to mention a wound just because he thought it had nothing to do with the cause of death?"

"Of course not. For a pathologist, the issue isn't simply the *cause* of death, but all the circumstances *surrounding* death. The very presence of a secondary wound makes it important. It would take the world's worst pathologist to make that kind of omission."

"Do you know what they call the guy who graduates last in his class in medical school? *Doctor*."

Riley shook her head. "I don't suspect Dr. Lassiter of incompetence."

Nick leaned forward. "What *do* you suspect him of?"

Riley said nothing.

"I know," Nick said. "You're 'not ready to answer that question.'"

She smiled slightly.

"There are three things that are significant about that wound," Nick said. "First of all, it was more of an incision than a wound—the edges of the tissue were too smooth to have been caused by any street weapon. Second, the wound was sutured closed—not surgically, like in a hospital, but the way your people do after an autopsy—just enough to hold it shut. Finally—and most important of all—Dr. Lassiter didn't make that incision."

"How do you know that?"

"Because there were larvae in the wound—we dislodged one of them, remember? I found two more still intact. If Dr. Lassiter made the incision during the autopsy, there would be no maggots present."

"Could the maggots have moved there from some other part of the body?"

"Not a chance. The only other infestation was still in the egg stage, and even if there were other larvae, maggots stay very close to where they're deposited—they don't go wandering around the body."

"Then the incision must have been made earlier—before our office picked up the body—and before dark, because you said flies cease activity at night. But, Nick, that pushes the incision all the way back to the time of death."

Nick nodded.

"Could it have been made even earlier? Say, the day before?"

"It's possible, but highly unlikely. For the wound to be infested, it had to be exposed. Don't forget, when flies approach a body they have a choice of egg-laying locations. All they need is warm, dark, and moist—that's why they like the mouth so much. But the only maggots on this body were on a wound near the center of the back. At some time after death, that wound was as open and available as the eyes, ears, or mouth."

"Then I have some questions," Riley said. "What role did this wound play in the overall death scenario? Why would anyone bother to suture a wound on a dead man? And most of all, why would Dr. Lassiter choose to overlook it?"

"Good questions," Nick said.

Riley slumped back against the sofa. "Then we're right back where we started from—we've got a bunch of questions and no answers."

"We've got a *different* set of questions," Nick said. "Now you have a second anomaly—an actual, physical anomaly—and now it looks much more certain that Lassiter's apparent negligence is intentional. I call that progress."

"So what do we do next?"

"It's a question of access. We can't go back to the crime scene, and we can't re-examine the body, so we go with Lassiter. Let's see what we can dig up about his possible motives."

"And the way we do that is?"

"I've got a couple of ideas."

Riley shook her head. "Why doesn't that surprise me?"

Neither one said anything for a minute.

"You kissed me," Riley said suddenly.

"What?"

"In the cooler. You kissed me."

"Are you just noticing this now? I've got to work on my technique."

Riley squinted at him. "The way I see it, Nick, there are only two options: either you're incredibly quick and able to think on your feet, or you're a big, fat coward."

Nick stared at the ceiling for several seconds, then slowly began to nod his head. "Yes," he said, "those would be the options."

CHAPTER 10

Nathan Lassiter stepped out his front door and tiptoed barefoot down the herringbone brick sidewalk that led to his driveway and the morning *Post-Gazette*. He wore a fading Penn T-shirt tucked into the powder blue surgical scrubs he always used as pajamas. The shirt did nothing to conceal his sizable paunch. His shoulders were narrowing and rounded, and his once-prized pecs—no longer able to be sustained by a dozen monthly bench presses—were fast becoming nothing but nipples. He was unshaven, uncombed, and thanks to Dr. Atkins, his breath reeked of ketones.

He stopped abruptly. In the center of his driveway was a bright orange pickup truck with a generic black insect on top, smiling and doffing its hat to passersby. The truck was empty, and the windows were rolled down. Lassiter looked around and noticed that the gate to his backyard hung open.

■

Halfway down the side of the house, Nick Polchak knelt beside the open door to the crawlspace that ran underneath the house. He wore blue coveralls with an embroidered logo representing a company called "Bug Off," and he was busy making notations on a silver metal clip box.

"Hey, you," Lassiter said, picking his way across the dewy grass. "What do you mean by just walking in here and—"

"You want the damage report?" Nick said. "You paid for it."

"What? I didn't pay for anything."

"Are you Nathan Lassiter? You got a five-year service contract with our company." Nick waved the paperwork in the air and then tossed it facedown on the grass. "Once a year we check under the house for termites, whole house wood bores, the whole shebang."

"I've never seen you here before."

Nick shrugged. "You never had a problem before. You think we'd knock on your door just to say, 'Everything's peachy'? If you got no problem, we're invisible—just like your termites."

"I never paid for any service contract."

"Is there a Mrs. Lassiter?"

Lassiter closed his eyes.

"Well, there you go," Nick said. "A smart woman, Mrs. Lassiter."

Lassiter glared at him. "What's this about termites?"

"Not just termites. You got carpenter ants—those are really tough to get rid of. I found powderpost beetles—with beetles you got to kill the eggs too, 'cause baby beetles can raise themselves, not like kids these days, huh, Nate? And then you got brown recluse spiders—I never seen so many of 'em. You ever seen someone bit by a brown recluse? I heard about a guy up in Blawnox, he crawled under to check his furnace, took a bite right here on his thumb. They say it looked like a gunshot wound, the whole hand practically rotted away—"

"Look, do I really need to deal with this right now?"

"Not if you don't mind your house being eaten out from

under you. Hey, you got a floor joist down there that looks like a twenty-foot loofah."

Lassiter muttered a colorful phrase to no one in particular. Nick watched him. His toes were hanging over the edge; all he needed was one more push.

"If it makes you feel any better, you already paid for it."

"What? When?"

"It's part of your service contract. You know how it works, sort of like a homeowner's warranty. You pay the cash up front; we cover the service if you need it. Some people win, some people lose—you're about to win big time."

"OK then," Lassiter shrugged. "Go ahead and spray."

Nick threw back his head and let out a laugh.

"Go ahead and *spray*? You look like a smart guy—what are you, a nurse? Let me explain something to you. A termite queen can lay thirty thousand eggs a *day*. Down along the Gulf Coast, Formosan termites can consume an entire house in just eighteen months. You have an *infestation*, my friend. You can only spray the ones you can see. The only way to kill them all is to fumigate."

"Fumigate? How does that work?"

"We tent the house. We wrap it up top to bottom with big yellow tarps—you should see it, Nate, it's really something— then we tape all the seams and lay sand snakes around the bottom to seal it up tight. Then we fill the whole thing up with *Vikane*—sulfuryl fluoride gas."

Lassiter groaned. "How long does all this take?"

"Not as long as you'd think. We can wrap a little place like this in, say, half a day. We blow in the gas—that doesn't take long—and then the whole thing sits for maybe a day. We pull off the tarps, open all the windows to air it out—that's it, you're done. A day and a half total. And there's hardly any prep work for you to do. Just be sure to remove the plants and the pets— 'cause that Vikane will kill every living thing under the tent. A couple years ago in Tampa, a woman committed suicide that way. Do you have a cat? You look like a cat person to me."

"I can't do this now," Lassiter said. "Maybe in a month or two."

"It's your call," Nick said. "I can fit you in late December."

"That's six months away!"

"The whole thing works on a big computer schedule. You know how it is. When we set up the service contract, we schedule the inspections and the repairs together. If you want to reschedule, you got to take what's available. I'll put you down for the weekend after Christmas."

Lassiter hesitated.

"Or I can do it tomorrow," Nick said. "A day and a half, the whole thing's out of your hair by the end of the week. Whaddya say? You head off to work tomorrow morning, but you get a hotel room tomorrow night. Or you could just find an empty bed at the hospital—hey, who's gonna know?"

"I'm a *pathologist*, you idiot!"

"It's OK," Nick said softly. "Hey, my wife's on Zoloft."

Lassiter turned and stormed off toward the driveway. "Do it tomorrow," he shouted back, "but I don't want to see any sign of your crew by the following afternoon!"

"Trust me," Nick called after him, "you'll never know we were here."

CHAPTER 11

Nick and Riley sat at a corner table at the Common Plea, just a short walk from the coroner's office at Fourth and Ross. The eatery was first-rate, one of Pittsburgh's finest, an authentically Italian establishment without a trace of checkered vinyl tablecloths or wax-rimed Chianti bottles. The pecan-stained walls were trimmed in ornate moldings and lined with elegant candelabra sconces and glossy oil paintings framed in gold. Riley looked at Nick, dressed just as casually as ever, looking as out of place as a fly on a china platter. He busied himself with a plate of Veal Veneziana while Riley looked on.

"You like Italian?" she said, picking at her own plate.

"I like food."

"Funny. Somehow I figured a bug man would be a vegetarian."

"Why? Insects are some of the biggest carnivores on the planet. Did you know that in Chile they have a spider that eats *mice*?"

She pushed her plate away. "Nick, I'm trying to eat here. Do you want to hear about my last autopsy?"

"OK by me."

"Look," she said, "I need you to explain this whole thing again. We go to Lassiter's house tomorrow, and the whole thing will be covered with tarpaulins. Then we just walk in dressed like exterminators and take our time looking around. Is that it?"

"Not too much time," Nick said. "We should be out by dark. It wouldn't do to have lights visible beneath the tarps."

"What about the sulfuryl fluoride? The gas is toxic."

"What gas?"

"I get it—you wrap the house, but you never fill it with gas. But then, how do you get rid of his termites?"

"What termites?"

Riley shook her head in disbelief. "How did you arrange all this?"

"I know a guy—an old classmate of mine at Penn State. He's doing pretty well for himself—he's actually making a living with an undergraduate entomology degree. He owns a pest control company in Oakmont. We worked out a deal."

"What's in it for him?"

"They don't tent and fumigate much around here—it's more of a Southern thing. When my friend wraps up a house with those big yellow tarps of his, it's practically a media event. He hands out cards all over the neighborhood. He tells them, 'See? This is what can happen if you don't do regular treatments.' It works out for both of us."

"Nick, has it occurred to you that this is slightly illegal? It's called *breaking and entering*."

"Why? Lassiter signed a release form that allows the exterminators access to his home."

"We're not exterminators! We're masquerading as exterminators in order to do an illegal search of his home."

"Details."

"Nick—have you ever been in trouble with the law before?"

He paused. "Define 'trouble.'"

"Do you know what a risk this is for both of us?"

"For both of us? Or for you?"

"OK," she grumbled. "For me. If I got caught, this would be the end of my career. It would end my fellowship—and even if they let me finish, who would hire a forensic pathologist who's a part-time burglar?"

"Not me."

"You seem to be taking this all pretty lightly."

"Look," Nick said. "I respect the law. We have the same goal in mind—I just find it necessary to take a different path to the goal sometimes. I like to think I keep the *spirit* of the law."

Riley rolled her eyes. "I'll bet the prisons are filled with people who kept the 'spirit of the law.'"

"I'm open to legal alternatives. Got any ideas?"

"No," Riley said sullenly. "I told you what happened when I tried to search his office. I guess this is not my specialty."

"Well, it's *my* specialty. I've taken risks with the law before, and let me tell you, this is a pretty good one. When you tent a house, people know that toxic chemicals are involved and they steer clear of it. The next-door neighbors generally clear out for the day, and you won't see a kid outside for a block in any direction. There's virtually no chance that Lassiter will return unexpectedly like he did at his office—and even if he did, what would he see? A house wrapped in plastic and a company truck in the driveway. And once we're inside—well, that's the best part. Lassiter knows that the exterminators need access to the house, and he'll expect a certain amount of disturbance—doors left open, objects rearranged, that sort of thing. As long as we don't do anything stupid, our tracks will be covered. It's a terrific setup. Personally, I'm hoping he has an indoor hot tub."

Riley's eyes widened.

"Hey, lighten up."

"Lighten up," she groaned.

"Look, if you feel this way, maybe you shouldn't come along."

"You mean let you do it alone?"

"Like you said, it's not your specialty. You almost got caught once; if something goes wrong this time, you'll be in the clear."

Riley watched him wipe a slice of Bruschetta around the edge of his dish.

"Nick, why would you do this? You barely know me. I'm not even paying you. You're not just offering to take a risk *with* me, now you're offering to take a risk *for* me. Why?"

Nick looked at her. "I'm not ready to answer that question," he said.

She shook her head. "Thanks, but I can't let you do this alone."

"I know you can't—I just wanted to see how loyal you are. I suspect that's what's driving this whole investigation of yours: some sense of betrayal on your part. As I suspected, you're a fiercely loyal person. You could never let me go alone."

"So your offer was just a test?"

"I think of it more as an experiment," he said. "Would you care to comment on my observations?"

"No," she said. "It just has to be the two of us."

"The three of us."

"What?"

Nick nodded toward the door.

Riley turned to see a short, barrel-chested man in a lambskin blazer and a white, ribbed crewneck. His narrow forehead supported a thick crop of shining, coal-black hair. His face bore a smile—no, his face *was* a smile, casting warm light wherever he turned like the glow of a miner's lantern. His eyes were dark and shining, squeezed tight by his constant smile until they glowed like black amethysts. He drifted from table to table, halting momentarily to squeeze a hand, rub a shoulder, or revivify a boring conversation.

"Does he own the place?" Riley asked.

"He owns every place—at least, you'd think he does. Brace yourself, here he comes."

He stopped beside their booth with both arms spread

wide, smiling and nodding like a salesman presenting a new line of cars.

"*Buona sera,* my friends! Ah, what an evening, what a city, what a life!"

"Riley McKay, meet Leonardo Lazzoli, known to his friends as Leo. Leo, this is Riley McKay."

Leo turned to Riley and did a dramatic double take. He looked stunned, astonished, and for a moment he said nothing at all; then the smile once again relit the lamp of his face, and he gestured toward her with outstretched arms.

"Now *this,*" he said. "*This* is a wonder. *This* is a thing of beauty. This is . . . *perfection.*" He turned to Nick with a look of contempt. "And what did you tell me? 'We're meeting with a *woman.*' A *woman,*" he spat. "You're a dead man, Nick. You have the soul of a goat. You spend too many hours poking around in dark corners. You need to look *up* once in a while, you need to see the beauty around you. Have you told this angelic being that she has the face of the Delphian sibyl and the grace of Michaelangelo's *Pieta*?"

"I was just about to," Nick said. "Grab us some dessert menus and sit down."

He took a chair next to Nick, still beaming and nodding at Riley with a look of profound satisfaction. "What a pleasure," he kept repeating, "what a very great pleasure." Riley smiled back, but could think of nothing at all to say.

"What the heck is *mascarpone*?" Nick said, flipping over the menu.

"Give me that, you peasant," Leo said in disgust. He beckoned to the waitress.

"Leo's coming along tomorrow," Nick said to Riley.

"Thanks for letting me know," Riley glared back. "Leo, are you an exterminator?"

"An *exterminator,*" Leo said with delight. "I've never thought of it quite that way before. Yes, you might say I'm an exterminator—I help people eliminate bugs. Nick tells me that you have one or two of your own."

"Leo has a doctorate in electrical engineering," Nick said. "He's a software engineer and a network specialist. Basically, he's your all-around tech head."

"All lies," Leo said with a wave of his hand. "I am an artist, a connoisseur of beauty, a lover of the finer things in life. But, like all artists, I must suffer—so I teach Information Technology at Pitt."

"Leo's a handy guy to have around when you're looking for *information*."

Riley looked at Nick again.

"He knows," Nick said. "I could hardly ask him to become an accessory to the crime without telling him why."

"It seems like everyone is taking chances for me tonight," Riley said. "Leo, has Nick told you the risks involved in this?"

"I doubt it. When Nick tells you there's no danger, he's lying. When Nick says there will be no problems, expect problems. This much I know about Nick Polchak."

"How's your sister?" Nick asked. "Does she still mention me?"

"Yes—when she has a high fever, or when she shuts the door on her hand."

"I should call her."

"I offer to help you, and you threaten me?"

"How do you two know each other?" Riley cut in.

"We grew up together, in Tarentum," Nick said.

"In different neighborhoods, of course," Leo added. "He grew up in the degenerate Polish section, while I was raised in the more fashionable Italian section. His family attended Holy Martyrs, whereas mine attended the more sublime Saint Peter's—where the pope himself would attend, given the choice."

"Not this pope," Nick said. "He can't wait to get back to Krakow."

"Your singular claim to glory—but in general, my people were launching the Renaissance while yours were still painting bison on cave walls."

"We met as teenagers," Nick said.

"After several encounters, we discovered that we shared the same penchant for . . . *adventure*."

"In other words: same high school, same detention hall."

"Hold it," Riley said. "This is not high school—and if anything goes wrong, they won't be sending us to detention hall. Leo, I have to ask you again: do you know what you're getting yourself into?"

"Do you?" he said. "If you're working with Nick, you probably don't."

"Then why do you want to come along?"

"Why, for the adventure, of course. Nick promised me a dragon to slay."

The waitress arrived at the table now, and Leo turned his attention to her. "Your tiramisu," he said to the waitress. "It's not the kind with custard, is it? It has the layers of mascarpone? And then we'll need something chocolate—something with ganache and a sprinkling of cocoa powder. You have cheesecake, of course; bring us a slice with some white chocolate slivers, or perhaps fresh strawberries. We'll need a nice dessert wine—perhaps a Vin Santo or a Black Muscat? That would be wonderful. And now," he said with a wink, "tell us your secrets. What are you holding out on us? You have something special back there, don't you, something you haven't told us about yet?"

The waitress smiled and winked back. "We do have a nice Panna Cotta with fresh raspberries," she said.

Leo groaned. "Please hurry—life is brief. We don't want to die before we taste your Panna Cotta."

"I usually skip dessert," Riley said.

"Skip dessert?" Leo looked around as though the voice had come out of nowhere. "Did someone say 'skip dessert'?"

"I don't eat very much."

"We don't *eat* dessert," Leo said. "What are we, gluttons? We *taste* dessert. The entrée feeds the body, but dessert feeds the soul. Dessert is for pleasure, and pleasures are meant to be tasted, not consumed. When you skip dessert, you leave with a full belly but an empty heart. Animals eat meat and vegetables, my dear Riley. Dessert is what makes us human."

"*Life is dessert*," Nick said. "You should hear his sermon on pasta."

"The goat-man speaks," Leo said with a toss of his head. "You know, I have watched him swallow an entire meal without even tasting it."

The waitress returned with four small plates, each a swirling patchwork of colors and textures and sheens. She arranged them in a square in the center of the table, and set out four gleaming forks.

"Where is the fourth?" the waitress said.

Leo picked up a fork and handed it back to her. "Should we take pleasure from you and give none in return? The first taste is yours."

The waitress smiled a sheepish grin, glanced over her shoulder, and took a quick mouthful of Panna Cotta before hurrying back to the kitchen.

Leo opened the Black Muscat and poured the rich, dark liquid into three small glasses. "And now, I'd like to offer a traditional Italian blessing."

"Here we go," Nick said.

"Do you mind?" Leo cleared his throat and stood up.
"May those that love us, love us.
And those that don't love us,
May God turn their hearts.
And if He doesn't turn their hearts,
May He turn their ankles,
So we will know them by their limping."
He held his glass out to each of them.

"That's a traditional Italian blessing?"

"Sicilian, actually. When Nick is around, it comes in handy."

Leo sat on the passenger side of the BugOff van, staring up at the two-story house wrapped completely in bright yellow plastic.

"Like an enormous Baby Gouda," he said. "Marvelous. Truly."

"Put these on before you get out of the van," Nick said, handing gas masks and hard hats to Leo and Riley.

"I thought there was no gas," Riley said.

"It just completes the disguise. This way, your own mother wouldn't know you."

Nick took a large toolbox and a plastic garden sprayer from the van, and they all went around to the back of the house. Nick searched the tarps, locating all the seams; at one point, just to the right of the patio, the duct tape stopped six feet above the ground and a vertical seam flapped loosely in the breeze.

"That should be the door," Nick said. "Good boy, Freddie."

They slipped inside and removed their masks and helmets. Nick opened the toolbox, took out a black garbage bag, and handed it to Riley.

"Start with the trash," he said. "Go room by room and round up everything, especially from the bathrooms and the study, if he has one. We'll spread it all out on the floor in the garage. Leo, you know your domain."

"I'm on it. I hope he wasn't too cheap to buy a decent computer."

"I'll look for files and other records," Nick said. "If anybody finds anything good, shout it out."

Nick wandered through the downstairs rooms, drawing general observations from the overall layout. It was clearly the house of a divorcé, and definitely a divorced male. The furniture, though contemporary in style and of a very high quality, had been selectively removed from each of the rooms, leaving gaping holes and awkward asymmetries everywhere. The family room was the most desolate; it contained nothing but an old recliner that faced off with a thirty-six-inch Toshiba resting on the carpet in the center of the room. On the wall, a rectangle of contrasting paint marked the spot where an armoire or bookshelf once stood. The mantel above the fireplace was barren, and every print and photograph had been removed except for one framed medical diploma that stood out on the empty wall like a beetle on a windshield. The dining room contained a table, but no chairs; there was a breakfront, but every cup and dish had been removed. It was still a functional house, but no longer a home. Every trace of warmth or humanness had been negotiated away in the final settlement.

"There is no trash," Riley said. "I checked the garage cans too. It must have been taken out."

Nick frowned. "I should have checked the collection day."

"What would we find in the trash?"

"Everything. Pay stubs, bills, phone numbers, credit card

numbers, purchase receipts—if you own it, it eventually ends up in the trash."

"Now what?"

"Upstairs," Nick said. "It's obvious Lassiter doesn't live down here anymore—the place looks like an empty museum."

The upstairs hallway branched off into four smaller rooms. On the left was the master bedroom and bath; near the center, a second bedroom contained nothing but an abandoned bed-frame and three empty corrugated boxes. Farther down, an even smaller room housed a Landice treadmill, a wobbly work-out bench, and a mismatched set of black iron dumbbells. Nick flipped the treadmill on and off quickly and watched the dust line move to the center of the roll.

At the end of the hallway, Leo sat smiling behind a black-and-mahogany computer workstation crammed with software boxes, user manuals, and other esoteric documentation. His fingers moved in a blur. Every few seconds he would stop, hum or whis-tle something to himself, and then his fingers would skitter off again like scorpions on a tile floor. On the floor beside him sat a squat, two-drawer file cabinet with brushed aluminum handles.

"You start in the bedroom," Nick said to Riley. "I'll go through this file cabinet."

"Why don't I start on the files?" Riley countered. "His bed-room gives me the creeps."

"Have it your way." Nick turned and headed down the hallway.

In the bathroom, he opened the mirror-front medicine cabi-net. The top two shelves were conspicuously empty; the bottom contained the expected toiletries along with a bizarre assort-ment of vitamins and herbal supplements. Nick searched first for antidepressants or signs of any questionable prescriptions or illicit drugs; there were none. Next, he carefully picked up each bottle and examined it, being careful to note the facing of the label before he removed it from the shelf. There was red yeast rice extract for his rising cholesterol, Ginkgoba biloba for his fading memory, and saw palmetto for his aging prostate. There was ginseng root for extra energy, Creatine for muscle growth, and Horny Goat Weed for—Horny Goat Weed? This guy's trying way too hard, Nick thought. It looked like a salvage shop for middle-aged men.

In the bedroom he checked the dresser and nightstands for journals, phone lists, or personal letters. There was very little of a personal nature anywhere. Was that the cause of his divorce, or the result? Many men, failing in love, choose to pour their entire lives into their work; Lassiter had obviously chosen this path. The only indication that his wife had ever existed was her conspicuous absence, and the fragmented home she left behind.

Nick headed back down the hall.

"Any security problems?" Nick said to Leo.

"Security, but no problems," Leo replied. "I was in in less than three minutes."

"How about you? Finding anything?"

"Bits and pieces," Riley said, the floor around her scattered with manila folders. "Most of this is obsolete financial records, old tax returns, auto repair histories . . ."

"Anything current? Anything that would tell us about his income or his financial situation?"

"I know what he makes," Riley said. "A pathologist in our office makes about sixty thousand a year."

"Sixty thousand? You people put in four years of medical school and six or seven years of residency just to take home sixty grand? And I thought professors were crazy."

"That's not all of it," Riley said. "Most of our pathologists have private autopsy practices and consulting services that can be very lucrative. The smaller counties can't afford to keep their own pathologists, so they hire ours on a case-by-case basis. And sometimes, when a local medical examiner gives them a verdict they don't agree with, they hire one of ours to get a second opinion. An autopsy here, a consulting fee there—it all adds up."

"No, it doesn't," Leo said. "That's the problem."

Nick and Riley stepped behind him and looked over his shoulder at the screen.

"Our friend does his personal finances and business accounting in Quicken and QuickBooks," Leo said. "Doctors are notoriously bad with money; his expense records are very spotty, but he does manage to keep track of his salary and receivables. He's not incorporated, so he's treating his private practice as part of his personal income. Riley, do you have his most current tax return?"

"Got it."

"OK, check his 1040 for total income. Does it come out to about . . . that?" he said, pointing to the screen.

"That's about right."

"Really? Then how do we explain . . . this?" Leo clicked on Quicken's Investing Center icon and switched to Portfolio View. There, in front of them, was an inclusive listing of Lassiter's investment holdings, complete with a record of individual transactions.

"Last year, his investments were modest and unfocused. A few shares of a tech stock, a little money in a high-yield fund— just your average dabbling day-trader. But this year all his investments have focused on a single company. And last year, his investments were roughly consistent with his earnings. But notice this fiscal year. Look at this transaction . . . and this one . . . and this one here. See? Those three transactions alone total a quarter of a million dollars. My friends, that's more than his entire income."

"Where is he getting that kind of money?" Riley asked.

"Is there any record of a loan, a second mortgage, anything like that?"

"There's no indication of where the money came from," Leo said. "However, we do know where it went." He pointed to the Security line within each of the three transactions. Each one read, "PharmaGen, Inc."

"Now look at this," Leo said, switching to Internet Explorer and pressing the History icon. "This is a record of all the Web sites he's visited in the last three weeks. There are the usual hits: eBay, Google, ESPN, plus a few that reveal a serious lack of character. But notice all these: *PharmaGen, PharmaGen, PharmaGen*. What's the old saying? 'Where a man's treasure is, there will his heart be also.'"

"What do we know about this PharmaGen?" Nick asked.

"I've heard of it," Riley said. "It's a Pittsburgh-based biotech startup in the field of personalized medicine. It's known as *pharmacogenomics*. Very new, very cutting edge."

"They're talking about this in my department," Leo said. "It involves a groundbreaking information field known as *bioinformatics*—taking genetic or biological information and putting it on computer for comparison and analysis."

"Has this PharmaGen gone public yet?"

Leo opened a separate window. A few quick keystrokes took them to the Web site of the Securities and Exchange Commission and its EDGAR database. "They haven't filed with the SEC yet," Leo said. "It looks like the company is still privately held."

"Then our boy isn't buying stock," Nick said. "He's trying to get in on the ground floor of this company *before* it goes public. Looks like he's betting the farm on it."

"He's betting the farm and then some," Leo said. "The question is, where is the farmer getting the extra money? And why this one company? This is not what one would call a 'diversified portfolio.' He's taking an enormous risk."

"Maybe," Nick said. He leaned forward and took the mouse, guiding it to the PharmaGen folder in the History list. He tapped the mouse, and a dozen specific links appeared underneath.

"He's been all over this Web site," Nick said. "What's the big interest?" He clicked on the link titled "PharmaGen.com: Welcome," and the screen went suddenly black.

The Web site opened with a low, tremulous tone, followed by a woman's voice as smooth and mellow as amber honey. "Welcome to the world of personalized medicine," the voice cooed. "Welcome to the future. Welcome to PharmaGen." In the right corner, a tiny Skip Intro icon appeared, and Leo instinctively reached for the mouse.

"Don't," Nick said. "This is what they want the public to see."

In the background, music began to rise: first the rumbling percussion, then the soaring woodwinds, then the stentorian brass proclaiming "The World of PharmaGen" in clarion tones. Now vibrant images began to flicker past like flashcards: a bald-headed child with dark, sunken eyes and a pleading smile; handsome men and women in white lab coats and gleaming silver stethoscopes; backlit vials and flasks of bright, multicolored liquids; crowded laboratories and computer rooms dotted with intense, concerned faces; and a stunning panorama of the Triangle taken from the exit of the Fort Pitt Tunnel.

"PharmaGen," the voiceover said. "The medicines of tomorrow from the knowledge of today."

Now the screen dissolved to black again, and the image of a multihued double helix appeared. The image began to tip and rotate, and the viewer's eye soared like a falcon over the connecting shafts and curling banisters that comprise the DNA molecule.

"Nice graphic," Nick said.

"Nice Web site," Leo added. "This was not cheap."

"*Pharmacogenomics* is the application of recent discoveries about the human genome to produce a bold, new world of pharmaceuticals, specifically tailored to individual needs. Environment, diet, age, and lifestyle all influence an individual's response to medication—but an individual's unique genetic makeup is the key. By tailoring medicines to individual genetic profiles, we can achieve far greater efficacy and safety than we can through the 'one size fits all' methods of today."

The image of a young girl was suddenly superimposed; she

was seated on an examination table, draped in an oversized hospital gown.

"A child is diagnosed with leukemia. As part of her treatment, she will receive a standard protocol of chemotherapy drugs. But a small percentage of Caucasian children lack a crucial enzyme that keeps those drugs from building up to toxic levels in their bloodstreams. Will her medications heal or harm? The drug that saves the life of one patient may take the life of another. Adverse reactions to medications kill an estimated hundred-thousand Americans every year and hospitalize two million more.

"Researchers at PharmaGen are studying the inherited variations in genes, known as 'snips,' that determine drug response in each individual. With this knowledge, we will be able to predict whether a medicine will have a helpful effect, a harmful effect, or no effect at all; we will be able to produce stronger, better, safer drugs and vaccines; we will enable doctors to determine dosages with much greater accuracy; and, by reducing the number of adverse drug reactions, we will play a major role in decreasing the soaring costs of healthcare.

"But it all begins with research. To accomplish these goals, PharmaGen faces a daunting challenge: we must identify as many of the genetic variations in the human genome as possible and trace them to specific diseases. To make this vision a reality, PharmaGen is forming a vital partnership with the people of western Pennsylvania. These visionary volunteers, half a million strong, are joining with us to accelerate our knowledge and help make the future a reality today.

"Won't you join with us? Visit the PharmaGen Web site now to find out how you can contribute, invest, or become a member our Keystone Club volunteer program.

"PharmaGen: the medicines of tomorrow from the knowledge of today."

At the tagline, the music rose once again, crescendoed, and ended with a clap of muted cymbals. The final image morphed to form a sleek, elegant, corporate front page.

No one said anything for a minute.

"Impressive," Leo said, breaking the silence.

"Lassiter thinks so," Nick said. "But how much of all this is just vaporware? Do they actually have a product yet?"

"I haven't heard of one," Riley said, "but they seem to have a great PR department. They're in the news all the time, talking as if the big breakthrough is just around the corner."

"They probably have an IPO coming up," Nick said. "You think all the talk is just smoke and mirrors?"

"There's no way to tell," Riley shrugged. "Pharmacogenomics is a promising field, but the problem is in doing the original research. Even with DNA micro array technology, looking for specific gene variations is a slow process. Then it's hard to determine which genes are involved with each disease or condition—it's hard to get the big picture. But the biggest problem is that, for their data to be reliable, they need an enormous population base to study. No one can afford to pay for it, so it all has to be done on a volunteer basis—that must be the Keystone Club they mentioned. PharmaGen's success depends on the sheer goodwill of half a million Pennsylvania residents."

"That's a lot of goodwill," Nick said. "Leo, check his e-mail. See if you can find any correspondence that might explain some of this."

"I already did," Leo said. "His e-mail has been selectively encrypted. I checked his installed program list; he's running PGP. It's a high-end encryption program. Without his key, we're not going to get into it."

Nick frowned. "I thought you guys could just type a few keys and hack your way into anything."

Leo mirrored his expression. "I thought you guys could just ask the flies and they'd tell you how long they've been there."

"So now what?"

"We can't see what he's e-mailed in the past," Leo said, "but we can see what he sends in the future. In fact, we can see a lot more than that." He took out a single, unlabeled disk and loaded it into the CD/DVD drive.

"What's that?"

"For want of a more honorable term, it's called *spy ware*. It hides on his computer, and it records every keystroke he makes. It records everything—e-mails, chats, instant messages, passwords—and it e-mails it all to us in tidy little reports. What's more, we can even set up a remote screen connection that allows us to see what he's seeing in real-time."

"You can do that?" Riley said.

Leo smiled. "I've impressed you! A most satisfying achievement. Yes, dear Riley, you can do that. Welcome to the world of corporate surveillance. Employers want to know how their employees are spending their office hours, and this is their answer. A lot of suspicious spouses and jealous lovers are finding applications for it too."

"But isn't this . . . illegal?"

Leo glanced around at their surroundings. "A moot point, don't you think?"

"So we can get his e-mails now? But won't they still be encrypted?"

"E-mails are encrypted when they're sent or stored. We won't be intercepting his messages, we'll be watching them as they're being typed, key-by-key."

"It sounds great," Riley said, "but what do we do now, just sit around and watch Lassiter surf the Web? Do we just wait until the right e-mail comes along?"

There was a long pause.

"You know," Nick said suddenly, "I feel a sudden surge of goodwill coming on. I don't know about you two, but I think I'll join the Keystone Club."

CHAPTER
13

Mr. Polchak? Mr. Nicholas Polchak?"

"That's me," Nick said, dropping his magazine on the side table and rising to meet the smiling young woman.

"Welcome to PharmaGen, Mr. Polchak. My name is Kelli. Thank you so much for your call."

Her expression was warm and welcoming, and her eyes were round and bright. She extended her hand; her long fingers, tipped in a perfect French manicure, came almost to a knife-point. Nick took the hand. It was as smooth and soft as Ultra suede, and he felt an almost irresistible urge to rotate it and study the surface more closely. Most impressive of all, she looked him almost perfectly in the eye. There was almost no hesitation at his enormous glasses, almost no fractional blink or subtle widening of the eye.

Almost.

"I'm a clinical research coordinator here at PharmaGen," she smiled. "Will you follow me, please?" She placed one foot behind the other and pivoted with perfect balance, heading for a doorway beside a smoky glass-and-chrome reception desk.

Nick watched her as she walked ahead of him. Her deep umber hair was pulled back tightly, except for one casual strand that curled across her right eye, creating the perfect synergy of professionalism and sensuality. Her immaculately tailored jacket was wide and sharp at the shoulders, tapering tightly to the waist before a deep back vent allowed it to curve around her hips. She was, like the lavish waiting room around her, a calculated image of precision and professionalism. She was the glossy cover on a soon-to-be bestseller, a story of imminent success.

They entered a small sitting room, much warmer and more intimate than the futuristic reception area. The lighting was all eye-level, without a trace of hospital-blue fluorescence any-where. Golden light poured through textured lampshades, casting fireside shadows across the lush green plants and over-stuffed furniture. On the walls, pastoral landscapes completed the image of friendship, trust, and security.

"Please have a seat, Mr. Polchak. Oh no, not there—try this one. It's full grain calfskin. Now, isn't that nice?"

"Like a big catcher's mitt," Nick said, settling back. He gave a quick thought to the ballpoint pen in his back pocket, but let it go.

"So—where did you come in from today?"

"Tarentum," Nick said.

"Tarentum. I don't believe I've heard of—"

"It's about twenty miles up the Allegheny, across the river from New Kensington and Lower Burrell." Nick leaned for-ward. "You have heard of Lower Burrell, haven't you?"

"Of course," she lied. "You know, you didn't have to drive all the way down here."

"You have offices in Tarentum?"

"We have offices in twenty-nine western Pennsylvania counties."

"That's remarkable for a company as young as yours," Nick said. "I hope you plan to buy stock."

"I'll be first in line," she said with a wink. She opened the chocolate-colored folder in her lap. "So you're here to join our Keystone Club."

"I'm here to learn more—this is all very new to me. I know the basics, of course: PharmaGen's goal is to develop personalized medicines by identifying disease-causing genetic variants in the general population."

"That's very good, Mr. Polchak."

"My mom says I have an aptitude for science. Tell me, does PharmaGen have a marketable product yet?"

"Not yet, but we're very, very close. Currently, we're focusing most of our resources on our population study. That's the Keystone Club."

"Half a million strong," Nick quoted. "That's an enormous research base. Do you have anywhere near that number signed up?"

"We will—with the help of people like you."

Nick nodded. "Tell me, how does one go about enlisting the cooperation of half a million people? They can't get that many people to vote."

"By making it easy to do, Mr. Polchak—that's the key. PharmaGen has formed a partnership with the University of Pittsburgh Medical Center. UPMC is the largest healthcare system in western Pennsylvania. Their facilities include twenty hospitals, four hundred doctors' offices and outpatient centers, fifty different rehab facilities—they even do in-home care. There are five thousand physicians in the UPMC network, and every one of them can sign you up for the Keystone Club. It's as simple as going to the doctor—even people who don't vote have to go to the doctor."

"Very clever," Nick said. "And what's in it for UPMC?"

"A big chunk of the company I'll bet—but you didn't hear that from me."

"OK, so I go to the doctor for my yearly exam. What happens then?"

"First of all, you'll find our brochures in every waiting area and exam room—brochures like this one." She handed Nick a slick four-color trifold with many of the same images and graphics from the Web site. "We also train nurses and phlebotomists to introduce our program to their patients, so you're very likely to hear about us face to face."

"And if I agree to participate? What happens next?"

"Here's the beauty of it, Mr. Polchak. All it requires of you is a signature, a blood draw, and a brief interview."

"The blood gives you the DNA sample—what about the signature? What exactly am I signing?"

"A simple release form, allowing PharmaGen access to your personal medical history."

"Whoa," Nick said. "I'm signing over my entire—"

"*Anonymously*," she interjected with surgical precision, anticipating the objection. "Your name is removed from all medical records and replaced by a numerical code—the same code is attached to your blood sample. Our researchers never know who you are, Mr. Polchak; they only need to know that *this* blood sample goes with *this* medical history. Complete confidentiality is assured."

"And the interview—what's that about?"

"It's a family history questionnaire. We want to know about your environment and background, especially the incidence of certain diseases and conditions in your family—but once again, the information is encoded and remains completely confidential."

"So PharmaGen has my blood, my personal medical record, and the history of disease in my family—and that allows them to search for predictable variants in my DNA."

"Variants that could predict diseases like asthma, diabetes, hypertension, and certain cancers—those are some of the ones we're working on first."

"Let's go back to the subject of confidentiality for a minute."

"Everyone does," she said with a reassuring smile. "It's perfectly understandable. Let me tell you this: The results of your DNA analysis will not be revealed to employers, insurance companies, or anyone else who doesn't have a legal right to know. In fact, PharmaGen has obtained a Certificate of Confidentiality from the National Institutes of Health. That certificate prevents our researchers from revealing any information that might identify you, *even if subpoenaed by a court*."

Her presentation was polished, and her enthusiasm was genuine. Nick smiled.

She was, without a doubt, a future stockholder.

"You're very good," he said. "Would you mind if I asked a couple of . . . *harder* questions?"

She gave him a mischievous grin. "I'm ready for you. Fire away."

"When is my name removed from my medical records—before they leave the doctor's office or after they arrive at PharmaGen?"

"Well, I . . . I have to admit, I've never been asked that—"

"Think it over. The doctor's role is merely to release the medical records and to obtain the blood sample. Who assigns the confidential numerical code?"

She knew this one. "PharmaGen does that."

"That means my records are *not* confidential when they leave the doctor's office, and *not* when they first arrive at PharmaGen."

"Perhaps—but immediately after arrival, they—"

"How *long* after arrival? And who specifically removes the name and assigns the numerical code? Do you know?"

The young woman said nothing.

"Let me try a different question. We have an aging population in the United States. In the future, the demand for safe and effective pharmaceuticals will continue to skyrocket. I can see how PharmaGen is poised to make an enormous amount of money—*if* they can come up with a product. My question is:

103

just how far away is the first *personalized medicine*?"

"We're very, very close—"

"It wasn't a fair question," Nick said, ignoring her stock response. "That's PharmaGen's deepest secret, now, isn't it? You haven't gone public yet, so you're surviving off venture capital and up-front investments—and to keep those investments coming in, success *has* to seem very, very close. This company survives on the promise of success, and you're very good at promising. The waiting area, this room, even you, Kelli—everything about this place says, 'I promise.'"

She did her best to maintain her confident smile, but she seemed to grow awkwardly self-aware.

"PharmaGen survives on trust," he said. "It's worth more to you right now than any amount of venture capital. For you to succeed, the public has to trust you. What I want to know is: can you be trusted, Kelli?"

The young woman closed the folder in her lap. "I think your questions are a little over my head," she said. "If you'd care to speak to my supervisor—"

"Better yet," Nick said, "who runs the company?"

She did an obvious double take now, the first real crack in her flawless image.

"Well . . . I . . . our founder and CEO is Tucker Truett, but—"

"Where can I find him?"

"Mr. Polchak, you can't just—"

"Is he here? Is his office in this building?"

"No. I mean yes, but you can't possibly see him without—"

"You never know. Let's give it a try," Nick said, rising from the chair and heading for the door. "Let's see: We came from *that* direction, so the offices must be . . . *this* way."

"Mr. Polchak! Wait!" As Nick disappeared out the doorway, she grabbed for the phone and dialed a single number.

Just a few yards past the reception area the cosmetic image of success suddenly fell away, revealing underneath the raw flesh and driving pulse of an ambitious young company. Nick picked up a coffee mug from the first unattended desk and walked confidently past a series of crowded desks and buzzing cubicles.

"Hey, Bob," he called to a man at a computer screen, snatching the appellation from a desktop nameplate.

"Hi, Jenny. Great sweater," he smiled at a passing woman. If you can't look familiar to them, he thought, make them think they look familiar to you. Nick could fake it with the best of them, but he knew this is where his eyes worked against him; the guy with the funny glasses never blends in. It was only a matter of time before someone called his bluff.

He moved quickly through the maze of cubicles and file cabinets, seeking the nerve center of the office, following his instincts like a blowfly tracing the scent of blood in the air. The CEO of PharmaGen would not have a cubicle; he would enjoy the privilege of an enclosed office. Tucker Truett would have a window; not just a window, a corner window; and not just any corner window, but the window with the best panorama of downtown Pittsburgh. Nick headed directly for the opposite corner, where a break in the surrounding buildings allowed an impressive overlook of the Allegheny River and PNC Park. He stopped at the administrative assistant's desk directly in front of the closed door.

"Is he in?" Nick said casually.

The young man cocked his head and squinted at Nick. "And you would be—"

"Just a quick question. I know he's busy today."

At that moment, a security guard hustled up behind Nick, with an anxious Kelli following a safe distance behind. Inquisitive coworkers began to fill in behind them, seeking the source of the disturbance. The security guard stepped squarely in front of Nick, then craned his neck backward to get the full effect of Nick's imposing spectacles.

"Can I help you *sir*," he said, the last word dropping like a flatiron. It wasn't a question at all; it was a shot across the bow.

"I'm a potential investor," Nick said. "I had a couple of

questions Kelli couldn't answer, so she suggested I take them up with Mr. Truett."

The guard glanced over Nick's shoulder; Kelli vigorously shook her head.

"I only need a minute," Nick said. "What's the big deal?"

"Do you have an appointment?" the guard said, folding his arms.

"For one simple question? He said if I ever had a question, I should just drop by."

"You're acquainted with Mr. Truett?"

"With Tuck? I've known him for years."

There was a long pause.

"No one calls him 'Tuck,'" the guard growled. "No one. Ever."

Nick nodded. "I thought that was probably over the top— but it was worth a try. Are you required to throw me out, or can I walk?"

The guard pointed firmly to the door. Nick turned to the crowd of onlookers and handed one of them the coffee mug. "If you people can find a variant in thirty thousand genes, why can't you make a decent cup of coffee?"

The crowd shuffled aside as he passed through.

"I'll be out of the office today, Bob," he called back. "Tell Jenny I meant what I said about the sweater."

CHAPTER
14

T his isn't how I thought I'd be spending the Fourth of July,"
Riley said.

Nick pulled hard on the oars, urging the skiff silently
forward on the black waters of the Allegheny River. Each time
he leaned back and pulled, Riley watched the lights of the city
flash blue or white or yellow off the face of his glasses. The
Boardwalk Marina disappeared into the shadows behind them,
and they passed under the lights of the Sixth Street Bridge and
out into the darkness of the river.

"Where *did* you expect to be on the Fourth of July?"

Riley shrugged. "Not on a rowboat in the middle of the
Allegheny, that's for sure. Maybe up on Mount Washington,
standing on the platform at the top of the incline, watching the
fireworks at the Point."

"Then this is a definite improvement. You're going to have
the best view of the fireworks you've ever seen."

Two hundred yards downstream, a fleet of boats large and small basked in the afterglow of the Bucs-Astros game earlier that day at PNC Park, dotting the river like a gaggle of geese. Within the hour the lights would die entirely, and the annual Fourth of July fireworks display would erupt from a series of barges opposite the Point at the mouth of the Ohio River. Nick pulled for the shadowy flotilla.

"That platform on top of Mount Washington," Nick said. "Did you expect to be there alone, or with someone else?"

"What?"

"You know, to watch the fireworks."

"With someone else, of course."

Nick said nothing for a minute. "Someone else like a boyfriend, or someone else like a family member?"

"Yes," she said. "Those would be the options."

Riley looked down at her feet. A half-inch of water puddled in the bottom of the boat, sloshing toward her shoes each time the oars caught the water and the boat dipped forward. She lifted her feet; they were her newest shoes, patent-leather slides, and she was not about to get them wet. She smoothed the front of her black silk spaghetti-strap dress, straightened her pearls, and shifted to the exact center of the bench. She picked up her beaded purse and set it on her lap, glancing over the side of the boat at the inky water.

"Nick, why this fixation on PharmaGen? Why are we going to so much trouble just to meet Tucker Truett?"

"You said you were interested in anomalies. As far as we know, PharmaGen is the only other anomaly in Lassiter's life. A quarter of a million invested in one company in a single year—don't you find that interesting?"

"So he's a lousy investor. What does that have to do with PharmaGen?"

"I can see why Lassiter might be interested in PharmaGen—but why is PharmaGen interested in Lassiter? A quarter of a million is a lot of money to your boss, but it's chump change to a group like PharmaGen. This is a high-stakes game; you don't sit down at this table unless you've got *millions*. Yet PharmaGen is letting Lassiter in on the ground floor. I'd like to know why. Besides," he said, filling his lungs with the night air, "this is a lot more fun than waiting for something to show up on the spyware."

"Is this your idea of fun?"

"Cheer up," Nick said. "You could have been stuck with some loser up on Mount Washington."

Riley turned and peered down the river. "Where is this yacht?"

"We can't miss it. It's seventy feet long, and it says *PharmaGen* across the stern. They say it's the biggest thing on the river from here to Cincinnati. Truett keeps it up at the Fox Chapel Yacht Club."

"Why couldn't we meet them at Fox Chapel and sail down together? I feel like an idiot rowing around in this little dinghy."

Nick said nothing.

Riley narrowed her eyes. "Nick—if there's something you haven't told me, this would be a good time."

"Did you know that it's exactly 443 feet, 4 inches from home plate to the river? A strong left-hander can reach the water on the fly—Daryle Ward did it just last year. If we had come earlier, and if we were in just the right spot—"

"Nick."

"You're a very suspicious person," Nick said. "It's very unflattering."

"I'm a pathologist. I'm paid to be suspicious. You're *here* because I'm suspicious."

"You have a point there."

They were approaching the rust-yellow trusses of the Roberto Clemente Bridge now, and the stadium loomed large on their right. Just past the bridge was the first circle of boats, the smaller craft dotting the perimeter of the flotilla like cruisers around ships of war. They could hear the rising sound of music and laughter now, and they could make out individual forms against the glowing deck lights.

"You told me we would spend the evening on Tucker Truett's corporate yacht," Riley said. "You told me you had arranged a meeting with Truett, and that we would get the chance to ask some questions about PharmaGen, and maybe get some insight into Dr. Lassiter's involvement."

"All true. The rest is just details."

"I want to hear the details."

Nick let out a heavy sigh. "OK," he said, "I arranged a meeting with Truett, but . . . he didn't exactly arrange a meeting with me."

"Oh, Nick. Oh, Nick, please . . . don't tell me that Truett doesn't know we're coming."

"What's a party without a few unexpected guests?"

Riley's jaw dropped. "You lied to me! You said we were invited to spend the evening on his yacht!"

"Actually, I said that we were *going* to spend the evening on his yacht. And we are—we just have to figure out how to get *on* his yacht."

They passed the first of the boats now, and Nick nodded a friendly "Evening" to the captain and his crew of one. He rowed a little closer than necessary to the next boat, hoping to keep Riley's temper in check. Like a lighthouse, her expression flashed between forced smiles at fellow seafarers and furious glances at Nick.

"Turn the boat around. Turn it around *right now!*"

"After we've come all this way? Come on, the hard part's over. We're almost there. See?"

As they passed the last row of medium-sized sport cruisers, they saw it. There, a respectful distance away, the gleaming hull of the *PharmaGen* stabbed up through the dark water like a white bowie knife. Its hull was so sleek and angular that it appeared to be in motion even at rest. A shining stainless steel railing outlined the contour of the deck from the tip of the bow to the stern. Three elliptical portholes poured orange light from the staterooms below deck, and a half-dozen extremely well-styled figures held champagne flutes and chatted on the sun pad and aft deck.

"Nick, we can't just row up and knock on the side of the boat!"

"That would be silly, now, wouldn't it?"

"You must have *some* kind of plan."

"Of course I have a plan. I wouldn't row all the way out here without a plan."

She waited for him to continue, but he said nothing. They were almost alongside the boat now. Riley looked up at the yacht towering above them; she saw cream-colored skin showing through the draped back of a scarlet evening gown. She turned back to Nick.

"You're going to humiliate me, aren't you?"

"I'm going to get you on the boat," Nick said. "Whether or not you're humiliated is up to you."

She gave him a searing stare.

"Let's look at this thing logically," he said. "As you pointed out, we can't just knock on the side of the boat. And we can't very well throw grappling hooks over the side and climb aboard either. One way or the other, they have to *invite* us to join them. Now I asked myself, what would make them do that? There are boats all around here, and no one's inviting *them* to join the party. And then it occurred to me: What if we were in distress? It's the first rule of the sea: Boaters always stop to help others in distress."

"What kind of distress? You mean like losing an oar?"

"That hardly qualifies as 'distress.' They could just hand us a spare oar."

"What are we supposed to do, set the boat on fire?"

"A fire? On a boat with no engine? That makes sense. 'Excuse me, can you help us out? We seem to have spontaneously combusted here.'"

"Then what?"

"It has to be genuine *distress*. Our situation has to be desperate, immediate, irreversible."

"Nick—are you suggesting that we jump in the water?"

"Of course not—If we fell in the water, we could climb right back into the boat again. Unless, of course, the boat wasn't here anymore."

Riley looked at him in horror. "Nick, do you know what you're saying?"

He nodded. "You're going to lose your fifty-dollar deposit at the marina."

For the first time, Riley looked at Nick's clothing. He wore a beaten pair of loafers broken down toward the insteps, and he had no socks. He wore a crumpled pair of khakis and a faded navy sports coat that showed white threads around the sleeves and collar.

"Look at you! The water would *improve* that outfit! But look at *me*—I'm wearing silk! Do you have any idea what this thing would look like wet?"

"It'll give us just the right touch of pathos. After all, who would help us if we fell in in our swimsuits? It's only fifty yards to shore."

"Turn the boat around," she demanded.

Nick released the oars, folded his arms across his chest, and cocked his head to one side. "I think it's time for my 'Commitment' speech," he said. "Whose cause is this anyway? Who's helping who here? How is it that I seem to be more committed to your cause than you are?"

"I *am* committed—but not like this. There must be other options."

"I'm all ears."

"We can meet with Truett some other way."

"How? I tried to make an actual appointment—not a chance, unless you've got an extra million dollars in your back pocket. I tried to drop in on him yesterday morning—he's got tighter security than the governor. We have to catch him when he's standing still, and a man like that is rarely standing still—except when he's on this boat, where he was certain to be on the Fourth of July. So here we are, and there he is. What do you want to do, Riley? It's your call."

She said nothing.

"OK," Nick said, "I didn't want to have to resort to this, but you leave me no choice. I *dare* you, Riley. You gutless pretender, I double-dog *dare* you."

Riley's eyes narrowed to slits. She shoved her purse between her legs and grasped the sides of the boat with both hands. "I had to hire *you*," she growled.

Nick held on too. "You get what you pay for," he said.

On the count of three, they turned the boat over and plunged into the darkness.

Hey! A little help down here!"

Nick and Riley bobbed in the water beside the PharmaGen yacht, just out from under the shadow of the hull, where they could be easily spotted by any of the guests on board. Beside them the overturned rowboat still floated, its ribbed aluminum bottom level with the surface of the water. Riley kicked, and one of her slides slipped off and disappeared beneath her.

"What if nobody hears us?" Riley said.

"Remember Cortez," Nick said. "There's no turning back now."

"Ho there! Need some help?"

Nick slowly turned in the water; behind them, a sixteen-foot Sylvan bass boat nodded in the water like a small bar of soap.

"Take us in a little closer, Doris! Move that cooler and make room for these folks!" The one barking orders, a large-bellied man with a full beard, reached over the port side and extended an aluminum gaff.

"No thanks," Nick said.

"What? You're kidding. Grab ahold now."

"No, really. We're OK."

"You just felt like taking a swim? What about your boat there?"

"Look, do you mind? We'd like to be rescued by a better class of people."

Doris shrugged and gunned the engine, drowning out the big man's colorful farewell as the bass boat motored away.

"What's the problem down there?" came a voice from above them.

"We had a little accident," Riley called back.

"Are you both all right? Is anyone injured?"

"We're OK—we just lost our ride."

"Swim around to the stern, then. I'll lower the swim platform. Climb on and I'll bring you aboard."

"There, now," Nick said in a low voice. "That wasn't so bad."

"Shut up," Riley whispered back.

They worked their way around to the stern, which seemed to take forever in the dark water. Riley curled her toes as she kicked in a vain attempt to hold on to her remaining shoe, but it was a hopeless task, and she finally allowed it to drift away in search of its mate. They could hear the hiss of a hydraulic lift; by the time they reached the stern, the swim platform was level with the surface of the water.

Nick grabbed one of the projecting handles and pulled himself up into a sitting position, facing away from the boat. Riley looked up at the small crowd gathered on the aft deck to observe their entrance. She glanced down at the front of her silk dress, then reached for the handle and dragged herself onto the fiberglass facedown.

"That was graceful," Nick said. "You look like Shamu."

"Do you mind? I'm trying to salvage a little dignity here."

"Good luck with that."

The platform immediately began to rise, and after a few

seconds it locked into place again. The gate to the aft deck swung open, and a young man slid down the railing to the platform below.

"Everybody OK? What happened out there?"

"We were hoping to see the fireworks," Nick said. "I warned her not to stand up."

"You can watch the fireworks with us," he said. "I'm Tucker Truett, and you're my guests. Let's get you out of those wet clothes."

"Nick Polchak," Nick said, shaking Truett's hand. His grip was fast and powerful. Truett stood eye to eye with Nick, but he was even broader in the shoulders and much thicker in the arms and chest. "This is Riley McKay." Truett turned and smiled at Riley, who stood with her arms pinned across her chest. He did not extend his hand.

Truett's face was square and very lean; when he turned, Nick could see the veins in his temples and the sinewy lines of his jaw. His eyes were a pale cerulean blue, and his tight, wavy hair glistened under the last of the stadium lights. He was barefoot, and his long toes seemed to almost grip the deck. He wore crisp white slacks with knife-edge pleats, and his black poplin shirt hung open to reveal a single strand of gold. Black and gold—the symbolism wasn't missed by Nick, nor would it be by anyone else in Pittsburgh. Tucker Truett was handsome, powerful, and he exuded confidence. He was an electrified, neon billboard for the city of steel—and for a rising new company called PharmaGen.

They were joined now by some of the other guests, who gathered around them with towels and long terry bathrobes monogrammed with the PharmaGen logo. Three elegantly clad women ushered Riley below deck. Nick stripped off his own dripping jacket and shirt, pulled on a bathrobe, then dropped his khakis around his ankles and kicked them away. He followed Truett up the steps to the aft deck and exchanged brief pleasantries with two other men, who then descended to the salon to check the satellite TV for the starting time of the fire-works display. Truett stepped to a refrigerator in the cockpit, opened it, and handed Nick an Iron City Beer.

"Thanks," Nick said. "Nice boat."

"It's a yacht," Truett said. "Technically, a yacht is any vessel that carries another boat on board. We carry a spare."

"I could have used a spare tonight. Is this yours?"

"It belongs to my company—PharmaGen. Ever heard of it?"

"Who hasn't? As a matter of fact, I stopped by your office the other day to join your Keystone Club—but you'd have no way of knowing that, would you?"

"Nope. I'm proud to say, you're just a number to us. But thanks for helping out."

"A population study of half a million—that's a researcher's dream."

"It's an IT's nightmare—but that's part of the challenge. This company is built on information."

"Funny," Nick said. "I would have said your company is built on trust." He ran his hand over the cool white fiberglass hull. "What's a boat—sorry, what's a yacht like this worth anyway?"

"With the extras? About two million."

"That must have taken a sizable bite out of your venture capital. What did your board of directors have to say about it?"

"It was their idea." Truett cocked his head and looked at Nick more closely. "What do you do for a living, Mr. Polchak?"

"It's *Doctor* Polchak—I have a PhD. Technically, a PhD is anyone who carries a student loan the size of a yacht. I'm just a lowly professor from the backwater state of North Carolina."

"My, aren't we humble," Truett said.

"Humility is a nice quality, don't you think?"

"Not in my business. This yacht is almost twice the size of anything on the three rivers, and that's no accident. Been to a Bucs game lately, Dr. Polchak? What do you suppose it cost PNC Bank to put their name on that stadium? This yacht sits right here every weekend, and especially for every home game.

117

We always turn the stern to face the park, and there hasn't been a game yet where the JumboTron didn't show the PharmaGen logo to thirty-eight thousand fans."

"When was the last time the Pirates had thirty-eight thousand fans?" Nick peered into the cockpit. The Euro-styled captain's chair looked like something from the bridge of the starship Enterprise. The instrument console was covered in high-gloss mahogany burl, and a soft blue light glowed from the radar and navigational monitors. "So this is all for advertising? Wouldn't a billboard have been cheaper?"

"This yacht is worth twice what we paid for it. The *PharmaGen* doesn't just sit in the river, Dr. Polchak; it dominates the river. We *own* the river, just as we will soon own the field of personalized medicine. As you said, this business is built on trust—on public confidence. You don't ask a man to invest by telling him, 'Someday we hope to be successful.' You tell him, 'We're successful *now*, and if you don't get on board you'll be left behind.'"

"*Are* you successful now? Where exactly are you in your population study? How close are you to your goal of half a million volunteers?"

"The research doesn't have to wait for half a million volunteers," Truett said. "Are you familiar with the Marshfield Clinic in Wisconsin? They're doing similar research, and their goal is only forty thousand volunteers—that's enough to produce statistically significant results. We have eight times that many now, and our research is well under way. It's a progressive effort: as the population study grows, so do the scope of the research and the reliability of the conclusions we draw. Once again, Dr. Polchak, it's all about *confidence*. Our study is so massive, so far beyond anything anyone else has attempted, that we will virtually *swamp* the competition."

"Big yachts swamp little boats," Nick said. "But size isn't everything; quickness counts. What if one of the little guys beats you to market with a product? And what about FDA approval, how long will that take? Just how far *are* you from a marketable product, Mr. Truett?"

Truett smiled.

"I know," Nick said. "Very, very close."

Just then, Riley emerged from the stateroom below. She was still barefoot, but she was now dressed in loose-fitting slacks and a breezy, open blouse with a camisole underneath. The clothes were casual, but very expensive; she was better dressed now than before her dive into the Allegheny. She stepped onto the aft deck, rubbing at her hair with a white terry towel. "Thanks for the hospitality," she said.

"Feeling better, Ms. McKay?"

"Much. I appreciate the clothes; I'll get them back to you."

"Keep them. Dana has plenty—I make sure of that."

"By the way," Nick said, "it's *Doctor* McKay."

"Another doctor? With all that education between you, you'd think you two would be better sailors."

"We all have our specialties," Nick said. "What's your specialty, Mr. Truett?"

"Vision, Dr. Polchak. I am an evangelist."

"And just what is your vision?" Riley asked.

"I see a world where no one ever dies from an adverse drug reaction; where physicians have an entire range of medicines to choose from to treat a deadly disease; where medications target tumors like smart bombs and leave surrounding tissues unharmed; where genetic susceptibility to disease can be determined in childhood, and possibly even prevented."

"Right out of the brochure," Nick said. "Where are the fireworks when you need them?"

"Why, Dr. Polchak—you sound like a cynic."

"Cynicism is the ugly cousin of humility, Mr. Truett. I don't think much of myself, but then I don't think much of anyone in *your* species either."

"My species?"

"What about you?" Riley cut in. "Surely you have a little *personal* vision in all this somewhere?"

"You bet I do. I see a world where patients think of medicines the way they think of coffee: they want it strong, they want it made their way, and they want it now—and PharmaGen will be there to serve the coffee. I see a world where aging baby boomers will pay anything to have the latest, strongest, and most *personal* medication. In other words, Dr. McKay, I see dollar signs—and I'm not ashamed to say it. I raised seventy million dollars to start this venture, and I plan to make a whole lot more in return. My goal is not to make money; my goal is to succeed—but if I succeed, the money will follow."

Nick watched him as he spoke. Truett would talk about PharmaGen all night, Nick thought. He was the genuine item, a true believer. He had willingly answered each of their questions, ignoring his invited guests for the opportunity to defend his dream to a couple of perfect strangers. His conviction and enthusiasm were hypnotic; he cast vision the way a dog sheds water, catching everyone within his reach. Maybe the yacht was worth two million, who knows? One thing was for certain—Tucker Truett was worth a whole lot more.

"I wonder if you know an associate of mine," Riley said. "Dr. Nathan Lassiter?"

"One of our early investors," Truett said. "A visionary himself."

"Oh? How so?"

"Most people invest their money in bits and pieces, a little here and a little there. They're trying to avoid risk—but that's investing out of fear, Dr. McKay, and that's no way to live. Life is a gamble, and you have to roll the dice. Dr. Lassiter is a visionary, he can see the future—*our* future. He placed his money on PharmaGen, and he was wise to do so."

"The dice don't always come up the way you want."

Truett smiled. "It's my job to see that they do."

One of the other guests emerged from the stateroom now, a young woman almost as long and as sleek as the yacht itself. She was the lady in red, the one they had glimpsed from the water below. Nick watched her; she moved smoothly, silently, flowing like the river around them. She leaned up against Truett, slipped an arm behind him, and nuzzled his ear—but Truett showed no awareness of her presence. *She's an early investor too,* Nick thought, but the return on her investment wasn't yet clear.

"Speaking of risk," Nick said. "What about this Keystone Club?"

"What about it?"

"You're asking people to give you a sample of their DNA— but no one really knows just how much information is locked up in the DNA molecule. We can read a certain amount of it today, but tomorrow we may find a way to unlock an entire library of genetic information about the individual."

"That's what we're hoping for; it means that even more extensive research will be possible."

"It also means that people have no way to know what they're really giving you. It's like asking them to sign a blank check."

"But the check is not from their personal account. Don't forget, Dr. Polchak, they give this gift anonymously. No one knows who you are."

"Yes—'PharmaGen promises complete confidentiality.' That's a big promise, Mr. Truett."

"As you said, this whole thing is built on trust."

Nick slowly folded his arms across his chest. "So I give you infinite knowledge of my genetic makeup, and in return you promise to keep it a secret—is that the trade? You called yourself an *evangelist*—if I remember my Latin, the word means 'messenger of good news.' You definitely are a messenger, Mr. Truett, the best I've ever seen. My question is: are you sure this is good news?"

Truett let out a laugh. He pulled the lady in red in close and planted a kiss on her, as though he just now became aware of her existence. She was a prop, Nick thought, just a visual aid in his presentation, and this was his way of making a transition. He was sprinkling pixie dust on everyone, trying to lift the ship out of troubled waters.

"I understand that you two might have some cautions about all this," he said. "I find that better-educated people often do. That's why, early on, PharmaGen established an ethics advisory board to advise us on controversial issues like genetic privacy."

"Your own ethics advisory board? Isn't that like asking senators to vote for term limits?"

"Not at all. These are professional bioethicists, very accomplished and well-respected in their fields. They are not employed by PharmaGen, nor are they remunerated by us in any way."

"Who sits on this advisory board?"

"Our founding member was Dr. Ian Paulos. He's a professor of ethics at Trinity Episcopal School for Ministry over in Ambridge. He's been with us from the beginning—he helped us shape all of our privacy policies. If you really want to pursue this issue of genetic privacy, you should take it up with him."

"Thanks," Nick said. "I just might do that."

To the west, in the distance, there was a cannon retort followed by a booming echo. Three seconds later a brilliant red starburst illuminated the sky, dropping sparkling silver tentacles on every side. It was the signal flare, the opening volley in the Zambelli Family's annual fireworks extravaganza at the Point. On board the *PharmaGen* it was all hands on deck now, and the whole group pressed against the starboard railing to witness the aerial display. Each couple pressed tightly together, holding hands and standing side by side or cheek to cheek. Nick glanced at Riley standing stiffly beside him, and he wondered what would happen if he put his arm around her. Not an all-out embrace, not even a perceptible squeeze—just his left hand resting on her left shoulder. What would she do? He took a mental accounting of the night's activities: he had lured her out to the middle of the Allegheny River in a rowboat, then dumped her in the water; he had caused her to lose her shoes and purse, and had ruined her dress; and he had forced her to stand almost naked and dripping in front of better-dressed women. Nick could imagine her taking out a scalpel and severing his hand at the wrist.

He glanced at her again. *I dare you*, Nick said to himself, *I double-dog dare you*. He lifted his arm and rested it gently across Riley's shoulders.

Riley did nothing.

Nick smiled. "I love fireworks," he said.

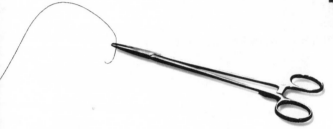

The *PharmaGen*'s twin diesels rumbled patiently, holding the boat steady in the water as the lower gates to Lock Number 2 slowly opened upriver. In the cockpit, Tucker Truett watched a handful of pleasure boats cautiously emerge, then gun their engines and curl off, leaving white streaks of foam in the black water behind them. Truett waited for a dozen or so smaller craft to enter the lock before him. It was more than civility that caused him to hold back. When the lock was filled and the great upper gates opened northward, the wake from the *PharmaGen*'s twin screws could turn smaller boats behind him into floating bumper cars.

Truett heard the lockmaster's go-ahead on his marine band radio. He nudged the throttle forward and pulled slowly into the lock, the great swan and her cygnets returning to roost upstream at the Oakmont and Fox Chapel marinas. He tossed a bow and stern line up to the lockmaster to secure his position, and then came the low, grinding sound of hydraulics as the lower gates swung closed behind him.

Truett had taken the *PharmaGen* up and downriver through the Allegheny's locks a hundred times. The process was as second-nature to him as riding an escalator. But this time when the lower gates locked shut behind him, sealed tight by the pressure of the rising water, a strange thought wormed its way into Truett's mind: Can the doors be reopened? Can the process be reversed? If he lay on his air horn, if he signaled the lockmaster, could he open the massive doors again and allow the *PharmaGen* to gently back out onto the peaceful lower river?

When is it too late to change your mind?

Truett sat alone in the cockpit now, staring silently ahead at the warning pattern on the black upper gates, watching the yellow stripes slowly dip into the water and disappear as the level began to rise. For the next twenty minutes, he had nothing to do but sit and stare and remember.

■

"To the ethics advisory board," Truett said, raising his glass in a toast. "May you keep us on the straight and narrow."

"And to fortuitous meetings," Zohar replied, raising his glass in return. "'When comets cross, do the skies illumine.'"

The two men sat across from one another at the S-shaped conference table in PharmaGen's newly commissioned boardroom. The flowing curves of the table accented the soft, organic shapes of the chairs and other furnishings, all washed in tones of olive and gold and sienna. On the walls, a row of stark black frames featured digital photographs of Heinz Field, PNC Park, and, largest of all, the *PharmaGen* yacht.

"I want you to know how much I appreciate your joining our board," Truett said. "I know what a busy man you are."

"I consider it a great privilege." Zohar smiled. "I'm never too busy to help with a strategic new venture. Perhaps you could tell me a little more about your vision for this board."

Truett leaned back in his chair and folded his hands across his stomach. "Ultimately, I'd like to have a dozen or so members—well-known, highly respected ethicists like yourself, from all different philosophical perspectives."

Zohar smiled. "Then you see this board as largely a public-relations effort. I'm disappointed."

"No, not at all," Truett said. "Our efforts here at PharmaGen are going to raise a lot of concerns about genetic privacy and bioethics. I want to meet those concerns head-on, and I want the ethics advisory board to spearhead that effort."

Zohar ran his index finger gently around the rim of his glass. "Have you ever served on an ethics panel yourself?"

"Can't say as I have."

"Let me tell you how they operate. They always begin very politely, everyone sharing the same goal, colleagues all. Then individual differences in perspective begin to appear—not superficial differences, mind you, but disparities in fundamental philosophical assumptions. Soon each member becomes entrenched in his own position, defending his own precious *a priori*, becoming more and more intractable and defensive.

"They're like a group of travelers who came to a fork in the road long ago, and each chose a different path. Now all they can do is shout to one another to abandon their path and join them on their own. No one is willing, of course; they've all traveled far too many miles to turn back now. Soon the members tire of all the bickering and the backbiting, and the panel begins to cool down and collapse like a dying sun. The truth is, Mr. Truett, asking a diverse group of ethicists to form a panel is like asking Congress to have a discussion about politics."

Truett rocked slowly back and forth in his chair. "Then what do you suggest?"

"As I see it, Mr. Truett, I have two things to offer this wonderful venture of yours. First of all, you were very wise to form this ethics advisory board. There will be many concerns, and it will be a tremendous advantage to be able to assure the public that you are addressing them. And you *need* to address them— but not by collecting a smorgasbord of ethical opinions. As a leader, Mr. Truett, I doubt that you make most of your own decisions by committee; that would bring your company to a grinding halt, now, wouldn't it? So there's the dilemma: you need to address ethical concerns, but you need to get things *done*. May I suggest a simple solution? You need to work from a single ethical perspective."

"*Your* perspective?"

Zohar smiled and spread his hands. "Why not? I think you'll find we have much in common, Mr. Truett—a vision for the future, an appreciation of technology, and most of all, a certain *force of will*. Like you, I like to make things happen. That's the first thing I can do for you, Mr. Truett—I can help you make things happen."

"And the second thing?"

"I can help you refocus your vision."

"Does my vision *need* refocusing?"

"If you'll forgive me, I believe it does. Do you know the difference between a dreamer and a visionary? *Focus.* Any child can conceive some grandiose scheme or utopian future; it takes a visionary to recognize the attainable part of that dream and bring together the necessary resources to make it happen. You are more than a dreamer, Mr. Truett. You've proven that already. But visionaries need to learn to *refocus* their visions, or their visions may end up nothing more than dreams."

"*Refocus* as in keeping a single-minded purpose? Keeping your eye on the prize?"

"Just the opposite, actually. You see, there's also a difference between a visionary and a fanatic. A fanatic focuses only on the destination; a visionary learns from the journey. The true visionary understands that, though he has a clear destination in mind, other opportunities may present themselves along the way that have even greater potential. The visionary must be determined, but he must remain flexible. How does the proverb go? 'The mind of man plans his way, but the Lord directs his steps.'

"Perhaps an example will help. When automobiles first appeared in our country, the railroad barons were kings—they had enormous wealth and power. When the automobile industry began to grow, the railroads were in a perfect position to buy them out—but they didn't. Do you know why? Because of a simple lack of vision. The railroad owners told themselves that they were in the *railroad* business—and what does a railroad have to do with automobiles? If they had only had the foresight to say, 'We are in the *transportation* business,' today we would all be driving Union Pacific Town Cars and Santa Fe SUVs."

"Interesting," Truett said. "So how does this apply to us?"

"I'd like to encourage you to think outside the box, Mr. Truett. Regardless of your current mission statement, despite what it says in your annual report, you are not in the business of personalized medicine."

"Oh? What business am I in?"

"The business of *applied genetic information*."

Truett let out a laugh. "I'm sorry, Dr. Zohar. That sounds like semantics to me."

"I assure you it's not. Your ultimate goal is to develop personalized medicines—but along the way to that goal, I think you've generated some other very lucrative possibilities for PharmaGen to explore."

"Such as?"

"Applied genetic information," Zohar said again. "You know, I really have to congratulate you on what you've already accomplished here."

"I wouldn't break out the champagne just yet. We need a salable product first. We need a clear path to cash."

"But you have a salable product right now. Don't you see? It's the genetic information you've collected from over a quarter of a million residents of western Pennsylvania."

"That information is strictly confidential."

"I couldn't agree more. The information you collect should never be sold, transferred, or released to any second party. However, the good people of Pennsylvania *have* entrusted PharmaGen with this information, which allows the possibility of certain secondary applications *within* your company."

Truett shifted uneasily in his chair. "What sort of *secondary applications* are we talking about?"

Zohar looked at him penitently. "I must confess something to you, Mr. Truett. Our introduction last week at that reception was not, strictly speaking, *fortuitous*. I intended to meet you there. You see, I've been observing the progress of your company from the very beginning. It's just the sort of pioneering venture I might have attempted myself, as a younger man. I've collected quite a bit of information on PharmaGen—not just from your brochures and glowing press releases, but from other sources—external sources. I have contacts among your major investors, and they tell me that PharmaGen has all but exhausted its original venture capital. The cost of your population studies has been enormous, and it's now a race against the clock to see if you can produce that salable product before your company goes the way of so many other promising tech start-ups. How many ambitious young entrepreneurs have faced the same dilemma? To attract ongoing investment, you have to promise success. But to deliver that success, you require ongoing investments. And so, like so many other young companies, you find yourself out of cash—and you're doing your very best to hide it, aren't you?

"The financial cost of failure would be enormous for you—but the *personal* cost would be even greater. You see, Mr. Truett, I've also looked into your *past* business ventures; this isn't your first attempt at a visionary startup, now, is it? There was that rather innovative multilevel marketing effort you attempted, followed by a most ambitious Internet venture. Each time you raised several million dollars in venture capital to get your project under way, and each time you failed."

Truett's face grew red. "That was not my fault."

"Of course not. There were unforeseeable market forces, unpredictable actions on the part of your competitors, but investors rarely bother themselves with such details, do they? Despite all their financial sophistication, investors tend to operate by a rather simple rubric: *three strikes and you're out*. To borrow a metaphor from your beloved Pirates, Mr. Truett, you are standing at the plate for the last time. If PharmaGen fails, *you* fail, and it will be time for you to retire to a nice, safe, *conventional* job—perhaps as an entry-level investment banker. That's a nice little career—though I doubt it comes with a yacht."

Truett looked at Zohar as though he had never seen him before. He had misjudged the man's abilities, and that was an error he rarely made. He ran his eyes over the old man again, quickly revising all of his initial impressions. Zohar was small in stature and unassuming in appearance—but he carried himself like a man much older than his actual years. Truett saw now that Julian Zohar was not old, he was cunning; he was not polite, he was calculating; he was not weak, he was restrained. Truett had thought of the man as little more than a doddering old academic, someone who could lend a scholarly aura to his company's sterile image—but now he saw him in a different light. Zohar was a serpent—a cobra—and Truett was unsure of his reach, his speed, or the power of his venom.

The old man reached across the table and gently patted Truett's hand. "My young friend," he said softly, "you're in such a fragile position. A virtual sword of Damocles hangs above your head—and I would hate to see that sword fall, Mr. Truett. I would deeply regret the demise of this visionary venture. I would do anything in my power to help keep this company alive. That's why I wanted to meet you; that's why I sought you out. I want to show you that *path to cash*."

Zohar smiled warmly. "Would a million dollars a month help? Tax free, of course."

The grinding of gears from the lockhouse brought Truett back to attention. There was a crackle from the marine band radio. In the smaller boats ahead of him, captains and their crews scurried over their vessels, coiling ropes and preparing for the remaining journey upriver. Truett glanced over the side of the lock at the lower river far below. When is it too late to change your mind? The question seemed strangely foreign to him now, a product of the black water and the darkness of the lock, and he cast the thought aside like a clinging bow line. There was nowhere to go but forward—and Tucker Truett was not a man to look back.

The water was at pool stage now, and the black-and-yellow upper gates began to groan open away from them. Truett stared at the warning pattern and watched as it disappeared into the dark of night.

CHAPTER
17

Dr. Ian Paulos ambled down the hallway at Trinity Episcopal School for Ministry, surrounded as always by an eager group of students who hovered around him like tugboats on a barge—a fitting image, since Dr. Paulos himself was built something like a barge. He was much too stocky to fit the expected image of a scholar, and he walked more like a long-shoreman than a doctor of divinity. His uneven mustache completely obscured his lower lip, and his gnarly salt-and-pepper hair looked as though it could shatter any mortal comb. He wore half-spectacles on the tip of his nose, causing him to constantly tip his head back and forth, depending on whom or what he wanted to include in his range of vision. Wherever he went, at any time of the day, his left arm seemed to be forever curled around a stack of books, and his right hand always carried an ancient brown leather briefcase.

His introductory ethics courses, intriguingly entitled "Right and Wrong 101" and "Telling Good from Evil" were the most popular in the seminary curriculum, and they were impossible to contain within four walls. Dr. Paulos had a habit of ending each lecture by simply turning and exiting midsentence; anyone curious enough to know how that particular sentence might end would simply follow after him. Discussions invariably ensued down hallways, across courtyards, through parking lots—sometimes even in crowded rest rooms, much to the chagrin of the female students.

"I still say love is the highest of all principles," one student passionately contended. "The most *loving* thing to do is the *right* thing to do. 'You must love the Lord your God with all your heart, all your soul, and all your mind,' he quoted. "This is the first and greatest commandment. A second is equally important: 'Love your neighbor as yourself.'"

"Read the book and saw the movie—loved them both," Paulos said. "So this 'highest principle' of yours, this 'love'— what exactly is it?"

"What is *love*? Doesn't everybody know that?"

"Do they? What about that woman a few years ago who backed her car into a lake and drowned all her kids? When they interviewed her later, she said, 'I loved my kids. No one ever loved their kids more than I did.' Do you think she loved her kids?"

"Of course not."

"How do you know? Are you able to somehow get inside her head and tell me what she did or didn't feel?"

"Maybe she felt the *feelings* of love," another student said, "but she didn't act in a loving *way*."

Without breaking stride, Paulos turned to the student, tipped his head forward, and peered at her over the top of his glasses. Trinity students learned to read Paulos the way a hunter reads a bear: When he leaned back and squinted at you through his lenses, that was good; it was a sign of consideration or even respect. But when he leaned forward and looked at you full on, it was time to climb the nearest tree.

"A *loving way*," he repeated. "Whatever does that mean?"

She shrugged. "You know."

"I don't know—and I don't think you do either."

"A way that's . . . you know . . . loving." That merited a laugh from the entire group.

"*Love* is a ruined word," Paulos said. "It's been gutted like an old trailer—stripped of objective meaning. When you say 'act in a loving way,' what you mean is 'act in a way that *feels loving* to you.' Isn't that right?"

"I guess so . . . yes."

"That's an *emotivist* ethic," Paulos said. "Start with David Hume and then read A. J. Ayer's *Language, Truth and Logic*—then we'll talk again. You see the problem here? The woman who drowned her kids *felt* loving. She *feels* she did the loving thing; you *feel* she did an unloving thing. Is that all we've got here, Ms. Stuart, a difference of feelings? Then how do you ever tell her she was *wrong*?"

Paulos arrived at his office door now. He shifted his briefcase to his already overloaded left hand, reached for the doorknob, then turned to face the group.

"Let me give you a BB to roll around in your puzzle: Five centuries ago John Calvin wrote, 'Love needs law to guide it.' In other words, the highest principle is not love, but God—because without God, love *has* no meaning. Think it over."

Paulos turned the knob and stepped forward, bumping into the door with a resounding thud. He stepped back again and fumbled in his pocket for the key.

"A truly great exit ruined," he grumbled.

He tried the knob again, pushed open the door with his hip, and backed inside.

"Does this mean the lecture is finally over?" one student quipped.

"The lecture is *never* over. Education is not a preparation for life, my young friends, education *is* life. Now take what I've taught you and get out there and do some serious good."

Paulos nudged the door shut behind him, turned, and stopped. Standing at his bookshelf was a tall man with very large glasses, leafing through one of his books.

"I hope you don't mind," Nick said, motioning to the open volume.

"Mi libro, su libro," Paulos said, dumping his own stack on the edge of his desk. "The way I see it, no one really owns a book."

"My students would agree with you," Nick said. "That's why the books keep disappearing from Ready Reserve."

Paulos smiled. "A fellow member of the Divine Order of the Underpaid? Welcome, brother."

"Nick Polchak," he said, extending his hand. "I teach entomology at NC State in Raleigh."

Paulos took his hand. "Oh yes—Tucker Truett's assistant called me about you. How do you know Truett?"

"We met on his yacht the other night."

"Lucky you. I got the tour once, plus a nifty PharmaGen windbreaker. Did you meet his girlfriend?"

"I saw a woman. Do you think she was the same one?"

"I doubt it. Please, have a seat—just dump those books off on the floor. Sorry about the mess. I could tell you that you caught me on a bad day, but as an ethicist I'm obligated to tell the truth: it's always like this."

"You should see my lab," Nick said.

"I like you already. Can I get you something? A Coke, some tea?"

"Nothing, thanks."

"I'm an Episcopalian—I can get you something stronger."

Nick shook his head.

Paulos took a seat behind his own desk, leaned back, and put his feet up on the corner. "So you have questions about PharmaGen," he said. "Fire away."

"I understand you're a member of PharmaGen's ethics advisory board."

"*Ab initio*," Paulos said. "From the beginning. I'm the founding member of an esteemed panel of—let's see, how many of us are there now? Oh yes—two."

"Truett says you guys don't get paid."

"I'm supposed to serve as a kind of ethical watchdog for this company, Dr. Polchak. I could hardly be expected to bite the hand that feeds me, now, could I?"

"Then what's in it for you? That is, if you don't mind my asking."

"I'm an ethicist. PharmaGen is creating one of the first industries based entirely on genetic information. That raises questions about genetic privacy, questions that up until now have been largely theoretical. This whole area fascinates me—and it worries me too. I want a voice in all this."

"And what is your voice saying?"

Paulos smiled. "I'd like to hear a little of your voice first. Why the big interest in PharmaGen?"

"I was considering becoming part of their population study. I've got some of those questions about genetic privacy."

Paulos tipped his head down and peered at him over the top of his glasses. "First you corner the CEO, and now you track down the ethics advisory board? I smell a journalist, Dr. Polchak—or maybe a competitor?"

Nick said nothing.

"OK," Paulos said. "Ethically speaking, withholding information is not the same thing as actually lying."

"Why did Truett decide to form an Ethics Advisory Board? What's the watchdog watching for?"

"That's easy enough. Ever since the Human Genome Project, there's been a growing concern about the possible misuse of genetic information: employers refusing to hire because of future health risks, insurance companies charging higher premiums for certain genetic types, that sort of thing. *Genetic discrimination*, that's what they call it. That's why the Project formed the Ethical, Legal, and Social Issues in Science group—to help develop guidelines for the security and proper use of genetic information.

"Now along comes PharmaGen, asking half a million people to give away their genetic information free of charge—that's what you call a problem of confidence, Dr. Polchak. People want to know if PharmaGen can be trusted—after all, there are guidelines about genetic privacy, but there are very few laws. PharmaGen anticipated this concern by volunteering to police themselves; they formed their very own watchdog group, and they make sure everybody knows about it. You should have seen the press conference when this board was first formed—quite the gala event."

"Are you saying the board is just for the sake of appearance?"

"I'm saying that appearance is a very big part of it. Don't misunderstand, we have a very real function—but to be honest, our biggest function is simply to let people know we exist. We're the dog that watches the henhouse. We help create the public confidence that makes PharmaGen work."

"Why you? Why were you asked to join this board?"

"Who better? I teach at a seminary, Dr. Polchak. Who better fits the image of guardian of the public welfare and enemy of moral turpitude? I'm an Episcopal priest *and* an ethicist—that makes me twice as nice. All modesty aside, I'm a well-educated and well-published ethicist—but I'm not kidding myself about my real value to PharmaGen."

"You're a very humble man."

"I'm a very realistic man. PharmaGen is a corporation, not a discussion group. They have places to go and things to do—they have money to make. They need my presence, but they hope I'll sit in the corner and act like a good little boy. But I've been a bad boy—I've forced them to ask some hard questions about the risks involved in what they're doing."

"Have they listened?"

Paulos shrugged. "I watch the henhouse from outside the

fence. I have no physical presence at PharmaGen. I serve as an advisor; how they implement my suggestions is up to them."

"What about the other guy? Who's the second member of the panel?"

Paulos folded his arms across his chest. "Now there's an interesting bird," he said. "His name is Julian Zohar. He's the executive director of COPE—the Center for Organ Procurement and Education here in Pittsburgh."

"Organ procurement?"

"You know, for transplants—hearts, lungs, livers, that sort of thing. The United States is divided into fifty-nine regions by the federal government. Each region has its own not-for-profit organ procurement office. Their job is to make the connection between potential donors and patients awaiting transplants. If you run your car into a bridge abutment, and if you've got a little red heart on your driver's license, then they call Zohar. Zohar checks the waiting list, takes the first guy on the list who matches your blood type, and zingo—you left your heart in Pittsburgh. Zohar runs our regional procurement office. It covers western PA and West Virginia, too, I think."

"So why Zohar? Why not another Episcopal priest?"

"You'd have to ask Truett that one. Maybe for variety—different ethical perspectives."

"Are your perspectives different?"

"Like night and day."

"How so?"

Paulos got up now, stretched, and walked around to the front of his desk. "Ethics is not just about right and wrong," he said. "It's about how you *get* to right and wrong. As an Episcopalian, as a Christian, I believe in the need for a grounded ethic—an ethical system that has its roots in unchanging values of right and wrong. I believe those values are found in the nature of God himself."

"And Zohar?"

"Like I said—a strange bird. Zohar did a doctorate in bioethics when the field was first emerging. He was very smart, very passionate, and very persuasive. He's an internationally respected bioethicist—or I should say, he *was*."

"What happened?"

"Transplant people are very concerned about definitions of death—they can't save a life until somebody else loses his, and the sooner he does, the better the odds of an effective transplant. The definition of death we use in America is a view known as whole-brain death: death is not pronounced until there is irreversible cessation of all functions of the brain and brain stem.

"But all the functions that make us really alive—personality, consciousness, memory, reasoning—they all involve the cerebrum, the so-called higher brain. If you lose all consciousness and personality, are you really alive? And if not, why should we wait around for all the lower-brain functions to cease as well? That was Zohar's position. He began to champion this view, known as higher-brain death."

"And that got him into trouble?"

"Not really—lots of people hold that view. He was just a little ahead of the curve on that one. It was what happened next that sank his boat. Zohar began to push an ethical view of organ procurement known as *routine salvaging*, a view that grants the state the right to harvest needed organs after death without the individual's permission."

"Wow."

"I agree. But think about it: when you set your garbage out on the curb, it's no longer your property. Anyone who wants to go through it can do so. Your rights over your garbage end at your property line. The routine salvaging view makes the same case for the human body: when you die, what's left over is garbage, and you give up your rights over it at death.

"You can see why a transplant person would love this view. His biggest headache is that he has to ask permission, and almost half the time he gets turned down. Wouldn't it be easier if he didn't have to ask?

"Zohar threw everything he had into this fight, but it was a no-win situation. In the Western world we place too high a value on the rights of the individual. We believe we have the right to control our own bodies, and that those rights continue even after death. To the Western mind, ideas like routine salvaging call up images of Dr. Mengele and Nazi medical experiments. When Zohar argued for a new definition of death, he was able to blend in with the crowd. But when he began to really push for routine salvaging—not just as an ethicist, but as a transplant officer—people recognized him for what he was: a pure utilitarian. The harder he pushed, the harder everybody else pushed back, until he finally gave up in disgust and just disappeared."

"Disappeared?"

"Dropped out of the ethical arena. Withdrew from panels and ceased publication. It's too bad, really. I used to read some of his stuff—very insightful. I lost track of Zohar completely until he suddenly turned up on PharmaGen's advisory board."

"Did that surprise you?"

Paulos shrugged. "I guess you can't expect burnout to last a lifetime. I was glad to see him again, actually—at least at first."

"The Christian meets the utilitarian," Nick said. "How has that worked out?"

"It hasn't exactly been a marriage made in heaven. Zohar is a big fan of PharmaGen—why wouldn't he be? PharmaGen is a utilitarian's dream: *the greatest good for the greatest number of people*. I don't get a lot of warm fuzzies from Zohar when I remind him about the rights of each individual, made in the image of God."

"You have concerns about where Zohar is taking the company?"

"I have concerns about a utilitarian approach to ethics. 'The greatest good for the greatest number of people'—what exactly does that mean? What *is* good, Dr. Polchak, and whose good are we talking about? I fear an ethical system that isn't tied down."

"Tied down?"

Paulos held up three fingers. "Three cowboys ride into town. The first cowboy ties his horse to the second horse, the second ties his horse to the third, and all three horses run off together. Why? Because none of the horses was tied to the hitching post. That's the problem with an ungrounded ethic, Dr. Polchak—no hitching post. Things have a way of running off without you."

"And who are these cowboys?"

"I suppose they change in every generation. In our day and age? I'd vote for information, technology, and efficiency—but that's just my opinion. There are a lot of new frontiers—and there are plenty of cowboys out there."

Nick slowly rose from his chair and extended his hand again. "Thanks for your time," he said. "Lots to think about."

"You might want to follow up with Dr. Zohar. You know—talk to the cowboy in person."

"I just might do that."

"So tell me—have you decided to participate in the population study?"

"Would you?"

Paulos grinned. "You're asking the watchdog if the henhouse is safe. All I can tell you is, I haven't seen a fox so far."

Nick returned the smile. "What if the fox is already inside?"

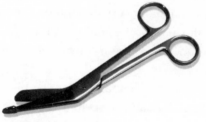

Riley pulled off the oven mitt and opened the door to her apartment. There stood Nick Polchak, his head buried in an open book.

"What do you know about organ transplantation?" he said without looking up.

"Nice to see you too," Riley said, heading back for the kitchen. "Do you want to come in, or are you going to finish the book first?"

Nick stepped slowly inside, leaving the door wide open behind him. He drifted toward the sofa like a sleepwalker and sat down, his eyes still glued to the pages.

"Water or wine?" Riley called from the kitchen.

"With what?"

"Food."

"Wine."

"I talked to Leo," she said. "I had him check the spyware reports from Lassiter's computer—"

"And there was nothing out of the ordinary," Nick cut in. "A few innocuous e-mails, visits to the usual Web sites . . . nothing we haven't seen already. I talked to Leo too—he said you called him twice today and three times yesterday. Give it some time, Riley. Have a little patience."

She poked her head around the corner and glared at him. "I spent the Fourth of July treading water in a Donna Karan because you couldn't wait to meet Tucker Truett. Are you going to stand there and lecture *me* on patience?"

Nick thought it was a good time to change the subject. "I saw Paulos today."

"And?"

"A very interesting guy."

"I should have come with you," Riley grumbled.

"We talked about this—you need to be at the office. You can't start disappearing all of a sudden. What would Lassiter say?"

"A senior pathologist is only on rotation eight days a month," Riley said, "but a fellow is on five days a week and every other weekend. How am I ever supposed to get away? When do I get to go with you?"

"You never take me out anymore . . . All I do is work. Didn't I just take you out on the Fourth of July?"

An oven mitt sailed through the kitchen doorway.

"What did you find out from Paulos?"

"I'm not sure yet. Did you ever hear of a guy named Julian Zohar?"

"I don't think so."

"He's the executive director of your local organ procurement organization."

"COPE? I've never met Zohar, but we work with COPE all the time."

"Really? Why is that?"

"There are about sixteen thousand deaths per year in Allegheny County, but we only do autopsies on about twelve hundred of them. Drug-related deaths, homicides, suicides, deaths in prisons or nursing homes—those are the ones that fall under the coroner's jurisdiction. Some of those people are potential organ donors—but our office has to view the body and sign off on it before COPE can claim the organs. You like garlic on your bread?"

"Sure."

Riley glanced at him as she set the plate down on the table. "You're not planning on kissing me again?" She paused. "Or putting your arm around my shoulder?"

Nick looked up from the book. Riley had already turned away and was headed back to the kitchen.

"Do you know how to tell male and female blowflies apart?" he called after her.

"What a fun evening this is going to be."

"It's their eyes. A male's eyes are very close together, almost touching. But a female's eyes are always spread wide apart."

Riley poked her head around the corner. "I'm waiting."

Nick shrugged. "I think females see more than males do."

"You needed a PhD to figure that out? Most males of all species are clueless."

Just then, a coal gray cat jumped onto the sofa and padded its way up onto Nick's lap, stretching and settling itself comfortably across his legs. Nick arched stiffly back and frowned down at the intruder. Riley returned from the kitchen, setting two glasses and a deep burgundy bottle on the table. She glanced at Nick's frozen posture, and at her cat contentedly stretched across his lap.

"Problem?"

"Your mammal is sitting on me."

"Nick, it's called a *cat*."

"Why do people keep mammals? What fun can you have with a mammal?"

"You keep poisonous spiders."

Nick looked up at her. "My point exactly."

144

Riley shook her head. "C'mon, time for dinner."

Nick looked down at the slumbering feline, its legs tucked invisibly under its overfed body. It seemed almost lifeless to Nick, except for the radiant warmth and the rumbling sound that came from somewhere deep inside. Nick frowned again; it looked like one big, amorphous, fur-covered blob.

"How do I pick it up?"

"How do you pick up an insect?"

"I use a sweep net, and then I drop it in a killing jar."

"That's a little hard on a cat," Riley said, scooping it off Nick's lap with one hand and dropping it onto the nearby recliner.

They sat together at the tiny dinette. Nick propped the book open against a stack of napkins, weighting down the curling signatures with the salt and pepper shakers.

"Tell me about organ transplantation," Nick said. "How does the system work?"

"I thought a forensic entomologist would know all this."

"Why? My species regenerates its own organs."

"Your species also gets stepped on a lot."

"That is a downside," he said. "This is good chicken. It needs salt."

Riley gestured to the salt shaker holding down the verso side of Nick's book.

Nick used it liberally, then extended it to Riley.

She shook her head. "I don't use salt."

Nick nodded slowly. "Tell me how the transplant system works," he said.

"Well, let's say you have a serious liver problem—"

"Let's say it's a kidney problem."

Riley paused. "OK, you have a *kidney* problem. So you go to a specialist, and he verifies that you need a transplant. Your medical information is entered into a database, and you're put on the national waiting list."

"Who runs that waiting list?"

"There's an organization called UNOS—the United Network for Organ Sharing, down in Richmond. They have the federal contract to administer the waiting list."

"Does that list include everyone who needs a transplant of any kind? All over the U.S.?"

"That's the whole idea. The list was created as a result of the National Organ Transplant Act of 1984. The goal was to ensure a fair and efficient system of organ allocation."

"How do you know all this?" Nick asked.

"People underestimate pathologists. We have to know something about every realm of medicine and surgery. We have to be familiar with every kind of procedure and its risks, and we have to be able to diagnose diseases by both tissue and fluid. Besides, in my residency I did a subspecialty in renal pathology."

"A national waiting list," Nick said thoughtfully. "All that information in one place. Who has access to that list?"

"Nobody."

"Nobody?"

"Not if you're talking about calling up the list and just looking it over. Nobody gets to do that. It's very private, and it's extremely secure."

"Then how is it used?"

"Suppose you have a motorcycle accident, and at the hospital you're pronounced brain-dead; that's when the local organ procurement organization goes to work. In western Pennsylvania, it's called COPE—the Center for Organ Procurement and Education. The hospital keeps you on a ventilator—they keep your *body* working—while COPE talks to the next of kin to request your organs for transplant."

"Do they always have to ask the family?"

"Not if you're over eighteen and you're carrying a donor card. But if you're underage or your wishes were never made clear, then somebody has to grant permission. So let's say they do—that's when COPE sends your medical information to UNOS, and UNOS sends back a matching donor list."

"And who's on that list?"

"Everybody in your local area that's a potential match, in order of priority. COPE calls the transplant surgeon in charge of the first person on the list and offers the organ; if he wants it, it's his; if not, it's offered to the second person on the list, and so on until the organ is placed. If no one wants the organ locally, it's offered regionally; if no one wants it regionally, it's offered nationally. That's how the system works."

"How is your place on the list determined?"

"The placement protocol is different for every organ. For kidneys, it's done by body size, tissue compatibility, medical urgency, and time spent on the waiting list."

"How long can you stay on the waiting list?"

"Forever," she said. "Some people are harder to match than others."

"So how do you beat the system?"

"You can't."

"Come on, Riley. What about our own governor a few years ago—what was his name?"

"Robert Casey," she said. "I was an undergraduate at Pitt at the time. Casey had a heart-liver transplant here at UPMC. He was on the waiting list less than a day, when the average wait for a liver was two months—six months for a heart."

"So it doesn't hurt to be first citizen of the state."

"It doesn't help either. They reviewed that case, Nick. Six people were ahead of Casey for a heart, and two for a liver. Casey jumped to the top of the list because he needed a multi-organ transplant—that's the only reason."

"You're telling me there's *nothing* the rich and powerful can do to manipulate the system in their favor?"

"Oh, there might be a couple of things. They could move to the transplant hospital with the shortest waiting list—the wealthy can afford to do that. Their surgeon could put them on the waiting list earlier than necessary, just to increase their seniority. And their surgeon could hospitalize them early, too, in order to make their need appear more urgent. But those are small things, Nick; none of them really tip the scales your way. For the most part, the rich and powerful have to just sit tight and wait—just like the rest of us."

Nick said nothing for a few minutes, busying himself with his dinner. Halfway to his mouth with a forkful of pasta and mushroom sauce, he stopped and set the fork down again.

"You said COPE sends the donor's information to UNOS."

"That's right."

"And COPE gets the matching donor list back."

"Right—all the potential matches in your local area."

"The size of that list would change from area to area. What about this area? They must do a lot of transplants in Pittsburgh."

"UPMC Presbyterian does. It's a huge transplant center."

"So when COPE gets a matching donor list, it could show most of the people at UPMC Presbyterian waiting for that organ."

"It could, yes."

"Think about it," Nick said. "Nobody gets to browse the waiting list, but every time COPE submits a donor's name, they get to see a *piece* of that list."

"In a way, yes."

"So if COPE wanted to, they could compile a list of all the people awaiting a kidney transplant in this area. And by comparing those lists over time, they could know how long each person has been waiting for their kidney."

"I suppose so—but why would they want to?"

"Listen to this," he said, turning to his open book. "'The French law on organ procurement adopted in 1976 is one that presumes the consent of persons who do not, during their lifetime, expressly refuse to have their organs taken on their death. The law states that "an organ to be used for therapeutic or scientific purposes may be removed from the cadaver of a person who has not during his lifetime made known his refusal of such a procedure."' According to this book, laws like this exist in Austria, Belgium, Finland, Italy, Norway, Spain, and Switzerland."

"It's called 'presumed consent,'" Riley said. "They *presume the consent* of the donor unless he says otherwise."

Nick frowned. "I thought I was going to impress you. OK, smart girl, try this one: 'Within the United States, at least two states have considered laws that would, if enacted, have properly been called presumed consent laws.' Maryland is one of those states; for one hundred dollars, name the other one."

"Pennsylvania," Riley said without looking up. "It didn't pass." She pushed her plate away and looked at him. "Where are you going with all this? Why the sudden interest in organ transplantation?"

"Julian Zohar," Nick said. "Executive Director of COPE. He's the guy who pushed for this law in Pennsylvania."

"Why wouldn't he? That kind of law would make COPE's job a whole lot easier."

"He's also a member of PharmaGen's ethics advisory board."

"So? What's the connection?"

"Ian Paulos told me that the ethics advisory board exists mostly to instill public confidence—to convince people that PharmaGen can be trusted to do the right thing. Paulos was brought on because he has the perfect image—he's an Episcopal priest. But Paulos gave me the feeling that his ethical input is not really valued. Paulos wants to talk about ethical concerns, and Truett wants to build a company.

"Then PharmaGen brought on a second ethicist: Julian Zohar. Zohar is philosophically much more to PharmaGen's liking—he likes to get things done. So the ethics advisory board stops with just two members, Paulos and Zohar. Publicly, they serve their function as symbols of moral uprightness. But privately, they butt heads. Zohar says 'go,' Paulos says 'slow.' I wonder who really has Truett's ear?"

"Where is all this taking us, Nick? We start with Lassiter, then we drop in on Truett, then you go to see Paulos, and now it's this Zohar guy. Aren't we getting off track here? What's the tie-in with all this?"

"Remember the blowfly," Nick said.

"The clueless one or the female?"

"The female. She finds a body by tracking molecules of blood in the air. First a single molecule, then a small cluster, then an even larger one, back to the source of it all. The blowfly follows the path of increasing concentration—that's what we're doing here. Follow your nose, Riley. We started with the anomalies in Lassiter's autopsies. Then we found that he's investing enormous amounts of money in a single company—PharmaGen. That's more than a wild investment. What gives Lassiter his confidence in PharmaGen? And why is PharmaGen willing to take on such a small-time private investor?

"Next we visited Truett. PharmaGen is about to make a ton of money—*if* they can keep public confidence long enough to produce a marketable product. But when we asked about things that could get in the way, pesky little things like ethical concerns over genetic privacy, who did he direct us to? Not Zohar, but Paulos—he never even mentioned Zohar. But Paulos tells me that he's mostly a figurehead, and that Zohar may be the real conscience behind the company."

"My head is spinning," Riley said, rising from the table. "I need to lie down for a minute—it's been a long day." She moved to the sofa and stretched out facedown. Nick turned in his chair and watched her. She seemed especially weary tonight, and she moved more slowly than usual. There was a sort of heaviness about her. She straightened slightly and grimaced, rolling her shoulders from side to side.

"Want me to rub your back?"

"What?"

"Your back seems to give you a lot of trouble. Want me to rub it for you?"

"It won't help."

Nick picked up his chair and carried it to the sofa, setting it down beside Riley. "Want to hear a wild idea? What if Zohar and Truett and Lassiter have found a way to create a black market in human organs?"

Nick watched Riley closely. She blinked once but said nothing.

"You're still not impressed. Now I'm really disappointed."

"The idea occurred to me," Riley said, "but it's crazy."

"Is it? There have been attempts before—in the Philippines, in India, even in England. We know that Julian Zohar is a big fan of 'routine salvaging' or 'presumed consent,' or whatever you want to call it. What if he found a way to pull it off? What if Lassiter refused to release that first kidney for transplant because he had some other use for it? What if you're being shut out of autopsies because Lassiter doesn't want you to see what's happening behind closed doors? What if Lassiter is 'salvaging' organs from cadavers for Zohar, and PharmaGen is acting as some sort of go-between?"

"C'mon, Nick," Riley said, sitting up slowly. "That's an old urban legend. It's just not possible."

"Why not?"

"There are a dozen reasons. How many people would it take to pull off something like that? Where would the organs be removed? At the coroner's office? We don't get bodies until hours after they're dead, and the organs would no longer be viable. And what does Dr. Lassiter do, just drop a kidney in a cooler and walk out like it's his lunch? Where would these organs get transplanted? What doctor would do that? What hospital would allow it?"

"What if—"

"Nick—there are a *dozen* reasons, and I'm just too tired to go into them all tonight." Riley stood up and stretched painfully.

Nick looked at her again. He saw the droop in her shoulders, and he heard the dullness in her voice. Riley McKay was strong and she was stubborn, but her exhaustion was showing through

151

like the bones behind her lucent skin.

"I'm worried about you," Nick said.

Riley stopped and looked at Nick. "I like you too," she said. "You can be a very sweet bug man. You don't know what your help means to me."

"No, I don't. I wish you'd tell me."

She put one hand on his chest and spoke slowly and deliberately. "Nick, I think it would be better . . . if we *both* tried . . . to keep this on a professional level."

Nick paused. "Want to know what *I* think?"

"No," she said. "I'm sorry, Nick. I'm just telling you the way it has to be. Now if you'll excuse me, I really need to get some rest. Can you let yourself out? Just lock the door behind you when you leave."

Nick watched her turn and shuffle slowly down the hallway toward the bedroom.

"I've got a long drive home," he called after her. "Mind if I use the bathroom?"

She reached in an open doorway and flipped on a light switch, then continued silently down the hallway, closing the bedroom door quietly behind her.

Nick shut the bathroom door and turned on the water in the sink. He quietly opened the white porcelain medicine cabinet and looked inside. There were three shelves containing cosmetics, deodorants, lotions, and a predictable array of items for personal hygiene and first aid. On the lowest shelf, front and center, were three prescription medicine bottles. Nick took out a pen and copied down the information from the label of each.

He flushed the toilet, turned off the light, and quietly let himself out.

Let me get this straight," Leo said. "Somebody dies, the coroner's office gets the body, and somebody strips it for parts before they release it for burial. Right?"

"Wrong—somebody strips it *before* it gets to the coroner's office."

Nick raised his head to get the waitress's attention. It wasn't difficult; she had been periodically glancing over at the man with the funny glasses for the last half-hour. Nick pointed to his coffee cup.

"Remember I told you about the guy in the cooler and the wound on his back, just below the ribs? It was tack-sutured shut. That's not a wound, Leo, it's an *incision*—and I found two maggots in that incision. That means it was made out of doors, and it was made sometime before dark—because blowfly activity tends to stop at night. The time of death was around dusk the night before the body was discovered; that means the incision was actually made at the time of death."

"Made by whom?"

"I don't know."

"Made *why*?"

"I think it was made to remove the kidney."

"For what purpose?"

"Again, this is just a theory: to offer the kidney for transplant."

"How? By selling it on eBay?"

"A guy actually tried that once, remember? I don't have all the details worked out, Leo, but look at the pieces. Zohar is the director of an organ procurement office. He knows who's waiting for a transplant locally, he knows how desperate they are, and with a little additional research he knows what they can afford to pay. PharmaGen collects genetic information from people all over western Pennsylvania. Truett could easily provide a match with someone on Zohar's waiting list."

"A *match*?" Leo glanced over both shoulders. "Nick, Truett isn't collecting information on *dead* people. Do you know what you're saying? If Truett is making matches with living donors, they're not just following these people around until they die of natural causes."

"No," Nick said. "They're killing them."

Neither man said anything for a minute.

"Nick, this is more than slightly illegal. Why would Truett risk such a thing?"

"Maybe to keep a startup afloat. He's got to keep the cash coming in until they get a product to market—and he's got an expensive lifestyle. Then there's Lassiter—he's a pathologist, he works in the coroner's office . . . If a kidney *was* removed at a death scene, who would be in a better position to cover it up? Think about it, Leo: This explains Lassiter's investments in PharmaGen—and where he's getting the money to make them. Lassiter's making sure that PharmaGen succeeds—and when they do, he'll be in a position to cash in big time."

"And Zohar? What would be his motivation?"

"That's what I want to find out," Nick said. "Leo, listen: Riley told me that no one has access to the UNOS waiting list. Do you think *you* could break into it?"

"Not likely. It's a federal database—a *medical* database—and privacy would be a huge priority. I would anticipate several layers of redundant security."

Nick thought for a minute. "Riley says that most of the transplants in our area are done at UPMC Presbyterian; wouldn't they keep a list of their own people waiting for transplants?"

"That would make sense."

"And isn't it likely that a single hospital's database would be easier to break into than the one at UNOS?"

"I would think so. Of course, I won't know for sure until I try." He lowered his voice. "I assume you're asking me to try?"

"I need a list of everyone at UPMC Presby who's waiting for a kidney transplant—no other organs, just kidneys. And if you find that list, Leo, I want you to look for *past* lists. Can you do that?"

"I can check for archived files," he said, "or for backups of the whole system. It could take a couple of days. What are you looking for?"

"I want to find out who used to be on the transplant list who isn't anymore. I want to know why they dropped off the list."

"Either they died, or they got their kidney. What other reason could there be?"

Nick shrugged. "Maybe they got a better offer."

"I don't know," Leo said. "This whole idea seems too fantastic to be possible. That guy in the cooler—are you positive his kidney was missing?"

"No."

Leo raised both eyebrows. "A minor detail."

"We didn't have time to check. The three deputy coroners came back with the pizza, and I had to kiss Riley."

Leo did a thoroughly Italian double take. "You kissed Riley? Where?"

"On the lips, of course."

"No—*where* did you kiss her?"

"In the cooler. At the coroner's office."

Leo leaned forward and thumped Nick on the forehead with the butt of his palm. "Let me explain something to you. A woman like Riley should be kissed over the Salmon Wellington at the LeMont, looking out over Mount Washington at the lights of the Golden Triangle. A woman like Riley should *not* be kissed in a cooler, at the coroner's office, surrounded by dead people in plastic bags."

"I had to think fast."

The waitress arrived and lifted the carafe to Nick's cup. "Bring my friend decaf," Leo said. "He's been thinking too fast."

"I put my arm around her too."

"Where? At a landfill?"

"No, on a seventy-foot yacht in the Allegheny, watching the fireworks display at the Point."

Leo looked at him. "How did you get access to a seventy-foot yacht?"

"We rowed up to it in a dinghy and then flipped the boat over."

Leo thumped him on the forehead again.

"Would you cut that out?" Nick said. "That hurts."

"It ought to hurt—I'm trying to knock a hole in it. Do you know your problem, Nick Polchak? You spend your whole life *up here*." He tapped hard on Nick's head with his index finger. "You're trapped inside this . . . this *charnel*, this *sarcophagus*. Your whole life is spent *thinking*; you have no senses—no sense of touch or taste or smell. And do you know why you have no senses? It's this business of yours—all these flies and maggots and decomposing bodies! You've shut down your senses, Nick—you've had to, just to survive."

"That's ridiculous."

"Is it? Let me ask you something: what does Riley McKay smell like?"

Nick paused. "Well, since she works at the coroner's office, I suppose she would smell like—"

Leo reached out to thump him again, but Nick ducked away.

"You see? Even when you try to use your senses, you're still *thinking*. Listen to me, Nick. Riley McKay smells like lavender. Have you ever noticed? And she uses Tresor from time to time, but she lets it wear off—it leaves just the slightest hint behind. Have you ever listened to the sound of her voice, Nick? Not the words themselves, but the *sound*?"

Nick's eyes floated upward behind the huge lenses. "It sounds like . . . a wind chime," he said distantly. "Even when she's angry."

Leo looked at him, then leaned forward and spoke softly. "Nick, let me ask you something: are you experiencing ordinary human emotions toward this woman? Because from you, I find that frightening."

"So do I," Nick said. "It's been a long time for me."

Leo paused. "You're serious?"

Nick said nothing.

"This complicates things."

"It gets worse. I was at her apartment tonight. I've been noticing some things about her. Her back seems to bother her a lot, and she tires out easily."

"She's a pathologist. What did you expect?"

"But I've noticed swelling in her ankles—she's too young for that. And she never uses salt; isn't that a little odd? So I checked her medicine cabinet for prescriptions."

"An excellent start to a relationship," Leo said. "Always check their meds."

"Leo, I stopped by a pharmacy on the way over here. Riley has some kind of kidney disease. It could be serious."

"How serious?"

Nick shook his head.

"This waiting list from UPMC Presbyterian," Leo said. "Is

there any particular name you're looking for?"

Nick said nothing.

"Nick, if this black market theory of yours is correct—if *Riley's* name is on that waiting list—then which side do you think she's on in all this?"

"I don't know," Nick said. "But I'd better figure it out. I need to know which side *I'm* on."

Julian Zohar ran his hand across the thick hardwood mantel, admiring the hand-carved woodland scene on the frieze that supported it. The fireplace beneath it was at least fifteen feet wide; the chocolate gray flagstone that covered it was hand-picked from the fields of Pennsylvania. Above the mantel, a formidable-looking man stared out from a full-length portrait framed in burnished gold. Twenty feet higher, the ceiling sprawled like the roof of a cathedral, a soft white canopy ribbed with thick veins of inlaid wood. The room below was awe inspiring. One corner was dominated by a Steinway concert grand, another by a life-size bronze; in between, rich upholstery and elegant furniture settings dotted the floor like luxuriant oases.

There was a sound at the doorway. Zohar turned to see a late-middle-aged woman in a motorized wheelchair approaching, escorted by a private nurse.

"Mrs. Heybroek," he smiled, "how nice to see you."

159

She extended her hand to him. He cupped it in his own right hand and patted it gently with his left.

"Have we met?" she said, cocking her head slightly.

"We have not; my misfortune. I'm Dr. Julian Zohar, executive director of the Center for Organ Procurement and Education here in Pittsburgh."

The woman's eyes widened. "Have you found a match? Is that why you're here?"

"Perhaps we could speak about that—in private."

The woman dismissed the nurse with a quick wave of her hand and watched until she disappeared through the archway into the darkness of the adjoining room. Then she turned to Zohar again—but Zohar was now occupied admiring an ornate mahogany breakfront.

"What a lovely home," he said. "What a *stately* home—a fitting tribute to all that you and the late Mr. Heybroek have accomplished in your lives: your charitable work, your sizable donations to the arts—and let's not forget your educational contributions. Wasn't Mr. Heybroek a member of the board of Sewickley Academy?"

"Mr. Zohar, have you found a *match*?"

Zohar turned to her and smiled sympathetically. "There's no match," he said. "I think you and I both know that there never will be."

He turned away again and continued his tour of the room, running his hand over the surface of a plush sofa, sampling the scent of a lavish flower arrangement, or stepping back to admire a particularly fine oil painting.

"This rural scene—it's an original, isn't it? A Pissarro, if I'm not mistaken."

"Mr. Zohar, what is the purpose of your visit? If this is not about my kidneys—"

"Oh, this is definitely about your kidneys," Zohar said. "It's an amazing thing, isn't it, the way our current transplant system works? Or perhaps I should say, *doesn't* work. Did you know that there are more than eighty thousand people just like you, hoping and praying for a kidney or a liver or a heart? Sixteen of them die each day without receiving it. It's tragic—But I don't have to tell *you*, now, do I?"

Zohar walked slowly back across the room now, taking a seat on a settee beside the woman's wheelchair. He leaned back, folded his hands neatly in his lap, and gazed intently into the woman's eyes.

"Do you know why this problem persists, Mrs. Heybroek? Do you know *why* you'll never get your kidneys? Because, despite all of the advances in medical technology, the current transplant system still requires us to ask *permission* to obtain an organ. Here you sit, waiting for a statistically improbable event—waiting for someone with your rare blood type to fall off a motorcycle or suffer a stroke—and even then, we have to *ask*. The fact is, Mrs. Heybroek, half the time the family will say *no*.

"And did you know that, even if a matching kidney *is* discovered, the law requires it to be offered regionally first? That means if someone in, say, Philadelphia falls off that motorcycle, his kidneys must be offered to someone in that region first, even if that person's need is less critical than your own—even if that person is less *deserving*. So many inconsistencies," he said sadly. "So much injustice."

Zohar stood up, put both hands in his pockets, and began to slowly wander around the room again, this time shaking his head sadly over each piece of furniture or work of art. "It's ironic," he said. "Despite all your power and influence, despite all your contributions to society, you will have to die along with the rest of them. Your money is of no help to you now. You're the victim of an arbitrary, outmoded set of bureaucratic regulations."

"Stop this!" the woman shouted. "Don't you think I know these things? Did you come here just to gloat?"

A look of profound compassion came over Zohar's face. "Is that what you think? No, Mrs. Heybroek, I didn't come here to gloat. I came here tonight to offer you your kidneys."

She looked at him in astonishment.

"I'm an ethicist," he said. "In my ethical system, organs would be allocated on the basis of *utility*—who would benefit from them most? Who could use them for the greatest good? In my ethical system there is a concept known as *social worth*. Look around you, Mrs. Heybroek. Who could seriously argue that your life is worth no more than that of, say, an indigent? Or a criminal? Someone who has spent his life taking from others, instead of making a contribution? You've contributed so much to this world, Mrs. Heybroek, and you have a lot more still to give. I want to help you make that contribution."

"How?" she said in almost a whisper.

"I believe you have the right to obtain a new pair of kidneys. And since you've worked so hard to amass a personal fortune, I believe you should be able to use that fortune to obtain them. Why not? You've *earned* the right."

"Stop these riddles," the woman said. "If you really have something to offer me, let me hear it."

Zohar smiled. "You are currently on the waiting list for a kidney transplant; you've been on that list for almost three years now. Next week you will announce to your physician that you have lost hope, and that you wish to be removed from the waiting list and simply go home to die in peace. And you will go home, Mrs. Heybroek, but you will not die. I will provide you with your pair of kidneys. Your transplant surgery will take place in a state-of-the-art surgical center. You will then return home to convalesce in seclusion for the next twelve months, during which time you will experience a miraculous 'recovery' from your end-stage renal disease."

"*You* will provide my kidneys? How? Where will they come from?"

"As an ethicist, I insist on a policy of strict confidentiality. I will not reveal the source of your organs, nor will the donor's family ever know who has received them."

"But you must be going outside the legal system."

"The *legal* system? I'm going outside the *unethical* and *unjust* system, Mrs. Heybroek; a system that's more than happy to let you die to protect the rights of someone with virtually no social value."

"I can't be a party to something like this."

"Can't you?" Zohar turned to the painting suspended over the fireplace. It was the focal point of the entire room. Two recessed halogen lights illuminated the painting, creating a fiery glare in the center of the glossy canvas. "James Ludlum Heybroek," he said. "Quite a man. He foresaw the decline of Pittsburgh's steel industry in the sixties, and he helped pioneer the transition from an industrial to a technological economy. He was a leading figure in Pittsburgh's second Renaissance, wasn't he? Three Rivers Stadium, the USX Tower, PPG Place, the Mellon Bank Tower . . . so many men were indebted to him—and he called in a few of those debts, didn't he? Debts that ruined other businesses, debts that even resulted in a couple of notable suicides."

"How *dare* you—"

"Don't misunderstand, Mrs. Heybroek. I have the greatest respect for your late husband. I'm simply pointing out that people of power and influence are accustomed to making hard decisions. I didn't just show up on your doorstep tonight. I've spent a good deal of time researching you and your family's history. You're an impressive person, Mrs. Heybroek, no less so than your husband. You didn't get where you are today through timidity and caution, now, did you?"

The woman narrowed her eyes and lifted her chin. "How much?" she asked.

"Three million dollars. By electronic transfer to a series of offshore accounts."

"*Three million—*"

"A small price, considering. Look at it this way, Mrs. Heybroek: I'm not really charging you, I'm empowering you.

Money is power, that's what they always say, but right now your money has no power. You're about to die with three million dollars in your pocket, and it will be of no value to you then. I'm giving you back the chance to get something for your money."

"I could have you arrested for this."

"You could—but you'd be signing your own death warrant, wouldn't you? I'm not offering you an option, Mrs. Heybroek, I'm offering you your *only* option. Where else will you get your kidneys?"

"I . . . I need to know where the kidneys will come from."

Zohar sat down beside her again, picked up her left hand, and cradled it gently. "Where did that lovely dress come from? Paris? New York? Where did your wheelchair come from? Mexico? China? Do you know? Do you really care? When you purchase a product, Mrs. Heybroek, you don't concern yourself with the process of production and distribution. That's what you pay other people for."

She said nothing but stared straight ahead.

Zohar reached into his coat pocket, took out a business card, and placed it in her hand. He rose and stepped to the doorway, where he stopped and turned back.

"You are a woman of great power," he said. "Please— exercise that power. I want you to live."

CHAPTER
21

Smoke poured from the toaster oven. Nathan Lassiter pawed the piece of blackened toast onto the counter, spit out an expletive, and shoved all four fingers into his mouth like his infant son used to do. He stood at the sink, scraping off the layer of crumbling carbon with a knife, when his cell phone rang. He dropped the toast into the sink and picked up the phone.

"Lassiter, what is it? Oh . . . it's you." He jabbed at the remains of the toast with the point of his knife until it folded like a little umbrella and disappeared into the garbage disposal.

"I'm fine, Margaret. No, I'm fine—I'm just a little busy, that's all." He felt the glass decanter in the coffee maker; it was cold. He pulled it out and stared at the thin layer of dark liquid in the bottom. He swirled it around twice, then sniffed it.

"Look, you didn't call just to see how I'm doing. What's on your mind? You got the check, didn't you? I know I wrote it." He pulled a cup from the stack of dirty dishes and examined the inside. He set it down and picked up another, then a third. He pinned the phone against his shoulder and wiped the rim of the cup with the tail of his shirt. He emptied the decanter into it, set it in the microwave, and punched a button. Nothing happened.

"I'm not starting something. I just asked about the check, that's all. I'm not arguing. Who's arguing?" He opened the fridge and scanned the barren shelves. There was a bulging, half-empty milk bottle with a thick yellow layer on top, and a series of opaque plastic containers all jammed to the back to the shelves. He slid one forward and began to pry off the lid, then thought better of it.

"What? No, I don't know why we always fight. I guess that's why people get divorced, isn't it?" He opened the pantry door and removed a promising-looking box from the shelf. He shook it and heard nothing; he dropped it on the floor and tried another. Behind one box he spotted a single granola bar wrapped in green and silver mylar. He took it.

"Look, can we get to the point? I've got a lot going on here. What is it you want? What?" Lassiter pulled the phone away from his ear and let out a laugh.

"You've got to be kidding. You got the bedroom suite, you got the oils and the Wedgwood—now you want the *plants*? Why don't you take the carpet too?" He flipped through the *Pittsburgh Post-Gazette* on the island, pulled out the sports and financial sections, and headed for the family room and his favorite recliner—his *only* recliner.

"No, I don't *need* the plants—I just don't think you'll want them anymore. Because they're dead, that's why. No, I watered them all right—*you* killed them. That exterminator you hired. That's right, he tented the house and fumigated. The gas killed every living thing in the house, including your plants. What? Yes, you did—you bought a service contract. I saw the paperwork. Well, maybe that's the problem, Margaret. You don't remember where the money goes. Anyway, the plants are yours if you want them—help yourself. Uh-huh. Well, I've got to go. Talk to you later. Yeah. Bye."

Lassiter dropped the cell phone on the carpet and leaned back in his recliner with a look of satisfaction. He set the paper on his lap and opened the sports page. As he scanned the headlines, his eyes drifted above the paper and focused on a mahogany plant stand near the doorway, supporting a leafy Boston fern.

It was in perfect condition.

CHAPTER
22

The silver Porsche roared into a parking space in front of the Fox Chapel Yacht Club and killed its lights. Jack Kaplan turned to the beautiful young woman sitting silently beside him and smiled.

"You know, Angel, when I saw you leaning up against that red Beamer the other night, I almost stepped out and helped you myself. I don't know who first spotted you, but you were the perfect choice for this job. I mean the face, the dress, the body—baby, you are the total package. Looks to die for, you might say."

"I didn't ask your opinion," the woman said.

Kaplan reached across and stroked her long, auburn hair. "I love this," he said.

She swung around and knocked his hand away. "Let me make something clear to you, Dr. Kaplan: This is a business relationship. I don't like you, I don't trust you, and I certainly don't need your help. Have I made myself clear?"

Kaplan thrust an imaginary dagger into his heart and twisted it. "You're killing me, Angel. But then, that's your specialty, isn't it?"

"One more thing: when we're out of sight, don't you *ever* touch me."

Jack looked her over once more and shook his head. "Your loss," he said. "Are you ready? It's showtime."

Kaplan stepped out of the car, fastened the top button of his sports coat, and moved around to the opposite side of the car. He opened the passenger door and extended his hand. Angel reached down at her feet and picked up a glossy black handbag and a bottle of champagne; she swung her slender legs from the car, then rose up to meet him, smiling and kissing him lightly on the cheek. They walked arm in arm down the sidewalk on the right side of the building, avoiding the glare of the streetlamps, heading directly for the marina and the wooden docks that projected into the river like gray piano keys.

Behind them, a second car rolled to a stop beside the Porsche. Two men sat silently, watching Kaplan and the woman called Angel work their way down the pier toward the farthest slip.

Nathan Lassiter turned to the driver. "I want to ride with Angel next time," he said. "I just got divorced, you know. What does this look like to people?"

Santangelo ignored him. "We'll give them another minute," he said evenly. "No sense crowding them."

Moments later, the two men emerged from the car and followed the same secluded path to the wooden quays lined with gently rocking sailboats, catamarans, and sport cruisers of all shapes and sizes—but none of them compared in size or luxury with the corporate yacht in the final slip, the seventy-foot *PharmaGen*.

There were hearty laughs and eager handshakes as the last two men stepped aboard, completing the party of six. The bow and stern lines were quickly cast off, the *PharmaGen's* twin

169

diesel inboards gave a guttural growl, and Tucker Truett backed the yacht slowly out of the slip and into the darkness of the Allegheny River.

As soon as the yacht passed out of range of the bright marina lights, the jovial pretense was dropped and the party fell silent. They traveled just over a mile upriver, to an isolated spot where Nine Mile Island and Sycamore Island lay side by side, dividing the river into three separate channels. They dropped anchor in the central channel, where the wooded islands blocked them from view from either bank.

Julian Zohar stepped into the center of the group and cleared his throat.

"Mr. Truett informs me we have refreshments tonight—please, help yourselves." They took seats on the U-shaped leather sun bench—all except for Truett, who remained seated in the captain's chair in the adjoining cockpit.

"I don't like this," Santangelo said. "All of us meeting together is a risk."

"We've been over this," Truett said.

"I still don't like it. I've got a lot to lose here."

"We've *all* got a lot to lose."

"Mr. Santangelo," Zohar said calmly, "I wouldn't take the risk of bringing this group together if it were not an absolute necessity. I am not simply a contractor handing out tasks to individual vendors. We're creating this venture *together*, and we need to learn from one another."

"We never should have met in person," Santangelo said.

"I considered other means of bringing this committee together, but all of them involved equal or greater risk. Mr. Truett entertains a different group of people on this yacht almost every evening—who would notice one more assembly? I decided that our safest course of action was to 'hide in plain sight,' so to speak."

"I don't like these people knowing who I am," Santangelo

said, gesturing to the group. "Knowing my name, knowing what I do for a living."

"You are Mr. Cruz Santangelo," Zohar replied, "special agent of the Federal Bureau of Investigation. I am Dr. Julian Zohar, executive director of the Center for Organ Procurement and Education. If something goes wrong, we all know where to find one another, don't we? I think that creates a certain incentive for *loyalty*, don't you? We've all cast our lots together, Mr. Santangelo. Why not just accept it?"

"This is old ground," Angel said. "Can we get down to business?"

Zohar nodded. "The first item on our agenda is to review our prior endeavor. We're on a learning curve here, and it's critical that we benefit from our mistakes and improve our perform-ance with each effort. Mr. Santangelo, you control the first phase; let's begin with you."

"The setup went off without a hitch," Santangelo said. "I scouted the location for a week—it was perfect for us. Homewood is a war zone. In that neighborhood I could have fired an assault rifle without anyone raising a blind. One thing," he said, looking at Angel. "Don't cover your eyes—never look away. He saw you, remember? One break in character is all it takes."

"Sorry," she grumbled. "I'm not a professional."

"Lady, you are now."

"I thought she was great," Kaplan said. "You guys should have seen her, standing beside that car all helpless and pouting— Please, won't somebody stop and help me? Man, a *monk* would have pulled over."

"That's another thing," Santangelo said, turning to face Kaplan. "If you ever crack another joke while we're waiting for the target, I'll kill you myself."

"Hey, lighten up."

"I will not lighten up," Santangelo said, enunciating each

word with icy precision. "You are undisciplined and unre-strained. I despise your sloppiness. It has no place in an operation like this."

"Take a valium," Kaplan said. "Doesn't the Bureau offer any therapy for ex-snipers?"

Santangelo began to rise, but Zohar put a hand on his forearm and prevented him. "Mr. Santangelo's comments merit consideration," he said. "Discipline and precision play a crucial role for *all* of us. Dr. Kaplan, perhaps you would like to report next."

"Well," Kaplan grinned, "doing the removal on-site was a real rush—but surgically speaking, it's a risk. The 'donor' has no worries, of course—he's a flatliner, thanks to the Terminator here—but there's an increased risk of contamination of the organ. I transferred it into sterile ice as fast as I could, but—hey, kids, I'm doing surgery on the side of a road here."

"There are bigger risks," Santangelo said, "like exposure. In our first attempt, I was out of there in two minutes. Kaplan did the removal at the other end."

"Very handy," Kaplan said. "Not as much fun, but very convenient. I had the donor in one room, and the recipient in the next. I'll bet that was the fastest kidney transplant on record."

"Now that we're doing the removal on site," Santangelo said, "there's more of a chance of being spotted. There are more variables that are out of our control."

Zohar turned to Kaplan again. "Is there any way to speed up the procedure?"

"Are you kidding? Not unless I reach down his throat and yank it out. This is still surgery, guys—I'm in and out in record time now. Nobody I know could do it faster."

Now Lassiter spoke up. "This is all a moot point. The first time, Santangelo and Angel drove halfway across town with an unconscious man in the trunk. What if they had a wreck? What if a cop pulled them over? And the surgical site was in a populated area, remember? Even late at night, sooner or later someone's going to spot you lugging bodies in and out of your trunk. Besides, there's the forensic side to consider. It's always risky to move a body from the place where death occurs. There are ways to tell."

"I thought you were taking care of all that," Santangelo said. "You cover the autopsies, don't you?"

"It's not that simple," Lassiter said. "We schedule these things when I'm on rotation, and only when our two boys are there to pick up the body—but there are police on the scene too, you know. The coroner has jurisdiction over the body, but the police have responsibility for the scene itself, and they collect their own forensic evidence. There's always a chance that somebody will spot something."

"Dr. Lassiter is correct," Zohar said. "We have no choice. Despite the potential risks, on-site removal is currently our best alternative. Mr. Santangelo, the onus is on you to find suitable locations and scenarios for these procedures. The last one seems to have served quite well."

"Angel and I are working on it."

Zohar looked at the group. "Suggested improvements for our next procedure?"

Lassiter turned to Santangelo. "These things have got to look like *accidental* deaths," he said. "You set the last one up to look like a drive-by shooting. That was acceptable, because our people don't expect to find a perp in a drive-by—but in the future it's got to look like an accident. A murder sets a whole different set of wheels in motion. We don't want investigators sifting through the evidence, trying to find some nonexistent killer—that's asking for trouble. And each scenario needs to be different; the police have people looking for crime trends, like serial killers and rapists. If you do two or three of these things the same way—even *close* to the same way—that raises a flag, and they'll be all over it. I hope the FBI taught you better than that. We can't afford that kind of screwup."

Santangelo narrowed his eyes.

"There will be no 'screwups,'" Zohar said, "simply because there can *be* none. We each need to do our job well, and we must encourage one another to do the same. Let me say again: This committee, this group, it's more than an organization—we are a team. A family, that's the way I like to think of it—we happy few, we band of brothers. We depend upon one another for our very survival. Think of this committee as a body; if one member suffers, we all suffer. It's in the body's best interest to make sure that each member contributes to the welfare of the whole."

There was the sound of a smaller boat approaching on the port side. Truett stepped to the railing, smiled, and waved as it passed. The rest of the group turned their faces away and waited until the drone of the engine disappeared into the night.

Zohar leaned back in his seat again and smiled. "On a more positive note," he said, "our previous client's payment has been received in full, and the appropriate transfers have been made into each of your offshore accounts, as you can verify as of noon tomorrow. And on a personal note, I'm happy to report that both of our prior clients are recuperating quite nicely in the seclusion of their homes. My congratulations to the entire team.

"Looking to the future, I'm pleased to announce that we are actively pursuing additional clients. Mr. Truett, I continue to be grateful for your organization's ever-expanding population data. I'll forward our potential clients' medical information to you tomorrow. If you will compile the potential donor lists, we can discuss our final selections."

Truett nodded.

"I suggest we spend our remaining time meeting as subcommittees. Mr. Santangelo, you and your team have donor scenarios to discuss. Why don't you remain on deck and enjoy the evening? Dr. Lassiter, I have an issue I would like to discuss with you and Mr. Truett in the salon below."

Lassiter nodded nervously.

Zohar smiled and looked at each member of the group. "The word *committee* comes to us from Latin," he said. "Its original

CHOP SHOP: A Bug Man Novel

meaning was 'one who has been entrusted'—one to whom something valuable was *committed*. That's what this committee is: a group of people who share a great responsibility. This bold venture of ours has the potential to be enormously lucrative; may I encourage you all to constantly remember the responsibility we share. We are *committed*, my friends. Please don't forget it."

CHAPTER
23

T ruett pulled the hatch door shut behind him and descended the handful of steps to the salon below. Dr. Zohar was already seated in the center of the L-shaped sofa, his legs decorously crossed and his folded hands resting lightly on one knee. Truett checked both the forward and aft staterooms, and glanced in both heads as well. Satisfied, he took a seat on Zohar's left.

Lassiter started toward the sofa himself, then reconsidered. The remaining seat placed him much too close to Zohar, and it blocked his view of Truett. The two men watched silently as Lassiter stepped back again, folded his arms clumsily, and leaned against the galley counter.

"So?" Lassiter said as indifferently as possible. "What's this all about?"

Zohar said nothing for a full three seconds; the silence had the impact of an air horn. After three decades of impromptu appeals to bereaved and grieving families, Zohar understood the power of both speech and silence, and used both with surgical precision.

"A problem has come to my attention," he said evenly.

"A problem? What sort of problem?"

"A potential breach of security. I hate to bring this subject up . . . again."

"That wasn't my fault!" Lassiter protested. "The first donor you picked was carrying a uniform donor card! When the coroner's office reported the death, his organs were requested by your own organization! What was I supposed to do, release the body and let them find a kidney missing? That would have ended this whole project! The best I could do was to refuse to release the organs for forensic reasons."

"As you say, it was the best you could do—but your method attracted undesirable attention. That's the last thing we want."

"Well, talk to *your* people about it. They requested the organs."

Zohar smiled. "Remember, Nathan, no one at COPE knows about this project of ours. Their business is to procure organs for people on the traditional transplant waiting list. I trained them myself, and they're very good at it. I can hardly stop them from doing their jobs now. But as a result of that first little mishap, I have made two corrections to our system: I will no longer select donors who carry traditional donor cards, and whenever we select a donor for our purposes, I will personally contact the next of kin to 'request donation'—and I will make certain that they decline. Those two steps should keep us from any further conflicts of interest with the traditional donor system."

"You'd better be right," Lassiter said. "I bluffed my way out of that one; I can't do it again. They'd be all over me—and like you said upstairs, I know where you live."

Truett began to speak, but Zohar gently placed a hand on his arm with a sideward glance, then turned back to Lassiter again.

177

"The issue I wanted to speak to you about is a different matter entirely. It appears, Nathan, that you are once again attracting undesirable attention."

"What? How?"

"As you so eloquently pointed out, the members of this committee depend upon one another—we live or die together. That kind of mutual dependency creates the need for a certain amount of *accountability*. In our case, the left hand must know *exactly* what the right hand is doing. For that reason, when you agreed to join us, Mr. Truett took the liberty of installing a type of surveillance software on your computer, both at your home and at the coroner's office. This software records every keystroke you make on your computer, and it reports the activity to us."

Lassiter opened his mouth to object, but Zohar raised his hand.

"You were not being singled out, Nathan. We took the same measures with every member of the committee. It was a necessary precaution, as I'm sure you'll recognize after proper reflection. You can see why this discussion needed to be held privately; you are the only member of our group who knows about this, and we're counting on you to keep it in the strictest confidence."

Now Truett joined in. "Last week, Dr. Lassiter, we noticed some unusual activity on your home computer. It appears that someone did a very thorough search of your personal records."

Lassiter blanched. "Which records? What sort of a search?"

"Everything, top to bottom. It was very careful, very thorough, very professionally done. Special attention was paid to your financial records."

"My ex-wife," Lassiter hissed. "She's looking for hidden assets."

Truett shook his head. "We don't think so."

"Why not?"

"If it was your ex-wife, she had help. They even searched for *steganography*—files hidden within other files, like child pornography files sometimes are. Does your wife have that kind of computer expertise?"

"Margaret? No way. E-mail and basic Internet, that's her limit."

"Well, here's the kicker, Dr. Lassiter: Before leaving, whoever it was installed another version of the same surveillance software that we use. They're not just interested in your finances, they're interested in your ongoing activities. Does that sound like your wife to you?"

"But—if it's not Margaret, then who? The IRS, maybe? Can you tell?"

Truett shook his head again. "The spyware uploads the reports of your activities to a server, and they're forwarded from there to the interested party. That's why it's called *spy*ware; we can track the reports to the server, but no farther. It's like a Swiss bank account: we know where the deposits are going, but there's no way to know who's making withdrawals."

Lassiter was beginning to pace now, growing more agitated by the minute. Suddenly he stopped and turned to Truett. "What day did this happen?"

"Last Tuesday, about midmorning."

Lassiter's eyes darted back and forth like two bees in a jar. "The plants weren't dead," he whispered.

"What?"

"The exterminator. He said he found termites; he said he needed to fumigate. He tented the whole house—wrapped it up in plastic and filled it with gas. He said the gas would kill every living thing—but I forgot to remove the plants, and the plants weren't dead."

Truett glanced at Zohar, then back at Lassiter again. "What was the name of the company?"

"I don't know. I mean, I didn't look. He said my wife hired him—some kind of service contract or something . . ." His voice trailed off as he spoke.

Zohar spoke up. "Nathan, listen to me. Do you know this exterminator? Have you used him before? Did you recognize him?"

Lassiter shook his head dumbly. "He was a tall guy with huge glasses."

Truett started. "Did you say *glasses*?"

"Big, thick lenses. Made his eyes the size of walnuts."

Truett slumped back against the sofa. Zohar turned and looked at him.

"I met this man," Truett said. "He had a little boating 'accident' on the Fourth of July, and we dragged him out of the water. He had a lot of questions about the company—questions about genetic privacy. He was with a woman."

"A woman," Lassiter said breathlessly. "Was it Margaret?"

"What does your ex-wife look like?"

"She's . . . she has . . . she's sort of . . ." Lassiter struggled to provide the most basic details about the woman he shared a bedroom with for seventeen years. "She has brown hair."

Truett shook his head. "This woman was a blonde."

"Did you get names?" Zohar asked.

"I didn't catch them. They were both doctors, I remember that. He said he was a professor somewhere in the Carolinas."

"And her?"

Truett squinted hard, searching for faded bits of memory. He shrugged. "All I remember is, she had remarkable eyes: one green and one brown."

Lassiter drew a sharp breath. He staggered forward, groping for the edge of the sofa. He sank down on trembling legs and sprawled backward, blinking at the ceiling. "Riley . . . McKay," he said in two gasps.

Zohar glanced at Truett, and Truett nodded.

"She's the one," Lassiter panted. "Pathology fellow . . . called me on the carpet . . . asked too many questions . . . had to get her out of the office . . ."

"Calm yourself," Zohar said sharply.

"Calm myself?" Lassiter struggled to an upright position. "Are you out of your mind? Do you know what this means?"

Zohar said nothing for a moment, staring directly ahead. "It means that someone's asking questions—questions about *you.* She's enlisted someone's assistance—or vice-versa—and they've gone so far as to break into your home and tap into your computer. That suggests a very high level of . . . *interest,"* he said, his voice trailing off into silence again.

"I'm out of here," Lassiter said, struggling to his feet. "We have to fold this thing right now."

"Sit down and be quiet."

Lassiter stared at him in astonishment. "Julian, someone is *on* to us. Somebody *knows."*

"Someone is asking questions—what we don't know is the answers they've come up with. We all have a great deal invested in this program, Nathan. It would be premature to abandon it over the first breach of security. Agreed, we have to take action—but remember, *whatever* action we take has its risks. We need to find out what they know, who knows it, and how they learned it. With luck, we'll be able to close those loopholes and have an even stronger system than before. What we have here is an unparalleled opportunity to learn."

Lassiter sank down again and buried his head in his hands.

"This exterminator," Zohar said. "You mentioned paperwork."

"I've got it—somewhere."

"Find it. When you do, we'll have Mr. Santangelo look into it."

Lassiter looked up. "Why him? Why does he have to know about this?"

"Now, Nathan," Zohar said with a minimum of reassurance, "Mr. Santangelo is a part of our team. He's on your side. Remember, Mr. Santangelo is an active FBI agent, and that allows him to do a certain amount of *investigating* without arousing suspicion."

"He's an assassin," Lassiter said.

"He's an authorized representative of your own federal government. Where's your patriotic spirit?"

"I'm leaving town. I've got vacation time coming—"

"You'll do nothing of the kind. Someone in your office is asking questions; this is hardly the time to do something out of the ordinary. You'll return to work tomorrow just as you always do."

"I've got to get that program off my computer—"

"You'd never find it," Truett said. "It takes a professional."

"Then *you* guys remove it."

"No," Zohar said. "It might prove useful. For now, I want you to use your computer as you normally would—but you are not to send e-mail, and you are to make no attempt to locate or remove that surveillance program. Do you understand, Nathan? If you do, they'll know—and so will *we*. You're to return to your regular daily routine, and you're to act as though nothing is out of the ordinary."

"I . . . I don't think I can do this."

Zohar looked at him. Beads of sweat dotted his forehead like dew on a leaf. The blood had drained entirely from his cadaverous face, and the pallid skin surrounded his eyes like two purple sinkholes.

"Nathan," he said evenly, "let me reiterate what I said earlier: this committee is a *body*. As you well know, there are times when a part of the body becomes diseased, and then surgery is required to remove the diseased member. It may be painful, it may be costly, but otherwise the disease could spread—and that wouldn't be fair to the rest of the body, now would it? Mr. Santangelo and I want you to understand: we are not above doing surgery, should it become necessary. Do I make myself clear?"

Lassiter said nothing.

Nick held the pole of the aerial insect net in his left hand, with the wire hoop parallel to the ground. With his right hand he pulled up on the tail of the net, holding it open like a giant gauze cone. Below the net, a forty-pound sow lay decomposing in the July sun, swarming with hundreds of cream-colored larvae, each vying with its neighbor to see which would reach the breakfast table first.

Nick watched the black dots hovering above the decaying sow. He lowered the net slightly, causing their instinctive escape behavior to lead them up and into the waiting net. Then he brought the net down with a swatting motion, finishing the stroke with a quick flip of his wrist. The net swung up and over the hoop, confining the tiny occupants in the tip.

The long meadow sat like a green cap atop the steep ridge comprising the town of Tarentum. The view from the field was spectacular; as a boy, Nick had spent many an afternoon here, gazing at the panorama of the Allegheny River below and watching the cars that crossed the Tarentum Bridge until they disappeared into the town of Lower Burrell. Down the hill, through the tips of the trees, he could almost see the back of his house. Nick thought of this field as his private property. His neighbors, aware of his strange entomological studies, were more than happy to let him have it to himself. Above the houses, exposed to the clearing winds, it was perfectly suited for some of his more malodorous experiments.

He opened a wide-mouth killing jar and draped the tip of the net inside. He sealed it again, allowing the ethyl acetate to do its work. Nick had already sent most of the predictable specimens to Sanjay for DNA analysis; he was hoping for something a little more unusual today—perhaps a *Phormia regina* or a Holarctic blowfly. In a few minutes, he would drop the specimens into an opaque jar of 95 percent ethanol to preserve them, and to prevent ultraviolet light from degrading their DNA.

From his backpack came a high, trilling sound. Nick took out his cell phone and opened it.

"Yes?"

"Nick? Nick Polchak?"

"Who's this?"

"Nick, it's Freddie, over at Bug Off."

"Hey, Freddie, how's the bug business? Did you pick up any—"

"Nick, we got a problem."

Nick paused. "I'm listening."

"The FBI paid me a visit this morning. Did you hear me? Not the police, Nick, the *FBI*."

"That's interesting. What did they want?"

"He wanted to know about a fumigation we did at 1874 Branchwater Trail. Sound familiar? It seems the FBI did a follow-up inspection and guess what? No termites and no sign of wood damage."

"Another satisfied customer," Nick said, swinging his net at a passing secondary screwworm fly.

"Nick, this is serious. He knows the job was a scam. He wants the names of my people who did the job—he wants to look at my service log. And if he does, guess what he'll find? All my people were on other jobs that day. How am I supposed to explain the extra crew?"

"Times are good. You hired on for the summer."

"Sure, and then he'll want to see employment records. I've got no tax IDs on you guys, no social-security records . . . and get this, Nick: He checked with neighbors, and he found somebody who *saw* you guys. He asked me about one of my employees, a tall guy with *big glasses*. Who have I got who looks like that?"

"That's your problem, Freddie. You don't hire enough good-looking people."

"Look, this is not a joke. He's threatening to pull my license. Did you hear what I said? *My license.* I did you a favor, and now the whole thing's blowing up in my face. Nick, what did you do? This is the FBI!"

"What does he want, Freddie?"

"He wants names."

"Did you call me on your cell phone?"

"Yeah. Sure."

"Then he's probably got my name—you've used it about a dozen times. Like you said, Freddie, this is the FBI."

"Nick, I've got until tomorrow morning to cooperate. He's coming back, and he says he's going to—"

"I'll take care of it, I promise. Did he leave a card?"

"I got it right here."

"Then give him a call, and let him know you'll be happy to cooperate."

"What do I tell him?"

"Tell him my name—and tell him I want to meet him." Nick paused. "Better yet—tell him he wants to meet *me*."

Dr. Polchak? I'm Special Agent Cruz Santangelo. Mind if I join you?" Nick and Riley sat side by side on the upper deck of the *Majestic*, the premiere riverboat of the Gateway Clipper Fleet. The wooden deck was scattered with tables, mostly empty on this early morning excursion that offered a panoramic one-hour tour of the Ohio, Allegheny, and Monongahela Rivers. The deck was surrounded by a white spindled railing, trimmed with touches of red and blue. Two black smokestacks protruded through the deck, completing the picture of a patriotic showboat from a bygone era. They sat in the full sun near the port paddlewheel; it was the noisiest spot on the upper deck.

Nick nodded toward the wooden bench opposite them, and Santangelo took a seat.

"I assumed we would be meeting privately," Santangelo said without taking his eyes off Nick.

"I think this is someone you'll want to meet. Special Agent Santangelo, this is Dr. Riley McKay of the Allegheny County Coroner's Office."

"Cruz," he said. "It'll save us ten minutes." Santangelo looked at Riley for the first time. Medium build, short blond hair, fair skin—and the unmistakable eyes. "Dr. McKay, it's a pleasure to—"

"May I see your credentials?" Riley extended her hand. "I'm the suspicious type."

Santangelo smiled. "We've noticed." He handed her the small leather folder. Riley laid the credentials open on her lap, took out her cell phone, and punched an autodial number.

"Sheila? Riley McKay. Yes, I know I'm late—I left a message for Dr. Lassiter. Look, I need a number for the FBI office over on East Carson."

"If I'd known you were coming, we could have met at your office," Santangelo said. "We're just across the river."

"Thanks, Sheila." Riley dialed the number and waited. "Good morning. Do you have a Special Agent Cruz Santangelo? No, don't connect me—he's sitting right here. I'd like to describe him to you: He's about six-foot, maybe six-one." Santangelo nodded at the latter number. "Midthirties, lean build, Hispanic mix, black hair, well-tanned, dark eyes. Sound familiar?"

Santangelo motioned for the phone. Riley hesitated, then handed it to him. "Stephanie? Cruz. Everything's OK. Go ahead, answer the lady's question." He covered the phone and held it out to Riley. "We're suspicious too," he said. "Those kind of questions can set off a lot of bells and whistles."

Riley listened intently, fixing her eyes on Santangelo's. "Thanks," she said simply, folding the phone and returning it to her purse.

"Well?"

"She says not to go out with you."

Santangelo let out a laugh. "They warned me not to date coworkers."

"Would you like to see *my* credentials?" Riley asked, lifting her gold coroner's badge from her purse.

"I trust you. I think trust is important, don't you?"

"I think trust has to be earned."

Santangelo turned and looked at Nick. "Dr. Nicholas Polchak," he said. "BS, MS, and PhD from Penn State University. Professor of entomology at North Carolina State University, member of the American Board of Forensic Entomology. It's a pleasure to meet you, Dr. Polchak. Man, do we have a colorful file on *you*."

"Shucks," Nick said, "those are just my federal offenses. How long have you been with the Bureau, Mr. Santangelo?"

"I've been a field agent for five years. Before that, I spent six years at Quantico."

"Six years at Quantico? That's too long for the academy."

"I was with the Hostage Rescue Team."

Nick sat up a little straighter. "I'm impressed," he said. "Dr. McKay, we're looking at a former member of the FBI's very own Delta Force, trained in urban warfare, special weapons tactics, close-in combat—even aerial assault. The HRT is the bad boys of the FBI."

"The *good* boys," Santangelo corrected. "'The minimum force possible, the maximum force necessary'—that's our motto."

"Five years as a field agent, and six years before that. Why, Mr. Santangelo, you must have been at Waco."

Santangelo barely nodded.

"I remember reading about that," Nick said. "It was almost a two-month standoff, wasn't it? There were three hundred FBI agents, including your own elite hostage rescue team, against a handful of ex-Seventh Day Adventists. You guys brought in snipers, tear gas, even a tank. By the time the smoke cleared, there were eighty people dead—including a bunch of kids. Not exactly a high point for the FBI, was it, Mr. Santangelo? I've always wondered: Where does an HRT member go after Waco?"

Santangelo paused, but his expression never changed. "Pittsburgh," he said simply. He turned his attention to Riley now. "And you, Dr. McKay—you must be the woman."

"What woman is that?"

"It seems we three share a common interest: a certain Dr. Nathan Lassiter."

Nick and Riley said nothing.

"OK," Santangelo nodded, "then let me get things started. On Monday of last week a pest-control service tented the home of Dr. Nathan Lassiter for fumigation—a fumigation that was entirely unnecessary and that did not, in fact, occur. The following day, a crew posing as exterminators illegally gained access to Dr. Lassiter's home, at which time they performed a thorough search of Dr. Lassiter's computer—including the installation of a surveillance program to allow ongoing monitoring of his investments and activities. How am I doing so far?"

"Impressive," Nick said. "How did you learn all this?"

"We watched them do it. The Bureau is conducting its own investigation into Dr. Lassiter's affairs; not long ago, we installed the same surveillance software on his computer. We watched every keystroke as it occurred."

"What does this have to do with us?" Riley asked.

Santangelo narrowed his eyes. "I figure you for a real smart woman, Dr. McKay. I'd appreciate it if you'd give me a little credit in return. We talked to one of Lassiter's next-door neighbors; she had a brochure from the Bug Off Exterminator Company. Yesterday, I interviewed Mr. Frederick Krubick, the proprietor of said company. That's where I got your name, Dr. Polchak. That same neighbor observed three figures enter the back of the house. She said one of them walked like a woman."

"I resent that," Nick said.

Santangelo looked at Riley. "By your presence here today,

I'm assuming that woman was you."

Riley hesitated, then slowly nodded. "Why are you investigating Dr. Lassiter?"

"Funny. I was about to ask you the same question."

"You first."

"Now wait a minute—let me explain something. The two of you are interfering with a federal investigation. You're already guilty of breaking and entering and illegal wiretapping—that's just for starters. I'm not here to answer *your* questions—got it?"

Nick shook his head in disapproval. "It's way too early for the fastball. Your curve ball was doing just fine."

"I could have you two brought up on charges."

"But you won't," Nick said. As he spoke, the riverboat began to pass under the span of the Smithfield Street Bridge, and the cool, gray shadow crept over the upper deck like a mist. Nick leaned back against the railing and stared into the sky. "This is my favorite part," he said, gazing up at the hundred-and-twenty-year-old maze of rusted trusses, pins, and eyebars less than twenty feet away.

"Why not?" Santangelo said.

Nick spoke without looking down. "If you charge us, our interest in Dr. Lassiter will become public knowledge—and that will tip off Dr. Lassiter himself, the very thing you want to avoid. If he looks for *our* software on his computer, he'll find yours too—and you don't want that, now, do you? You can end our investigation, Mr. Santangelo—but in the process you'll end your own."

The bridge passed overhead now, and the midmorning sun streaked the deck again with blinding yellow light. Nick squinted hard and turned back to Santangelo. "Besides," he said, lifting his glasses and rubbing his eyes, "you didn't come here just to tell us to back off—a phone call would have accomplished that. You're here because you want to know what *we* know."

"You're a hard man to intimidate, Dr. Polchak."

Nick looked at him. "I thought you read my file."

Santangelo turned to Riley. "Why is a pathologist investigating her own colleague? What would motivate you to break into his house? And how did the two of you get together on this?"

Riley glanced at Nick. He nodded.

"I'm in a fellowship program at the coroner's office," Riley said. "Dr. Lassiter is my supervisor. A few months ago, I began to notice some strange anomalies in his work—and when I asked about them, he became extremely defensive. He 'protested too much,' you might say, and it made me suspicious. I met Dr. Polchak at a . . . professional function, and I asked him to help me look into it."

"I'm good at peeking through keyholes," Nick said.

"What sort of 'anomalies' are we talking about?"

"Lassiter refused to release organs for transplant due to a head trauma—that was the first one. Then I asked Dr. Polchak to do an entomological evaluation on an acute myocardial infarction victim."

"And?"

"The body had been moved," Nick said, "shortly after death. It was transported from the city to the country, where it was later discovered."

"So it was dumped," Santangelo said. "It happens."

"It happens to murder victims," Riley said. "Lassiter wrote it off as a death by natural causes."

Santangelo nodded. "Any more?"

"Just one. Dr. Polchak helped me reexamine one of Lassiter's autopsies—the victim of a drive-by shooting in Homewood. The cause of death was a gunshot to the back of the head, but we discovered another wound—an incision on the lower back, just below the rib cage."

"An incision?"

"It was sutured shut," Nick said, "and it all happened at the murder scene."

Santangelo did a double take. "You can tell that?"

191

"You'd be amazed what I can tell. For example: I can tell that you already know most of this—maybe all of it."

"I'll bite. How do you know that?"

"Because you're a federal agent. The FBI wouldn't get involved with a simple medical misadventure—that's for the local authorities to take care of. Your very presence here indicates the violation of some federal statute or regulation—say, the National Organ Transplant Act, which makes it a federal crime to buy or sell human tissues."

Santangelo sat motionless.

"Thanks," Nick smiled. "Now I know for sure."

Santangelo held up both hands in protest. "I'm not at liberty to discuss details of an open investigation. All I can tell you is, your observations are . . . *consistent* with our own discoveries. What else can you tell me?"

"Like you said, we searched his computer, and I'm sure we found the same thing you did: Lassiter has been investing enormous sums of money in a company called PharmaGen—money that he never earned. Where's that money coming from, Mr. Santangelo?"

"Sorry."

"Come on, *Cruz*, I thought we were all friends here. We answered some of your questions; you can answer one of ours."

"I'm asking you to help confirm details of the Bureau's investigation, Dr. Polchak, but I'm not free to answer your questions in return. You know how it works—a need-to-know basis."

"Some friend you are."

"So what about this PharmaGen? Has he mentioned the company at work, Dr. McKay? Can you explain his heavy involvement?"

"No," she said. "At this point, all we have is speculation."

"I'm open to speculation. Let's hear it."

Riley took a deep breath. "PharmaGen has collected genetic

information on a few hundred thousand people in western Pennsylvania. They have a man serving on their ethics advisory board—his name is Julian Zohar, the director of western Pennsylvania's organ procurement organization. We think he . . . it's possible that . . ." Her voice trailed off here, and Nick leaned forward.

"We think he could be creating a black market for organs, using PharmaGen's database to facilitate matches between donors and recipients."

Santangelo looked at both of them, then slumped back against the bench.

"Like we said, it's only speculation."

"Can you *prove* any of this? Do you have anything tangible for me?"

Nick shook his head. "You look surprised, Mr. Santangelo. Was your investigation taking you in a different direction?"

"I . . . I can't say," Santangelo stammered. "I'm just . . . amazed that you've . . . made these connections."

No one said anything for a minute.

"That's all we've got," Nick said at last.

"I can't tell you how much we appreciate your cooperation," Santangelo said, his mind still racing.

"So what do we do now?"

Santangelo looked at both of them. "I can tell you this much: We have several people under surveillance. We suspect the involvement of a number of parties, and we won't do anything until we identify all of them and have enough physical evidence to prosecute—that's when we'll close the net."

"What do you want us to do?" Riley asked.

"You've already done it. You've told me what you know, and you've turned the investigation over to the FBI—right? Here's what I *don't* want you two to do: no more breaking into houses, no more tapping into computers, and no more poking around in Dr. Lassiter's affairs. The worst thing you could do is let Lassiter get wind of you—or of *us*. The minute somebody lets out a yell, everybody scatters. We don't want anyone to get away, understand? You need to let us complete this investigation our way, on our timetable. If you do, we'll both be satisfied."

"Just what is that timetable?" Nick asked.

"You'll know when we know. In the meantime, Dr. McKay, you go back to the coroner's office and finish that fellowship program. Talk to *no one* about what we've discussed here. And if you do observe any more irregularities in Dr. Lassiter's conduct—if you even have further speculations—you're to call *me*, understand?" He handed both of them a business card embossed with the black-and-gold seal of the FBI. "One more thing—Dr. Lassiter's neighbor reported seeing *three* people enter the house. Who was the third party?"

They said nothing.

"You're a pathologist, and you're an entomologist," he said, looking at each of them. "I assume the third party was your computer expert."

"An interesting assumption," Nick said.

"The Bureau would really like to know."

"Like you said, Mr. Santangelo—a need-to-know basis."

Santangelo glared at him. "Enjoy your stay in Pittsburgh, Dr. Polchak. Take in a few ball games. Work on your tan—you could use it. Like I said before, you know how the system works: your government thanks you for your cooperation; now keep quiet, stay out of the way, and let us do our job."

Santangelo rose from the bench, shook hands with each of them, and headed off across the deck. Nick and Riley watched until he descended the opposite stairway and disappeared from view.

Nick turned to Riley. "He didn't read my file," he said.

CHAPTER 26

The curving hull of the *PharmaGen* lay in the black water, drifting slightly in the gentle current. The three men sat in a circle on the aft deck, staring in opposite directions at the moonless sky.

"So what do you think?" Santangelo said.

Zohar sat in silence for another moment. "I think we've had an epiphany," he said. "We've learned three crucial lessons from your interview today, Mr. Santangelo: first, we've confirmed Dr. Lassiter's complete ineptitude; second, we've learned that Dr. McKay is a very bright woman indeed; and third, we've learned that we must make a concerted effort to disguise the link between the coroner's office, PharmaGen, and myself. Now that our relationship is well established, Mr. Truett, I think it might be prudent for me to resign from your advisory board. I suggest that you recruit instead more members with Dr. Paulos's reassuring image."

"Never mind the future," Truett said, "what about now? They *know*, Julian—they figured it out."

"What do they really know? Think carefully. They know about Lassiter's foul-ups, but they are unaware of the reason behind them. They know about Lassiter's investments in PharmaGen, but they don't know the source of his funding. And as for the connection to me, that's the weakest correlation of all. As they said to Mr. Santangelo, they're only guessing."

"But they're guessing *right*," Santangelo said. "They don't have to be able to prove anything. They just have to raise the right questions."

"I agree," Zohar said. "But I believe we took care of that today. Where would they raise those questions? To the authorities, of course, and today they did exactly that. They spoke to the authorities—and not just any authority, a federal authority —the FBI. They now believe that their concerns have been heard, that a federal investigation is under way, and that they have no reason for further involvement."

"That's good for now," Truett said, "but what about later on? Cruz promised them an end to the investigation. What happens when six months or a year goes by and it's still business as usual? They won't wait forever, Julian; they're going to want closure."

"And closure they shall have. Please understand me, gentlemen. This situation will have to be dealt with. All I'm suggesting is that we proceed with caution and that we take advantage of this opportunity while we have it."

"What opportunity?"

"Mr. Santangelo made it quite clear: if they learn anything else, they are to call *him*. Don't you see? If there are any more holes in our system, they will find them—and they will report them directly to us. These people are our very own U.N. inspection team! I think we should regard this as a divine opportunity."

CHOP SHOP: A Bug Man Novel

"When *do* we deal with the situation?" Santangelo asked. "The sooner the better in my book."

"I think that would be wise. But one thing is crucial: We must identify the third member of their party. As you told them today, Mr. Santangelo, we don't want to close the net until we have identified all parties involved. If we act prematurely, whoever remains will most certainly return to haunt us. Can you do this? Will you be able to identify the remaining accomplice?"

"It could take a few days," Santangelo said reflectively. "I don't have the resources of the FBI for this—I'll have to do it the hard way."

Zohar nodded. "As you said—the sooner the better."

"What about the next procedure?" Truett said. "Do we go ahead, or do we call it off and lay low until this situation is taken care of?"

"I say call it off," Santangelo said.

"I agree," Truett nodded. "The risk is too great."

"Gentlemen," Zohar said in his most reassuring voice. "We must be careful not to let our fears cloud our usual acumen. If we are to test our system for flaws, we must continue as planned with our next procedure. Besides, we must remember that our waiting client also poses a risk. How are we to raise her expectations, only to suddenly postpone without explanation? Believe me, her courage is fragile; if we show the slightest sign of caution or hesitation, she will back out of our arrangement, and then we'll have a risk of a different kind. The only safe client is a satisfied client—and she will not be satisfied until she gets her kidney. We have a week before the next procedure; let's see what Mr. Santangelo can learn in that time."

The men grew silent again, lost in thought. Truett sat slumped forward, his forearms resting on his knees, rolling an amber bottle back and forth between his hands.

"What about Lassiter?"

"What about him?"

"He's been paid well for his part in all this—*very* well. But that wasn't enough for him; he had to invest that money in the company, he had to try to make an even bigger killing. It was his greed that allowed them to make the connection to PharmaGen. It was his stupidity that got them asking questions in the first place. From where I sit, Dr. Lassiter is becoming a greater liability than an asset."

"Lassiter is a loose cannon," Santangelo agreed. "He makes me nervous."

Zohar nodded thoughtfully. "A contact within the coroner's office is a necessary part of this process—but Dr. Lassiter does not have to be that contact. I share your concerns, gentlemen. This situation just might prove a double blessing. I think I see a way to improve our system and to replace our weakest link at the same time."

Zohar reached down to the table in front of him and lifted his wineglass. He glanced at each man, then held the glass aloft. "Any man makes a sailor in calm seas," he said. "Into the storm, gentlemen. Our port awaits on the other side."

CHAPTER
27

Riley parked her car beside the river and took the winding, rust-red walkway over West Carson Street to the lower station of the Duquesne Incline. She loved the hundred-and-twenty-five-year-old building, with its rose-red brick and violet slate roof with gingerbread trim. Nineteen inclines once lined Pittsburgh's formidable hills, transporting workers, vehicles, and coal up a thirty-degree pitch that even horses couldn't master. Now only two inclines remained, the Duquesne and the Monongahela, both offering passengers a silent ascension from the river's southern edge to the peak of Mount Washington. As a little girl, Riley's father brought her often to ride the inclines, but by then they had been reduced to little more than tourist attractions. But it never failed to take her breath away when the red-and-yellow car rose out of the station and the three rivers came into view below.

She always took a seat at the very front of the car, turning to face the glass in anticipation of the stunning panorama—but this morning she moved directly to the rear of the car and took a seat beside a beaming, wavy-haired man.

"The lovely Riley McKay," Leo said. "Truly, the Golden Triangle offers no more beautiful vista than you."

Riley leaned over and gave him a peck on the cheek. "Let's make this a regular thing," she said. "Every time I'm having a bad day, I'll meet you right here."

"I will be your incline, lifting you from the depths of despair to the celestial heights where a woman like you belongs."

There was a small jolt as the incline's twin cables drew taut, and the car began its silent climb up the long track. The lower station began to shrink away, leaving a square, black hole where the car had been.

"I got your call," Riley said. "Sorry if this seems a little cloak-and-dagger, but after our meeting with the FBI, I thought it might be wise if we tried to be a little more . . . discreet."

"Just the way I like things," Leo said. "Discreet."

"What's on your mind?"

"Nick Polchak is on my mind. Is he on yours?"

Riley hesitated. She began to speak but stopped short. She glanced around the empty car, then back at Leo again. All the while, Leo watched her eyes.

"I see," he said.

Riley felt the rush of blood to her face. "What do you see?"

"I see that you care about Nick. But I sense that things are . . . complicated."

"You have no idea."

"Pour out your soul to me; I am your confidant."

"I wish I could, Leo, I really do. But—"

He nodded. "I think you should know, Nick cares a great deal for you. I tell you this because he will have a great deal of difficulty telling you himself."

"Did he tell you that?"

"He said your voice reminds him of a wind chime."

Riley smiled. "That's kind of sweet."

"In a sixth-grade sort of way, yes. But you have to start some-where, and for Nick, that's really quite remarkable."

"I've tried not to . . . encourage him."

"Nonsense—you've encouraged him by your very existence. You're beautiful, you're intelligent, and you're comfortable with your arms up to the elbow in human viscera. You're Nick's kind of girl."

"Nick is a wonderful man. But he's kind of—"

"Strange? Twisted? Demented? Take your pick. Nick Polchak is all of these and more."

"Leo—I thought you were Nick's friend."

Leo looked affronted. "I love Nick Polchak like my own brother. What am I saying—I *hate* my own brother. I love Nick Polchak like no other man in this world."

Riley grinned. "Leo, is there anything that you just . . . *like*?"

"What would be the point? That's like stopping halfway up the incline. Italians have two emotions, Ms. McKay: we love, and we hate. Everything else is just pasta."

Riley let out a laugh. "Well, I hope you don't hate *me*."

"I adore you—and so does Nick, which brings us back to the subject. Nick is like a man trapped in a great ship, staring out two giant portholes at the world passing by. I believe he wants out—but I don't think he knows how to *get* out. For that, he needs the help of someone else—someone like you. Nick Polchak, you see, is a tortured soul."

"I was always warned not to get involved with a man like that."

"There is no other kind. But why should that discourage you? We're *all* tortured souls—aren't we, Riley?"

She looked down at her feet.

"Leo, what happened to Nick? What hurt him?"

"I think he should answer that question for himself. But I can tell you this much: Tarentum was a very tough town when Nick and I were growing up. The mills and factories were all closing down, people were out of work. Lean times can make mean-spirited people; Nick's father was one of them. He abandoned the family early, but he kept on return-ing like a plague—seemingly just to torment Nick. And then there was Nick's obvious visual impairment—people can be very unkind, can't they? That's the world Nick grew up in, Riley. Early on, he discovered two things: that he had a most unusual intellect, and that—once he got his glasses—he could see things other people couldn't see."

"What sort of things?"

"My family liked to do jigsaw puzzles. We had lots of puzzles, and we would assemble them again and again—but over time we lost the boxes, and then we would store the pieces in plastic bags. So when we began a puzzle, we had no idea what the final image would be. Is it the lighthouse? Is it the old mill? It was always a kind of competition to see who could rec-ognize the subject first. One evening Nick came over for dinner, and after dinner he joined us to start a new puzzle. Nick watched us lay down the first three pieces, and then he said, 'It's a clipper ship with three masts.' And you know what? He was *right*. And after that, my family didn't want Nick to help with the jigsaw puzzle anymore. Do you know why? Because Nick takes all the fun out of it. He sees things that other people can't see, and that puts him in a world of his own."

"Does he really think of himself as an insect?"

"He has no love for the human species—at least, not the members of it *he's* met. Human beings can be so unpredictable, so irrational—so *hurtful*. I think Nick came to appreciate the orderliness and predictability of the insect world. I believe there's a cure for his malady—but I don't think it will come in the form of a pill or a therapy. I think it will have to have a human face."

"Leo, I need to ask you something: what do you think of Nick's theory, this whole idea of a black market in human organs?"

"I would call it absurd," Leo said, "except for the fact that it's *Nick's* theory. Remember the clipper ship, Riley. Nick has a kind of intuition that he borrows from the insect world; he makes connections in a most remarkable way. He may be wrong about this, but I would not discount his instincts."

Now Leo took Riley's hand and looked her full in the eyes. "I want to tell you why I really called," he said, lifting a folder from the wooden bench beside him. "Nick asked me to see if I could hack into the patient database at UPMC Presbyterian."

"What? What for?"

"Because you told him that most of the organ transplants in this area are performed there. He asked me to find a list of patients awaiting kidney transplants there. He also asked me to search for *old* lists; he wants to compare them, to see if anyone has dropped off the list without having their surgery. If anyone has, he plans to check them against the obituaries. Nick is putting his theory to the test, Riley. If anyone is still alive who shouldn't be, he wants to know why. "

Riley said nothing. Leo squeezed her hand a little tighter.

"How long have you been on the waiting list, Riley?"

She turned to him with a look of both sadness and relief. "Six years, eight months, and seventeen days."

"That's a long time to wait—a long time to *hope*."

"I have a rare compatibility problem, Leo. There's very little chance a kidney will ever turn up for me."

"And if it doesn't?"

"I was diagnosed with chronic kidney failure; when my kidney function fell below 10 percent, it became end-stage renal disease. Dialysis can buy you some time, but a transplant is the only cure." She turned to the window. "The word among doctors is that kidney failure is a pretty good way to go. Your blood becomes more and more polluted, and you just sort of run down like a battery. My battery is pretty low."

"Are there no family members who can help?"

"I have one sister; she's not a match."

Leo put his arm around her, pulled her close, and kissed her hair. "I can see why things are complicated."

"I think Nick suspects anyway."

"Nick knows you're ill. When he was at your apartment the other night, he looked through your medicine cabinet and found your medications."

Riley straightened. "He had no right!"

"Breaking and entering, hacking into patient databases—the question of 'rights' here is a little slippery, don't you think? The point is, Riley, when I hand Nick this list, he's going to see your name on it. He's going to know the full extent of your illness. He's going to *know*, Riley. Is that what you want?"

"What choice do I have?"

Leo opened the folder and took out several sheets of paper. "As a friend—as someone who *loves* you—I'm offering to remove your name from this list."

Riley stared at him. "Would you be willing to do that?"

"I might—but first you have to answer some questions for me: Why are you involved in all this, Riley McKay? What's your true motivation? And what does this have to do with your own need for a kidney transplant?"

Riley took a minute to collect her thoughts. "When Lassiter refused to release that man's organs for transplant, I thought, 'Those could have been *my* kidneys!' And even if they weren't, they could have saved *someone's* life. People die on the waiting list every day, Leo. Someday soon, I will. I had to know why Lassiter would do that. It just triggered something inside me; I didn't know where all this would lead." She looked into his eyes. "Do you believe me?"

"Without question," he nodded. "Nick lives in a world of the mind—but *I* happen to know hearts. If you were lying to me, I would have known it before you finished your first sentence. Now, about this list—what do you want me to do?"

"What do you think I should do?"

"If Nick knows you're dying, he'll either throw himself at you or run away. Either way, it could no longer be an ordinary relationship—and that's what I want for him most. The time may come when you have to tell him yourself, Riley, but I want you to have the freedom to make that choice."

Leo tore the top sheet of paper in half and put it back in the folder.

She kissed him on the cheek again. "That's the nicest thing anyone has ever done for me."

They looked out the back window; the car was approaching the end of the steel track. Their piece of the jigsaw puzzle was about to slide into place, completing the picture of the upper station with its white beveled siding and twin towers with violet caps. Riley began to turn toward the door as the car came to its final stop—but Leo held on to her hand until she turned back to him again.

"I don't know if you'll be the cure for Nick," he said, "but I hope you won't contribute to his disease."

"I'll try not to."

"You know, Riley, it isn't enough for you to be Nick's cure—he has to cure something in you as well."

"Oh, Leo—I don't know if that's possible."

Leo kissed the back of her hand. "You never know," he said. "Love heals all kinds of wounds."

Make a right on 19," Riley said, studying the MapQuest directions.

Nick pushed harder on the gas as they started up a long hill; the engine made a whining sound, coughing and wheezing like an old man climbing stairs. Each time one of the four cylinders missed, another puff of blue smoke belched out behind them, punctuating the still morning air.

"Nick, I've heard model airplanes that sound better than this."

"That's because they cost more. I got a deal on this."

"Somebody got a deal. How old is this thing?"

"Car talk bores me. Which way at this intersection?"

"Left." Riley sipped her Starbucks and glanced at her watch: *five-thirty*. She was giving up her every-other-weekend-off for *this*? Her only consolation was that Nick had no way of flipping the car over and dumping her onto the roadway—but looking at the shuddering car around her, she wasn't entirely sure. She picked up a half-eaten croissant from her lap, nibbled at it, then wadded it up in her napkin and turned to Nick. "What do I do with this?"

"There's a place for trash in the backseat."

She turned and looked. The backseat and floor were piled high with faded textbooks, drab-looking journals, and glutted three-ring binders spewing disheveled papers. There were two knapsacks, wadded-up articles of multicolored clothing, and a strange assortment of lidded plastic and foam containers.

She looked back at Nick. He took the napkin from her hand and tossed it over his shoulder. It bounced off something that looked like a butterfly net and came to rest under the rear window.

"Has anyone ever told you you're a slob?" she said.

"Only rude people."

Riley folded her arms tightly and settled back in her seat, trying her best not to touch anything around her. "You sure know how to treat a girl," she grumbled.

"Stop complaining. Aren't I taking you to Upper St. Clair? It's the classiest neighborhood in all of Pittsburgh."

Riley looked out her window. Through breaks in the tall hedges she began to catch passing glimpses of sprawling private estates with manicured shrubbery, sculptured fountains, and winding driveways paved in sulfur-gray Pennsylvania flagstone.

"Look at this place," she said. "I've never seen anything like it."

"You're not from around here?"

"Hardly. I grew up about forty miles south of here—a little coal-mining town called Mencken. My father was a coal miner from the time he was old enough to go to work until the day he died."

"What did he die of?"

Riley shrugged. "A coal mine is a toxic place—so are the towns that grow up around them. There's coal dust, fly ash, cadmium, iron oxides—take your pick. My father just began to waste away one day. A month later he was dead. The cause of death was never determined. I think that's one of the reasons I went into pathology: it's nice to know why someone you love died."

"Mencken—why does that sound familiar?"

"Probably our underground coal-mine fire; it's been burning for forty years now."

"Forty years?"

"There are places where the coal vein comes right up to the surface. The miners' families used to go there to gather our own coal to use in our furnaces. People dumped their trash there too, and years ago someone got the bright idea to burn it. That set fire to the coal seam, and the fire's been smoldering underground ever since."

"That's bizarre."

"There are underground coal-mine fires all over Pennsylvania—five in Allegheny County alone. Of course, what makes Mencken so special is that we've got a bony pile fire too."

"A what?"

Riley looked at him. "You're from Pittsburgh, and you've never heard of a bony pile?"

"My family was in steel," he said. "The Carnegies and the Polchaks."

"A coal mine produces a lot of scrap—shale, coal tailings, old timbers, stuff like that. In the old days, when the miners came out of the shaft, they just dumped it all beside the mouth of the mine. Over the years those piles grew to enormous sizes. The Mencken bony pile is two hundred feet high and half a mile long; it went right past our back door. The problem is, those piles contain a lot of low-grade coal, and sometimes they catch fire just like the mines do. Our bony pile has been burning for years now."

"Like a giant pile of charcoal briquettes?"

"Only it burns from the inside out. To look at it, you wouldn't even know it's on fire. I used to play on it all the time as a little girl."

"You used to *play* on it? Isn't that a little dangerous?"

"It is if you don't know where you're going. A man from the Department of Environmental Protection came out once. He climbed halfway up the bony pile and stuck a temperature probe into the ground by his feet. A foot and a half below the surface it was eight hundred degrees. He came down off that pile *fast*."

"And you used to *play* on it?"

"Like I said, you just have to know where you're going. Every winter, when it snowed, the bony pile looked like a ski area. The snow would melt off all the hot spots, and stick to all the cold ones. It made a sort of map; it told us where it was safe to walk."

"And you just hoped it stayed that way until the following winter."

"I'm a coal miner's daughter. We didn't have it soft like you steel tycoons."

"So the mine is on fire, and the bony pile is on fire. That's got to be a little hard on property values."

"My sister and I still own the house, if that's what you mean. How could we sell it? Mencken is a ghost town. The basements collect carbon monoxide, smoke seeps out of cracks in the ground, and after it rains the bony pile steams like a giant compost mound. It's not exactly Upper St. Clair."

"So you and your sister are blue collar girls. Somehow I thought the blue was in your veins."

"Why's that?"

"You're a doctor. I don't imagine many Mencken High graduates went on to medical school."

"Sarah and I both went into medicine. We thought it's what our father would have wanted."

Nick looked at her. "Your father would have been very proud of you."

She met his eyes. "What about your father? Was he proud of you?"

Nick turned away. "Boyce Street. What do we do here?"

"This is it. Make a right—it should be just a couple of houses down."

They passed a series of tall brick posts capped in limestone finials the shape of chess pawns. The posts were connected by sections of intricate wrought-iron fence; in the center of each was a flowering fleur-de-lis. After the sixth post there was a wide, arching gate that spanned an immaculate crushed-stone driveway. Nick pulled to the center of the gate and stopped the car. At the end of the long driveway, visible between a colonnade of stately elms and poplars, was the seemingly endless English Tudor estate of Mr. Miles Vandenborre.

"Five million at least," Nick whistled.

"Nick—don't stop here!"

"Why not?"

"Look at that place—and look at this car."

"OK . . ."

"Do I have to spell it out for you? Their garbage is worth more than this car!"

"I hope so," Nick said. "That's the whole idea." He stepped out of the car and lifted the trunk with a rusty groan. To the right of the gate, two thirty-gallon garbage cans stood sentry, surrounded by a series of smaller white plastic bags neatly twist-tied at the tops. He flipped the lid off each can, pulled out the black cinch-top bags, and carried them to his trunk. He rounded up the white bags in a single armload, and in less than two minutes they were under way again.

Nick glanced over at Riley, who was slumping even lower in her seat. "Now you know why I wanted to bring *my* car—the right tool for the right job."

"Just drive," she said, cupping her right hand over her eyes.

"Your first time Dumpster diving? I guess you've never been a teacher."

"What are we going to do with all this stuff?"

"We're taking it to Leo's. Mr. Vandenborre is a rich man in need of a kidney transplant, but for some reason he removed himself from the waiting list—yet he's still alive. I want to know why."

"And you think his trash is going to tell us."

Nick glanced at the backseat. "You can tell a lot about a person by his trash—don't you think?"

■

They parallel parked in front of Forest Hills Apartments. Riley took the two black bags; Nick gathered the assortment of white bags and closed the trunk behind him. They disappeared through a stone archway and up a flight of stairs.

Across the street, Cruz Santangelo set his binoculars on the dashboard, took a pen from his coat pocket, and jotted down the address.

Set them there, on the kitchen floor," Leo said.

Riley set the two black bags side by side on the linoleum. Nick was right behind her with an armload of bulging white plastic.

"Don't get them mixed up with your own trash," Nick said. "Mr. Vandenborre could turn out to be *really* weird."

"I'll get the door," Riley said, crossing back across the living room.

"Don't bother," Leo called after her. "I never close the door— to my apartment or to my heart. It helps with the electric bills."

"You have an electric heart?" Nick said.

Leo turned to Riley with a look of disgust. "Have you spent the entire morning with . . . *this*?"

"I had to ride in his car too."

Leo grimaced. "How could you tell it from the trash? Why didn't you drive the whole thing up here?"

212

Riley looked around the apartment. The entry door was braced open by a small entertainment center; she wondered if he ever closed it at all. The windows were open too, and the summer breeze caused the drapes to flutter in like flags. The room was sparsely furnished, but the walls were crowded with framed reproductions of the masters of the Italian High Renaissance. Along the far wall was a long workbench covered with computers, monitors, storage drives, scanners, and devices that Riley had never seen outside the coroner's own forensics lab. In the center of the workbench, a flat-screen plasma display hung under a copy of Titian's *Sacred and Profane Love*. Behind a high-speed optical scanner stood a marble reproduction of Michelangelo's *Bacchus*. The entire room was an endless anachronism: it was a computer lab within an art museum, a brave new world under the watchful eye of the old.

At the end of the workbench, a charcoal gray flat-panel monitor displayed the PharmaGen logo. As Riley watched, the image changed to the company's most recent corporate report.

"Why are you watching the PharmaGen Web site?"

"I'm not," Leo said, "Lassiter is. I have our spyware configured for remote viewing; whatever Lassiter is looking at, we're watching in real-time. You're seeing what he's seeing right now."

"That's a little creepy," Riley said. "Anything out of the ordinary? I tried not to call for a few days—Nick said to give it a rest."

"He should talk—Nick never gives anything a rest. Don't worry; I check the keystroke logs every hour. There's been nothing of interest to us so far."

Riley stopped, took a deep breath, and bent over slightly.

"Are you all right?"

"I carried those bags up three flights of stairs," she said, stretching her back. "I have to be careful about that kind of exertion."

"Do you need to sit down?"

"I'm OK. I just needed to catch my breath."

In the kitchen, Nick gently patted the sides of the white plastic bags until he came to one. "Bingo," he said, tossing it to Leo.

He tested it himself. "I think you're right." He laid the bag down on the kitchen counter and carefully slid a knife up the side; a tangle of paper strips bushed out through the slit. Leo turned and gave Nick a beaming thumbs-up.

"But it's shredded," Riley said. "What good is that?"

"Shredding is good," Leo replied. "Shredding tells you that they have something they want to hide—something that might be worth looking at." He reached into the slit and carefully pulled out a handful of paper. "See this? This is approximately five documents, and they can be reassembled manually in about ten minutes. That's the beauty of strip-shredders, Riley. They only create the *illusion* of security. They separate a document into narrow strips, then they drop them side by side into the waste receptacle. It doesn't take a genius to put them back together again. It doesn't take a computer specialist either," he said, turning to Nick. "You can do this yourself."

"Come on, Leo, I've got things to do. Don't you have some work-study kids you can give it to? Besides, we're definitely going to need you for *this*." He handed Leo a second bag. He felt along the bottom; it was filled with paper, too, but it was much heavier and more compact. He carried this bag to the kitchen table and carefully slit along the bottom. Thousands of tiny white-and-black squares poured out in a soft mound of paper confetti.

"Don't tell me you can put *that* back together," Riley said.

Leo looked up at her with a pained expression. "Still you doubt me. Still I must prove myself to you. Of course I can put this back together. It just takes a little longer—and it does require a computer specialist. Fortunately for you, I just happen to be one." He shook the bag until no more came out, then carefully searched the inside of the bag for tiny pieces clinging to other objects. Then he began to spread the bits of paper evenly on the table so that no two were touching.

"Next I lay down sheets of a special transparent plastic," he said. "The bits of paper adhere to them. Then one by one I place the sheets on an optical scanner and scan both sides of each sheet. The program does the rest."

"What program?"

"I originally developed it for the FBI. It looks at the image on each bit of paper, and it also notes the exact shape of every edge. Then the computer goes through millions of permutations, matching images and edges until the original document is restored. It's like working a hundred-thousand-piece jigsaw puzzle at warp speed."

"Your family would be proud of you," Riley said.

"But even at warp speed, this will still take a little time."

"How much time?" Nick asked.

"The rest of the day should do it. And what if this should turn up something—something that confirms this theory of yours? What happens then?"

"Then we call Special Agent Santangelo. We tell him what we've learned, and we turn over the physical evidence—that should speed up his investigation."

"He's not going to like it," Riley said. "He told us no more poking around."

"He said no more poking around in *Lassiter's* affairs—I always listen very carefully when people are threatening me. And we're not poking around in Lassiter's affairs anymore."

"We're still monitoring his computer activity."

"Yes, but the FBI has no way of knowing that—all we're doing is watching, just like they are. And all we did this morning is snatch someone else's trash. That's perfectly legal, as long as the trash is curbside."

"Nick, we're reassembling shredded documents. What would the FBI say about that?"

"They're using Leo's program—what could they say? Look, Riley, you're the boss here. We can stop what we're doing right now and leave the rest to the FBI. Would you be happy with that?"

Riley thought for a minute. "No," she said. "With the FBI, it's always going to be a 'need to know' basis—even when their investigation is over. They might not ever tell us what was really going on here."

"I don't want to interfere with a federal investigation," Nick said. "I just want to finish what we've started. We can't call the FBI with every little detail we come up with; if we do, they'll tell us to back off for sure. I think we should finish what we're doing here, and *then* turn over what we have—because the next time we call Santangelo, we're finished."

Nick and Riley stood by the table, watching Leo sort and arrange the thousands of bits of paper into an enormous, miniature mosaic. He looked up at them.

"Don't you two have things to do?"

"Right," Nick said. "I should get going."

"It is my day off," Riley nodded. "What's left of it anyway."

Five minutes later they were still watching.

Leo walked around the table, took both of them by the hand, and led them to the open window.

"Look out there," he said to Nick. "What do you see?"

Nick shrugged. "Pittsburgh."

He shook his head in disgust and turned to Riley. "Please, rescue this lost soul. Look out the window and tell him what you see."

"Life," Riley said.

Leo threw both hands in the air. "A heartbeat! Faint, but barely audible. For you, there's hope. Your friend here has no pulse at all—he may be beyond resuscitation. You know the problem with you two? Your whole existence is work, and you've forgotten entirely how to *play*. You find you have a few precious hours off, and still you hover around my table like two old prisoners afraid to leave their cells. Go on, get out of here while there's still some hope of redemption for both of you. And *you*," he said, pointing a finger at Nick. "Don't come back here until you *feel* something. Help him with this," he said to Riley, "even if you have to defibrillate him."

He ushered both of them to the doorway, gave them a solid push toward the stairwell, and returned to the apartment.

They stood in awkward silence for a moment.

"He gets like this," Nick said. "He won't let us back in for a while."

"How long?"

"It's hard to tell. Maybe the whole evening."

Riley nodded. "Might as well go, then."

"Might as well."

They slowly turned to the stairwell, with no idea where they were going next.

You make a mean *kielbasa*, Mrs. Polchak," Riley said, pushing away her plate.

"All Polish food is mean," Nick said. "Just give it a few hours."

Mrs. Polchak looked at Riley's half-finished plate. "This is how you eat?" she said disapprovingly. "No wonder they think you are a *fellow*."

They took their coffee in the tiny family room. Mrs. Polchak settled into an upholstered rocker that dominated the room like a throne. On her left was a small taboret, a maple magazine rack, and a portable writing table; on her right was an end table and a reading lamp with a moveable arm. The only other seat in the room was a small love seat directly across from the recliner. Nick and Riley took a seat side by side and stared silently into their cups. Mrs. Polchak turned the reading lamp until it cast its light directly on them.

"So tell me," she said to Riley, "how are things going with you two?"

"Uh—" Riley looked at Nick for help.

"No way," he said. "She asked *you*."

"Oh . . . well, things are . . . they're sort of . . . things are kind of—"

"She doesn't like me, Mama," Nick said. "God knows I've tried."

"That's not true," Riley said. "I *do* like him."

"Nicky," Mrs. Polchak smiled, "there is a nice lemon torte in the refrigerator. Go and fetch it for us, that's a good boy."

"Why don't we wait awhile before we—"

"Fetch it for us. Slice it up for us in nice little pieces. Take your time."

"Mama, Riley doesn't really like—"

"Nicky!" she said with a quick glare. "Go away so I can talk about you behind your back."

Nick set his cup on the coffee table. "I'll get the dessert," he said. "I may never come back."

They both watched until he disappeared behind the swinging door, then Mrs. Polchak turned to Riley again.

"We have a nice walnut tree," she said. "Do you like walnuts?"

"Walnuts? Yes, I—"

"Walnuts are a lot of trouble. The shells are very thick, and they stain your hands. But they are worth the trouble, don't you think?"

"Mrs. Polchak, it isn't your son, it's *me*—"

"It's him," she said, shaking her head. "Women take too much blame. When a man does not love us, we say, 'It's me.' When we cannot love a man, we say, 'It's me.' Sometimes it's *them*. Nicky is hard to love. I know; his father was hard to love."

Riley set her own cup down. "Mrs. Polchak, what happened between Nick and his father? Can you tell me?"

"Nicky's father was a very strong man, but he was

ignorancki—he was not very bright. Nicky was just the other way; he was very smart, but he was weak—his eyes, you see. It is hard for men to have sons; they are like little mirrors. I think Stanislaw did not like what he saw in Nicky's eyes."

"That's so very sad."

"What about you? Do you like what you see in Nicky's eyes?"

Riley slowly nodded.

"Me, I like walnuts," Mrs. Polchak said. "But it takes time to open them up. It takes a big hammer too."

"I wish I had the time," Riley said softly.

"You young people! Is your time so short?"

"I'm afraid it is."

"Then use the time you have."

"Mrs. Polchak, I want to be fair to Nick. I don't want to lead him on."

"And why not?" she said indignantly. "I led three men on, and then I picked the best of them. Stanislaw was the lucky one, and the others survived. What do you think men are, little pastries? Life is not fair; love is not fair; but time, as you say, is short."

Riley considered her words. "You know, I think you're right—Stanislaw was the lucky one."

Just then Nick reentered the room with a small tray containing plates, forks, and a badly mauled lemon torte.

"Why do you embarrass me?" Mrs. Polchak said, grimacing at her beautiful dessert. "You can slice open those little worms of yours, but you can't find the center of a lemon torte? What did you cut this with, your elbow?"

"It's OK, really," Riley said. "I don't think I could touch another bite right now. I could use a walk first."

Mrs. Polchak brightened. "A walk is just the thing. Why don't you two take a nice walk, while I go in the kitchen and throw two hours of hard work in the garbage?"

"This is what's known as a 'guilt trip,'" Nick whispered to Riley. "C'mon, let's get out of here."

They left by the back door. Twenty yards away, tucked in the trees against the hillside, the greenhouse glittered like a faceted jewel in the passing moonlight. They followed a well-worn path toward the greenhouse door.

Nick glanced over at Riley. "So what did she say about me?"

"She said you're a nut, and if I want to open you up, I'd better have a big hammer."

"That's better than I hoped for," Nick said. "Wait here a minute." He stepped into the greenhouse and emerged a moment later with two shining objects. He handed one to Riley; it was a small mason jar with the lid ring holding a coffee filter in place across the open mouth.

"Come on," he said. "I want to show you something." He turned and headed for a second path that curved slowly uphill and disappeared into the woods. Riley followed him to the edge of the trees, stopped, and peered into the darkness.

"Where are we going?" she called after him.

"This way. You've got to see this."

Riley took a deep breath and plunged into the shadows after him, where strips of bright moonlight illuminated the path in a zebra pattern. She caught up to him at a place where the trees suddenly gave way to a great, open meadow.

They walked together to the top of the rise. "Welcome to my world," he said.

The hill sloped gently away from them to form a vast, shadowy meadow that seemed to rise and fall like the ocean at night. Thin pockets of mist lay in the hollows, and around the edge of the woods, thick stands of locust and maple stood guard in uniforms of deep blue and violet. And everywhere, as far as the eye could see, were the gentle, silent, floating green lights of a thousand fireflies.

"It's beautiful," she whispered.

Nick reached slowly into the air and clapped his hands together once.

"Look." He opened his hands to show a glowing smear of light across his palm. "Luciferase. It's the enzyme that produces their light. Did you know that 95 percent of the energy used by an incandescent light bulb is given off as heat? A hundred years of technological advancement and that's the best that your species can do. But this little guy gives off almost 100 percent *light*. Incredible!"

He reached his arm into the air again and a moment later brought it back, holding out the edge of his hand to show a single black insect, tipped with orange and glowing with soft green light. "You're looking at the state insect of Pennsylvania," he said. "New Mexico's is a *wasp*. Fireflies are really beetles, not flies at all. In a few weeks, they'll all be gone." He slowly extended his hand to her. She held out her own hand, and Nick took it, allowing the tiny creature to crawl off of his hand and onto hers. But Nick held her hand a little longer.

They waded forward into the ocean of soft green lights.

"I'll bet I know how to tell the males from the females," Riley said. "It's the eyes. The females see everything going on around them, and the males are all clueless."

"Nice try. The truth is, every one you see is a male. Most people have never seen a female firefly." Nick dropped to his hands and knees and began to search through the thick grass. "Look—here's a female."

Riley saw a tiny green glow coming from the tip of a blade of grass.

"The females stay on the ground. Each species of firefly has its own flash pattern. The females flash their signal, and the males fly overhead and flash back. When there's a match, that's *amore*—most of the time."

"Most of the time?"

"See that one?" He pointed across the meadow. "That's a Big Dipper firefly—a *Photinus pyralis*. He lights his lamp, dips, and then curves up again—see? He writes the letter J over and over again. Now, somewhere in this meadow is a female *Photinus*—but there are also a few *Photuris* ladies too. They're much larger than the Dippers, and they've learned to mimic their flash pattern perfectly. If the male *Photinus* picks the wrong lady, it's dinnertime—and he's dinner."

"Love is a risky business in the insect world," Riley said.

"In the human world too. Get attracted to the wrong female and you can get eaten alive."

"Is that your personal experience or just a scientific observation?"

Nick removed the lid from his jar and began to move among the tiny lights, reaching and bending and scooping at the air.

"At the beginning of the firefly season, there are hundreds of males for every female. The male soars over the meadow, flashing, searching, like Diogenes with his lantern. He spots females everywhere, but none of them are for him. Suddenly he sees it—can it be? Yes! It's *his* signal! After endless miles of flying and thousands and thousands of flashes, he's found his ladylove. He soars down into her waiting arms," he said, with arms extended, "and she bites his head off."

"Why do you think they keep trying?"

"Because they have brains the size of pinheads," Nick said. "What's *our* excuse?"

Riley sat down now and watched Nick as he moved about the meadow. Sometimes he stretched and sometimes he stooped. Sometimes he stood perfectly still and waited. Then he would start again, almost running across the field, arms sweeping back and forth before him. Riley smiled, imagining that even after the fireflies were gone he might come to this field late at night and run, like a child, for the sheer joy of movement.

The moon was bright, but the sky was littered with clouds. At one moment she could see him perfectly, a cobalt figure with a gleaming glass jar. An instant later he was only a silhouette, barely visible at all.

"Riley," he called out. "Where are you?"

Riley sat perfectly still.

"Riley!" he called louder.

Silence.

"So *that's* the game," he said, and began to retrace his steps back across the field toward the rise. There was a flash of moonlight and he whirled around, taking a quick accounting of every potential shape and shadow—then darkness again. Riley sat in a small hollow, blending almost perfectly with the ground around her. He was now very near, and once he passed so close that she could hear his breathing, so close that she felt the hair stand up on the back of her neck. Still she said nothing.

He stopped and turned. He was looking almost directly at her. He stepped forward, stopped, and stared more closely, as if by concentrating he might somehow draw extra light from the coal black sky. He stepped closer; closer; now he was only a few feet away, and the air seemed supercharged between them. Riley held her breath and stared up at him. Another step, and then he bent slowly forward, staring into the strange shadow before him.

At that moment the moon slid out from behind a black cloud, and Nick found himself staring into Riley's green and brown eyes, ablaze in the blue white moonlight. They both found themselves strangely short of breath. Riley rose to her knees; Nick dropped to his and took her in his arms. She blinked hard once, and he instinctively blinked back.

"It's been a long time," Nick said. "What do I do now?"

"I think you're supposed to kiss me."

Nick hesitated. "I think I forgot how."

"They say it's like riding a bicycle."

"I was never any good on a bicycle—I used to fall off a lot."

"Like you said—love is a risky business."

And then they both remembered.

They were interrupted by the sound of Nick's cell phone. He slid it out of his pocket and opened it. "What?" he said with obvious annoyance.

"Nick, it's Leo. Have you felt anything yet?"

"I was starting to. What do you want?"

"Is this a bad time?"

"The worst. Hang on a minute." He motioned to Riley; she edged up beside him, and he held the phone away so she could hear as well.

"I finished the shredding," Leo said. "The program just ended and printed out a copy of all the original documents. Most of them were ordinary financial records—a Visa charge summary, a mutual-fund statement of activity, health insurance explanation of benefits—that sort of thing. But there were a few items in the confetti shredding that I thought you should know about. One was a brochure from an outpatient surgery center in Penn Hills. You don't suppose your boy had a knee repaired or a wart removed, do you?"

"It's possible. What are the other items?"

"Three prescriptions from a Canadian online pharmacy. The drugs are called Neoral, Immuran, and Orasone. I have no idea what they are."

Nick looked at Riley.

"Neoral is a cyclosporine," she said. "Immuran is an azathioprine, and Orasone is a corticosteroid. They're all immunosuppressants, and they're commonly prescribed together—after transplants."

CHAPTER
31

How can I help you, Mr. Polchak? The receptionist tells me you have some concerns."

"Are you a doctor?"

"No, sir. My name is Allen Reston. I'm the COO—more like an office manager, really. You could say I run things here at Westmoreland Surgery Center."

Nick glanced around at the office. The room was precise in every detail, lit with the same antiseptic fluorescence as a procedure room. The desk was a curving slab of white maple with a contoured laminate base. The desktop was bare except for a matching black desk set and a flat panel monitor. The computer itself, like all other functional components of the room, was tastefully hidden from sight. The walls were dutifully adorned with three sterile landscapes, which provided about the same warmth and assurance as the teddy bears on a phlebotomist's smock. Nick's plum-colored chair, ergonomically designed, forced him to sit more erect than he liked; it made him feel as though someone were pushing him from behind.

"I blew out an ACL on the tennis court," Nick said. "Now my doctor says I need laparoscopic surgery."

"Did the same thing myself," Reston said. "I guess it's the weekend warrior thing; you think you're still twenty-five, but your knees have other ideas."

Nick nodded. "I'm a little uncomfortable about having the procedure done here."

"Oh? Why is that?"

"Well, it's not a hospital. I mean, if something goes wrong in a hospital, you've got state-of-the-art medical facilities."

At this, the man broke into a smile. "You're a little behind the times, Mr. Polchak. How much do you know about freestanding surgery centers?"

"Very little, I'm afraid."

"These places started popping up everywhere about a dozen years ago. Hospital ORs were increasingly overcrowded, and they realized they could lighten the load considerably if they began to conduct minimally invasive surgeries off site."

"That's what I was afraid of—I get bussed to relieve someone else's overcrowding problem. I get second-rate care."

"There's nothing second-rate about Westmoreland Surgery Center," Reston said. "A decade ago, ambulatory surgery centers only performed the simplest procedures: endoscopies, breast biopsies, lesion excisions—and that's all that some centers still do. But more aggressive facilities—like this one—developed into full-fledged, freestanding surgery centers. At Westmoreland, we now do an entire range of surgical procedures: gynecological, urological, vascular, and orthopedic. We're constantly increasing the number of procedures we can perform."

"But you can't compete with a hospital for quality of care."

"Why not? Our surgeons are on the staff of several local hospitals; if you choose to go to a hospital, one of our surgeons may perform your procedure there."

"But surely hospitals have better facilities—the equipment and all."

"Westmoreland Surgery Center has two state-of-the-art surgical suites. They are identical to the ORs in any major hospital—except for the instrumentation, of course."

"The instrumentation?"

"The cost of medical equipment is enormous—a single surgical laser can cost almost a hundred and fifty thousand dollars. Hospitals have the funding to purchase their equipment outright; we avoid the capital outlay by using an equipment outsource company. Suppose you need a procedure that requires the use of that surgical laser; instead of buying one—and charging *your* insurance company for it—we can lease it for a single day. The outsource company can provide blood bypass equipment, instrument trays—anything we require, depending on the procedure we're doing."

"Clever," Nick said. "That would allow you to do almost any procedure a hospital can do."

"Almost."

"Just out of curiosity, what keeps you guys from going all the way? What keeps you from performing, say, brain surgery?"

Reston leaned as far back as his ergonomic chair would allow and considered this. "In theory, we could—that is, we could at least set up to perform the procedure—but what we're not set up for is long-term convalescent care. No intensive care unit, no month-long hospital stays. This is an *ambulatory* center, Mr. Polchak—strictly outpatient."

"So you knock out a wall and add a few beds. Surely brain surgery is more profitable than vasectomies."

"You'd think so—but the problem is liability. Surgery centers can only expand as far as liability insurance will allow them to. Think about it: We do a brain surgery, something goes wrong, and the attorneys all scream, 'Inadequate care! It wouldn't have happened in a hospital!' One suit like that would be the end of us."

"The end of who? Who owns this place anyway?"

"It's privately owned; that's all I'm allowed to tell you."

"By individual doctors?"

"Sorry. But I can tell you that doctors commonly own these places. Let's be honest, Mr. Polchak, there's a second reason these facilities began to develop: doctors took a good look at the fee structure in hospitals and realized they were missing out on a lot of money. Check a hospital bill—there are professional fees, and there are hospital fees. The professional fees go to the doctor, but the hospital gets the rest. Doctors realized they would never get the lion's share until they owned the facility itself—and outpatient surgical centers were born."

Nick glanced around the room. "I imagine these places are very profitable."

"There's a very definite profit motive behind these places—and I don't mind telling you, because it's to your advantage. Those profits allow us to compete with any other kind of healthcare facility—hospitals included. At Westmoreland you get state-of-the-art facilities, top-of-the-line surgical staff, privately employed nurses, and a lot more attention than you're going to get in a hospital ward with a hundred beds. You have nothing to fear here, Mr. Polchak. We're on the cutting edge."

■

Nick steered his car onto the Penn Lincoln Parkway and waited until he emerged from the Squirrel Hill Tunnel before punching the button on his cell phone.

"Riley McKay, please." He waited. "Riley—Nick. Can you talk? I just stopped off at Westmoreland Surgery Center and asked a few questions. What? Yes, I was tactful—aren't I always tactful? The COO at Westmoreland told me that they can set up to perform almost any technical procedure there. The only thing that limits them is liability—but if there is no liability, then there are no limits, are there? I think we've got the last piece of our puzzle—and I think it's time to call Santangelo. Are you OK with that? Then you make the call and tell them everything we've found—but keep Leo's name out of it, will you? Right. I knew you would.

"What's your caseload like today? When do you get off? Then let's meet tonight at Leo's, and we'll put a few notes together and collect all the physical evidence. Ask Santangelo what he wants us to do with it, and we can drop it off. Maybe the three of us can grab dinner together—you know, to celebrate. I'm afraid it'll have to be Italian.

"Hey, about last night. That talk you had with my mom seemed to do some good. What did she tell you? What? Well, pity is underrated. No, I'm not proud—I'll take pity any day.

"You know, it's been a long time since I've . . . ridden a bicycle. We sort of got interrupted. Too bad—it was just beginning to come back to me."

CHAPTER
32

T he yacht's twin diesels had barely rumbled to a stop before
Cruz Santangelo leapt to his feet.

"They know everything," he said. "They hacked into
UPMC's patient records and got a list of transplant patients.
They picked the ones who dropped off the list and compared
them against death records. They took the richest guy and
searched his trash. They've identified a client, Julian—they
found Vandenborre."

"Ingenious," Zohar said. "Really quite impressive."

"Did you hear me? They know everything!"

"What *don't* they know?"

"What difference does it make? They've found a client! All
they have to do is—"

"What *don't* they know?" he repeated patiently.

Santangelo sat down hard. "They don't know about my
involvement. They still believe there's a federal investigation
going on. That's why they called me."

"As we expected," Zohar nodded.

"And they don't know about Kaplan or Angel—but those are just details, Julian. They've made the connection between Lassiter and Truett and you. They know enough to put us away for life—what difference does it make what they *don't* know?"

"It makes a great deal of difference. Remember, Dr. Polchak and Dr. McKay are helping us to identify vulnerabilities in our system. They're working for us, not against us—not yet anyway."

"Santangelo is right!" Truett shouted, charging from the cockpit. "These people can destroy us with a single phone call."

"Which they already made—to the FBI, just this afternoon."

"But all it takes is one word to somebody else. I say it's time to shut them down—I've got too much at stake here."

"You have everything at stake here; we all do, Mr. Truett."

"Then we deal with this *now*."

"I agree!" Santangelo said.

Zohar paused to allow their emotions to subside. Then he smiled and spoke even more softly than before. "I agree. I think it's time, as you say, to *shut them down*—assuming, of course, that we know who *they* are. Mr. Santangelo, have you been able to identify the third member of their party?"

"I have—and I know where he lives."

"You've reviewed his vita? You've considered his education and background? You're convinced he was capable of providing the necessary computer expertise?"

"He's the one, all right. This guy has even developed software for the Bureau."

"And you're satisfied there's no one else? No fourth member?"

"There will be if we don't get moving. Who knows who else they might involve in this? The more time we spend here talking, the greater the risk."

"On that point I disagree; the more time we spend here talking, the *smaller* the risk. Remember, gentlemen, we're talking about 'shutting down' three human lives. If Dr. Lassiter were here, he would remind us that a careless course of action now will 'raise all kinds of flags' with the authorities."

"We don't have time for this," Truett said. "We've got to do it *now!*"

"We *do* have time for this," Zohar corrected, "but I agree that we should not delay. All I'm suggesting is that we proceed just as we've always done—according to *plan*, not out of passion. Mr. Santangelo, you know what to do?"

"I'm ready."

"Please keep me posted on your progress."

"What about the next procedure?" Truett said. "It's coming up fast. Are we still on?"

"Of course. I'll inform the rest of the committee about the details. Remember, we have a client who's depending on us—and I think Mr. Santangelo can guarantee that there will be no more prying eyes."

"You got it," Santangelo said.

Zohar smiled and looked at both of them. "Our last two meetings on this beautiful vessel have been so . . . *depressing*. May I suggest that our next gathering here be a kind of celebration? The end of one era and the beginning of another. What do you say, gentlemen? I'll bring the champagne."

CHAPTER 33

A toast," Leo said, raising is glass. "To the finest team of forensic exterminators ever assembled."

They touched their glasses together and drank. Leo's kitchen table was crowded with paper: strip-shredded documents reassembled into tiny woven mats, thousands of bits of confetti sandwiched between plastic sheets, and one neat stack of computer-generated reproductions. Beside the table, a mound of black-and-white garbage bags still rested.

"And now," Leo said with a flourish, "I would like to invite both of you to join me in a triumphal feast."

"Great idea," Nick said. "There's a little Polish deli just around the corner."

Leo twisted from side to side, as if searching for a place to spit. "How have I offended you? How have I sinned, that you would assign me this penance?"

"OK then, we'll let Riley decide."

They turned to her. Riley folded her arms.

"Has it ever occurred to you two that I'm *Scottish*?"

Nick squinted at her. "You want to go to McDonald's?"

She turned up her nose to him. "Just for that, I vote for Italian."

Leo raised his hands to the sky. "I promise you an unforgettable evening. Cost is no object, thanks to the good Mr. Vandenborre."

"Mr. Vandenborre?"

Leo picked up the top sheet of paper from the table. "Mr. Vandenborre has been kind enough to loan us his Visa card for the evening. I find this to be a poetic justice not even the FBI can attain."

Nick turned to Riley. "That reminds me: How was Santangelo when you told him?"

"Stunned. He didn't say anything at all for a minute—I thought we got disconnected at first. Then he kept asking me to repeat myself, asking for more and more details. Boys, I think we flat-out wowed the FBI."

"No complaints? No rebukes? No requests to give up your trivial pathology career and join the FBI?"

Riley laughed. "I wish I could have been there when he reported this to his superiors. I hope we didn't embarrass him too much."

"All authorities need to be embarrassed from time to time," Nick said. "It keeps them humble."

"I hate to change the subject," Leo said, "but I need my kitchen table back. What do we do with all of this?"

"I told Santangelo I'd call him again once we had time to organize it. Is this everything?"

"I should include a copy of the entomological evaluation I did for you," Nick said. "I need to polish the report and get the specimens mounted."

"This is everything I've got," Leo said, "except for the keystroke logs from Lassiter's computer. I saw no reason to include those, since the FBI has been monitoring them as well."

"We should throw those in too," Nick said. "We want them to know we're holding nothing back; better to give them too much than too little."

"It will only take a minute." Leo sat down at the computer and began to call up the spyware reports and send them one by one to the laser printer. Suddenly, he stopped and studied the screen. "Nick," he said. "Is this what I think it is?"

Nick stepped up behind him and peered over his shoulder. "What have you got?"

"An encrypted e-mail Lassiter sent less than an hour ago. Take a look."

The message read:

NEXT PROCEDURE AS SCHEDULED

DONOR: SARAH JEAN MCKAY

3162 ROCKFORD AVE APT 17 / MT.
LEBANON

O POSITIVE

"Riley," Nick called back to the kitchen, "isn't your sister named Sarah?"

"What's she done now?" Riley said, grinning as she stepped into the living room—but her smile instantly vanished when she saw the look on both of their faces. She charged to the computer and pushed Nick aside.

"Oh no," she whispered. "*Sarah!*"

"Was your sister part of PharmaGen's population study?" Nick asked.

"She's a *nurse*—half the medical people in the city are a part of it!"

Leo examined the screen again. "It says next *procedure*. She's referred to as a *donor*, and even her blood type is listed. There can be no doubt what this is."

Riley covered her face and turned away from the screen.

"Easy," Nick said. "Everything's OK."

Riley spun around. "Everything's *OK*? Dr. Lassiter did autopsies on three people who are *not* OK—three people who walked into the wrong alley or stopped to change a tire or felt a little needle prick in the back of the neck—and they never woke up again! Well, my sister is *not* going to be the next one!"

"Riley, listen to me," Leo said. "The FBI is monitoring Lassiter's computer just like we are. They've seen this message too."

"Have they? What time do federal agents knock off for the evening? You got this message less than an hour ago—what if they *haven't* seen it yet? The message says, 'Next procedure *as scheduled'*—scheduled when? What if it's scheduled *tonight*?"

She rushed to the kitchen counter and shoved her hand into her purse, fumbling for her cell phone. She turned the purse upside-down and dumped its contents onto the counter. She flipped open her wallet and pulled out a business card with a black and gold seal.

"Who are you calling?"

"Special Agent Santangelo. I'm going to make *sure* they've seen this message." She dialed the number and waited an eternity for it to connect.

"Hi there," the voice on the other end said.

"Special Agent Santangelo?"

"Mmhmm."

"This is Dr. Riley McKay."

"Of course it is. I've been expecting you to call."

"Mr. Santangelo, are your people still monitoring Lassiter's computer? Did you intercept the e-mail message he sent out tonight?"

"Can you hang on a minute? Coffee's ready."

"No! Wait a minute, you idiot! This is urgent!" She pulled the phone away, stared at it in disbelief, and shoved it against her ear again. It was a full thirty seconds before the voice came back on the line.

"There we go. I find it gets bitter if you brew it too long. Now, you were saying something about a message. What message would that be?"

"A message from Dr. Lassiter—*Next procedure as scheduled—Donor: Sarah Jean McKay*! That's my sister, Mr. Santangelo! These people are targeting my sister next!"

"Dr. Lassiter sent that in an e-mail? That was awfully careless of him, wasn't it? And he probably thought that was a safe thing to do because it was *encrypted*. But you saw the whole thing because you were watching his keystrokes, weren't you? Well, I guess that's what I get for working with morons."

Riley froze.

"I really do want to thank you for your cooperation. Why, without your help, I would have had to *guess* what you kids have discovered—but you were kind enough to keep me informed every step of the way. As a way of saying thanks, Dr. McKay, may I give you a piece of advice? I wouldn't worry about the 'next procedure' if I were you—I'd worry about my own health."

Riley began to tremble so hard that she dropped the phone. She stumbled back away from the counter and into Leo's arms. Nick picked up the phone.

"Santangelo? Nick Polchak."

"Oh yeah, our Bug Man friend. You know, Dr. Polchak, I really didn't appreciate your comments about Waco. The whole thing started when those idiots killed four ATF agents searching for illegal firearms. The truth is, no FBI agent fired a single shot at Waco—did you know that? But I wanted to, believe me. I would have killed them all if I had been given the order—but no, we had to let them set fire to the compound and burn themselves to death, then take the blame for everything."

"So you're the bad boy of the FBI after all," Nick said. "Tell me something: just how many bad boys are there?"

"It's not nice to talk about other people; let's talk about me. You asked me where HRT members go after Waco, remember? Well, I went looking for a more lucrative way to apply my hard-earned skills. And I found one, right here in Pittsburgh."

"You're the one who's been killing these people," Nick said. "The phony cardiac arrest, the drive-by shooting in Homewood. You were trained for this. You're an assassin."

"An *assassin*," he said thoughtfully. "Really, that's like calling Mozart a 'piano player.' No, Dr. Polchak, I'm much more than that—as you and Dr. McKay are about to discover."

"What happened to 'the minimum force possible'?"

"Sorry—this time the maximum force is necessary."

There was a click, and the line went dead.

Nick slowly turned and looked at Riley. "We told him everything," he said. "What was I thinking? Why didn't I see it? We thought we were shutting them down—we've been *helping* them."

Riley grabbed the phone from his hand and started punching numbers.

"Who are you calling?"

"The *real* FBI."

"Stop," Nick said, pulling the phone from her hand.

"What are you doing? Give me my phone!"

"Riley, he *is* the real FBI. Remember when we first met Santangelo on the *Majestic*? You called the local FBI office to check him out. Santangelo is an actual field agent, Riley. We have no idea who else in his office is involved."

"We can't just sit here! Sarah's life is in danger!"

"Maybe—maybe not. When you told Santangelo about Lassiter's e-mail, what did he say?"

"He acted like he knew nothing about it. He said Lassiter shouldn't have sent it, and he called him a moron. Why?"

"Santangelo has been working *with* Lassiter; that message may have been nothing more than a plant."

"But why would they plant a phony message? What would they have to gain? They already know what we know, and they know where to find us—why feed us information about another procedure? And why Sarah, of all people?"

"Exactly—why Sarah? Doesn't the coincidence bother you?"

"Nick, listen to me. Lassiter *is* a moron—we know that. We've both witnessed his past mistakes. Maybe he *wasn't* supposed to send that message—maybe Sarah *is* the next victim. If we assume the message is phony, and we're wrong, then Sarah is dead. We can't take that chance—I *won't* take that chance." She took the phone from his hand and opened it again.

"No," Nick said, covering the phone with his hand. "There's no one to call. Think about it, Riley: The FBI? We've been there. The coroner's office? Hardly. The police? They work closely with the coroner's office—who would be safe to call? You're right about one thing: we have to assume that the message is legitimate—but whatever we do about it, we have to do it ourselves."

"What do we do?"

"We get your sister to safety, that's the first thing—and we get *ourselves* to safety at the same time. Now that Santangelo knows everything, he'll come after us. That's his next order of business."

"Where do we go?"

"You can stay here," Leo said. "My house is your house."

"Not a chance," Nick said. "Santangelo referred to 'you and Dr. McKay.' He still doesn't know who you are, Leo, and we've got to keep it that way. There's no sense in endangering you, and we may need your help back here. In the meantime, get the rest of this evidence organized as fast as you can. Somebody's going to want it—we just don't know who yet."

"We can't go to my place," Riley said. "They'll know where I live for sure."

Nick shook his head in frustration. "They're a step ahead of us—they've been a step ahead of us all along. What we need most is time to *think*."

"Nick—we don't know how much time we have."

"How far is it to your sister's place?"

"Ten minutes, maybe less."

"Let's go. First we grab Sarah, then we find some place where we can figure this thing out."

■

"Here they come," Santangelo said, pointing at the two shadows emerging from the arched doorway into the yellow glare of the streetlamp. Riley climbed into her car, gunned the engine, and pulled away from the curb; Nick followed close behind in his own car, marking his parking space behind him with a glistening black puddle.

"Third floor," Santangelo said. "Down the hall, on the right—look for an open doorway. You know what to do?"

She nodded. "Away from the door and away from the windows."

"Good girl, Angel. I'll be right behind you."

CHAPTER
34

Riley knocked again, this time harder. The apartment door opened until the chain stretched tight, and a single eye appeared in the crack.

"Riley?" a woman's voice said. "Is that you?"

"It's me, Gabriella. Can we come in?"

The woman peered around the door's edge and discovered Nick, glaring impatiently at her from over Riley's right shoulder. Her eye widened at the sight of Nick's enormous eyes.

"It's late," she said uneasily. "I'm not exactly dressed for company."

"Gabriella, please. This is important."

The chain made a scratching sound and then dropped away. The door slowly swung open with Gabriella still behind it, peering around the edge at Nick, who followed Riley quickly through the open door.

"Sarah!" Riley called out, hurrying toward the hallway and the two back bedrooms.

"She's not here," Gabriella said.

"Where is she?"

"Why? What's wrong?"

"Gabriella—*where is she?*"

"Sarah's at the grocery store. What is it? What's happened?" She shut the door and chained it again, then hurried over to Riley, making a wide arc around Nick.

"It's a little late for grocery shopping," Nick said.

She jumped. The combination of Nick's deep voice and over-powering eyes had an unnerving effect on Gabriella. Riley stepped close, put her arm around her shoulders, and squeezed her tight.

"Gabriella, I want you to meet Nick Polchak. Nick is a friend of mine—a good friend. Despite those big buckeyes of his and his terrible taste in clothing, he's a nice guy, really."

"Does your roommate always do her grocery shopping at night?" Nick plunged ahead, ignoring Riley's attempt at warmth and reassurance.

Riley rolled her eyes. "Nick, Gabriella is Sarah's roommate. They're both nurses at UPMC—they often work late."

"Do you know anyone around here?" Nick said. "Family? Friends? Somewhere you can go for a few days?"

Gabriella stared at Nick. "You guys are scaring me. I need to know what's going on."

Riley turned her away from Nick and led her to the sofa. They sat down side by side, and Riley took her by the hands. "Gabriella, you know that I work for the coroner's office, right? Well, something has come up—something that I can't tell you about right now. There's a chance that Sarah is in danger—and you could be in danger too, because you share this apartment. We think it's best if you get away from here for a few days. Can you do that? Give me your cell phone number, and I'll call you when it's OK to come back. Is that OK?"

Nick sat down on the other end of the sofa. "What store does your roommate shop at? Does she go at the same time each

243

week? Does she follow a predictable route to the store? Does anyone else know that route?"

"*Nick*," Riley said with a quick glare.

"When should I leave?" Gabriella asked nervously.

"The sooner the better," Riley said gently.

"First thing in the morning?"

"*Now*," Nick said. "The longer you stay here, the greater the risk."

Gabriella scrambled to her bedroom; Riley followed her to the doorway, then then turned back to Nick.

"What's wrong with you? Do you want her to jump out the window?"

"That would be a little counterproductive; I just wanted to hurry her along. Do you know where your sister shops?"

"There's a Giant Eagle just a couple of miles from here. Should we go there and look for her?"

"We can't both go—if we missed her she'd come back here, and then she'd be alone in this apartment. I can't go by myself—I don't even know what she looks like. And *you* can't go."

"Why not?"

"What if you find Sarah and she's in trouble?"

"What if *you* find Sarah and she's in trouble?"

"Better me than you," Nick said. "Besides, if you leave me alone with Gabriella, she *will* jump out the window."

Riley picked up her purse from the sofa. "Stop trying to protect me."

Nick stepped between her and the door. "Isn't that the whole point here?"

"The point is to protect Sarah first. Get out of my way."

"The point is to protect all of us."

She took a step closer. "Don't make me walk over you. I will, you know."

Nick raised both hands. "You wouldn't hit a man with glasses, would you?"

"This is my sister, Nick. You don't know how it is for me."

Now Nick stepped closer. "You don't know how it is for *me*."

Just then, there was the sound of a key fumbling in the lock. The door opened a few inches and then stopped, with a paper grocery sack wedged in the opening.

"Gabriella, get the chain!" a voice called from behind the door. "I'm losing this bag!"

Riley unlatched the chain and swung the door open wide. Sarah stood in the doorway, mouth open, blinking at her sister. "You look like someone I know," Sarah said. Then she looked at Nick. "Whoa—who's the big guy?"

Nick stepped forward and lifted both bags from her arms.

"Watch that one," Sarah said. "It's got eggs."

"Get in here!" Riley said. "Where have you been?"

"Is this a double date? You could give a girl a little more notice."

Riley gave her a quick embrace, pulled her into the apartment, and shut the door.

Sarah watched Nick as he disappeared into the kitchen. "Cute," she whispered. "Has he tried contacts?"

"I tried them," Nick said, returning. "They were the size of paperweights—kept stretching out my eyelids."

"Sarah, I want you to meet Dr. Nick Polchak." Riley slid her arm behind Nick's back and looked intently into Sarah's eyes.

Sarah nodded slightly and turned to Nick. "It's really nice to meet you, Nick. Welcome to the McKay Coal Mine—duck your head as you enter."

Behind them a bedroom door opened and Gabriella appeared, lugging a black Samsonite carry-on in one hand and a small cosmetic bag in the other.

"What's going on?" Sarah said. "Are you two moving in?"

"We asked Gabriella to spend a few days with her family," Riley said.

"What? Why?"

Gabriella stepped past Sarah and opened the door. "Oh, Sarah—be careful."

"You too," Sarah replied. "Will somebody tell me what's going on here?"

Gabriella turned to Nick and Riley. "Should I go in to work tomorrow?"

"Go to work as you always do," Nick said. "Keep an ear out for anyone asking questions about Sarah's whereabouts. We'll check in with you—and *don't* come back here until we tell you to, understand?"

Gabriella nodded, gave Sarah a quick peck on the cheek, and pulled the door shut behind her.

Sarah turned to Nick and Riley. "Well, this is interesting. My sister and a tall, dark stranger mysteriously appear in my apartment late one night, and two minutes later my roommate moves out. What are you, Nick, an immigrations agent? I'm pretty sure Gabriella's got a green card."

Riley shook her head. "Sarah, there's so much to explain, and there isn't time. Do you trust me?"

"The last time you said that you set me up for a blind date with an anesthesiologist. I've been drowsy ever since."

"I want you to pack a bag. Pack enough for—" She looked at Nick.

"A few days. A week at most."

"A *week!* You know, this is a little sudden for a road trip. What's going on?"

"I can't explain it all now."

"So I'm supposed to just disappear for a week—from my job, from my friends, from the club—and just head with you two to parts unknown?"

"That's about the size of it," Nick said. "We can talk on the road."

"We can talk *now*," Sarah said. She strolled to the sofa, plopped down, and picked up a magazine from the coffee table. "I've got lots of time—I *live* here."

Riley charged over to the sofa, ripped the magazine from her hands, and threw it across the room. "You pack that bag," she said. "You pack it *now*. This is your big sister talking to you, and if you give me any more trouble, I swear I'll throw you over my shoulder and carry you out of here kicking and screaming—I've done it before, and you know I can do it again."

Sarah looked at her, then turned to Nick. "Are you sure you know what you're getting yourself into?"

"I'd do what she says," Nick said. "She's been very belligerent tonight."

Sarah gave her sister a bored look, shrugged, and headed for her bedroom.

"Five minutes," Riley called after her. "Don't make me come looking for you!"

"We'll take two cars," Nick said, "yours and Sarah's, if it's OK with her. Stop at an ATM and take what you can out of your checking account—no more credit cards, OK? I'll do the same, but I'll find an ATM in the opposite direction. If they check our bank activity, they'll know we're on the run—but they won't know where. Let's meet at the motel in thirty minutes. And build a fire under Sarah, will you?" Nick turned and headed for the door.

"Nick," she called after him.

He turned.

"You can't protect me."

"Thirty minutes," he said. "Don't make me come looking for you."

■

It was just after midnight when they checked into the King's Motel, a sixties-era relic complete with flat, gravel-covered roof and open hallways fenced in by black iron railings. Riley and Sarah checked in first; they took a room together on the second floor overlooking the street. Nick watched from the parking lot until they disappeared behind a peeling orange door; then he entered the small office himself and requested a room nearby. He paid in cash, and he registered under the name of William F.

Burns. Five minutes later, he knocked softly on their door. Riley quietly slipped out and shut the door behind her.

"I put her to bed," she said. "I think she's a little overwhelmed."

Nick took her by the arm and led her down the hallway to a place where the elevator blocked them from view from the street. He reached up and twisted the incandescent bulb once, and the hallway instantly went dark.

"Your sister doesn't seem the type to easily overwhelmed," Nick said.

"Sarah? She's as tough as an old razor strop."

"Sounds like someone I know."

Their shadows came together and touched once, then drifted apart again.

"This is a key to my room," Nick said. "I'm in 213, just a few doors down. If you need me, call. If the phone doesn't work for any reason, you come straight to my room—understand?"

She nodded. "Nick—what are we going to do next?"

"You're going to get some sleep. I'm going to do some thinking."

CHAPTER
35

Riley slipped the key into the lock and turned it gently; she felt the bolt give way. She pushed on the door, and it begrudgingly opened. The rubber weatherstrip dragging along the short-pile carpet made a sound like a stretching balloon.

She stepped quietly inside. It was just before six a.m., but every light in the room was on. In the center of the room, Nick straddled a wooden desk chair. His chin rested on his folded arms, which draped across the back of the chair. He sat utterly still; he stared directly ahead at an empty spot on the dingy wall, and his floating eyes were as still as two rafts on a glassy sea. Riley started forward in alarm, then stopped, recognizing telltale signs of life. Every day at the Coroner's Office she was reminded of the infinite difference between even a coma and death; Nick was lost in the depths of thought, but, thank God, he was still very much alive.

She approached him head-on, but there was no look of recognition or even awareness of her presence. She leaned down and looked into his face; at this distance his eyes were truly overwhelming, and for the very first time she saw them motionless. She felt a sense of gratitude, as though some rare or endangered species had allowed her to approach unchallenged. They were soft and dark, and Riley understood why few people could bear to look at them directly. But somehow she loved them; she loved the way they floated over her, calming her, like a groom with two soft brushes.

She reached out and stroked his chestnut hair. His eyes jumped suddenly like awakening birds and began to slowly take the room into focus. At last Nick straightened up and looked directly at her, but it was several seconds more before he spoke.

"I'm going to Leo's," he said. "You two stay here until I get back."

"Good morning to you too. Do you always sleep sitting up?"

Nick was still too lost in abstractions to engage in pleasantries. "I thought about it all night—what do we do next? We did the right thing first by grabbing Sarah and by sending Gabriella to her parents. But we can't stay on the defensive forever; the only way to eliminate the threat to us is to expose the ones who are threatening us."

"But how do we do that?"

"That's what I spent the night asking myself. Whoever we call next, whoever we choose to trust, we'd better be right about it—because making that contact will be like sending up a flare. Our problem is that we don't know who to trust. Santangelo is with the FBI; surely the entire Pittsburgh field office isn't in on it—at least, I hope not—but we don't know who would be safe to call. Your own office has been compromised—it may have been Lassiter's lone involvement, but then again he may have had help. It seems possible that at least two of your deputy coroners are in on it; they pick up the bodies at the death scene. And that raises the question of the police. They're at the death scene too—at least in cases like the drive-by shooting. Who can we trust within the police department? Who can we trust *any-where*?"

"And the answer is . . ."

"The newspaper. We go to the *Pittsburgh Post-Gazette*."

Riley looked aghast. "Nick, that seems incredibly risky. First they're going to think we're nuts, and then they're going to start calling around to make inquiries. That will stir up everything."

"I hope so. Look, we've only got two things going for us: first, they don't know where to find us; and second, *we have physical evidence*. We have the shredded documents that prove that Mr. Vandenborre picked up a spare kidney somewhere along the way. And we also have my entomological report and specimens, remember? That report could raise all kinds of awkward questions. The trick here is to reveal the physical evidence without exposing ourselves."

"How do we do that?"

"I'm going to swing by Leo's and grab the reconstructed documents. Then I'm going to drop them off at the *Post-Gazette* and head back here."

"Why can't Leo bring them here? Or why can't he take them to the newspaper himself?"

"Because I can't reach him. I've left messages, but I haven't heard back from him. This can't wait, Riley. They're searching for us right now, and they're looking for Sarah too. The sooner we get this out in the open, the safer we'll be—and the sooner I get this out of Leo's hands, the safer *he'll* be."

"I wish I could go with you," Riley said.

"You know better—Sarah needs you here. There's a very rich person somewhere waiting for one of her kidneys, and you need to make sure she doesn't do anything stupid. Don't dial out. If the phone rings, don't answer it. If it's me, I'll let it ring once, and then I'll call again. Got it?"

"Got it." She stroked his hair again. "Are you OK? You didn't sleep a wink."

"My species requires very little sleep."

Riley frowned. "If you're not careful, your species will be extinct."

■

Nick stopped half a block from Leo's apartment. He considered whether to park several blocks away and walk over, but he wanted to remove all the evidence at once, and it occurred to him that the sight of someone carrying an armload of trash bags several blocks would raise far more eyebrows than one quick trip to the street. He pulled his car into the same space he had occupied just the night before.

"Leo," he called out as he rounded the corner into the ever-open doorway. "Hey, Leo!" He headed directly for the bedroom. It was still early, and even tireless Leo might still be in bed. But the bedroom was empty, and the bed was unslept in—unless Leo was more fastidious than Nick remembered. He had hoped to find Leo here, to set his mind at ease and to brief him on their plans, but it didn't really matter. Right now all he needed was to collect the evidence and deliver it to the proper person at the *Pittsburgh Post-Gazette*.

He pushed open the bathroom door; it was empty. On a whim, he slid open the shower curtain and felt the inside; it was perfectly dry. It was possible that Leo made his bed *and* skipped his morning shower, Nick told himself. It was *possible*—but he moved to the kitchen with a crawling feeling on the back of his neck.

The kitchen table was completely bare; even the black-and-white trash bags surrounding it had been moved. But where had Leo taken them? Nick had asked him to *organize* the evidence, not to remove it. He assumed it would still be here on the kitchen table, where it had always been. Now he would have to search the whole apartment for it. Now he would have to—

He stopped.

Over the Formica counter, on the white ceramic kitchen floor, Nick saw the edge of a crimson pool.

He sat down hard on one of the kitchen chairs and stared at the wall below the counter that blocked his view of the kitchen beyond. He didn't need to look on the other side. He knew what was there—he could see it in every detail. He could see Leo's body stretched out facedown, just as it had first fallen, with a small slit below the rib cage or a gunshot wound through the occipital bone—or maybe even a crushed skull, depending on the savagery of his attacker. And somewhere on the floor there would be a wine bottle or a shattered cup of sugar, some small favor that Leo had been asked to fulfill that would cause him to pause momentarily in a vulnerable and accessible position. And in his mind he could hear the sound of the falling body, lifeless before it hit the floor without reflex or recoil, and the dull, flat sound of flesh slapping tile. Nick cringed and covered his ears with both hands.

He turned and looked across the room at the long computer workbench. The monitors were still in place, and the printers and scanners too—but the two computer towers had been removed, and their hard drives with them, along with all digital record of the reconstructed prescriptions. Nick ran his hand over the empty kitchen table. Leo didn't move the evidence—it had been removed by his attacker, and by now it was all completely destroyed.

Nick rose slowly to his feet and stumbled toward the kitchen. He had already seen it all in his mind—why did he have to look? But he knew he had to be a witness to the horror of his oldest friend's death—to do less would be cowardice. He owed it to Leo; somehow he knew that Leo would want him to look. "Drink it *all*, Nick," Leo would say. "If you leave any behind, you'll only regret it later." When he remembered the sound of Leo's voice, he felt alternating waves of rage and nausea. Why did he ever get Leo involved in this? How did he let things go this far? Leo was the most *alive* person he had ever met. He was all heart—he was *Nick's* heart. And now his heart was dead, and all he wanted to do was climb back up into his skull and lock the door forever.

He stepped into the kitchen and looked at the floor. He felt no additional shock, no fresh grief over the reality before him. Why should he? It was just as he knew it would be, down to the shattered bottle of claret and the deep green shards of glass lying in a stain of purplish red. He knelt down beside him; there was a trickle of red from the base of his skull. He leaned over the body and gently brushed back the wavy hair. Around the entry wound was the tattooing of gunpowder, indicating a close-range shot. There would be no exit wound; it was a small-caliber shell, intended to ricochet off the inside of his—Nick shut his eyes and pushed back the thought.

He began to stroke Leo's hair now. Teardrops gathered at the tips of his eyes and fell away into his glasses, pooling in the great lenses and washing all the terrible details from the image before him.

Nick sat back on the floor. It would have been quick and painless—he was sure of that, because pain produces noise, and noise is something no assassin can afford—especially from a victim who lives with open windows.

Open windows.

Nick looked up at the cream-colored walls. Above the sink he saw a tiny black speck, and two more above the counter. He struggled to his feet and hurried out into the living room; there were dozens more, dotting the walls above the computer work-bench, surrounding the paintings like tiny visitors to an art gallery.

Mosquitoes.

He rushed to the door and down the hall, down the three flights of stairs to his waiting car. He leaned through the back window and pulled out his aerial sweep net. They would not stay long; they were female *Anopheles* or *Culex* mosquitoes, both late-night biters, who had engorged themselves on a meal of human blood. All night long they had rested, using the blood proteins to allow them to produce their eggs—but when the daytime temperatures rose again they would depart, searching for a source of standing water and a place to deposit their clutch.

Back in the apartment, Nick swung the net back and forth across the walls, allowing none of the tiny specks to escape. He was grateful that mosquitoes are slow fliers, reaching speeds of no more than a mile and a half per hour; Nick was used to netting far faster and more elusive carrion flies, and this was comparative child's play. The important thing was that he let none escape. He searched the walls carefully, waving his hand through the air to stir up any late risers, continuing until the walls were spotless and the tip of his net was flecked with gray-black specks.

He hurried back to the kitchen and began to open drawers, searching for a rubber band or clothes pin, something he could use to close off the tip of the net and trap its occupants until he could process them.

Suddenly he heard a quick knock on the doorframe and the sound of footsteps approaching from behind. Nick spun around.

"Hey, neighbor, I was wondering if you had any—"

The young man stood in the kitchen doorway. He looked at Nick, then down at the body lying in the crimson pool, then back at Nick again. There was a moment of horrified silence—then the man began to back away, his eyes still glued to Nick's.

"Wait," Nick said. "It's not how it looks."

The man held up one hand and continued to back across the living room; at the doorway, he turned and bolted down the hallway.

Nick took a last look at Leo, grabbed the aerial net, and ran for his car.

Nick rapped twice on the door, then stepped back from the peephole so he could be clearly seen. In his left hand he carried the aerial sweep net; his right arm encircled two plastic containers and two metal tins.

A moment later the door swung open. Riley smiled up at him, but Nick refused to meet her eyes. He brushed past her and charged into the motel room, heading directly for the small kitchenette.

"What happened?" Riley said.

Nick said nothing. He stepped to the counter and with a sweep of his arm sent a collection of small objects clattering onto the floor. He set down the net and peeled the tops off the two plastic containers.

"Nick—what's wrong?"

Sarah stepped out of the bathroom in a knee-length robe and a terry towel wrapped around her blond hair. "What's going on?"

Nick unscrewed the lid from the metal tin and poured the acrid liquid into one of the containers. In the bottom, an inch-thick layer of gypsum absorbed the fluid and kept it from spilling.

"This is ethyl acetate," he said without looking up. "Don't breathe it."

Riley stepped closer. "Nick, look at me."

"Somebody hasn't had his coffee yet," Sarah said, dabbing her ears with a towel.

Nick took the sacklike end of the sweep net and shook its occupants down into the extreme tip; then he draped it into the plastic container and pressed the lid on tight. Now he opened the other metal canister and poured the transparent fluid into the second container.

"I have to get them into ethanol as fast as possible," he said. "I've got to dry them out—moisture degrades the DNA."

Riley stepped up close to him now. She put her hand on Nick's arm and stared at him intently until he could no longer continue. He dropped his head and closed his eyes.

"Whatever it is, you have to tell me," she said gently.

Nick slowly turned his head and looked at her—and when his eyes met hers, she instantly knew.

Her knees buckled. Nick turned and caught her before she could fall. He pulled her in tight against him, and her body began to shake. She buried her face against Nick's chest and sobbed.

Sarah's eyes widened. "You guys are freaking me out. Will somebody tell me what's going on?"

But it was several minutes before anyone could speak.

"Leo's dead," Nick said to Sarah.

"Leo? The computer guy?"

"He was killed sometime last night."

Riley looked up at him. "How did it happen?"

"It doesn't matter."

"I want to know."

"The pathologist in you wants to know—but *you* don't. Just let it go, Riley. He's gone."

Sarah sunk down on one of the beds. "Last night? But you two were just there last night."

"If we had stayed any longer, they would have caught all three of us together."

Riley took a towel and wiped her eyes. "We thought they didn't know about Leo. How did they find out? How did they know where he lived?"

"I've underestimated them every step of he way," Nick said. "Not anymore." He turned back to the specimens again. He removed the net from the killing jar and shook its lifeless contents into a tiny black pile in the very tip of the bag. Then he placed the container of ethanol into the net and gently tipped the contents into the clear liquid. They floated to the bottom like tiny pieces of ash.

"What are you doing?" Riley asked.

"I'm going after Santangelo."

"What?"

"These are mosquitoes. I collected them from the walls in Leo's apartment—he always left his windows open, remember? These mosquitoes were there last night when the killer arrived—and I'm betting it was Santangelo. At least one of these mosquitoes drew blood from the killer, and that blood sample is still in its gut. I'm taking these specimens to Sanjay at Pitt; he'll do a DNA sequence on each of them. Now all I need is a sample of Santangelo's DNA, and if there's a match, we can prove that Santangelo was present at the murder scene."

"Now wait a minute," Sarah said. "You want to go *after* this guy? Aren't we supposed to be running away here? He just killed your friend *last night*."

"We have no choice—the physical evidence is gone. Santangelo took it all with him—the shredding, the computer hard drives, the trash bags—everything. Now what are we supposed to show the newspapers? What are we supposed to show anybody? If this mosquito evidence works out, we can shift to the offensive again."

"*If* it works out? How long will it take to find out?"

"A few days, tops . . . I think."

"You *think*?"

"Well, this has never actually been done before—at least, it's never been used in a court case. But it's been proven possible in a laboratory."

"And in the meantime we're supposed to stay here? Nick, we're still in Pittsburgh—surely they'll check the local motels. This guy knows more than you think he does—you said it yourself. He's just one step behind us. I think we need to put some distance between us."

"Sarah had an idea," Riley said. "I think it's a good one. We can go to our house in Mencken, remember? The place is deserted; no one would ever look for us there. There are no utilities, but there's a working pump in the backyard—and we can take food and supplies with us."

"It's perfect," Sarah said.

"I'm not going into hiding," Nick said. "I'm taking the fight to *them*. They started this—I'm going to finish it."

"I know I'm a newcomer here," Sarah said, "but it's my life, too, you know. I think we should get away from here."

"Then we split up."

"No!" Riley said. "Whatever we do, we do it *together*. There will be no splitting up!" She glared at both of them until their countenances softened.

Nick slumped down on the edge of the bed and lay backward. He rubbed his temples in long, slow circles, staring at the ceiling above. "Maybe you're right," he said. "Maybe we could—" He sat up suddenly. "We're going to Tarentum."

"Tarentum? But you just said—"

"Listen to me—Santangelo knows *everything*. He knew about the shredding, and he knew about Leo—and he knows about my entomological report and the blowfly specimens in my greenhouse in Tarentum. Santangelo has to destroy all the physical evidence; how long will it be before he heads to Tarentum?"

Riley looked at him in horror. "Oh, Nick—your mom."

Nick jumped up from the bed and began to gather the containers and canisters. Some clear fluid dripped down the edge of the specimen container; Nick wiped his hand on his trousers and turned to Sarah.

"Have you got something I can put this in? Something watertight?"

Sarah searched through her suitcase and found a Ziploc bag. She opened it, dumped out a hairbrush and a comb, and handed it to Nick. He sealed the leaking specimen container inside and set it with the others.

"You two get packed. I'm taking these specimens to Sanjay— I'll be back in a couple of hours. Then we're heading to Tarentum." He took out his cell phone and pushed an autodial number.

"Wait," Riley said. "Use the motel phone. They could be listening—"

Nick held up one hand. "Mama? Nick. Look, Riley and I are headed up there this afternoon. We need a place to get away for a couple of days. And I need a favor, OK? I need you to pack a bag and stay with a friend; we need the house to ourselves. What? No, it's not like that. No, really. Look, if it makes you feel any better, we're bringing a chaperone along with us, OK? What? I don't know, how about Mrs. Drewencki? Well, then, try Mrs. Teklinski. I don't know, Mama, you figure it out. You're the Queen of Poland, just tell them you're coming and they have to obey. Right. Now don't forget, I want you out of there by this afternoon. I'll call you when it's safe to come back. What? No, I said when it's *time* to come back—give your hearing aid a thump. I've got to go now. Thanks. Me too." He folded the phone and dropped it back in his pocket.

He turned to Sarah. "You're right, Sarah, we *do* need to put some distance between us—and we're going to need a day or two to hide out while these samples are being processed. We'll go to Tarentum, and then we'll head for Mencken—but after that, I go after Santangelo."

Nick gathered up the containers and turned for the door. Riley stepped in front of him.

"*We* go after Santangelo," she said.

It was late afternoon before they arrived in Tarentum. Nick and Riley drove together, and Sarah followed in her own car close behind. They made the long drive up Route 28, with the Allegheny River winding beside them on their right like a long, green snake. At some points it came almost up to the roadway, then suddenly curved away and disappeared behind clusters of houses and trees and factories, only to reappear just as suddenly a few miles ahead. The rivers of Pittsburgh are the city's vascular system, and life surrounds the waterways like clusters of living cells around blood vessels. Opposite the river, narrow roads cut back through the steep, wooded hillsides, lined with gray-shingled houses that huddled close against the cold Pennsylvania winters.

They led Sarah to a small motel on the outskirts of town, where she checked in alone under an assumed name. Now it was dark, and Nick and Riley stood at a pay phone in the corner of a BP station across from the motel.

"No answer?"

"She must have packed up and left," Nick said. "Good girl."

"Now what?"

Nick thought for a minute. "I wish I could sneak in the greenhouse just long enough to grab those specimens."

"We can't chance that. What if Santangelo shows up and finds you? What if he's already there and waiting?"

Nick frowned.

"Why didn't you ask your mom to take them with her?"

"The greenhouse is filled with specimens. What was I supposed to tell her? 'Grab the *Phaenicia sericata* and the *Calliphora vicina*, but forget the *coeruleiviridis*.' My mom can't tell a palmetto bug from a pierogi."

Riley shivered. "That's the last time I eat her pierogies."

"Come on—we'll stick with our original plan."

They took a winding road to the very top of the hillside. They parked at the edge of the woods and made their way down on foot, approaching Nick's house from behind.

They emerged from the trees behind three sea green water tanks that sat like giant sentinels atop the Tarentum Plateau. The tanks were ancient, built before anyone could remember, holding a million gallons of water in reserve for the citizens of the town below. They were the tallest structures on the steep Tarentum hillside, boilerplated together from long, curving sheets of steel and welded together in rippling seams. From the rims, long brown lines of rust and corrosion dripped down the sides like icing on a cake.

"That one," Nick said, pointing to the tower on the right. "My house is on the other side."

Riley placed her left foot on the first rung of the metal ladder and looked up. Fifty feet above her, the curving rim of the water tank cut a dark slice from the evening sky. She climbed two rungs. Nick reached around her legs and grasped the sides of the ladder.

"Keep going," he said. "I'm right behind you."

263

Riley glanced down. She could already see the roof of Nick's house, the tiny backyard, and the shimmering glass of the green-house beyond. By the time they reached the top of the tank, they would have a perfect view of Nick's home—and of everything else in Tarentum as well. Riley checked her grip again; though she was no more than twenty feet off the ground, the hillside plummeting away to her left created the illusion of staggering height. She pulled herself tight against the ladder and looked at the rusting rivets that secured it to the side of the tank.

"Are you sure this is a good idea?"

"Trust me," Nick said, stepping up close behind her.

"The last time I trusted you I ended up in the Allegheny River."

"That's gratitude for you. Didn't I tell you I'd show you the town?"

They were only ten feet from the rim when Riley felt an over-whelming sense of exhaustion and a familiar dull ache in her lower back. She wrapped her arms around the ladder and shut her eyes.

"I have to rest," she said, panting. "It's the climbing—that's the hardest thing for me."

Nick climbed to the rung just below her and pressed his body tight against hers. "Take your time," he said softly. "Let me know when you're ready."

A few minutes later they pulled themselves up and over the curling rim and proceeded on hands and knees to the opposite side of the tank. Nick swung himself upright and casually draped his legs over the side of the tank; Riley approached the edge with considerably more caution.

Nick looked at her. "I thought you were queen of the bony pile."

"You can't fall off a bony pile," she said warily, but already she was feeling more accustomed to their lofty perch. She glanced back at the hillside rising up close behind them, which thankfully helped to diminish the sense of height. She sidled up beside Nick and took a seat, still focusing on the metal surface to help hold her fear in check. Now for the first time she raised her eyes and drew in a sharp breath.

The panorama before them was spectacular. Far below, the Allegheny River glistened blue white in the crystalline moonlight. Beyond the river, the dark bluffs of Lower Burrell and New Kensington ascended to heights equal to their own, the crest lined with glimmering dots of blue and gold. On their own side of the river, angular edges of boxcars, warehouses, and scrap-yard conveyors cut sharp silhouettes against the white water. As the hillside rose to meet them, dots of light became individual streetlamps, and vague geometric shadows became houses and fences and yards. The streets around Nick's house were awash in orange light and visible in every detail, and the house and backyard lay at their feet. No one would be able to approach from any direction without their knowledge.

"I could get used to this," Riley said.

"I spent a lot of time here as a boy. In those days the tanks had no tops; I used to climb up here at night and walk the rim."

"Did your mom know?"

"Did you tell your dad you were climbing on the bony pile?"

She shook her head. "For some things, it's easier to ask forgiveness than permission."

"That's my life motto."

Neither one said anything for a few minutes. Reverential silence seemed to be the most appropriate response to the awesome vista before them.

"Do you think Sarah will be OK at that motel?"

"She'll be safe there—that's where *you* should be."

"Don't start," Riley said.

They heard the sound of an engine; a car approached from the left and pulled over to the curb just two blocks away. A man got out, locked the door, and entered the adjacent house.

"Mr. Jankowski," Nick said. "When his dog died a few years ago, I asked him if I could have the body. He's never looked at me the same way since."

Riley studied his face; the lenses of his glasses glowed like two white shields in the brilliant moonlight. From up here Nick could study the world's inhabitants like the insects in one of his terraria, but maintain a protective distance from all the pain and risk of personal contact. She wondered if anyone had ever shared this lofty vantage point with him before. She thought about Leo; she felt a hollow ache in her stomach, and tears flooded her eyes again as they had throughout the day.

"About Leo," she said. "Nick, I am so sorry—"

"Leo was not your fault."

"He was my *responsibility*. If it wasn't for me—"

"I asked him to help, not you. Leo was *my* responsibility."

Riley stroked his back. "Where did he live? Can you see his house from here?"

Nick pointed to a house several blocks closer to the river—then he pulled his hand away quickly, as if the contact had produced a painful spark. "It was Santangelo's fault," he said, "and I'm going to make sure he picks up the check."

"What about the rest of them? What about Lassiter and Zohar and Truett?"

"We only need one; he'll give us all the others."

Riley wiped the corners of her eyes and looked at the house below. "How do you know he'll come tonight?"

"That's what the phone call was for. I used my cell phone—they're bound to be listening in. And I left a forwarding address and phone number at the motel desk; I might as well have put up a billboard. Santangelo knows where we were headed, and he thinks we're planning to be here tonight. He won't pass up a chance to catch us here—and I don't think he'll come until night. He needs the cover of darkness to get in and out of here unseen."

For the next two hours they sat in silence, watching every

passing car until it disappeared from sight and tracking every wandering pedestrian until a door closed securely behind him. About ten o'clock, a silver sedan approached from the direction of the river and pulled over about three blocks away. The engine stopped, the headlights blinked off, but no one emerged from the car for several minutes. Then the driver's door quietly opened; a single figure stepped out and glanced around. Nick and Riley both recognized Santangelo instantly.

Then the passenger door opened, and a young woman emerged with long auburn hair.

"Who is she?" Riley said.

Nick nodded slowly. "I was wondering about that. Unless I miss my guess, she's the lure."

"What lure?"

"Think about it: The murder of each of the 'donors' had to be carefully planned—a specific location, very precise timing. Now, how do you make sure your victim is in the right spot at the right time? What makes a man pull over to change a tire at night in the worst part of town? How do you get a man to hold still while someone sneaks up behind him and injects him with a syringe? The answer is: you use a lure. I have a feeling we're looking at the last thing Leo ever saw."

Riley looked at her again, squinting hard. They were too far away for the features of their faces to be visible, but in the still of night sound traveled readily. As they approached, even their footsteps became audible; his were flat and dull-sounding, hers were sharper and higher in pitch. Santangelo cleared his throat once, and even that muffled sound drifted up to Riley's ears. They moved quickly toward the house, pausing in shadowy areas just long enough to search for prying eyes. With every step they came closer—closer to the street, closer to the house, closer to *them*. Riley felt terrified, but at the same time strangely exhilarated. It was like being an angel, floating passively in the sky above, looking down from the heavens on the sins of foolish men.

Suddenly, Santangelo looked directly at them.

CHAPTER
38

Can they see us?" she whispered to Nick.

"I doubt it. The moon is on the other side of the river."
He lifted one hand slightly and waved. Riley grabbed his arm and jerked it back down.

Santangelo and the woman hesitated at the corner opposite the house. They stood for several minutes in the shadow of a tall hedge, watching the house and glancing up and down the street. When they finally moved, they moved quickly—not toward the front door, but around the house to the left and into the darkness of the backyard. They approached the back door silently and stopped, and Santangelo removed something from his coat pocket. While the woman stood watch, he bent over the doorknob and seemed to freeze like a statue.

Riley was almost directly above them now, looking down at the tops of their heads. Suddenly she began to feel faint. She felt herself being drawn irresistibly toward the edge of the water tower, and she imagined herself falling headlong and landing facedown on the grass just yards from the woman's feet. Riley propped herself up on wobbly arms, and there was the blank-faced woman staring at her; the woman turned to her companion, who slowly reached beneath his coat again and—

Riley's eyes began to droop shut—and then she felt two large hands grab her by the shoulders and pull back.

"Try breathing," Nick whispered. "You'll find it helps." He held her while she took several long, deep breaths. She looked at him and nodded.

Below them, the back door opened a crack. A streak of yellow light fell across the yard and disappeared into the trees. Santangelo stepped quietly inside and the woman followed. She pulled the door shut behind them.

"That's my cue," Nick said, rising to his feet.

Riley turned to him with a look of panicked protest. "Take me with you."

Nick shook his head. "What if we have to run? Sudden exertion is not your forte. I'll be OK; I should have plenty of time. And you'll be safe here—but stay back from the edge, will you? We can't catch these guys by falling on them." She watched him move quickly across the tower, turn, and back down the ladder.

Riley turned back to the edge of the tower; this time, she lay on her stomach and propped herself up slightly, with only her head protruding past the metal rim. She looked down to her left and saw Nick working his way around the side of the tank. She checked the back door of the house; it was still shut. Nick darted across the yard, around the side of the house, and momentarily disappeared from sight. A moment later he appeared again, standing under a streetlight on the front sidewalk, staring back at the house.

"Get out of the light!" Riley whispered. "They can see you!"

As if in response, Nick turned and hurried down a small alley between two houses.

Just then, the back door opened wide, and light flooded the backyard. Santangelo stepped out of the brightness and looked around; the woman was right behind him. Riley wriggled back from the edge until only her eyes were visible. Santangelo glanced to his left and spotted the greenhouse. He snapped his fingers and motioned to the woman; they turned together and headed directly for it, stopping briefly in the doorway before disappearing into the darkness inside.

Riley looked back at the streets and searched for Nick; he was nowhere to be found. Suddenly he emerged from a side alley less than half a block from Santangelo's car. He glanced both ways, then approached the passenger side. He tried the door, but it didn't open. He hurried around to the driver's side and tried again; still nothing.

From the corner of her eye, Riley glimpsed a flash of yellow light. She turned to the greenhouse and saw a light reflecting off three of the glass panes. She searched from side to side for the source: a flashlight, a passing car, a neighboring house. Suddenly she realized that the light was not reflecting off the glass—it was shining *through* it. The light appeared in a fourth pane now, then a fifth—and it grew brighter all the time.

Fire.

She looked back at Nick. He was on the passenger side again, but now he was facing away from the car. Thirty feet ahead of him was a house; shielding the house from the street was a tall hedge, and in front of the hedge was a short retaining wall. He seemed to be doing something with the retaining wall. He was holding on to it—no, he was *tugging* on it. He stumbled back away from the wall and looked down at something in his hand. He turned, raised his arm, and brought his hand down against the passenger-side window.

An instant later a sound like crunching gravel reached her ears, and right behind it came the shrill, piercing scream of a car alarm. Nick reached through the window, opened the door, and slid into the passenger seat.

Riley turned back to the greenhouse. She could hear the sound of the ceiling panes shattering from the heat and tinkling to the ground. Now the woman appeared in the doorway, silhouetted against the rising flames. She turned her head from side to side, searching for the source of the shrieking siren. She turned back to the greenhouse now and pointed urgently in the direction of the car. Santangelo bolted through the doorway and stopped, listening; he took two halting steps forward, then took off running toward the street, with the woman not far behind.

Riley jumped to her own feet now, oblivious to the ominous edge and the fifty-foot plunge beyond. She searched frantically for Nick; he was out of the car again, standing on the sidewalk beside it, waving something in the air at her. She waved back with both arms, urging him away from there, desperately trying to warn him of the danger coming his way. She could see him clearly under the orange streetlamps—but could he see her? "I doubt it," Nick had said. "The moon is on the other side of the river."

Santangelo was on the street now, headed for the corner, and the woman was less than ten yards behind. In another few seconds they would round the corner, and Nick would be clearly visible less than two blocks away. Riley dropped her arms to her sides and staggered closer to the edge. Her utter helplessness almost overwhelmed her.

Moments from now Santangelo would round the corner and discover Nick standing by his car. Nick would turn and try to run, but Santangelo didn't need to overtake him. He only needed to get within firing distance, and then he would pull his gun and put an end to Nick's life, just as he had done to Leo—and all she could do was watch.

Riley took a deep breath, threw back her head, and screamed.

The sound rivaled the car alarm in intensity. On the street, Santangelo and the woman both skidded to a halt and turned to search for the source of the scream—but echoing off the hillside, it must have seemed to come from everywhere at once. Two blocks farther away, Nick heard the scream too. He started down the sidewalk toward the corner, then spun to his right and ducked into the tall hedge.

The thick brush rustled and shook, and an instant later Nick appeared on the other side. Riley held her breath, waiting for him to dart across the yard to safety behind the house—but to her dismay Nick remained where he was, kneeling in the darkness behind the hedge directly across from the car.

Nick! Get out of there!

Santangelo rounded the corner and raced down the sidewalk to the car. He threw open the driver's door, ducked inside, and silenced the wailing alarm. Riley could hear everything now—*everything*. The piercing siren had flayed her auditory nerves like sandpaper on the fingers of a safecracker, sensitizing her to even the tiniest sound. She heard the angry slam of the car door, the whispered curse from Santangelo's lips, and the grinding sound his soles made as he stepped through the bits of glass by the smashed-in passenger window. He pulled out a dangling piece of shattered safety glass and threw it aside; it landed like a beaded purse on a kitchen counter.

Hands on hips, Santangelo turned and surveyed the surrounding area: down the street toward the river, up the row of cars that lined the far sidewalk, over the shadows between the houses on the opposite side of the street. Now he turned to the hedge. He was looking almost directly at Nick now—there was no more than ten feet between them.

Half a block away, the woman with the long auburn hair had stopped running. She kicked off her shoes, picked them up, and continued at a walk. As she approached the car, Nick began to crane his neck up and down, trying for a better look.

Suddenly the porch light behind Nick went on, flooding the front yard with blinding luminescence. A storm door opened and an old man stepped out. "What's the problem out there?" he called to the street.

Nick jumped to his feet and spun around.

"Somebody broke into my car," Santangelo called back from the sidewalk. "Have you seen anybody around here?"

The old man looked at Nick. Nick gestured frantically for the old man not to answer.

"Nick, is that you? Nick Polchak? What are you doing out there?"

Without a word, Nick took off around the side of the house and disappeared into the shadows.

On the sidewalk, Santangelo began to dart from side to side, searching through the thick hedge for a glimpse of Nick—but he was staring directly into the blinding porch light. He turned away in anger and kicked the passenger door, leaving a noticeable dent.

The old man walked to the end of his porch and peered around the corner after Nick; then he slowly shook his head and turned his attention to the street again. "You want me to call the police?" he called over the hedge.

"No thanks," Santangelo said. "My insurance will cover it."

He hurried around the car and motioned for the woman to follow; she opened the passenger door, brushed off the seat, and climbed in. The engine raced, the car pulled away from the curb, and they headed back down the road toward the Allegheny River.

Riley sat down hard and rolled onto her back. She lay staring at the spinning stars above, trying to bring her breathing under control. The hollow water tower amplified her throbbing pulse like a massive bass drum.

CHAPTER
39

Where have you *been*?" Sarah said frantically. "You've been gone for hours!"

Riley slipped through the motel door, and Sarah quickly shut it behind her. "Pack your things," she said. "We're leaving."

"Right now? In the middle of the night?"

"It's an hour and a half to Mencken. We want to arrive before daylight."

"Doesn't this boyfriend of yours ever sleep?"

"We'll talk about it in Mencken. Right now we need to hurry."

"I've been worried sick about you! What happened out there? Where did you go?"

"We'll talk about it in *Mencken*." She tossed Sarah a pair of jeans and opened her suitcase on the bed.

They split up as before, with Nick and Riley driving one car and Sarah following behind—but this time they took an altogether different route. Route 28 was the single major artery in and out of Tarentum, and the one place Santangelo could lie in wait for them. Instead, they turned right across the Tarentum Bridge and into Lower Burrell, heading for Mencken by a series of convoluted back roads that Santangelo could never follow. Even Pittsburgh natives cursed the bewildering tunnels, endless bridges, and cratered roads in the area; for the first time, they provided a measure of protection. Nick knew the back roads halfway to Mencken, and Riley and Sarah could lead them home.

"You're quiet," Nick said, glancing over at Riley.

"I'm tired. My species sleeps—most higher life forms do." She glared at him. "I'm also angry. What's wrong with you anyway?"

"We've only got an hour and a half. Can you be more specific?"

"Why did you stay behind that hedge? You scared me to death. I almost fell off the water tower!"

"That seems to be a recurring problem for you. Do you suffer from vertigo?"

"Santangelo was less than ten feet away from you. He could have reached through the hedge and grabbed you by the throat."

"He didn't know I was there. It's the last thing he would have expected. Sometimes the safest thing is the most unexpected."

Riley rolled her eyes. "You must be the safest person on earth."

"Besides, I was in darkness, and he was under a streetlamp. He couldn't see me."

"And when that old man turned the porch light on?"

"Mr. Davidek? I didn't count on him."

"But why didn't you just run in the first place? Why did you stay? What was the point?"

"I wanted to get a better look at the lure."

"What if Santangelo came after you? He would have killed you for sure."

"Out of doors? In front of Mr. Davidek? The one thing Santangelo fears most is exposure. That's why he wanted to catch us at home."

They cut through New Kensington and headed east on 56, then south on 66 toward the town of Greensburg. The narrow roads curved back and forth between the rounded hills, following the paths of ancient creek beds and valleys. Under the shadow of a hillside the road would lie in utter darkness, but just around the bend the asphalt would glisten in the bright moonlight.

"So what did she look like?" Riley asked.

"Who?"

"You know who."

"I never got a look at her. Mr. Davidek turned on the porch light before she got close enough to see. I only saw what you saw; she had long red hair." Nick glanced at her. "And great legs."

Riley stuck out her tongue at him.

"If you like that sort of thing," he added.

"Please, spare me. What did you take out of Santangelo's car?"

Nick held up a half-filled Aquafina water bottle.

"I get it," Riley nodded. "Saliva."

"If we run this through a centrifuge, we've got a sample of Santangelo's DNA. Now that we've lost the blowfly specimens, this is the only physical evidence we've got left."

"Sorry about your greenhouse. Won't the police figure out it was arson?"

"I doubt it. Santangelo knows his business—besides, I kept gallons of ethanol and ethyl acetate in there. The police will just think I left the cap off the wrong bottle. All it takes is a spark."

Riley glanced down at the water bottle. "How do you know it's Santangelo's? How do you know it's not *hers*?"

Nick held it up again. "No lipstick."

"Do assassins wear lipstick when they're on the job?"

"She's the lure," Nick said, "and lures need to be attractive."

They followed I-70 west almost to Washington, then headed

south again on 79. They were well south of the city now. The area took on a much more rural look, and the names of the towns along the way reflected it: Lone Pine, Prosperity, Ruff Creek. At the town of Lippincott, Sarah flashed her lights at them and signaled for a left turn.

"Sarah's turning off," Nick said. "Should we go back?"

"She's just stopping for food. The last grocery store is in Lippincott. She'll meet us at the house; she knows the way."

"Mencken has no grocery store?"

"Mencken has no people."

Ten minutes later they came to a stop in front of two black-and-white barricades that completely blocked the road.

"It's not exactly the Welcome Wagon," Nick said.

Riley opened her door and stepped out. A moment later she appeared in front of the bright headlights; she lifted the end of each barricade and walked it slowly out of the way. Nick pulled ahead, and Riley slid back into the car. She winced as she stretched her back from side to side.

"I could have helped you with those," Nick said.

"I'm not helpless, you know."

"Never thought you were."

They drove slowly forward. Mencken was, in fact, a ghost town; it looked more like a movie set than a place of human habitation. The yards, untended for years, had reverted to coarse yellow buffalo grass. Tall brush grew in clumps right up to the roadside, and in places pushed its way up through cracks in the pavement.

"Stop here," Riley said.

Directly ahead of them, a jagged crack cut across the road, and wisps of smoke seeped out of it and vanished into the darkness.

"Problem?" Nick said.

"That wasn't here the last time I came. We've got a little ground subsidence problem here in Mencken. The coal vein runs right under the town. When they mined it out, they left huge columns of coal in place to help support the roof; but as the fire works its way through, it consumes those columns. Now there are huge areas that have no support at all, and they can collapse at any time."

"That's what you call a 'little problem'? Where are these areas?"

"There's no way to tell. Pull forward."

Nick drove slowly across the hissing crack. Riley watched through the rear windshield until the smoke appeared again behind them. She turned to Nick and smiled.

"That wasn't one of them."

Nick blinked at her and continued on.

They passed through the town itself now, with abandoned stores and offices lining the road like empty boxes. The structures themselves still looked solid, but badly in need of paint and repair. Most of the glass had been broken, courtesy of the Lippincott teenagers, and there were even charred patches where fires had apparently been set. The town ended just as abruptly as it began, and the storefronts gave way to a cluster of small single-family dwellings—all just as vacant as the town itself.

"Take a left here," Riley said. "It's just a little farther."

A quarter of a mile ahead, the road ended in front of a two-story white frame house. At first, it appeared to be on level ground, standing out like a beacon against the midnight sky. But as they drew closer, the blackness behind the house began to sparkle in the headlights. Nick leaned over the steering wheel and peered up, and far above he could see where the blackness ended and the true night sky began. It was the bony pile, and it was the size of a small mountain.

"No offense," Nick said, "but why have you kept this place?"

"What are we supposed to do with it? The town is condemned."

"Condemned? All of it?"

Riley nodded. "No one could afford the subsidence insurance, and no one wanted to live with the health risks. First the families left, then the store owners, then everybody just pulled out. There was a little money from the government, but not enough to go around. We're not the only coal-mine fire in Pennsylvania, you know."

To the left of the house was a large slatted shed. Nick pointed to it. "Is that empty?"

"Everything's empty. We can hide both cars in there. If we keep the drapes closed when we light the lamps, we'll be practically invisible."

"You've got drapes?"

"All the comforts of home."

They walked to the house together and stepped up onto the wooden porch. The boards under Nick's feet sagged ominously. He rocked from heel to toe and the boards produced a squeal like rusty hinges.

"A real fixer-upper," Riley said. "Priced to move."

She took a key ring from her purse.

"You keep it locked?" Nick said. "Is security really a problem around here?"

"It's still our home. We don't want it turning into a crack house."

They stepped through the doorway and into the darkness of a large open space; the hollow echo of their footsteps told them the room was empty. A pinpoint of white light appeared on Riley's key ring; she pointed the tiny flashlight quickly around the room and brought it to rest on a doorway on the opposite wall. Through the doorway, on the right, was a closet door; it opened with a complaining groan and the pungent odor of mothballs. Riley handed Nick a Coleman lantern, matches, and a box of white candles. She took out two sleeping bags wrapped in plastic and a pair of ragged towels.

"You're well stocked," Nick said. "Come here often?"

"This is my water tower. I come out here from time to time to think things over."

"I've got a better view."

Riley headed for the wooden stairway. "You don't really climb up on that water tower to look at the river, do you? And I don't come here to stare at the bony pile. We both get away for the same reason, Nick—to look *back*."

They started up the narrow stairway—Riley first, then Nick. At the top of the stairs, the hallway led to three small bedrooms.

"Take your pick," Riley said. "They're all the same."

They entered the first room, facing the front of the house. On the right was a bare wooden dresser; on the left, a simple head-board and footboard with nothing but a metal bedframe in between. Riley stepped to the window, turned off her flashlight, and pulled open the dusty drapes. Moonlight colored the room with an even wash of greenish gray. She turned and looked at Nick, standing in the center of the room.

"You're a hard man to love," she said.

"So I've heard. Apparently I'm not a project for beginners."

"You almost died tonight."

He shrugged.

"I hope not." He walked across the room to her, brushed back the hair from her face, pulled her close, and kissed her. A moment later, she pulled away.

"You know," he said, "you're not easy to love either."

"Nick, I want to be fair with you."

"I don't want you to be fair; I want you to love me."

"The two go together."

"No they don't. When a woman say she wants to be fair, that's when everything starts to fall apart."

"Nick—we need to talk about the future."

"The future is an odd concept," he said. "It's a word we use for an imaginary collection of predictions, probabilities, and wild guesses. The strange thing is, we let our fears about that imaginary world take all the enjoyment out of this one. Now does that seem *fair*?"

"Nick—there's something you don't know about me."

"What? After all the time I've known you?"

"Stop joking! I need to tell you something." She struggled for a way to begin.

The lenses in Nick's glasses flashed with a glaring light, then darkened again. He stepped past her to the window and looked out. He saw a car slowly turning off toward the open doors of the shed.

"It's Sarah," he said. "Let's grab something to eat; then we could all use a few hours sleep." He headed for the door.

"Nick," Riley said. "We need to have a talk."

"We'll have time for that," Nick called back.

"I hope so," she whispered.

"ood morning," Sarah said, stretching as she entered the kitchen.

Nick looked up from his coffee. "Good afternoon is more like it—it's after eleven."

She pointed to his cup. "Is there any more of that?"

"It tastes like rust," Nick said.

"You have to let the pump run for a while. It's a deep well, but iron from the mine gets into everything."

She stepped to the counter and reached into an open bag of bread. She took a spoon from a jar of strawberry preserves and absent-mindedly wiped it across the bread, then tested the side of the metal pot on the small camping stove. Nick watched her. She was a little taller than Riley, and her hair was an identical shade of blond. Her eyes were blue—both of them—and she had the same high cheekbones and fair complexion. She was quite beautiful—like her older sister—but minus a few of the lines and wrinkles awarded with a medical degree and residency. She was barefoot, and she wore a loose-fitting T-shirt over powder blue surgical scrubs. She pulled out a chair across from Nick and sat down.

"So you're the boyfriend," she said.

"Did Riley tell you that?"

"She didn't have to. How long have you two been an item?"

"That depends on who's doing the counting. I think I'm still trying to convince her."

"I think she's convinced." She stopped for a moment to sip her coffee. "What is it you do for a living, Nick?"

"I'm a forensic entomologist."

She looked at him blankly.

"I'm a bug man. I study the insects that inhabit human bodies when they die: blowflies, flesh flies, carrion beetles . . ."

Sarah shivered. "The things people do."

"Riley tells me you're a nurse. In what area?"

"OR, ER, ICU—I've done it all at one time or another. I'm in pediatrics right now. It's a lot more humane."

Nick looked around the room. It was long and narrow, with the cabinets and counters at one end and their table at the other. Behind them, a large window looked out on an ebony hillside. "So this is where the two of you grew up."

"Right here, in beautiful downtown Mencken."

He pointed over his shoulder. "And that's the volcano you used to climb on."

"Not me—you couldn't get me up on that thing. That was Riley's playground."

"With or without your dad's permission?"

Sarah smiled. "My sister has what you might call a stubborn streak—but I suppose you've noticed that by now."

"I've had a taste."

"Riley's like a weather vane. She has a way of always turning into the wind—she seems to follow the path of greatest resistance." She pointed out the window. "It's two hundred feet to the top of that thing, and the ground around here is fairly flat.

When Riley climbed up there, she could see for miles. She could see out of Mencken; I think that's what she really wanted."

"And you?"

"Me? I didn't care. Our dad died when we were still teenagers. Riley raised us both—she was both parent *and* sister. She made me go to college, and she made sure I got a good job. Then she went on to medical school and then a residency and now the coroner's office." She peered out the window again. "You know, I think she's still climbing."

"You love your sister, don't you?"

"Do you?"

Nick shifted in his chair. "That's . . . not an easy question."

"Sure it is. You just don't want to tell me yet. That's OK; I'm just a little overprotective."

"She seems to feel the same way about you."

"It's just the two of us, Nick. That's the way it's been for a long time. We look out for one another."

"I guess that makes me the third wheel."

"Wagons have four—one more and we've got a set. Have you got a brother?"

"Sorry."

Sarah snapped her fingers. "Just my luck."

"A woman like you can't be short of men."

"Ordinary men, sure—but the McKays settle for nothing but the best. Riley makes sure of it. You know, that says a lot about you."

"Do you ever get tired of your sister's influence?"

"Riley's more than my sister—she's my hero. Can you say that about anybody?"

"Not anymore."

"Well, it's a nice thing. A little overbearing at times, but nice."

Nick leaned closer across the table. "Can I ask you something about your sister?"

"Sure. I'm an expert."

"How is she? I mean, how is her health?"

284

Sarah paused. "How much do you know?"

"I know about her kidney disease. I've seen the edema in her ankles, and I know that she tires out easily—sudden exertion almost paralyzes her. What I want to know is, how serious is it?"

"What has Riley told you?"

Nick sat back in his chair. "You do look out for one another, don't you?"

She looked intently into his eyes. "Nick, I would do anything for Riley. Would you?"

"Would he what?" said a voice behind her. Riley tousled her sister's hair and headed straight for the coffee. "It's not decaf, is it?"

"It's the good stuff," Nick said. "Plus iron."

"Good. I'm fighting off anemia."

She poured herself a cup, turned, and leaned against the counter. "Were you two talking about me behind my back?"

"That's the best way," Sarah said.

"What did you tell him?"

"I told him about the guy who took you to the prom. I told him he got a little too forward, and you broke his hand."

She looked at Nick. "Did she really tell you that?"

"She did now."

"So you'd better be a gentleman," Sarah said.

Nick held up both hands. "There's not a mark on me." He pushed back from the table and began to collect his things. He walked over to the counter and gave Riley a peck on the forehead.

"Where are you going?"

"I'm late for work."

"What work? I thought we were hiding out here."

"I need to take the sample to Sanjay at Pitt. He'll run a DNA sequence on it, and in a day or two we'll know if we have a match."

At the table, Sarah set her bitter coffee down and slid the cup away from her. In the center of the table was a half-filled Aquafina water bottle.

"Well, be careful," Riley said. "Don't do anything *unexpected*."

"There is one 'unexpected' thing I plan to take care of," Nick said. "I just thought of it last night."

"What's that?"

Sarah twisted off the cap and lifted the bottle to her lips—

"Stop!" Nick shouted.

Sarah froze.

Nick gently took the bottle from her hand and replaced the cap. "That was close. You almost let the genie out of the bottle."

CHAPTER
41

Julian Zohar held up the Money section of *USA Today* and searched the multicolored columns. Featured prominently on the second page was a story about the breathtaking progress in PharmaGen's research and development program and enthusiastic speculation about the much-anticipated date of their initial public offering. Zohar nodded and smiled.

He felt the table in front of him jostle slightly; he lowered the paper and looked across the table at an unexpected visitor.

"Do you know who I am?" Nick said, touching his glasses.

Zohar shook his head in astonishment. "You never cease to amaze me, Dr. Polchak. It's a pleasure to finally meet you." He extended his hand across the table. Nick ignored it.

"Your Web site photo is misleading," Nick said. "Photoshop does wonders."

"We all need a little touching up from time to time, don't we? So now we know how you recognized me; how did you know to find me here?"

"I followed you from your office. You don't strike me as the sort of man who packs his own lunch."

A waiter approached the table now. "Will you be joining us today, sir? Can I get you any—"

"Go away," Nick said without taking his eyes off Zohar.

"Perhaps just a glass of—"

"*Now.*"

The waiter glanced at Zohar, who smiled and nodded reassuringly. He turned and waded back through the sea of bustling lunchtime tables.

"Dr. Polchak, I hope you're not planning to do anything embarrassing or physically violent—I abhor violence."

"Somehow I thought you would. That's why I figured it might be safe to drop in on you like this."

"I'm glad you did. We're overdue for a visit."

Nick glanced around the restaurant. "I don't suppose any of your henchmen are joining you here."

"*Henchmen*? I'm not a Mafioso, Dr. Polchak—I'm simply the proprietor of a small business enterprise."

"Have you joined the Chamber of Commerce yet?"

Zohar smiled. "As long as we're airing our suspicions, I don't suppose you're wearing a . . ." He gestured to Nick's shirt.

Nick unbuttoned his shirt partway and pulled it open. "No wires, no tape recorders—just me and you. What's the matter, Dr. Zohar, don't you trust me?"

"Forgive me. I sense that we're both a bit . . . *tentative*. But there can be no relationship without trust, now, can there? So why don't we both throw our cautions to the wind and dive right in?" Zohar cocked his head to one side and studied Nick. "Another man might come here today with a demand or an offer or a plea—but you, Dr. Polchak, you're not like other men, are you? I believe you came here with some *questions*."

"How many people are involved in this 'business' of yours? How far does it go?"

Zohar grinned. "It involves every policeman, every federal

agent, every person in any position of power or influence— that's what you need to believe right now. That's what keeps you from going to the authorities, isn't it?"

"Is this all about money? Is that it?"

"For some of our members, yes—it's all about money. Take our crime-scene investigators, for example. Do you know what a CSI makes in our city? Twenty thousand dollars a year. Can you believe that? The men and women who are responsible for collecting forensic evidence at a crime scene, the ones who may decide whether a killer is convicted or goes free."

"Welcome to capitalism," Nick said. "I thought you were a businessman."

"I despise a purely capitalistic system. It caters to the worst in all of us. It fulfills our every whim, but ignores our greatest needs. Think of it: an economic system where a man who can do nothing more than throw a little ball through a hoop is rewarded with millions, while someone like yourself—a college professor, a holder of a graduate degree—survives on a relative pittance."

"And you're planning to correct this system?"

"I'm planning to *use* it, simply by applying the law of supply and demand."

"What about the rest of your people—is it all about money for them too?"

"Motives are mysterious things, Dr. Polchak. Who can really say why a man does what he does? For Dr. Lassiter, yes, I suppose it's all about money. His cupidity never ceases to astound me. For others in our little group, it has more to do with excitement and danger—they simply enjoy living on the adrenaline edge. For Mr. Santangelo, I think it's largely about money—but then, Mr. Santangelo is by nature something of a predator. I suspect he would work for far less. As for the rest of us—well, there are *personal* motives involved."

"But it's not about money for you, is it?"

"Thank you for recognizing that—I was afraid you were

about to insult me. No, Dr. Polchak, it's not about money for me. You might be interested to know that I do not benefit financially from our endeavors in any way."

"How noble of you."

"Not at all; I have nothing against making money. I simply have other motives."

"Such as?"

"Justice."

Nick slumped back against the booth. "Routine salvaging," he said. "That's what this is all about, isn't it?"

"Very good, Dr. Polchak. That's one of the things I admire about you—you have the most remarkable facility for making *connections*."

Nick leaned closer again. "As I understand it, routine salvaging has to do with dead people. These people you're stealing organs from—they're still alive. I find it slightly ironic that you call yourself an *ethicist*."

"Really? Why?"

"Has it ever occurred to you that what you're doing is . . . *wrong*?"

Zohar let out a sigh. "Let's talk about right and wrong, shall we? Suppose a man puts a gun to his head—a man with an otherwise healthy body. That one man's organs, tissues, and corneas could benefit more than *two hundred* people—and yet that man is allowed to take his life-saving tissues to the grave, simply out of selfishness or neglect. He's allowed to kill himself *and* someone else."

"That's his right."

"Two wrongs don't make a right, Dr. Polchak. Let me describe the scenario another way: A wealthy man lies dying; he calls his three closest friends to his bedside. He tells them, 'I'm going to take it with me.' He hands each of them an envelope containing a million dollars in cash. He says, 'At the graveside, as they're shoveling in the dirt, I want each of you to throw in his envelope.' At the funeral, each of them does as the man requested—he dutifully tosses his envelope in with the casket. Later, the three men meet to confer. The first one says, 'I have a confession to make: I kept fifty thousand dollars for myself.' The second says, 'I kept a hundred thousand.' The third man says, 'I'm surprised at both of you—I threw in a check for the full amount.'"

Nick said nothing.

"I'm disappointed. I thought you would have more of a sense of humor."

"I guess I'm not in the mood for jokes right now."

"It wasn't a joke, Dr. Polchak, it was a parable. The question behind the parable is: would *you* have thrown in the envelope? Because people do it every day—and I consider it a crime."

"More of a crime than what *you're* doing? Taking the lives of innocent people?"

"Innocent people? Look a little closer. The donor who lost his life in an apparent drive-by shooting—he was a family man, yes? A husband and a father. Did you also know that he was compulsively violent? That his loving wife refused to leave him, even though she had to undergo plastic surgery *twice* to repair the damage to her face? In time, he might have taken her life; instead, he saved one.

"And the donor who suffered the apparent heart attack, the one who was discovered lying facedown in a gutter—did you know he spent most of his adult life in a gutter? That's right, he was a hopeless alcoholic. His liver was almost certainly cirrhotic; fortunately, we're only in the kidney business—for now, that is."

"How do you know all this?"

"Do you know what I do for a living, Dr. Polchak? Do you know what I've done for the last forty years? I collect information about people—and I make connections, just as you do. And just like you, I'm very good at it."

"And that's how you justify all this? As some kind of social cleanup campaign?"

"Not at all. I'm simply saying that our selection process involves far more than financial considerations; there are ethical concerns as well. Yes, Dr. Polchak, *ethical* concerns. You may find it hard to believe, but I have an ethics board of my own, and we meet before every donor selection. I'm not a barbarian, you know. I simply draw a moral distinction between *worthwhile* lives and *useless* lives—between givers and takers. My goal is to save worthwhile lives—ideally, by taking the most worthless life I can find in trade. And with three hundred thousand people to draw from, I'm finding quite a few."

"How can you decide whose life is useless and whose is worthwhile? What gives you the right?"

"I have no *right*, as you call it; what I have is what Nietzsche called 'the will to power.' We live in a society that lacks the will to do what's best for its citizens—so I'm doing it *for* them. Try to see the larger picture here; try to understand what I'm after. This is about infinitely more than whether rich Mr. Vandenborre gets his kidney or not. Remember Prohibition? The Volstead Act declared the consumption of any alcoholic beverage to be illegal. If you think about it, it was a perfectly good law. Think of the reduction in alcohol-related crimes, automobile accidents—even domestic violence. The problem was with *demand*; the sheer demand for alcohol eventually led to the repeal of Prohibition through the Twenty-First Amendment.

"That's how it works, Dr. Polchak—demand creates law. I've shown a handful of the very wealthy that they can do more than wait around to die like dumb livestock; their demand can create a supply. I am, if you will, a kind of biological bootlegger. And as I extend this offer to more and more of the six thousand people who die on the waiting list each year, the victims of an antiquated ethical system, the demand will grow—and when it does, the laws will change. That's what I'm after, Dr. Polchak. I want to save six thousand lives a year—and if I have to do it at the expense of a handful of miscreants and reprobates, then so be it. You may call that unethical; I call it a greater good."

"I've got a parable for you," Nick said. "Three cowboys ride into town. The first cowboy ties his horse to the second horse, the second ties his horse to the third, and all three horses run off together. Why? Because none of the horses was tied to the hitching post."

Zohar shook his head. "You've been talking with Dr. Paulos, haven't you? I'm afraid he's infected you with a rather old-fashioned ethical system."

"I've always thought there was a difference between *old* and *old-fashioned*. Ian Paulos believes that all individuals have value—not because of their performance, but because they're made in the image of God. I find something very timely about that; it seems to keep the horses in check."

"Horses are born to run, Dr. Polchak."

"Horses need riders, or there's no telling where they'll run. How many times in history has someone looked past the individual to see some *greater good* that later turned out to be a disaster? Sorry, Dr. Zohar, I don't buy it."

"So you're adamantly opposed to what I'm doing? You think I'm misguided? Demented? Deceived?"

"I think you're a murderer—nothing more."

"Let's put this philosophical commitment of yours to the test, shall we? After all, 'virtue untested is not virtue at all.'"

"Don't tell me—you're going to offer me a position with your company."

"I wouldn't insult your intelligence. Tell me: how is Dr. McKay's health?"

Nick stiffened.

"I only ask, of course, because of the seriousness of her situation. You're aware, of course, that Riley McKay is dying."

Nick almost stood up. He caught himself and did his best to regain the appearance of ease. "That's a lie," he said.

"I can show you the transplant list for the University of Pittsburgh Medical Center if you like—a list she's been on for more than six years now."

Nick paused. *Leo.*

"Are you just learning this now? How very awkward. I have to say I'm a little surprised, since I understand that your relationship with Dr. McKay has become . . . personal."

Nick suddenly realized that he was slowly shaking his head. He stopped.

"End-stage renal disease is such a sad affair. The body begins to run down, the kidneys no longer able to purify the blood of all its pollutants. Like the rivers of Pittsburgh used to be—yes, that's a very good analogy. Choked with pollution, poisoned by toxins, life slowly ceases. What a tragedy that would be, considering what an outstanding human being Dr. McKay has become—but I don't have to tell you that, now, do I? I'm afraid she's in quite a predicament; she has a very rare compatibility problem that will make it virtually impossible for her to obtain her transplant in time—by conventional means."

"What are you asking me to do—trade someone else's life for Riley's?"

"I'm not asking you to do anything at all. All I'm saying is: Don't underrate your influence. Never underestimate the power of love. And let's not forget the influence that Riley McKay's death would have on *you.* Why, you've just barely come out of your cocoon, haven't you? Your new wings are barely dry. You've entrusted your heart to someone for the first time in—how long has it been, Dr. Polchak? And now she's going to be taken away from you, and who knows what you'll do then. You might very well crawl right back into that shell of yours and never come out again—and who could blame you?"

Nick stared at Zohar's face, but his eyes wouldn't focus. In his ears he heard an even, buzzing sound.

Zohar smiled. "That's another skill of mine—I know people. When you walk into a hospital waiting room; when you interrupt a family freshly grieving over the loss of a loved one; when you have less than an hour to find a way to say to them, 'I want your husband's liver and pancreas—someone is waiting for them across town'; then you learn to read every facial expression, you learn every nuance of posture and voice. And when I look at you, Dr. Polchak, do you know what I see? I see *fear*."

"Funny," Nick said, "that's what I was about to say to you."

"Me? And why should I be afraid?"

"I'd say you have plenty of reason. My friend Leo—the man you had murdered—he always left his windows open. When I found his body on the floor, I noticed mosquitoes all over his walls. I collected those mosquitoes, and I extracted the blood from their guts—blood from the man who killed my friend. When your boy Santangelo followed us to Tarentum the other night, I broke into his car and took his water bottle. I have a sample of his DNA, Dr. Zohar, and when I match it against the blood from those mosquitoes, I'll be able to prove that he was in the room the night my friend was murdered."

Zohar clapped his hands in delight. "Dr. Polchak, believe me, you have my most profound respect and admiration. But let's reexamine this little plan of yours. You say you'll be able to prove that Mr. Santangelo was in the room the night your friend was murdered—But why shouldn't he be? After all, you were interfering with an FBI investigation—he had contacted your little group before. And these mosquitoes of yours—can they tell you if Mr. Santangelo arrived *before* or *after* your friend expired?"

Nick said nothing.

"That seems a rather important point. And one other little item: have you considered that those mosquitoes may also contain samples of *other* DNA: your friend's, Dr. McKay's . . . even your own? Now what will the authorities make of that?"

Nick's thoughts raced, but they settled on nothing. His mind was a fog; Zohar's words ricocheted inside his skull like small-caliber bullets.

Zohar looked down at his plate again and picked up his knife and fork. "I wouldn't worry about Mr. Santangelo if I were you; I'd worry about Dr. McKay. Because she's going to die, Dr.

Polchak, she is most certainly going to die—unless *we* do something about it."

Nick slowly rose from the table. To his surprise, his legs were unsteady. He looked down at Zohar. "One last thing: What about Sarah McKay? What's her social drawback? Why was she chosen as one of your donors?"

Zohar squinted at him. "Is it possible that you're not as clever as I thought?"

Nick stared at him blankly, his eyes darting like the fireflies on the Tarentum Plateau.

"Well, I could talk all day," Zohar said, "but as you can see, my lunch is growing cold. And besides—don't you have some mosquitoes to catch?"

Nick turned to the door and staggered out.

CHAPTER
42

Nick looked at his watch again. It was almost six o'clock now, ten minutes later than the last time he looked. He folded his arms and slumped despondently in the chrome-and-plastic chair. Across the hallway, a bulletin board was push-pinned full of departmental notices regarding fall registration, graduate teaching schedules, and a hundred other bits of minutiae relevant to graduate-student life. Nick had read all of them—several times.

He heard a sound; he jumped up from his chair. A student rounded the corner and padded quietly down the long corridor toward Nick, thoroughly absorbed in a fall course catalog.

"Have you seen Sanjay Patil?" Nick called out to him.

"Excuse me?"

"Dr. Sanjay Patil—he's a professor of molecular biology here."

"Sorry. I never had him."

"You don't have to take a class from him to know who he is. Have you seen him? I'm trying to locate him."

"Have you tried his office?"

Nick slumped down on the chair again and rocked back against the wall. "Try his *office*—now, why didn't I think of that? Look in the most obvious place first! And here I picked the most obscure place I could think of, just hoping he might wander by. Thank heaven you happened by—I might have been here all week."

The student avoided eye contact as he passed by.

Nick glanced at his watch. He bolted out of his chair again, sending it clattering across the linoleum floor. He turned to the door beside him and tried the knob; it was locked, just as it was the last six times he tried it. He cupped his hands and peered through the glass into the darkened room. The laboratory was a molecular biologist's toyland, complete with an ultracentrifuge, an electron microscope, a PhosphorImager, an X-ray diffractometer, and two state-of-the-art Applied Biosystems PRISM 377 DNA sequencers. The lab had everything a researcher could ever want—except for one critical, missing element: Dr. Sanjay Patil.

Nick began to pace the long corridor, his footsteps echoing behind him in the evening stillness. He thought again about Julian Zohar's words. Was it true? Was Riley really dying of her kidney disease? Would Leo purposely remove her name from UPMC's transplant waiting list, hiding the truth from him? He thought about Leo, and he knew instantly that he would. He would have done it to protect Riley—he would have done it to protect *him*. That was Leo—always trying to protect someone, but in his trusting and unsuspecting manner, unable to protect himself.

Riley. Is that what she tried to tell him last night? Is that what she meant when she said, "There's something you don't know about me"? Is that why she constantly pulled away from him, half-surrendering and half-resisting his advances? But why didn't she tell him long ago? Why didn't she trust him with this? Did she think he'd run away, refusing to get involved with a doomed woman? Or maybe she thought he would love her all the more—like a martyr—out of pity—as a service. Somewhere in his mind, a light began to dimly glow. He remembered something Leo used to say: "The heart has reasons that the mind knows nothing of." Zohar was right: Nick had a remarkable facility for making connections—but not connections like this.

Was it true what Zohar said—that Riley would never find a kidney through the official allocation system? "She is most certainly going to die," he said, "unless we do something about it." He felt a bead of cold sweat run down his back. He had been asked to make a deal with the devil himself—hadn't he? "I'm not asking you to do anything," Zohar said—but wasn't he? *The devil never asks,* Nick thought; *he just reaches into your mind and creates fear or panic or desperation, and before you know it, the deal is done.*

For the last four hours Nick had visited a very dark place within himself—a place he barely knew existed. Could he sit idly by and watch Riley die, her precious lifeblood slogging to a standstill like some toxic river? Nick had risked his own life a hundred times, but the life of someone else—the life of someone he *loved*—that was a different matter. Would he do nothing to save her? Wasn't her life worth more than that of some despicable wife-abuser or a hopeless gutter bum? Wasn't her life worth more than . . . *anything*? "Let's test this philosophical commitment of yours," Zohar said. Nick shivered; the stench of sulfur was all over him.

And what if she did die? What then? Zohar's words flew in his face like a spray of acid. "She's going to be taken away from you, and who knows what you'll do then? You might very well crawl back into that shell of yours and never come out again." Did Zohar really know what was in Nick's heart? Had Nick become that obvious, that transparent? Or were his insights just an educated guess by a master manipulator, an off-the-cuff cold reading by the king of all con men? It didn't matter; either way, his words hit way too close to home.

Nick felt like an embarrassed child exposed in some shameful misdeed. He felt ravaged, he felt violated. He *felt*; that was the problem. For the first time in years he had opened his heart, and where had it got him? His work was sloppy, his thinking muddled. He had been a step behind Zohar from the very beginning —no, not a step, a *mile*. Now here he was to drop off Santangelo's DNA, the last of his physical evidence—and was it all for nothing? He tried to remember Zohar's words. Did Santangelo have a perfect excuse for being there that night? Could he claim that he visited Leo *before* the murder—could the blood from the mosquitoes prove nothing more? Worst of all, could Leo's death be blamed on Nick himself? He tried to focus his mind; he tried to sort out all the complexities of these options. But he was so tired, and he was in so much pain—more pain than he had felt in years. All he could do was push on and hope to somehow sort it all out along the way.

He heard footsteps from the opposite end of the hallway. He turned to see Sanjay Patil rounding the corner toward him. "Nick," he said simply.

"Where have you been?" Nick shouted. "I've looked everywhere for you—I've been waiting for hours!"

"Let me see." Sanjay handed his attaché case to Nick, who held it out for him like a tray. He flipped the brass latches, lifted the lid slightly, and peeked inside. "There it is—yes, I thought so—I have a *life*." He closed the lid and took the attaché back again. "You should get one yourself," he said. "I recommend it highly." He turned to the laboratory door and searched for his keys.

"Sanjay, this is a matter of life or death!"

"That is what your messages said—*all* of them—the ones you left at my office and on my pager and on my e-mail and with my research assistant and the *four* you left on my answering machine at home."

"Where have you been all day?"

"Have you ever heard of a *day off*? It is a fascinating new concept introduced to the Western world sometime in the last three millennia."

"I thought you'd come in *some* time today."

"Ah. You see, you misunderstand the concept of the *day off*. The idea is to *not* come in—to not work at all, all day long. A radical idea, is it not?" He pushed open the door and looked at Nick. "Do you know that you *filled* my answering machine with your messages? My wife called. She tried to leave me a message, a reminder to pick up my daughter from cello practice. But she could not, because of all *your* messages."

"So your daughter got an extra hour of cello practice."

"*Two* hours."

"Oh. Well, that's how you get to Carnegie Hall."

Sanjay squinted at him. "What is my daughter's name?"

"What?"

"My daughter—what is her name? What is my *wife's* name?"

"Mrs. Patil?"

"You see? That is the problem with you, Nick Polchak. Everything is *work* for you—everything is life or death. You will never respect the lives of other people until you get a life of your own."

"Sanjay, I'm *trying* to get a life of my own—but I'm about to lose it if you don't help me."

Sanjay studied his face. "Truly? Life or death?"

"Truly."

He stepped into the lab and flipped on the light switch. Bank after bank of fluorescents hummed on, flooding the room in blue white light. Nick picked up the water bottle from the floor beside his chair and followed.

"I have the results for you," Sanjay said. "We were able to identify four separate DNA sequences from the mosquitoes you captured."

"Great. Now I want you to do a sequence on this." He handed him the water bottle.

"What is this?"

"It should contain trace amounts of saliva. I want you to separate it in your centrifuge and then run it through one of your sequencers. I'm looking for a match with one of the four DNA samples from the mosquitoes."

Sanjay frowned. "But we already have a match."

"What are you talking about?"

"You brought me the mosquitoes preserved in alcohol, sealed in a plastic bag—yes? You said you were searching for a match."

"That's right—a match with *this*."

"I assumed you had given me all your samples. We already found your match."

Now Nick looked confused. "A match with what?"

Sanjay turned to the counter and picked up the Ziploc bag. He slipped on a pair of latex gloves, opened the bag, and carefully removed a single blond hair.

"With this," he said. "There were four of them in the bag with the specimen jar."

Nick turned for the door and ran.

CHAPTER
43

You throw like a girl," Sarah said. "Watch me."

She sailed the walnut-sized rock toward the side of the building; it struck the corrugated siding with a metallic *clack* just inches from the single remaining windowpane. They stood in the road beside the Mencken Breaker, the multitiered structure once responsible for crushing large, sooty lumps of anthracite into smaller, cleaner nuggets. True to its name, at any given time half the windows in the Breaker were broken. Now, years after the mine had been abandoned and the building closed down, just a single piece of glass remained. Sarah reached down for another stone.

"Let it be," Riley said. "If it's lasted this long, maybe it deserves to live."

Daylight was almost gone now. The bony pile, hiding the sun behind its jagged crest, cast a premature gloom across the roadway. They started back toward home, past the old barracks where the single miners once lived, taking the same path their father had taken ten thousand times on his way home from the Mencken Mine. Riley stared at the gravel path, imagining that she was placing her feet in exactly the same ruts and furrows that her father once followed. Ruts and furrows—that's what a coal town was made out of—and once in them, it was almost impossible to escape.

"Remember summer mornings?" Sarah said. "If you slept with the windows open, you woke up with a ring of soot around your nose."

Riley nodded.

"And the water in the sink always had a layer of coal dust on it. Remember that?"

Riley said nothing. Sarah frowned.

"And the mountain lions—they used to sweep down from the hillsides and carry off the small children for dinner."

Riley nodded, then stopped abruptly. "What children?"

"Where *are* you? You haven't been paying attention all day."

"I've got a lot on my mind."

Sarah shook her head. "You always were a worrier."

"It's part of being a big sister. It comes with the territory."

"No, it's part of being a *mom*—that came with the territory too, didn't it? But you're not my mom, Riley—you never were."

Riley hooked her arm through Sarah's. "Can't a girl look out for her baby sister?"

"I'm not your baby sister anymore; I should be looking out for you now."

"For me? Why?"

"Well, let's see. Hmm. That's a tough one. Wait—I know. How about the fact that you're dying, and I'm not?"

Riley dropped her arm. "I'm not dying," she said.

"C'mon, Riley, get real. Have you heard anything from UPMC Presby?"

"You know I haven't. The odds are a million to one."

"So what are you going to do?"

"What can I do? It's called a *waiting* list, Sarah—there's a reason for that."

They walked in silence for the next few minutes.

"I like Nick," Sarah said.

"Really? What do you like about him?"

"He's intense. Especially those eyes of his—they're spooky."

"I like them. When he really looks at you . . ."

Sarah nodded. "I think Nick's the best one you've brought home in a long time. Do you love him?"

Riley looked mildly annoyed.

"What's the matter?" Sarah said. "Can't a girl look out for her big sister?"

"It's just that . . . it's kind of hard to say."

"Stop being a weasel. Do you love him or not?"

Riley glared at her, but her countenance slowly softened, and she finally nodded.

"Then say it. Say, 'I love Nick.'"

"Cut it out, Sarah."

"Go on—tell the truth and shame the devil."

"I don't have to say it."

"You don't mean it 'til you say it."

"I thought you weren't a baby anymore. You can be so *annoying*."

"Chicken. Coward. Yellow belly."

"OK!" Riley said, turning to face her. "I love him! There, are you satisfied? I love Nick Polchak!" She stopped abruptly, stunned by the force of her own admission.

Sarah paused. "Does he love you?"

Riley rolled her eyes. "How am I supposed to know?"

"He hasn't told you yet?"

"Well, not in so many words."

"Not in *words*? How did he tell you, in smoke signals?"

Riley turned away and started down the road again. "I don't want to talk about this anymore."

"Well, *I* do," Sarah said, following right on her heels. "So you think he loves you?"

"I think he has a hard time saying it."

"Why?"

"I don't think love is his primary language."

"That's a crock. Men always say that."

"He didn't say that—that's just what *I* think. Nick comes from a pretty rough background."

"What is *this* place, Shangri-la?"

Riley stopped and looked at her. "Sarah, Nick has been hurt in the past."

"Oh, Riley, not another three-legged dog."

"No, it's not like that. He just needs . . . we *both* need to take it slow, that's all."

Sarah put her hands on her hips. "You haven't told him, have you? Nick doesn't know you're dying."

"He knows I'm sick—nothing more."

"He has a right to know, Riley."

"It's not that easy," she grumbled.

"'Nick, I'm dying—I thought you should know.' Sounds easy enough to me."

"Easy for you, maybe—you're not the one who's dying. When was I supposed to say this, Sarah? 'Hello, Nick, I'm Riley. It's so nice to meet you; by the way, I'm dying, so don't get too close.' Or maybe after the first date: 'I had a nice time tonight, Nick. If you want to ask me out again, you'd better make it fast—I'm dying.'"

"Come on, Riley, you know what I mean."

"I didn't want his pity, OK? And to be honest, I didn't want to run him off either. For the first time in years I met a perfectly wonderful guy, someone who's just as weird and twisted as I am, and I wanted to know if we had a chance together—just as *people*. Is that so wrong?"

"Would you?" Sarah said. "Have a chance together, I mean?"

"I think we would," Riley said, "if only."

Sarah paused. "All the more reason to live."

"Do you think I *want* to die?"

"Everybody talks about the weather, but nobody does anything about it."

"What is it I'm supposed to do, Sarah? You tell me."

"OK, I will. How about moving to another transplant region—rich people do it all the time. Somewhere where you can be higher on the list, somewhere where there's more placement activity."

"More activity than Presby? You must be kidding—it's one of the top transplant centers in the country. Besides, Sarah, I can't just pack up and move—I've got a career to think about."

"Dead women don't have careers. How about moving overseas, have you ever thought of that? Someplace where the procurement laws are more flexible—somewhere where your odds might improve."

"You expect me to move *overseas*? Be serious."

"I *am* being serious. You said it yourself, your odds are one in a million here. Well, that's not good enough, Riley. You can't just sit around and wait to die."

Riley kicked stubbornly at the ground. "Well, it's my life."

"Sorry—it's not that simple. I love you, Riley, and so does Nick. That means a piece of your life belongs to me, and a piece belongs to him. You can't just take your ball and go home—you have a responsibility to both of us."

"I'm *sick* of responsibility."

"Well that's just too bad. Welcome to Mencken, Riley, welcome *home*. It's a world of responsibility—it always has been and it always will be. You have to *do* something to improve your chances. You've gone the conventional route—now you need to consider extreme measures."

"This all seems so simple to you, doesn't it?"

"You think it's hard to be the one who's dying? Try being the one who has to live—the one who has to stay behind. You're all I have in the whole world, Riley. Did you ever think of that? If you die, my whole world dies with you."

Riley looked into her sister's eyes; she saw the love, the devotion, the same furious intensity that used to fill her own eyes before her blood began to grow tainted and her spirit began to leech away. Now the last of her energy was leaving her—even her grief—and exhaustion weighed her down like a suit of armor. Her head throbbed, and her entire body felt like one dull ache. She threw her arms around her sister's neck—less out of affection than to support her own failing legs—and she began to gently weep.

"Oh, Sarah, what am I going to do?"

"You're going to live," Sarah said, "even if it kills us both."

They turned together toward the house, Sarah half-dragging, half-carrying her sister the last quarter mile. They struggled up the front steps together.

"When was your last dialysis?" Sarah said, pushing open the front door.

"Five days ago."

"That's too long. We need to—"

They stopped.

Standing in the center of the room, pointing a handgun directly at them, was Cruz Santangelo. He looked at Sarah.

"Hello, Angel," he said.

CHAPTER 44

Santangelo motioned them into the room.

"Ordinarily, I'd tell you to shut the door," he said. "But out here in the sticks I don't suppose it matters—does it, Angel?"

"Shut up, Cruz," Sarah said.

Riley looked from her sister to Santangelo and back again. She stared at Sarah wild-eyed, but Sarah refused to meet her gaze. Slowly, understanding began to break over her in pummeling waves.

"You're the one . . . the woman with the red hair. But then you must have . . . oh, Sarah, what have you done?" Riley sank down on the floor.

"Those were lousy directions," Santangelo said. "I thought I made a wrong turn somewhere. Do you know this place isn't even on the map anymore?"

Sarah lifted her sister to her feet and helped her to a chair—then she turned to Santangelo and held out her hand for the gun.

Santangelo shook his head. "Sorry—you *are* sisters, after all."

"You won't need the gun," Sarah said.

"I hope not—but then, that's up to you, isn't it?"

"We have a deal, remember?"

"Sure—the same deal we had in Tarentum." Santangelo looked at his watch. "You've got ten minutes."

Sarah helped Riley struggle to her feet again; they turned toward the back hallway.

"Whoa," Santangelo said. "Where do you think you're headed?"

"The kitchen," Sarah said. "Do you mind? This is personal—we'd like a little privacy."

Santangelo shrugged and took a seat on Riley's chair. "Make it fast. There's not much to do around here."

In the kitchen, Sarah deposited Riley in a chair and stood at the counter across from her. Riley looked up at her sister in unbelieving horror.

"Tell me it's all a mistake," Riley said. "Tell me he's confusing you with someone else."

"*You're* confusing me with someone else—with a baby sister who doesn't exist anymore. I've grown up a lot lately, Riley."

"Oh, Sarah—in God's name *why*?"

"To get you your kidneys, of course. Didn't you hear what I said back there? It's time to consider extreme measures."

"Like killing someone else to save my own life? Did you think I'd ever agree to something like that?"

"You were never supposed to *know*. When we found a match for you, all we had to do was make sure he had a donor card—we could have let his kidneys come up for transplant through the regular system. With your compatibility problem, you would have been number one on the match list. You would have gotten your kidneys, Riley, and you never would have known. That was the deal I made; that's why I agreed to work for them."

"And who would this 'donor' have been, Sarah? A mother? Someone's husband? A woman my age with a sister just like you? Would you really trade my life for someone else's?"

"You don't understand. When they pick a donor, they consider more than medical factors. The man in the drive-by shooting—he was a wife-beater, did you know that? Do you know why he pulled over in that alley in Homewood? Not to change *his* tire, to change *mine*. I stood there by my car in a low-cut dress looking helpless—looking *available*—and he practically skidded to a stop. Do you think he would have stopped if I was old or ugly or overweight? Not a chance. That guy owed his wife a debt he could never repay, but there he was trying to hit on a younger woman. Are you asking me if I would trade that scumbag's life for yours? I'd trade *ten* of him for you."

"And what about your *clients*?" Riley said. "What do you know about them? Is Mr. Vandenborre some kind of angel? How does he treat *his* wife? Does he have an eye for younger women too—or is he even worse than that? You have no idea at all, do you?"

"I don't know—and I don't care. I know *you*, Riley. I love *you*. You've been my whole world since I was a little girl. What was I supposed to do, just stand by and watch you die?"

"So you find a match for me, and you help commit another murder; then I get my kidneys, and I marry Nick, and we all live happily ever after—is that the picture? Only we wouldn't all be happy, would we, Sarah? Because you couldn't live with yourself. You'd end up just like this town—burning underground, smoke seeping out through cracks, ready to collapse at any time. How many people have you helped murder?"

"No more than necessary."

"*Necessary*? Necessary for what—for me to live? For you to keep your happy family? Remember that verse from Sunday school: 'What does it profit a man to gain the whole world, and lose his own soul?'"

"First we save your life," Sarah said. "I'll worry about my soul later."

"I worry about *my* soul all the time—it comes with dying."

"You need to start thinking about the future."

"Dying *is* the future—it's everybody's future. So now what, Sarah? Why are we here in the kitchen? What is Santangelo expecting you to do? Are you supposed to try to change my mind about all of this? Are you supposed to *convince* me? Is that what these ten minutes are for?"

Sarah pulled out the chair across from Riley and slowly sat down. "It's a little more complicated than that. I didn't *ask* to work for these people, Riley—I never knew they existed. They asked *me*. Now, why do you suppose they did that? They liked the way I looked, sure. They also liked the fact that I've been a surgical nurse; but most of all, they knew I would have a motive. They knew about *you*, Riley. These people know everything—they're incredibly thorough."

"You could have said *no*."

"Could I? Remember about a week ago, that wealthy woman from Sewickley—the one who drowned? What was her name . . . Heybroek, wasn't that it?"

"I remember," Riley said. "I assisted on her autopsy."

"Funny, isn't it, a woman in a wheelchair falling into her own swimming pool? How careless of her. She didn't slip, Riley, she was pushed—but I don't suppose that showed up in the autopsy, now, did it? Do you want to know her *real* cause of death? She said *no* to Julian Zohar. He approached her about being a client, and she turned him down. But then she knew about the system, and Zohar couldn't have that—so she had to have an 'accident.' Do you understand what I'm saying? That's what happens when someone tells them *no*."

"You could have agreed at first—then you could have gone to the authorities later."

"I could have; I didn't *want* to. They knew me, Riley; they did their homework well. They offered me a chance to save your life—without you ever knowing about it—and I jumped at it. I *wanted* to say yes." Sarah reached across the table, took both her sister's hands, and looked intently into her eyes. "I wasn't talking about me, Riley. I was talking about you. *You* can't say no."

Riley jerked her hands away. "What are you telling me—that they're offering me my kidneys, and if I say no they'll kill me? Are you joking? Sarah, I'm dying anyway! What difference do a few months make?"

"It's not that simple. They're not just offering you your kidneys, Riley—they're offering you a *job*."

Riley's jaw dropped open.

"It's Lassiter," Sarah said. "He's an idiot. He's put the entire process at risk—he's the reason *you* caught on in the first place. They need a person at the coroner's office, Riley. They need someone to replace Lassiter."

"And what happens to Lassiter?"

Sarah shrugged. "Does he own a pool?"

"So that's the deal: I get my kidney, so I can no longer turn them in; then I spend the rest of my life working at the coroner's office, covering up strange little anomalies, passing off deliberate murders as accidental deaths. Are you out of your mind, Sarah? What in the world would ever motivate me to do such a thing?"

Sarah's eyes brimmed with tears. "Try this for starters: If you don't, they'll kill us *both*."

Riley stumbled out of her chair and reached for the counter to steady herself; Sarah was right behind her.

"When you and Nick started poking around—when you uncovered the system—they knew they had to deal with both of you. But with you they saw another option; they saw the chance to replace Lassiter. That's why they agreed to give me a chance to talk with you. That's why we came after you in Tarentum."

"You *called* him," Riley said. "You called Santangelo from the motel in Tarentum—and *you* were the one who wanted to come to Mencken!"

"They wanted us to get away. They wanted a quiet place where we could have some time together, where we would have a chance to talk."

"And if things didn't work out, they wanted a quiet place where they could *kill* us! And what about Nick, Sarah? What deal are they planning to offer him?"

Sarah said nothing.

"That's just great. Do you understand the choice you've given me? To live with you or to die with Nick. Well, I love Nick too, Sarah."

Sarah glanced nervously at her watch. "I tried to save your life," she said. "Now you have to save us both."

Riley turned on her. "Don't you put this on me! I was the only one dying here. Now you've killed us both—*and* Nick—and *Leo*! Oh, Sarah, Leo! If only you'd *known* him. I'll *never* forgive you for that!"

"It would have worked," Sarah grumbled.

"Then what would have happened, Sarah? Did you really think they'd let you stop working for them? That they'd let you *retire*? What would have happened when you started to get a little older, or when you gained a few too many pounds—when the men would no longer pull over just to get a better look? You would have turned up in some swimming pool yourself."

"I didn't care," she said. "It was for a greater good."

Riley took her sister by the shoulders. "Listen to me. The greatest good is the good that's right in front of your nose. You cannot take an evil path to a good goal."

"All I did was love you."

"That's the problem, Sarah—all you did was love *me*. You've got to love something *more* than me, something greater, or even love gets twisted."

Sarah held out her watch. "Time's up. What are we going to tell Santangelo?"

Riley paced back and forth across the kitchen, her mind racing. "We have to buy some time," she said. "We'll tell him I agreed—that I bought the whole thing."

"These people are not idiots, Riley. Santangelo doesn't *want* this to work out—he despises loose ends; he'd rather kill us both and be done with it. If he detects the slightest hesitation on your part, if he picks up any hint of deception . . . all he wants to do is go back to Zohar and say, 'It didn't work. I took care of it.' Can you look Santangelo in the eye and convince him—unless you really mean it?"

Riley shook her head, trying to sort through the barrage of thoughts.

Sarah took her by the arm. "This can still work," she whispered. "You're right, we need to buy time—so take your kidneys, Riley, do that much—we can negotiate from there. Even about Nick—who knows what we might be able to work out?"

Riley twisted her arm free.

"Nick is coming back here," Sarah said. "If you say no, he'll be dead the minute he walks in the door. Do you really love him, Riley? You're the only one who can save him—you're the only one who can save us all."

Riley lunged for the back door.

"Where are you going?"

"I'm going to save my soul," she said. "I'll worry about my life later."

"You can't run—not in your condition."

"It's a world of responsibility, Sarah—I can do anything I *have* to do."

"He'll follow you."

"Not where I'm going."

"Riley, he'll *follow* you—you don't know him."

She started out into the darkness.

"I won't be here if you make it back," Sarah called after her. "When he realizes you've run, I'm finished."

Riley didn't look back. She kept moving forward with all of her remaining strength, heading for the base of the bony pile. Now she was just a distant shadow, and Sarah called out to her sister for the last time.

"I love you, Riley."

Santangelo charged into the kitchen and saw Sarah alone, standing in the doorway, facing the empty darkness. "Where is she?" he demanded.

"She ran."

She heard his footsteps approach quickly. There was a moment of silence, and then she heard the click of a revolver hammer behind her head. She closed her eyes and waited . . .

She heard a second click, and then he pushed by her into the doorway. "I'm going after her," he said. "You wait here. If that Bug Man comes back, you do anything you have to do to hold him here until I get back, understand? No more screwups, Angel. Do this right, and I just might let you live."

He disappeared into the darkness.

CHAPTER
45

Nick plowed through the barricades without stopping. They seemed to explode, sending splintered chunks of black-and-white wood clattering across the hood and over the roof. He kept the gas pedal to the floor, racing through town, the empty shanties whipping past like shuffling cards. As he rounded the last corner, his headlights played across a clump of brush just thirty yards from the house. Hidden behind the brush was a silver sedan with the passenger window open.

He's already here.

He killed his headlights and pulled in behind the sedan. If they were watching for him, it was already too late—in the perfect darkness of Mencken, approaching headlights would stand out like signal flares. He approached the house on foot; no sound of voices came from the house, no flicker of lantern light, no sign of life at all—maybe because there was no life. Nick tasted acid in the back of his throat.

He started to work his way around to the side of the house to try to get a look through a window—but just then, the front door opened and Sarah stepped out. A flashlight swept the ground in front of him.

"Nick! Is that you?"

"Where's Riley?" Nick called back.

"She isn't here! Come inside, we've got to talk!"

"Uh-uh," Nick said. "We'll talk out here."

Sarah ran wildly to meet him; Nick was startled by her apparent recklessness. He searched the surrounding brush, expecting to see an armed figure step out of the shadows at any moment—but Sarah arrived alone. She threw her arms around his neck and let out a sob. "I have to tell you something," she said.

Nick pried her arms from his neck and shoved her away. "I know who you are, Sarah. The mosquitoes that I took to Sanjay—the container was leaking, remember? I asked you for something to put it in. You handed me a plastic bag, but you took out a hairbrush and comb first. You left some of your hair in the bag, Sarah—your *real* hair, not that wig you wear on the job. Sanjay matched your DNA with the blood in the mosquitoes. It was *your* blood, Sarah—you were in the room the night Leo was killed. You're the lure, aren't you? You're the woman with the long red hair."

"That's what I was going to tell you."

"Save it," he said. "There are only two things I want to hear from you—where is Riley, and where is your partner Santangelo?"

"She's climbing up the bony pile—and Santangelo is right behind her! Come on, we've got to go after them!"

"You expect me to *follow* you? Where, Sarah? To some quiet spot where your partner is waiting for me?"

"Nick, this whole town is a 'quiet spot.' If I wanted to kill you, you never would have made it this far. You've got to trust me."

"*Trust* you? The way Leo trusted you?"

"Look, you can think whatever you want about me—but right now someone is trying to kill my sister."

"I know—*you* are."

"Don't be an idiot! Look, there isn't time to explain. Riley is about to *die*, Nick. Now maybe I'm lying to you—but if you love her half as much as I do, you won't be willing to take that chance."

Nick hesitated for only an instant. "Let's go."

"Do you have a gun?"

"Don't *you*?"

"Then how are we going to stop him?"

"I don't know," he said, "but we sure won't stop him standing here."

Nick took off running toward the bony pile, and Sarah was close behind.

Riley stumbled two hundred yards along the mountain's base before finding the first familiar landmark. As a six-year-old girl she had trampled down a sycamore sapling to point the way up—the safe way up. Now it was a full-grown tree, still bowing to the ground in memory of that day. She glanced back over her shoulder and started up the hillside.

The slope felt infinitely steeper than she remembered. Loose bits of coal and shale crumbled under her feet; she seemed to slide back half a step for every one she moved upward. She felt a surge of panic; she was trapped in a childhood nightmare, running as hard as she could to escape an approaching storm, but going nowhere. It was the wind—it wouldn't let her go. It kept tugging on her, holding her, pulling her back.

Even before she had reached the sycamore, her head was pounding and her back was throbbing with pain; now her exhaustion was almost overwhelming. Dull, aching pulses

319

radiated from her failing kidneys like sonar waves, bouncing off the cap of her skull and down through her leaden limbs. She sank down on the hillside, panting, gathering the energy and summoning the will for the next upward advance.

"*Ri-i-i-ley!*"

She spun around in horror.

"*Ri-i-i-ley!*"

The voice sounded distant. He was still at the foot of the mountain, searching for the path she took upward—or was he? Did he only sound distant because he was calling in a quiet voice? Or was it all just a trick of the wind—was he right behind her in the darkness, just a few steps away? She held her breath—but her heart beat so loudly that she was sure the sound alone would give her away.

"I'm coming after you, Riley. I'm not far behind. You can't get away, not in your condition. Don't make me come up there after you—I'll be even angrier when I find you."

She looked down at herself. Thank God her clothing was dark, blending in against the ebony hillside—but her skin! She dug her fingers through the sooty coal, then rubbed her face and neck and arms until only her golden hair stood out in the moonlight—but she had no cap or hood to cover it. She looked up into the sky; ominous clouds passed intermittently across the face of the moon, momentarily blocking its light. Beneath the shadow of each cloud she vanished into the hillside—but when the moon slid out again, her hair lit up like a carbide lantern. She felt a drop of water on her face. She quickly rubbed the spot to cover it again.

She looked farther up the mountain, searching for the next marker: an ancient tangle of wheat-yellow brush that had somehow found a way to survive in the dusty soil. The hillside was dotted with such pockets of life: thorny brambles, twisted trees, and coarse tufts of buffalo grass enduring in meager deposits of soil and clay dumped along with other mine debris.

CHOP SHOP: A Bug Man Novel

Riley spotted the brush, about twenty yards up and as many yards to her left—and then it suddenly disappeared.

To her dismay, Riley saw that in the shadow of a covering cloud *everything* disappeared—every tree, every bush, every life-saving pointer and mark. The only time it was safe to navigate the smoldering hillside was when the moon shone bright—but that's when she herself was most visible. There was only one safe course of action: she would take her bearings in the moonlight, then move as fast as possible the instant darkness fell.

She scrambled for the scraggly brush, but not directly toward it; that was dangerous ground, she remembered—or was it? It had been almost two years since Riley sat on the back porch on a winter day, wrapped in a blanket, sipping coffee, and watching the falling snow map the contours of the underground fire. It had been far longer since she was *on* the bony pile, and from up close all the distances and proportions seemed to change. Was her memory reliable—and how much had the fire progressed in two years' time? She wasn't sure it was safe to move any farther—but she knew it would be fatal to remain where she was.

She headed straight up the mountain until she was even with the brush, then turned at a right angle and moved directly toward it. She ducked down behind the thick growth and listened.

"*Ri-i-i-ley!*"

He was on the hillside now. Riley traced her path back down the mountain; her sliding footsteps looked like craters in the undisturbed coal. And the *sound* she made—her feet, struggling through the crumbling slurry, seemed as loud as a car on a gravel driveway. What was the point in hiding? A blind man could have followed her.

"*Ri-i-i-ley!* Come on, Riley, my shoes are getting dirty. I only want to talk with you—didn't your sister tell you that? If I wanted to kill you, I could have shot you the minute you walked in the door."

Riley looked up the hillside again. Her next goal was a dishwasher-sized lump of limestone thirty yards away. She looked back down the mountain, straining her eyes against the darkness—and she saw movement. In the moonlight, she could almost make out Santangelo's contour not far from her last stopping point. She turned to run—but then she stopped. She looked back at the path between her and Santangelo—not the path *she* had taken, not the *safe* path, but the one that *he* might take—if she called to him.

The idea seemed unthinkable—but what else could she do? She couldn't run from him forever; she could barely run at all. In another few minutes he would close the gap between them, and then—

"Here I am!" she called out from behind the brush. "Come on up and let's talk!"

There was a sharp crack. Riley heard a quick hiss and the sound of scattering rock behind her. Once again darkness fell, and she scrambled up the hill toward the lump of limestone. She heard a second crack—but this time she didn't hear the bullet hit. He was firing wildly, aiming at the sound of her footsteps.

She collapsed behind the boulder and waited. She could hear the *crunch-crunch-crunch* of his footsteps coming up the hill. They stopped; then they started again, moving away from her. Riley pounded her fist against the stone. In the darkness, he had followed the only thing he could see—her own footsteps, leading him safely across cooler ground.

She felt a raindrop on her arm, and then another one. She wiped furiously at the spots with coal dust, but then the drops began to come more quickly. Seconds later, it was a downpour. Washed by the cleansing rain, her fair skin began to reappear like a seashell in a receding tide.

She looked around her. The cloudburst was exposing her

skin, but it was obscuring almost everything else—shapes, motion, even the raking sound of her footsteps. She had to take advantage of this blessing from above; she had to put distance between them—but which way? Up, of course—but there were no longer any markers visible, no signposts to guide her safely on her way. She closed her eyes and tried to assemble a mental map—but it came to her only in fragments and pieces. She sensed the cloudburst already beginning to lose intensity, and she knew she had to go, blind or not. She struggled to her feet and started climbing.

Twenty yards up the hill, then right; forward ten yards—no, a little more than that—then up again. Twenty yards, thirty yards—now left, leaving a wide berth for an especially dangerous section of ground. She stopped; this should be a safe spot. She sagged to her knees, exhausted—and felt a searing pain shoot up both legs. She leapt to her feet again.

Her pants were burned away at the knees, and the skin beneath was charred and blistered. She leaned down and extended her hand; a foot above the ground, the air was like an oven. Did she turn the wrong way? Did she travel too far—or not far enough? Or had the fire beneath her feet eaten away even more of the hillside, rendering her memory useless? She turned one way, and then the other . . . and then she stopped.

Riley stood paralyzed, utterly spent, her entire body throbbing with pain. She could see her heartbeat pulsing in her eyes. She tasted iron in the back of her mouth—was it the coal dust, or was it her own blood? She felt as though she were drifting away from the scene before her, becoming strangely distant, like a woman stepping back from a great picture window. It amazed her that she was somehow still standing. She wondered: don't you fall down when you die?

The rain stopped just as suddenly as it began, leaving her completely exposed on the open hillside. She looked at the sky; the last of the clouds slipped past the moon now, bathing the entire mountain in brilliant light. She looked up the slope; she was almost at the crest of the hill now, standing out in stark relief against the nighttime sky. She looked down at the abandoned buildings of Mencken, standing like little card houses in a darkened room. She saw the stores and the houses and the Breaker and even the old entrance to the mine itself. She saw her entire childhood all at once—and on the horizon, in the distance, she saw the lights of Pittsburgh.

She looked down at the base of the mountain. She imagined two tiny figures, scurrying from side to side, searching for the pathway up the hillside. She knew that they would never find it in time; Sarah didn't know about the sycamore. Sarah never climbed the bony pile as a child; Riley wouldn't let her. You have to look out for your baby sister; that's what big sisters do.

She lowered her eyes again. Just twenty-five yards below her, Cruz Santangelo searched for her in a patch of tall weeds.

"Not there," Riley called. "Not even close."

He turned. His own face was blackened with soot, just like hers, but at this distance Riley could see little white lines coursing down the sides of his face that freshets of sweat had washed clean. He stared up at her. She was so calm, so perfectly at peace. He whirled and pointed his gun at the darkness around him.

"There's nobody else—just me."

Santangelo turned back to her again. He widened his stance, squared his shoulders, and cupped the butt of the revolver in his left hand.

"Come on up," she said. "I'm not going anywhere. You could miss from there."

Santangelo raised the gun and took careful aim. "I bet I wouldn't."

"You're an expert—do it right. You owe me that much."

Santangelo slowly lowered the gun. "You know, you're a lot of trouble."

"I've always been that way. It's a specialty of mine."

He started forward, picking his way slowly across the shifting coal. Ten yards away from her, the ground stopped crumbling under his feet; it became hardened, encrusted, like the excess asphalt they dump on the side of a new road. The soles of his shoes began to make a peeling, sticking sound.

"You're sure you won't change your mind?" he said. "It seems a shame to lose a woman like you."

"It's a great offer—I just don't think I'd like working with a moron like you."

Santangelo smiled. "I have a specialty too. Want to see it?" He flipped open the cylinder of his revolver and slid in two brass cartridges.

Riley's body was like clay now, senseless, unfeeling—but somehow her mind was perfectly clear. Her thoughts seemed to her like the last high-pitched trill a television makes when it blinks off at night and the picture fades away. She raised her eyes and looked past Santangelo, over his shoulder, at a point halfway down the side of the mountain. She saw a solitary figure scrambling up the hillside toward them, oblivious to his own danger.

"I love Nick Polchak," she whispered.

Santangelo slowly raised the gun and pointed it at her head. "I'm going to enjoy this," he said.

She shook her head. "I bet you won't."

She tried to jump—her legs refused. She had no strength left, no power to move at all—so she simply told her legs to go ahead and die. An instant later they gratefully yielded, folding under her like strips of cloth, and she came down hard on the brittle mantle at Santangelo's feet.

■

Halfway up the mountain, Nick heard a howling scream. It was the voice of a man—or was it some kind of animal? It was impossible to tell; at that level of agony, all species seem to share a common voice.

He looked up the hillside near the crest—there, at the place where a moment ago two shadowy figures had stood, was a gaping, orange hole in the side of the mountain. The heat that belched from the jagged opening shook the air, and white-hot embers swirled above it and disappeared into the midnight sky. The glow from the inferno illuminated the hillside all around. Nick searched everywhere.

There was no one.

He sank to his knees and buried his face in his hands.

CHAPTER
46

Nick and Sarah sat across from each other on the wooden floor of the great room, leaning against opposite walls and staring at the empty space between them. They had spent most of the night pacing their own private prisons of grief and regret—but from time to time they talked. During those times Sarah poured out her heart, openly weeping, longing to explain her motives and actions. But if it was understanding she wanted, she didn't get it from Nick.

It was morning now. Their anguish, dulled by utter exhaustion, had begun to cool and crust over like the gaping hole on the crest of the bony pile. Nick lifted his eyes and looked at Sarah, curled in a fetal position against the wall.

"So there was no one else?"

"I already told you."

"Tell me again."

Sarah stiffly raised herself into a sitting position. "Julian Zohar—he's the organizer, he's the one who has access to the waiting lists. Tucker Truett provides genetic and medical information from western PA. Jack Kaplan—he's an ER surgeon at UPMC—he does the removals and transplants. Lassiter is the inside man at the coroner's office. There are two CSIs on the payroll too, but they don't know the whole system. That just leaves Santangelo."

"And *you*," Nick said. "Don't be so modest, Sarah. You were a valuable part of this team."

Sarah said nothing.

Nick leaned back against the wall and stared at the ceiling. It was a smaller operation than he ever imagined. Santangelo was the only contact at the FBI—and there were *none* in the Pittsburgh Police. He and Riley had no idea who they could turn to—they weren't sure that *anyone* was safe—but as it turned out, almost *everyone* was. Zohar was bluffing. He was just a little man who was adept at casting a very large shadow. Nick shook his head in disgust; he felt like vomiting.

Sarah looked at him. "What happens now?"

"Now? That's easy—I turn you over to the police, along with the DNA evidence that puts you in Leo's room the night he was murdered. Then you start squealing like a pig—you start naming names, you try to cut the best deal you can for yourself. Santangelo's already dead—you can blame most of it on him: a deranged federal agent, an ex–Hostage-Rescue-Team member who went over the edge—he *blackmailed* you, he threatened to *kill* you if you didn't help. That's good, Sarah. That just might play—except for one little problem: *me*. I'll be right there, telling them the rest of the story, making sure you get everything you deserve."

"I don't blame you for hating me," Sarah said.

Nick glared at her; his eyes were more than *intense*; they were like two great coal drills, piercing her black walls. "Last night—while you were sitting there—I thought about walking across the room and killing you myself. I *thought* about it, Sarah. I don't mean the idea just passed through my head—I mean I actually considered it."

"So why didn't you?"

"It's too quick," he said. *"Eight hundred degrees*—that's the temperature inside that mountain, did you know that? And it isn't fire exactly—it's more like a barbecue pit, that's what it is. I wonder: Is your body consumed immediately, or do you sort of *cook* first? How long can someone survive in that kind of heat— five seconds? Ten? Santangelo seemed to scream for an awfully long time—but pain is like that, isn't it? It seems to last—"

"Stop it!" Sarah buried her face in her hands and began to weep again.

"Might as well," Nick said. "You'll be thinking about it for the rest of your life anyway—and I hope it's a long life, Sarah, I really do. When the DA pushes for the death penalty, I plan to be there, pleading for leniency. Have pity on the poor girl, make it a life sentence instead—make it *two*—one for Riley and one for Leo. And I plan to visit you in prison, Sarah. I want to see you as the years go by. I want to watch you age *way* before your time; I want to see the way regret eats away at you—I guess that's what they mean when they give you *two* life sentences."

Sarah shuddered. "I can't do that, Nick. I can't."

"You'd be surprised what people can do—when they *have* to."

Sarah looked at him. "What about all the others—what about all the innocent people? Are you willing to destroy all of them too?"

"What innocent people?"

"Come on, Nick, think about it. Zohar is the chief executive officer of COPE—a legitimate organ procurement organization. They're the people who find organs for everybody else—the *honest* way. They're the ones who might have found Riley's kidneys for her, if only the odds had been better. COPE didn't go bad, Zohar did—he's like one of the execs at Enron. Are you planning to punish the whole organization because of what one man decided to do?"

"I guess it can't be helped."

"Can't it? COPE depends on public confidence, Nick. They

need people to donate organs, they need people to *trust* them. They have to fight for every donation, because they're dealing with people's fears. If this whole thing comes out in the open, the loss of confidence will set their work back ten years—not just here, but everywhere. And you know who will be hurt the most? People like Riley; people on waiting lists, praying that other people won't lose faith."

"You picked a fine time to start thinking about all this," Nick said.

"I've been thinking about it all night. What about PharmaGen, Nick? It's a good company—if it survives. Personalized medicines, wonder drugs, new vaccines—I like that vision. But Truett took a shortcut; he needed cash. *Truett* made a mistake, not the whole company—but when this leaks out, the company is finished. What does that do to the future of personalized medicine? What does it do to other companies like PharmaGen, companies with their own population studies in other parts of the country?

"And what about the coroner's office? Lassiter deserves what he gets—but what about the rest of them? These are Riley's people, Nick—she was one of them. What will happen to their budget, their staffing, their fellowship program?"

"It's like a bomb," Nick said. "Innocent bystanders will get hurt." He leaned forward and looked into her eyes. "But whose fault is that?"

"It's *my* fault!" Sarah said. "I'm not blaming you for anything."

She paused.

"I'm just asking you to let me do something about it. Nick, I have a favor to ask."

CHAPTER 47

My friends, I'd like to propose a toast."

Julian Zohar lifted his champagne flute; it sparkled gold and white against the nighttime sky. It was a perfect summer evening at the Point. Every dot of light from the Pittsburgh skyline stood out with crystalline clarity, perfectly reflected in the glassy water of the Allegheny River. The *PharmaGen* yacht lay floating at anchor directly in front of PNC Park. The Pirates were away on a three-day road trip, and the stadium lay black and cavernous before them. The hour was late, and there were no other boats in sight; they were alone on the river, minus the clinging barnacles that tended to collect around their splendid hull.

"To a new day," Zohar said, "and to ever more distant horizons."

They drank together.

"I love this boat," Kaplan said. "I've got to get one of these."

"Well, park it somewhere else," Truett said. "It won't look so good if we all pull up side by side in matching yachts. Besides—these are the hottest wheels in town. Go find your own strip to cruise." They both laughed.

"Where is Santangelo?" Lassiter asked. "What about the—you know—the problem? I want to hear the full report."

"Now, Nathan, calm yourself," Zohar said. "Angel is below deck right now, changing; she assures me that Mr. Santangelo will be joining us shortly. Her preliminary report informs me that everything went according to our expectations. I'm sure she will be more than happy to give us a complete account of her activities presently."

Just then the hatch swung open, and Sarah stepped up onto the deck. She was dressed in red, dressed as she had often been in Santangelo's company—except for the auburn wig. Tonight her blond hair drifted out behind her in the evening breeze.

All the men stared, but Kaplan was the only one to whistle. He held up one hand to block his view of her face. "*This* part I know," he said, "but I'm having a little trouble with the hair."

"Give it a chance," Sarah smiled, walking over to him. "You may learn to like it." She winked, then gave him a quick kiss on the lips.

"Whoa," Kaplan said. "Who lit *your* fire?"

"I do love red," Truett said, admiring her.

She turned to him and ran a finger down the buttons of his shirt. "I know—I wore it just for you." Now she slinked across the deck to where Zohar and Lassiter were standing. "Nathan." She nodded. "You're looking good tonight—as always." She turned to Zohar and offered her hand; he took it, kissed it, and smiled. She gave him a wink and reached for the ice chest. She lifted a champagne flute and drained it.

Now she turned, and every eye was on her.

"Do I have everyone's attention?" she smiled. "I do hope so—I'd hate to think I'm losing my touch. Dr. Zohar has asked me to make a report, and that's just what I'd like to do—only I'd like to expand it a bit. I get so tired of just *business* all the time, don't you? I think a moment like this calls for a few *personal* comments. I do hope you'll all listen. I promise not to bore you."

The men settled back against the railings and grinned.

"I want to thank you," she began, "each and every one of you. This last year has been—how can I describe it? An *education*. I have learned something from each of you, something of inestimable worth, and I want each of you to know what it is.

"Nathan, from you I've learned that no matter how much you have in life, you can always want more. I've learned that greed is really not about money or things at all—it's about *desire*. It's the wanting, not the having. You long for something, you think you'll die if you don't get it—but then when you do, you don't want it anymore. The *desire* is gone, and that's all you really wanted in the first place. The things themselves are insignificant, almost arbitrary—they're just hooks to hang our passions on, aren't they?"

Lassiter glanced uncomfortably at the other men.

"Nathan, you've taught me that it's worth sacrificing everything in pursuit of your desires: your friendships, your family, your reputation, your professionalism. I learned all that from you, Nathan, and I'm a different person because of it."

She held up her glass to him—and then she turned to Kaplan.

"And, Jack—what can I say? From you I've learned that it's possible to treat human beings as if they were inanimate objects—even in a caring profession! Your level of objectivity is astonishing, Jack—you really are above it all, aren't you? I've watched you cut into a man who's been dead for less than three minutes as though he were a med-school cadaver—that's really remarkable. That's what's allowed you to become what you are; that's what's permitted you to reach your incredible level of efficiency. You never let yourself get bogged down in the distractions of compassion or empathy or pity." She raised her glass again. "*Salud*, Jack. Because of you I know what I want, and I know how to get there—and nothing is going to stop me."

Now she looked at Truett.

"Tucker Truett—if ever there was a poster boy for success, it's you. You have so many remarkable gifts: intelligence, vision, business savvy, and let's not forget the package—women do love a nicely wrapped package, don't they? When you take all those gifts and pack them in tight together, it creates a kind of critical mass—an energy source, a *heat*." She held out one hand and wiggled her fingers. "I can feel it all the way over here. You don't lead people, you *compel* them. You're like . . . you're like this boat." She stepped into the cockpit, placing her hands on the wheel as if she were steering. "You're big and you're fast, and wherever you go you draw people into your wake."

She turned and looked at him. Truett smiled back and bowed slightly.

"What I've learned from you, Tucker, is that with the potential for success comes the *need* for success. You're like that big crystal ball in Times Square on New Year's Eve; everybody knows it will drop, everybody waits for it to drop—if it didn't, people would be so disappointed. That's you, Tucker. You're the crystal ball—so bright and so shiny and so ready to drop. You just *have* to make good, don't you? Because if you don't, there will be *shame*—and shame just doesn't fit in that perfect package of yours."

She raised her glass in tribute.

"To you, Tucker. From you I've learned that success is not an option."

Finally, she turned to Zohar. "And how could I forget you? Julian Zohar, our mentor, our founding father—from you I've learned so *many* things. Where do I even begin? I think most of all, I've learned from you that ethics is not about right and wrong or good and evil—it's just a way of talking. It's a way of getting *around* good and evil, really, a way of getting what you want. I've learned that almost anything can be justified in the name of some greater good—and the greater good itself never has to be justified at all. You're a kind of shaman, Julian; you give moral force to people. You give confidence, you give permission—to do right *or* wrong. But then, there's no such thing as *wrong*, is there?

"From you I've learned that you should always pursue the greatest good for the greatest number of people. And if someone is not a part of that 'greatest number,' well, he's just out of luck—because good can't slow down for individual people. You've given me the greatest gift of all, Julian: you've given me power—*moral* power—the kind that only comes once you abandon all sense of morality."

"Now, hold on," Kaplan said. "What about you, Angel? Let's not leave *you* out of this little roast of yours."

"You're right, Jack. That would be a terrible oversight—because I've learned more from myself than I have from any of you. I've learned that when you love something desperately—when you love something more than *anything* else—you'd better be careful what it is. I've learned that there's a kind of 'order of events' in the universe. If you put the right thing first, everything falls in line; if you get it wrong, everything falls apart."

She looked at each of them; no one was smiling now.

"Oh, please don't get the wrong idea. I'm not putting myself above any of you. In fact, that's the lesson I've learned most of all—I *belong* here. We really are a family, aren't we? We really belong together, and I have never felt more a part of this group than I do tonight."

The men began to relax.

"And now," Zohar said, "if we can get on with the—"

"Wait!" Sarah said. "I've forgotten someone—my very own partner, Cruz Santangelo. I have so much to thank him for. None of us appreciates him enough, you know—he's such a multitalented man. From him, I've learned how to kill—something every girl needs to know. I've learned how to do it quickly and quietly and with complete surprise; it's amazing what you can learn, spending a year in the company of a trained assassin.

"For example: I've learned that boats smaller than forty feet in length usually run on gasoline. Not this one; big yachts like this run on diesel fuel because it's less dangerous—because diesel fuel doesn't explode, it just burns. But big yachts like this, ones that carry Jet Skis or smaller boats on board, they often carry gasoline tanks—like this one does."

The men began to straighten. They looked at one another.

"The tanks are made of aluminum. They're nice and soft; you can punch right through them with an ice pick, and you can shove a little hose inside and let all the gasoline drain down into the bilge—right down into the engine room. Then all you have to do is remove one of the spark plugs, and leave it hanging in the air . . ."

Kaplan and Truett started toward her. Zohar stood frozen. Lassiter looked down at the river, contemplating the distance. But Sarah looked into the sky with a look of perfect peace.

"Forgive me, Riley."

She reached down to the console and turned the ignition key.

■

A hundred yards upriver, Nick Polchak sat in a small rowboat, watching the meeting on the PharmaGen yacht. He saw four men on the aft deck, leaning against the railings, transfixed. He saw a figure dressed in brilliant red standing in the cockpit, the object of everyone's attention. He watched her lift her face to the heavens . . . and then he saw a massive fireball erupt in the water, sending pieces of fiberglass and steel as far as the opposite bank. The blast shattered the stillness of the night, echoing off the buildings and the hills of Mount Washington beyond and sending a rippling shock wave in circles out across the river. A moment later, there was nothing left but a burning pool of diesel oil.

Nick sat motionless in the boat, his mind recording the event but his emotions untouched by it. The lenses of his glasses flashed from black to blinding white to orange and then back to black again.

MEA CULPA

As a writer of fiction, my job is to tell lies—but to use enough truth to make the story sound as though it just might happen. All of the characters in *Chop Shop* are fictional, though most of the settings are very real. There is a Pittsburgh, a Tarentum, and an Allegheny River. PharmaGen does not exist; the Fox Chapel Yacht Club does. The coal-mining town of Mencken does not exist; the Duquesne Incline does. In this kind of blending of fact and fiction, there's a chance that some very real person or group might inadvertently fall under the shadow of its fictional counterpart. This is potentially the case with two very fine organizations, and I wish to clarify any misconceptions here.

The Allegheny County Coroner's Office—The Allegheny County Coroner's Office appears in my story under its actual name—no pseudonym seemed to do. In the real world, the Allegheny County Coroner's Office is one of the top forensic pathology facilities in the United States, under the leadership of internationally known pathologist Dr. Cyril Wecht. The professionalism and skill of their staff are known and respected nationwide, and I wish to thank them for their forbearance and good humor toward my fictional tale. You can learn more about the real Allegheny County Coroner's Office by visiting their informative Web site at www.county.allegheny.pa.us/coroner.

The Center for Organ Recover and Education (CORE)—My story involves a fictional organ procurement organization based in Pittsburgh. In fact, there *is* an organ procurement organization based in Pittsburgh—the Center for Organ Recovery and Education. Since its inception twenty-five years ago, CORE has helped to provide more than 300,000 organs, tissues, and corneas for transplantation. They have saved innumerable lives and done immeasurable good, and I in no way wish to cast doubt or generate fear about legitimate organ donation. I have requested a little red heart to be placed on my driver's license, and I encourage my readers to do the same. You can learn more about organ donation and procurement by visiting CORE's Web site at www.core.org. Be sure to visit the link titled "Donation: Separating Fact from Fiction."

...TO BE CONTINUED

If you liked *CHOP SHOP*, you'll love *SHOOFLY PIE*

WANT MORE MYSTERY?

Lizbeth, Bennu, Len, and Angie are misfits who are often overlooked and ostracized. When bullies attack them, the four friends find themselves suddenly thrust into an alternative dimension—the realm of Welken. Several mysterious adventures reveal that weaknesses in their own world are powerful weapons in Welken. Unless the misfits find the courage to wield their weapons and turn the battle, Welken will fall.
ISBN: 1-58229-355-4

Fame has created a glimmering facade in Shanna O'Brian's world, but when the spotlight fades, even her success fails to penetrate the darkness of reality. With Shanna's ex-husband now in control of her record label, Shanna's life careens out of control. Shanna's need to reclaim possession of a life she's too often surrendered to others leads her down a path of self-discovery that is cruelly threatened by unseen forces.
ISBN: 1-58229-342-2

www.howardfiction.com

WANT MORE ROMANCE?

Hanna Landin's past holds her captive, but Micah Gallagher, the rugged mountain guide she hires to help the family's floundering mountain lodge, makes her wish she could move beyond it. Together Hanna and Micah face the past. But it's more horrifying than either of them feared, and Hanna faces the ultimate challenge.

ISBN:1-58229-358-9   www.denisehunterbooks.com

Welcome to Oak Plantation, an expansive rice plantation in the Old South. When the overseer's daughter, Camellia York, accidentally causes the death of the plantation owner, she is haunted by guilt. But when she finally tells the truth about what really happened in the cook-house, she discovers a startling truth about her family's past.

ISBN: 1-58229-359-7

WANT MORE INTRIGUE?

After learning a horrific secret, Meagan Juddman is consumed with guilt and bitterness—guilt over a shameful secret she harbors and bitterness over a suspected government cover-up. After escaping to her hometown of Twisp, Washington, she meets Tharon Marsh, a decorated officer in the Gulf War. Their friendship grows toward something deeper, until Meagan discovers that Tharon harbors a horrific secret that ties their pasts together.
ISBN: 1-58229-391-0

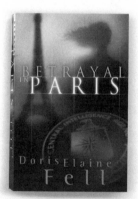

Amid the trauma of the September 11 Pentagon tragedy, twenty-seven-year-old Adrienne Winters fights to clear the names of her brother and father, who were victims of a double betrayal on foreign soil. As she pursues her quest, Adrienne discovers a gentle romance as she sorts out her family's history and her faith in God.
ISBN: 1-58229-314-7

www.howardfiction.com

Enjoyment Guarantee